A LAND IN FLAMES

Also by David Marcus

A LAND NOT THEIRS
TO NEXT YEAR IN JERUSALEM
THE MIDNIGHT COURT
(translation from the Irish)

A LAND
IN FLAMES

David Marcus

BANTAM PRESS

LONDON · NEW YORK · TORONTO · SYDNEY · AUCKLAND

The author wishes to acknowledge his indebtedness to
'Memoirs of Constable Jeremiah Mee' by J. Anthony Gaughan
(Anvil Books, 1975) on which some of the incidents in
Chapter 15 are based.

TRANSWORLD PUBLISHERS LTD
61–63 Uxbridge Road, London W5 5SA

TRANSWORLD PUBLISHERS (AUSTRALIA) PTY LTD
15–23 Helles Avenue, Moorebank NSW 2170

TRANSWORLD PUBLISHERS (NZ) LTD
Cnr Moselle and Waipareira Aves,
Henderson, Auckland

Published 1987 by Bantam Press,
a division of Transworld Publishers Ltd
Copyright © David Marcus 1987

British Library Cataloguing in Publication Data

Marcus, David
A land in flames.
I. title
823'.914 [F]   PR6063.A624/

ISBN 0–593–01336–0

Typeset in Great Britain by
Phoenix Photosetting, Chatham
Printed in Great Britain by
Mackays of Chatham Ltd

For Louis and Chookie

1

IT WAS AN INCONGRUOUS SCENE: a dusty country road with neither chick, child nor conveyance in sight, the gorse-spattered hedges becalmed in the still air, and the iron gates at the mouth of the long rhododendron-lined drive leading to Odron House closed and padlocked as if all the inhabitants of the centuries-old mansion were away on some extended visit, or on holiday, or had even fled – but drawn up outside the gates, carbines in hand, and intermittently shuffling their feet with nervous impatience, were twelve men of the Royal Irish Constabulary under their officer in charge, Sergeant Driscoll.

Any other time – the sergeant was lamenting to himself – any other time and he'd have welcomed such a pet day, blue skies as clear and clean as the Virgin's robe, the sun like a plate of gold coins baked solid in a furnace, banks and ranks of flowers in the gardens of Odron House sweetening with their incense the tang of the tobacco in his pipe and ambushing his gaze every time he turned in his pacing of the road. But inside the stiff high collar of his braided coat his neck was beginning to feel clammy with perspiration; the cruel weight of the spiked helmet he wore only on ceremonial occasions or when he wanted to impress his authority on potential trouble-makers was having a more dismaying effect on himself than it was likely to have on Tim O'Halloran and his band of agitators, and the tight belt around his middle might be helping to shape the stern appearance of an upholder of law and order not to be trifled with but, Lord above, it was the devil's bite on his digestion.

Such physical distresses were, however, his only immediate worries, for he had no fears about the impending confrontation. Certainly O'Halloran and his supporters would have by far the greater numbers – there might be a hundred or so of them against the twelve men that were all he could muster, eight from his own barracks and four others who had cycled in from a neighbouring station to lend their assistance. But *his* men had their carbines and bayonets, while the demonstrators would be weaponless. He reckoned it was highly unlikely they'd have disturbed the illegal arms he knew were bedded away under their floorboards or lying hidden in secret dumps; they wouldn't be so foolhardy as to sport them in daylight when the word was that they had no intention of using them. Banners and flags they'd probably have, even a band – for their aim would be just to draw attention to their grievance, not to start any trouble. Not yet anyway; if fighting was on the menu, that would come at a later date. Besides, Sunday morning wasn't the best time to raise a rumpus, just after they'd have been to Mass and would all still be wearing their best suits.

Sergeant Driscoll paced slowly once more to the centre of the road and gazed into the empty distance. All he could see was a heat haze at his vision's limit. He screwed his eyes up and peered fiercely ahead, drawing his bushy brows together in an almost angry quest for sharper focus. He feared to trust his sight completely, aware for some time that it wasn't what it used to be. More than once he had been tempted to drop in casually on the travelling oculist who visited the district every few months. He'd have no trouble trumping up some excuse for his call and then he could suggest, as if for a bit of sport, having his eyes tested while he was there. But he knew there'd be no way of keeping the story from the local gossips – the news would be scattered within the hour, and they'd have him blind before the night was out. Besides, what sort of a sketch would he present to his men if he had to don a pair of spectacles every time he wanted to read a paper or peruse the Orders and Acts and Regulations that lately seemed to be flooding his desk. Doubtless it was the years having to pick his way through the thickets of tiny print in these same official documents that forced him now to look twice where before a mere passing glance was sufficient to take everything in.

He plucked his pipe from his mouth and impatiently swatted at the rings of slow-curling smoke that wreathed his head. No, there was nothing; nothing to be seen. And nothing to be heard, either, except for a gang of crazy blackbirds crowding into a nearby tree and cawing away as if dawn had only just broken. Good luck to them, the lazy buggers! But wasn't it a curse that it couldn't be always like this? Wouldn't you think, to look around, that nothing but peace and tranquillity held sway throughout the land?

The sergeant strolled back to the verge, knocked his pipe against the demesne wall and hoped he'd be able to return quickly to the barracks, to be on hand if Lucy needed him. He had left only young Francie O'Leary to hold the fort, with strict instructions to pedal like mad for Dr Harvey if herself gave the word.

'Oh, I will, Sergeant, I will, to be sure. I'll go for the doctor immediately,' Francie had almost stammered in confusion and fear. Francie had four brothers and three sisters of his own, but he was the youngest of the brood, and the idea of being left alone with a pregnant woman would surely rout any thought of making his own judgement or using initiative. Which was all the sergeant required – he didn't want Francie taking any chances. Lucy and he had been trying all their married life for a child, only for Lucy to suffer a succession of miscarriages and still-births, and Dr Harvey had warned that the odds were flowing more and more against them as time passed. He hadn't allowed Lucy to rise from her bed for the past three months, so if ill-fortune were to dog them again on this occasion the sergeant knew he'd have to accept it as God's will that they were to remain childless.

He felt he'd be able for such a disappointment, if it came to it. He had already got through twenty years of wedlock without any family, so if it was destined to stay that way, having to face a barren future would at least be nothing new. But it wouldn't be the same, would it, for gone for ever would be the hope that had made it possible for him and Lucy to bear with their childlessness up to now.

Sergeant Driscoll studied the twelve young constables waiting patiently for something to happen, waiting with their future ahead of them. He closed his eyes as if to shut out recollection of the early plans he and Lucy had had, before year by year they had gradually withered away. He knew that after hope there'd be only hopelessness; they were twins living in the shadow of each other. What then? *He'd* still have his work of course – fifteen more years to serve in the Royal Irish Constabulary, responsibility, authority, respect, the daily routine to fill the empty hours. But what would Lucy have, living in two rooms of a dismal barracks, washing, cooking and cleaning for other women's sons instead of for a family of her own? How would *she* face up to a future deprived even of hope? Oh, if only this time their child would survive. Boy or girl, he didn't care which – beggars couldn't be choosers – and he no longer dared entertain the luxury of preferring one over the other. Earlier, much earlier, when they had played at the game of testing each other about the family they'd like, he had said he wanted their firstborn to be a boy. Now, a girl would be every bit as much a blessing; perhaps even more, for with the country the way it was, with fighting and pillage everywhere, no misfortunate Irish father could feel happy about a son's future. What prospect would a growing boy have? What path could he take but that of rebellion and be shot by the British, or support for the Crown and be shot by Sinn Fein? Or sail off on the boat to America and probably never see his parents again. But that was today's picture, and Sergeant Driscoll couldn't believe that things would never change. Surely it wouldn't be long before there'd be some resolution and peace would return. In five years? In ten certainly. By 1930, now, there'd be bound to be a different Ireland. But a better one? Who could tell? Nothing could be relied on in such a topsy-turvy world. So, whether or which, he still felt that if the Lord granted him and Lucy the blessing of a child, and if he was given the choice this day, he'd choose a girl.

And yet. . . . When the sergeant stood in the middle of the road, the smoke from his pipe barely shifting in the air, and gazed through the whorled iron spaces in the gates of Odron House, he had to admit to some doubt. There were daughters and daughters in it. Beyond the balmy gardens, beyond the lazily curving driveway, inside the mansion that stood hidden behind its screen of protective oaks, was a pair of young ladies who had had every material advantage of upbringing, the two daughters of Amelia Odron, the colonel's widow, yet two more contrasting sisters it would be hard to find throughout the length and breadth of the land. So different were they in everything – looks, temperament, manner, behaviour – oh, certainly in behaviour – that it was difficult to believe they came from the same parents. Victoria, the younger, was a jewel; the sergeant would have counted himself a blessed father if he had had a daughter in her mould. But the other one, that Elizabeth. . . . Sergeant Driscoll threw his head up in a disdainful resigned gesture. There was hardly a person in the district who didn't whisper behind his hand, bandying her exploits from ear to ear. Servants' tales there had been in profusion of how, even when only in her teens, she was already making free at frequent house-parties with young blades over from London and officers invited from the local garrison. These shenanigans came to an end when the Great War wasted the young blades and the troubles in Ireland put a tether on the soldiers' comings and goings, but by all accounts their suspension didn't discommode that young lady. It was then that the reports began to grow of her carry-on with Ambrose Mercer, the Odron land steward. Shocking stories they were but, judging by the way that same steward had turned out once the colonel was in the ground, Sergeant Driscoll could well credit them. Wasn't he the cause of having the sergeant and his men sweltering in the middle of the road under a boiling sun on this summer Sunday morning and, if his latest boast had any substance at all, the sergeant knew that local opposition would go much further than just a demonstration.

Could Mercer really be telling the truth? For weeks past he had been crowing that he was going to marry Elizabeth Odron. It might have been just drunken braggadocio of course, for it was during one of his evening sessions in the local pubs that the declaration was first made. Sergeant Driscoll wasn't inclined, however, to blame the porter; certainly the steward was a hard drinker, but he had always been able to hold his drink and wasn't given to idle talk under the influence. On the other hand, it might have been something he had concocted on the

11

spur of the moment just to stir up the locals and then persevered with when he saw how agitated it made them. That was his style without a doubt. He derided the cause and political ambitions of Sinn Fein, which by this time most of the men around had espoused, and continually riled his landless neighbours with the bitter taunt that it wasn't the colonel they had to deal with now, but him.

The colonel, for some years before his death, had been selling off parts of his estate to his tenants through the recently established Land Commission, but once he was gone these sales stopped, and Mercer swore that the tenants had as much of the Odron land as they would ever get. What was left would stay in the family as long as he was in charge. And in charge he'd be for just as long as he wanted, for the widow had no knowledge of estate management and depended on him completely. Indeed, from all accounts she seemed to submit to his will even in matters in which she might have been expected to exercise her normal authority as mistress of Odron House. No one had forgotten – no one ever would – the terrible winter three years before when conditions were so bad that a deputation led by Tim O'Halloran had waited on Amelia Odron, pleading that the poor of the neighbourhood be allowed to raise some food for themselves on two fields of hers that weren't being used. Fair play to the widow, she had said yes – but when Ambrose Mercer had walked in on their discourse and heard what she promised he made her go back on her word immediately and sent the supplicants packing. That was the brand of customer he was. If he meant to marry Elizabeth Odron, and if only half the stories told about her were true, then like as not marry they would. Ambrose Mercer would be virtual master at Odron House, and if that happened the locals could go and whistle for what was left of the land. Sergeant Driscoll wasn't surprised at the fury such a vision of the future generated locally; it was a heaven-sent cause for Tim O'Halloran and his Sinn Fein members right on their own doorstep. Bad enough that the estate should still be in the hands of an Ascendancy family, even though the colonel's ancestors had come to Ireland two centuries ago and he himself had been the best of landlords, widely revered – but times had changed since his death, and throughout the country the trend had been for much of the land to be restored to the native Irish, so for an interloper to start putting down roots now was something no one could stomach.

O'Halloran, judging the situation, had seen no need to make any secret of his plans for this morning's protest demonstration. Not that a demonstration itself would change things. The sergeant knew that, and he had no doubt O'Halloran knew it, too. But O'Halloran was not the sort of individual to indulge in empty gestures, so it would be wise to take it as certain that something more forthright was being plotted and that this Sabbath-morning outing was his way of warning the Odrons that he and Sinn Fein meant business. Well, Sergeant Driscoll also meant business, which was why he had gathered together as full a muster of men as he could. That was *his* warning. It would also put O'Halloran's mind at rest as to whether the local RIC's loyalty lay with the Crown or with the people. Disaffection and desertion might be rife among the sergeant's colleagues in other stations, but when he first donned uniform thirty years earlier he had taken an oath, and John Driscoll was a man of his word. He'd happily let O'Halloran know where he and his men stood: he wasn't going to brook any lawlessness, and if Sinn Fein had in mind using force at any time they could expect to find him and the Royal Irish Constabulary barring their way.

And bar it they would; for, though they were only a handful in number, the sight of them standing there, ready for anything, made the sergeant proud and confident. He had drawn them up in three rows of four, their backs to the locked demesne gates so that if it came to anything as unlikely as a physical fracas they knew they had no ground to give; the only direction they could go was forward. The four men of the neighbouring barracks formed the middle row. The sergeant calculated that keeping them together would get the best out of them – they'd be anxious to uphold the pride of their own barracks, they wouldn't want to fall back on the men behind them, and they'd have the front row, the pick of the sergeant's force, to bolster their courage.

Constables Fahy, O'Sullivan and Power were in the van along with Pat Howell. Sergeant Driscoll had no hesitation in putting Howell in front despite the youngster's inexperience in this sort of situation. He had been transferred only six months

13

before from a sleepy north-western village station, but he had been in the Force for nearly two years, he was keen, intelligent, tough, and possessed of plenty of moral courage. Of course, if events turned nasty, it was physical courage that would be needed, but the sergeant was well aware that without the former you couldn't have the latter. And certainly Pat Howell had buckets of moral courage, perhaps too much for his own good, as he had proved by his support of the Police Union, his pet hobby-horse. To the authorities, such support in the face of their implacable opposition amounted to insubordination at best, treason at worst – which was why they had transferred him. A busier district where he'd have more duties to fulfil, more to occupy his mind, and stricter discipline might make him lose interest in trying to keep the Union alive. Under Sergeant Driscoll he certainly had more to do and more to think about, but that had by no means snuffed out his determination to work for a radical review of the policeman's situation. On the contrary, being in a bigger station gave him the opportunity to spread his gospel even more effectively, and he had succeeded in gaining the tacit support of most of his colleagues even though elsewhere in the country enthusiasm for a Police Union was ebbing. His activity in this direction was not something Sergeant Driscoll could prevent. For one thing, the sergeant had quickly grown to like his new member; for another, he was not without a good deal of sympathy for the particular message Constable Howell was spreading, though in the sergeant's position and with his responsibilities he couldn't dare do any more than turn the blind eye.

Well, maybe a bit of real action will give him something to occupy his mind for a while, Sergeant Driscoll thought as the sound of distant bells began to billow on the air. Instantly the waiting constables became alert, as if suddenly recalling what they were there for. Conversation was abruptly stilled – except for Constable Fahy, who gave a jaunty nod as he winked at his companions. 'Here goes, lads,' he half-whispered, relishing the moment, like a schoolboy embarking on an audacious prank.

The sergeant paced to the middle of the road, took off his helmet and waved it up and down, blowing into it to hasten the cooling process. Replacing it carefully on his head, he drew out a heavy silver watch from inside his tunic.

'Won't be long now, men,' he assured them. 'Mass is just over.'

That was the signal for the policemen to take a firmer grip on their carbines. Whatever their feelings about the dangers the next half-hour might bring, they weren't showing any doubts or fears to each other. If some of their reassuring smiles were grimmer than they were meant to be, they took their cue from Constable Fahy's light-hearted pose, winking back at him as they exchanged brisk nods and growls of mutual encouragement. Sergeant Driscoll ran his eye over them and lazily, almost ostentatiously, relit his pipe and puffed out a spiral of smoke. He might almost have been in collusion with Constable Fahy in his determination to spread the feeling that there was nothing to worry about. A man like Fahy was great to have at such a time; a bit of a devil-may-care he might be, but his inability to let anything put him off his stroke could always be relied on whenever it was needed. And it certainly was needed now, for although since early-morning muster the sergeant had tried to suggest by his confident, even indifferent demeanour that O'Halloran wouldn't give them any serious trouble, he'd nevertheless be much happier when the whole exercise was over and they were back in barracks. There'd still be the nuisance of drawing up his report, of course, and he hated paperwork, but at least it would give him the opportunity of praising his men and perhaps putting in a special word for young Howell. That might help a little to balance things for him in the authorities' books.

A mark for good behaviour was, however, the last thing Constable Howell was interested in. Whichever way the confrontation went – whether force would have to be used or not – he saw this as just the sort of situation that made a Police Union essential. It was plain crackers: the country in turmoil, daily IRA attacks, and here they were, a handful of policemen, being forced to carry arms and act as if they were soldiers, while all the time there were scores of garrisons and thousands of British troops all over the place. Where was the sense in it? The unprotected police stations were easy targets for arms raids, frequently resulting in Irishmen shooting at and killing fellow-Irishmen. And the brass hats at the top couldn't, or wouldn't, see the stupidity of their policy. That they weren't

15

even consistent about it often made Constable Howell's anger boil over into a passionate rage.

'Look,' he would repeat to his colleagues, being as patient as he could and doing his best not to raise his voice, 'do you ever hear of attacks on police stations in Dublin? No. And why? Because the Dublin police aren't armed. Doesn't that sum it up for you, lads, doesn't that just sum it up?'

'Why don't you apply for a transfer up there, then?' Constable O'Malley would ask with a broad wink, ever watchful of the chance to break the monotony of their humdrum routine with a little stir of the pot; and Fahy, on cue, would put in: 'Sure you know the Dublin Metropolitan Police wouldn't take a midget like our Pat.' Constable Howell, at just under six feet, was no midget, but it was a recognized tradition of the Dublin force that every man jack of them was well over that mark.

'Laugh if you like. I know most of you agree with me, but silent agreement is not enough. You've got to do something about it. If fellows like you shook yourselves a bit and took an active interest in your own welfare, we'd have a strong Union in no time. Otherwise, you mark my words. . . .'

Constable Howell's warnings weren't long being fulfilled. Far from withdrawing the RIC's arms and so putting an end to the constantly increasing attacks on countryside police stations, early in 1920 the authorities reinforced their policy with the shock announcement that Brigadier-General Byrne, the only Catholic ever to have been appointed head of the RIC, was being relieved of his post.

'And who did they put in his place?' Pat Howell accused, as if it was solely his colleagues' inactivity that had brought down this latest blow on all their heads. 'I warned you, lads, don't say I didn't warn you,' he moaned, for the new inspector-general was Thomas Smith, an Ulster Protestant with a reputation as an iron-fisted disciplinarian, whose almost first action was to reject out of hand an application for a meeting to discuss all the RIC's grievances, including their objection to the carrying of arms. Now, as Pat Howell stood outside Odron House waiting for the demonstrators' expected onslaught, a single resolve dominated his thoughts: come what may, nothing would ever persuade him to shoot an unarmed man, be he Irish or British or Hottentot savage. To have a gun was one thing, to

16

use it another. Indeed, that morning as he and his companions had made their way on their bicycles to Odron House, grunting and mouthing oaths as they bumped along the broken road with the sun beating down on them and their Martini carbines slung across their backs, Tom Fahy's comment, squeezed out between breaths, that they were like a band of Red Indians riding out to scalp some white men had provoked him to reply: 'I wish we *were* Red Indians. Then it'd be bows and arrows we'd be carrying instead of these cursed guns.' Now, as he took a firmer grip on his weapon, he crossed himself quickly and said a prayer that there'd be no blood on his hands before the day was out.

The church bells ceased ringing, but for a moment or two their echo lingered until that also died away and the silence, like a strange new sound they had never heard before, filled the men's ears. Then, from over the intervening fields, came the muffled boom of a bass drum. Four steady sturdy beats, and immediately the band struck up.

'"The Wearin' of the Green" bejay,' Fahy joked. 'Now that's a tune you could do a jig to.'

Sergeant Driscoll turned to face them.

'Silence there now.' And then, briskly and firmly: 'Attention. Fix swords.'

'Thank God,' Constable Howell murmured to himself. At least there'd be no bullets used this day.

Did a wayward breeze momentarily carry the sound of the music in another direction? Or was it the rasp of the swords being drawn from their scabbards and affixed to the carbines that for a second drowned the brass notes of the band so that some of the men looked up wildly, imagining the demonstration was moving away rather than towards them? But any such notion was illusory, for now the music was clearly swelling, and at last in the distance the procession came into view.

Sergeant Driscoll expected that the band would be preceded by Tim O'Halloran, and indeed it was, but the sergeant could not suppress a smile when he saw that O'Halloran, flamboyant as ever, was not marching but was driving in a horse-drawn open carriage. There he sat, upright and prideful, his plump cheeks ripe with resolve, his firm lips almost obscured by the curtain of a thick brown moustache. It was just the style of the man to take such an opportunity of advertising to all the excellence of his craftsmanship as a carriage-maker. Not, indeed, that any advertisement was necessary, for he was the last of his trade left in the county and so anyone from miles around who needed repairs to his own carriage or a new one made had to go to Tim O'Halloran, where, if he wanted the best of attention, he'd be wise to put up with a homily on the twin advantages of nationalism and the ancient traditions of the native Gael.

As the procession drew nearer, the sound of the band was augmented by the singing and shouting of the crowds in its wake. Sergeant Driscoll's apprehensions grew as he saw that their numbers were even greater than he had feared. Packed tightly into the narrow road, they spilled out on to the adjoining fields, the green sashes that many of them wore blending with the darker green of the grass. They appeared to be unarmed but almost all carried ash plants which they waved menacingly in the air. Ash plants could be frightening enough customers, the sergeant thought, as the noise of their hissing tore fiercely through the familiar strains of the music. But at least they were harmless – they weren't guns. And then another thought – a far more disturbing one – suddenly occurred to Sergeant Driscoll, making him fear that he could have misjudged the situation. Flamboyant Tim O'Halloran might be, but he was also the craftiest of men – and ruthless when need be. Supposing the carriage he was riding in was not there for a bit of show-off but had a sinister purpose. Supposing that hidden in its belly were the arms the sergeant had no doubt the local Sinn Fein possessed, and that as soon as the procession was near enough they would be speedily grabbed by the leading members and turned on the unprepared policemen?

He took a quick glance at his men to see how they were responding. They all stood at the ready, one leg bent in front of the other for solid stance, the blades in the carbines glinting and winking in the sunlight. The men themselves stared apprehensively at the approaching demonstrators, the sweat of tension and heat gathering on their foreheads and a tightness in their throats that no amount of swallowing could loosen.

Sergeant Driscoll quickly turned back to the procession. It was now no more than fifty yards away, so that he could clearly

18

recognize every face in the leading group. As he kept his eyes fixed on them, O'Halloran suddenly reined in his horse and dismounted from the carriage. He leaned over one of its wings, his arms disappearing into the carriage's depths as if to lift something out. Followers gathered around him, pressing forward eagerly, hands outstretched. The band had stopped playing, and the marchers were crowding up together, their ash plants held in check. They might have been waiting for some signal.

'Ready there, men.' Sergeant Driscoll threw the command back over his shoulder.

O'Halloran straightened, lifting something from the carriage and handing it up to those nearest him. Sergeant Driscoll moved a pace to one side, trying to make out what was afoot. He had to be certain. A false decision, a misguided command to his men to remove their swords and be ready to shoot – it could end in carnage. But the broad body of the Sinn Fein leader obscured his view until O'Halloran turned to face him and the front line of his supporters spread apart, unrolling between them a huge banner: THE LAND FOR THE PEOPLE, THE BULLOCK FOR THE ROAD. Immediately, a loud chorus of cheering issued from the demonstrators, and the renewed tumult of the waving ash plants broke over the policemen like a suddenly released dam, making them almost reel back from its force. Constable Howell felt a trickle of perspiration course down the back of his neck and he had to take a tighter grip on his carbine to offset the dampness of his palms. His heart was pounding, its tattoo reverberating in his head. The band hadn't resumed playing, but the beat of the drum persisted, its monstrous booming gradually drawing the shouting together into one sustained rhythmic repetition of the waving banner's message: 'The land for the people, the bullock for the road.' It was the slogan of the landless peasant, the slogan that had been adopted by Sinn Fein and spread throughout the country. It was a call that many a land steward had been met with as he tried to collect his master's rents and that many a landlord had heard ringing in his ears as his mansion was going up in flames.

Sergeant Driscoll stood firm, letting the demonstrators' chant continue for a minute before lifting up a hand to them in

19

a signal for silence. In response O'Halloran turned to his men and waved furiously, but it took some moments before his message found its way to the back of the crowd and the whole throng was still. Constable Howell and his colleagues exchanged glances. The sudden slackening of tension was a relief, but what next? What was the sergeant up to?

He stood in the middle of the road, motionless, waiting, his eyes fixed on Tim O'Halloran. Half a minute passed before he advanced a few paces and then he stopped again. O'Halloran, as if reading his thoughts, turned to the band, silent now apart from the lone drummer who, his vision completely blocked by the huge drum carried on his chest, was relentlessly repeating his one booming note. At a sign from his leader, the bandsmen on either side of him motioned to him to stop, and gratefully he lowered his drumsticks, letting them dangle by their thongs from his wrists, while he mopped the perspiration from his face and brow.

Sergeant Driscoll, satisfied that he at last had everyone's attention, moved a few more paces forward and then calmly took off his spiked helmet.

'Bejay, the heat must be getting to him,' muttered Constable Fahy.

'Don't be a gom,' Constable Hogan, the oldest and most experienced of the group, whispered back. 'Don't you know your regulations?'

If Fahy had forgotten, he was immediately reminded, for the sergeant put a hand inside his helmet and drew out from its lining a folded sheet of paper. With almost exaggerated care he replaced the helmet, opened the document and read from it, his voice loud, his tone grave, his pace measured.

The demonstrators listened, and Tim O'Halloran waited patiently, almost respectfully, as if he would be the last man to hinder an officer in the execution of his ceremonial duty. In fact, however, he and his supporters welcomed Sergeant Driscoll's action, for they had heard reports from other parts of the country that any time a demonstration threatened real trouble the officer in charge of the opposing police detachment was required to read out the Riot Act without delay. If that was the form elsewhere, they wanted it applied to themselves as well. It was no more than their due. Even if nothing further was achieved, they had been taken seriously, and in their estimation that put them a point up.

For the twelve policemen waiting in the hot dusty road behind the sergeant it was also the first time *they* had heard the Riot Act. Except that they couldn't quite hear it because of the distance between them and the sergeant and the fact that his voice was being directed away from them. They caught odd words and part of a sentence, and then, as the sergeant appeared to raise his voice, they did hear the charge 'to all persons gathered to disperse upon the pains contained in the Act made in the twenty-seventh year of King George III to prevent tumultuous risings and assemblies'. Then they saw Sergeant Driscoll refold the piece of paper and return it to its niche inside the lining of his helmet. Would the demonstrators respond to the order? Would they turn and disperse as charged? Nothing happened. The policemen strengthened their hold on their carbines and tensed themselves for possible action, awaiting Sergeant Driscoll's command.

When his command came, however, it was not addressed to them.

'O'Halloran,' the sergeant called. And then again he called, a shade less publicly this time, certainly a shade less officiously. 'Tim! Tim O'Halloran!' And he started, slowly and steadily, to walk towards the crowd.

Tim O'Halloran hesitated for no more than a second before striding out confidently to meet the sergeant.

They met when they had reached what each judged to be the half-way point between them. One step further would be to enter enemy territory, and any such mismeasurement would be looked upon by both contingents as a concession. Besides, the further both O'Halloran and the sergeant could get from the opposing groups, the less chance there was of their exchanges being overheard. So, silent as both groups remained as the parleying went on, and hard though they strained to glean some whisper of the negotiations, they could hear absolutely nothing. They had to be satisfied with the sight of the two principals, heads close together, sometimes nodding in unison, at other times one head nodding and the other shaking from side to side, until after some minutes they shook hands, saluted, turned, and started to retrace their steps.

21

When O'Halloran reached his supporters, he climbed into his carriage and stood up to face them.

'Attention!' he called. 'About turn. Quick march.'

Docilely, and with a proud show of order, his instruction was obeyed. The crowd parted to allow the band make its way to lead the procession back. Then it regrouped behind the bandsmen who, instruments to lips, closed ranks, waiting for the drummer to give them the beat, and then off they set. O'Halloran cast one look back at the sergeant before urging on his pony, content to bring up the procession's tail.

Sergeant Driscoll was content, too.

'Unfix swords,' he ordered his men. 'Right turn. Dismiss.'

The policemen, feeling theirs had been the victory, quickly sheathed their swords and ran to retrieve their bicycles which rested side by side against the wall. Joking and laughing in relief as if to make little of the almost intolerable test they had but a moment ago faced, they jumped on their machines and pedalled off.

The sergeant still stood in the middle of the road. Calmly he took out his pipe, relit it and lazily puffed away for a few moments, cocking his head on one side to listen to the receding sound of the band.

'"A Nation Once Again,"' he muttered, recognizing the tune it played.

He pivoted towards the still locked gates of Odron House.

'Maybe,' he said, looking around at the countryside that once more appeared as innocent and uninvolved as it had when he first arrived on the scene that morning. 'Maybe,' he said again.

Then, removing his helmet and strolling to his own pony and trap waiting some yards away, he followed his men back to the station.

Five minutes later, when the road, from end to end, was completely empty and the only sound to be heard was the renewed chatter of the crazy birds, a tall dark-visaged man with a large black hound padding beside him strode down the driveway of Odron House, unlocked the gates, and swung them wide with a powerful heave of each arm. He walked to the middle of the road, looked for a moment both ways, and then contemptuously spat into the dust.

22

'Come on,' he shouted at the dog as he marched back up the drive towards Odron House. 'Come on, there, Brutus. That's the end of these Shinners' fun and games. I don't think we'll be having any more trouble from such scum.'

But Ambrose Mercer was soon to discover how wrong he was.

2

It seemed to Amelia Odron that she was the only one who remembered her husband, probably the only one who ever even thought of him. It could hardly be otherwise, for she never mentioned him in conversation. Elizabeth had been five when he died, Victoria barely one, nineteen long and lonely years ago. To them their father was no more than just a tall uniformed stranger who stared out from the various stiffly posed regimental photographs on the drawing-room walls. Family pictures of him when they were babies, along even with wedding photographs, were kept locked up by Amelia in her dressing-table, and any curiosity they had shown about him when they were growing up had been actively discouraged or only grudgingly and inadequately satisfied. But how could she talk to them of the twin forces that led him to cut short his army career after a quarter-century of distinguished service and settle in his family home in Ireland? How could she speak of the love he had borne her? It would have been embarrassing – for them as well as for herself – even to hint at the heat of their passion, the fire of their love-making. And that was what dominated her memories, day and night. It had been his secret and hers. Now it was hers alone, and to share it – even with their own daughters, the very fruit of that passion – would somehow have made it less precious.

As for his other obsession, the land of his birth and his

concern for the worsening plight of the Odron estate tenants whom his parents, preferring to spend their time in London, had sucked almost dry – to speak of that would have been no less than offering hostages to fortune. Neither Elizabeth nor Victoria had ever taken any special interest in the affairs of their country, but Amelia feared that if she revealed to them the depth of their father's devotion to it she might revive their curiosity about him, and who knew what that could lead to? They might end up held fast in this luckless land, just as she was.

She still shuddered to recollect the desolation of her first four years spent in Odron House. There was no joy in being the bride of Colonel Odron when her husband was hundreds of miles away fighting foreign wars most of the time. Odron House was miles from its nearest neighbour, and with its echoing empty rooms it had been like a mausoleum after the cosiness and intimacy – especially the intimacy – of the small terraced house she had lived in with her parents and brother and sister in Colchester. She had felt utterly lost and bewildered, taking weeks to learn even the location of all its rooms. Leaving the breakfast room in the mornings, she had to stand for half a minute in the marbled chill of the great hall, hesitating over which of the many doors might be that of the sitting-room. Much of the time she guessed wrongly, and whenever she found it was the library door she had opened she would go in and choose a book at random, pretending, for the benefit of any of the servants who might have seen her, that she was going to spend the morning reading.

The servants, too, made her quake with fear. They were respectful and kind but, being local and new themselves to Odron House, they were as ignorant as she was of how such an establishment should be run. They kept coming to her for instructions and directions, and she had the greatest difficulty in understanding their accent. So she kept out of their way as much as possible, going for walks in the grounds when it wasn't raining or too wild, getting up late so as to shorten the day, doing embroidery until her eyes burned and her fingers ached.

Worst of all during these four years, worse even than the absence of old friends and the lack of congenial company, was the spiritual isolation, the thought that perhaps Alex had packed her off to this gloomy mansion in a far corner of Ireland so as to put as much distance as possible between her and their respective families. She had seen how uncomfortable he had been with her family on their few meetings – unsure and restrained, anxious to ignore the social chasm between them, but by this very over-politeness making it more obvious. And as for his own parents – at least having to spend time with them was one ordeal she had been spared, for they had contrived not to be on hand until the wedding ceremony itself and she knew they had been very upset with their son's choice.

She supposed at the time that she could hardly blame them. What had she but her beauty, the beauty that had first attracted Colonel Odron when they had met on that distant summer afternoon so long ago? Amelia never forgot the date: 15 July 1891. Or the circumstances: the local gymkhana which his regiment always supported and where she had been selling her needlework for charity at one of the many colourful stalls. She recalled also what she had been wearing: a pink floral high-bosomed dress that she had made herself, and a pink-ribboned bonnet tied under her chin. The sun blazed down pitilessly, and for relief she had taken off the bonnet and allowed her long auburn tresses to fall around her shoulders. She blushed when a tall soldier who had been passing her stall and had seen her action stopped to say: 'Too hot a day for tight bonnets, eh?'

As she smiled her agreement, he went on: 'Lucky you. I wish I could take off this cap of mine, but if I did I might get into trouble. Do you know what I'd be accused of?'

She shook her head forcefully, anxious that her example should not lead him into any transgression.

The soldier laughed. 'Oh, nothing more serious than being improperly dressed. But that's bad enough, don't you think?'

She made no answer to that, feeling somewhat overawed by the splendour of his appearance. His tall athletic build was handsomely suited to uniform, and though she couldn't construe the epaulettes on his shoulder or the battle honours on his breast pocket, she guessed that they betokened a high rank. His demeanour, too, suggested to her a man born to authority, the firm jaw and thick but impeccably clipped fair moustache softened by the easy jocular manner. Her unconsciously admiring gaze had not embarrassed him. Instead, when the twinkle in his eyes had suddenly awakened her to the openness of her stare, she sought to cover her confusion by taking up her bonnet and attempting to don it once more.

'Don't do that!' he protested. 'Such lovely hair shouldn't be imprisoned.'

She had blushed again at that, but his words had encouraged her to hope that she might perhaps have found a willing customer for her work.

'Would you care to buy something?' she asked. 'It's all in a very good cause.'

'Indeed.'

He smiled again, and as he stroked his chin in pretended confusion at the variety on display she noticed how long and elegant his fingers were. Hers were long and elegant, too, adept at the needlework which was her main domestic activity.

He was still nodding as his eyes moved from item to item on the stall.

'My mother used to do a lot of this, so I reckon I'm a bit of a judge. She was quite good at it but not up to this standard, I'd say.'

'Thank you for the compliment,' she had replied.

He glanced up quickly in evident surprise.

'Oh, is this *your* work, then? I say, you *are* talented.'

'Oh, it's not much really,' she said self-deprecatingly, and then, with some audaciousness: 'It's very kind of you, but compliments are all very well. . . .'

The soldier threw back his head in open laughter.

'A cheeky maiden, eh? Taking the bull by the horns. Always the best tactics, in my opinion. You're right of course, I should put my money where my mouth is. And I certainly will. Yes, I'll buy your wares, my lady. One of them anyway.'

'And which one would you like, kind sir?' she said, echoing the courtly tone he had adopted.

'I'll tell you what. Which is your favourite piece? Whichever it is, I'll have it. Is that a bargain?'

She *did* have a favourite piece. Among all the hearts and flowers, the intricate patterns, the embellished mottoes and old saws, there was one composition that she was especially proud of, one that had involved more care and concentration than the others. It depicted a splendid mansion – not a fairy-tale castle

27

but a real dwelling-place – set in a field of rolling green thread flecked with spots of daisy white, and dove-grey birds circling in the cloudless sky above it. It had taken her months to do, mainly because she would pause so often as it took shape to wonder about its origins. Had she read of such a place, had she seen a picture of it, or was it perhaps the embodiment of some subconscious fantasy that any girl of her station might harbour? Wherever it came from, it meant something special to her that she couldn't explain, and she hadn't at first wanted to include it in the sale objects. Her mother, however, soon changed her mind – her mother, practical and straight-speaking as always, upbraiding her for hankering after the unattainable.

'Don't nurture a viper in your bosom, young lady,' she had said in a tone which Amelia recognized as the start of a homily. 'It's only a bit of needlework, no more. That sort of place is not the destiny of your sort of girl. If you let yourself covet it, you'll build up your expectations and then you'll never properly appreciate less – and less is all you can expect. But it's a good piece of work, I'll say that for it. Artistic. It might be worth a few shillings to someone, so put it in the sale and out of your mind.'

And Amelia, dutiful daughter as she had been taught to be, had put her dream house in the sale, half-hoping it would catch nobody's eye. But, when the tall handsome soldier had offered to buy whatever she considered her own favourite, pride in her artistry contended with the special attachment she felt for the product of her own inspiration, an attachment which her mother's strictures had only served to strengthen. Nobly, however, she had dismissed 'the insubstantial in favour of the practical, and pointed to her masterpiece, telling herself, as she had told him, that it was all in a good cause.

'I say,' he had immediately responded, 'that *is* charming. Most accomplished. I'll have it. I'll pay you now, but would you put it aside for me? I have to see some friends here before I leave, but I'll return for it within the hour.'

He *had* returned for it; in a sense she had, too. At least he later often teased her with the accusation that marrying him was the only way she could repossess her precious piece of embroidery.

When he brought her to Odron House and installed her as its mistress, they had hung his purchase in the master bedroom where they might see it immediately they awakened every morning. It had brought them together, he said, and its rightful place was where they could both look at it together. She had never removed it, and as she sat gazing at it now, the afternoon sun bathing the room and making the large bed – so much too large for one – seem emptier and more bereft than ever, she pined for her dead husband's love.

How wrong her mother had been! Odron House was even bigger than the mansion she had created, even more resplendent; and, though she couldn't have guessed it at the time, it seemed to have been her destiny from the moment he returned that day to her stall to claim his purchase. That was when he had claimed her, too.

'Look,' he said with straightforward military directness, 'there's a bit of a party in the mess tonight, music, dancing, it'll be fun. I'd like to take you. You'll come?'

It had all been like that, a whirlwind pace, difficulties – real or imagined – swept aside or not even mentioned. He had dismissed her hesitations almost as if she hadn't even voiced them. When they exchanged names he said he didn't much care for Amelia and would call her Melly. That had decided her to accept his invitation. At home she was always Amelia, which to her ear had a dull correct sound, the kind of name that branded a girl as strait-laced and sparkless. But Melly was bright, there was an adventurous ring to it, and it answered to the fun-lover in her, the girl who secretly wished not to be tied for ever to the role of dutiful daughter, but to break the rules now and again and see what the world was like outside the shadow of strict convention.

Within months they had been married. He wouldn't delay; he wanted to take her to his home in Ireland and honeymoon there as soon as possible before he was posted abroad again. She had been glad of his haste, not only because she had fallen in love with him but also because the prospect of escaping from the humdrum life that had stretched ahead of her at home was exhilarating. She quickly abandoned herself to the new attitudes his carefree youthful behaviour encouraged. When proposing, he had told her his age – 'because,' he had said, 'you may decide I'm too old for you.' The gap of sixteen years

29

between them had at first been quite a shock. The unexpectedness of his proposal after an acquaintance which, though exciting and flirtatious, had been very brief was itself a surprise; to learn there was such a disparity between their ages was almost unbelievable. Forty-two seemed very old to her, yet he did not look forty-two or act forty-two.

'You know what they say,' he had joked. 'You're as young as you feel.'

'That applies to a man,' she had corrected him. 'A woman is as young as she looks.'

He gave a little laugh of triumph. 'Then, we're the one age. I *feel* eighteen and you *look* eighteen.'

'Flatterer,' she had responded.

'Certainly not' – in mock dudgeon. 'As an officer and a gentleman I'll swear that you look no more and that when I'm with you – or think of you, and that's all the day and most of the night – I feel no more.'

'Well, just to show what a bad judge you are, my colonel, let me tell you that I'm twenty-six.'

He smiled. 'Twenty-six! All of twenty-six! I'm not sure that I should believe you but, if I did, what's sixteen years? What are years at all? It's how we feel about each other that counts. I feel I want to marry you.'

'Why?' she had asked mischievously.

He paused, a hint of a smile on his lips.

'I need someone to polish my buttons; it's such a chore,' he answered slowly and mock-seriously.

They stared into each other's eyes for some seconds before simultaneously breaking into laughter. Then he put his arms around her and his cheek against hers. But she pushed him off, saying: 'Now, you're just trying to take my mind off the difference in our ages.'

She was joking. She didn't care a jot for the difference in their ages; she just wanted to prolong the exhilaration of the moment. Exchanging banter with him was not mere dalliance but the way they had, up to now, conveyed the warmth of their feeling for each other. It was a game she had never played with a man before, had never even suspected she was capable of, but under Alex Odron's encouragement she had taken to it quickly, eagerly and expertly.

She waited to see what effect her comment would have on him. But her colonel was too experienced a soldier to walk into an ambush, too canny to betray any doubt he might have as to whether she was serious or joking. He paid her back in like coin.

'Of course I'm trying to take your mind off our ages. I don't give a fig for the difference in years between us, so obviously I wouldn't want you to dwell on it. But, then, if it *does* worry you, that's an end to the matter.'

He turned his head away, but a sly twinkle flickered in the corner of his eye. Her bluff had been called, and she knew it.

'No, of course I don't care. Age means nothing to me. As you said, it's how we feel about each other that counts.'

He nodded, then suddenly drew in his breath.

'Oh, there is *one* difficulty, one little embarrassment I should reveal before you commit yourself.'

'Whatever might that be?' she asked, unperturbed, somehow suspecting that this might just possibly be another of his jests. He seemed to like taking every opportunity of teasing her; she wasn't sure whether it was his natural temperament breaking through the straitjacket of military training, or a trait many soldiers developed to relieve the tedium of having to spend so much time in exclusively male company.

'What's your little embarrassment? I just can't imagine.'

He swallowed hard, as if in acute discomfort.

'It's my name,' he admitted shamefacedly.

'Your name? But your name is Alex Odron. That's what you told me.'

'That's *all* I told you. Actually it's Henry Alexander Osbert Granville Odron. Do you think you can live with that?'

Oh God, how happily, how ecstatically she *had* lived with it, especially when he eventually retired from the Army and was able to spend so much time with her. Even though his days were mostly devoted to the business of the estate and to improving the lot of his tenants, they were not always separated, for he often encouraged her to accompany him on his rounds. 'They want to see you, Melly dear,' he used to say. 'They *like* seeing you. The colonel's lady, y'know. They want to feel that you're as interested in them as I am.' Certainly the tenants always appeared to welcome her visits and often

31

insisted that she drink 'a sup of tay' with them and sample their freshly baked bread. On these occasions she did her best to hide her feeling of strangeness because she knew how much it pleased Alex to see her play the role of lady of the manor, but what made her especially proud was the genuine respect and affection he inspired in them. Landlord he might have been, but he behaved with them as if they were his partners rather than his tenants, sometimes even his teachers, for he often made it a point to ask their advice on some farming matter about which he suggested they would be far more knowledgeable.

It was a relationship which to Amelia was completely unexpected, not at all what she had been led to believe was the way Anglo-Irish landlords and their tenants looked on each other. When she expressed her surprise to Alex, he reminded her that in the less-populated western half of Ireland things weren't as closely regulated as they might be on the other side of the country. 'You have the Castle society there – Dublin Castle, I mean – and their style is much more British than we can sustain in these parts. There aren't as many of us around here, so it's only natural that our relationship with the native people would be very different. More friendly, I suppose you'd call it. Do you know what was said of the Normans not very long after they first invaded Ireland centuries ago? It was said that they became "more Irish than the Irish themselves". Do you think you might end up like that, eh? Melly MacOdron!' He laughed. 'I like that. It has a ring to it.'

That was the happy, good-humoured, playful Alex she so often recalled. Now his playfulness was only a memory, but a memory so poignant that nineteen years after his death its loss was becoming harder rather than easier to bear. And she felt she had nothing of her own playfulness left, either, that she had allowed herself to relapse into the sort of ageing woman she would probably have become anyway if the whole course of her life had never been changed by that one summer afternoon at the gymkhana.

But had she really nothing left to raise her spirits, to make her believe that the memory of the girl she had once been was real and true, not just a 'good old days' picture that conveniently rubbed out the shadows? Was there nothing at all to hope for or look forward to? She still had her daughters – hers and Alex's. How different they might have been if he had lived to give them his love and guidance when they were growing up – or if she had not put such a barrier between them and herself, leaving them virtually motherless as well as fatherless. Was it too late now for her to affect their futures? Victoria needed a strong influence to make her see that the reward her goodness deserved would not come automatically, but had to be sought out and courted, even fought for. Elizabeth, on the other hand, required no instruction on how to fight for herself; no one would ever do *her* down, but her hard calculating sort might easily be betrayed by its own pitiless streak. Such disadvantages, such difficulties – and so compounded by the continuing decline of the ·Odron fortunes. Now, in addition to all that, there was something even worse to contend with: the very physical threat they faced. As yet that threat had not been overtly directed at her or at her home – not until today and the Sinn Fein demonstration.

As Amelia sat in her bedroom she could hear the music of the band, its raucous sound scraping her nerves until her flesh was frozen with tension and she feared that the terror she now expected nightly had begun to engulf her. Eventually the music faded away and at last she was able to relax. In exhaustion as much as in relief she threw herself on to her bed, her face buried in its pillows, and soon tears came as the present dissolved and her body began yet again to crave the worship it had for so long been without. Nothing – neither time nor fear – could banish the memories of the love it had known. She was a widow, fifty-one years old, the mother of two grown-up daughters, the mistress of a mansion and an estate however reduced in wealth and regard – surely such a hunger should play no part in her thoughts or her feelings. It was unseemly, almost obscene. But she had learned from the long fallow years without Alex that the passion he had awakened in her would not die simply because he had. From their very first night, on their arrival at Odron House after the marriage ceremony, his love-making had been intense, insistent, insatiable. On that first night, when he had eventually desisted, leaving her quite overcome both by his masterfulness and by the unsuspected reservoir of response and inventiveness that had welled up in her, she had told him, only half-jokingly, that she believed his rush to marry her was not because he feared an early posting but because he couldn't wait to get her into bed.

'Have a care, my love,' he had replied, his fingers searching her out once more. 'Any insubordination and I'll start all over again.'

Since soon after his death, when the numbness and shock had eventually abated, she had dreaded the lonely nights when daylight's realities and demands did not attend her, when there was nowhere she could go and nothing she could do except endure the long dark hours in the bed of their love with only ghostly memories to assuage her need.

Now, as she lay face down on that bed, the burning sun bursting through the window to enfold her body, she felt all resistance melt away. He was back again, here in the room with her, impalpable, invisible, expectant, demanding. No longer in control of thought or reason, she feverishly tore off her clothes and stretched out on the counterpane, her fists clenching and unclenching as the heat of the sun played on her trembling limbs. For minutes she lay thus, struggling with her body's hunger, knowing too well that hunger's power – what it could do, had done, might make her do again.

Then suddenly, as tears forced their way through her closed lids, she turned over violently on the bed as if trying to crush the desire that would not let her rest. Her sobs were muffled by the pillow; muffled, too, the words she whispered in her anguish. But hoping that somehow he might hear them, whether his spirit was still with her in the room or lay with his bones in their mouldering grave, she repeated over and over again: 'Forgive me, darling. Forgive me, forgive me.'

'Did he give you much trouble?'

'Trouble? Is it Tim O'Halloran? Sure what trouble could that man give me?'

'Tch, tch, John Driscoll. Stop treating me as if I was an invalid. I'm no such thing. Tell me now, what happened down at the House?'

Lucy Driscoll was sitting up against two pillows, with Saucy, the cat, snuggled into her side. Her face was turned to the window, and the bars of the brass bedstead behind her caught the sun's rays so that they looked like a row of yellow strokes painted by an artist to set off her head of jet-black hair. Dr Harvey had insisted that she spend most of her pregnancy in bed and the lengthy confinement had dulled her normally apple-red cheeks, but she had prepared herself for her husband's return by pressing a wet cloth to her face so that her skin now looked fresh and windblown.

The sergeant sat on the side of the bed and took her hand.

'Francie saw after you all right, did he?'

'What was there for him to do at all? I've been sitting up here all morning like Queen Maeve waiting for you to come back and tell me how it went. Come on now.'

'Sure don't you know how it went? I'll bet Pat wasn't in the door but he was straight up to you to give you the news.'

'Ah, he was too excited to tell me anything but that it never came to any shooting or fighting. Thank God for that. The poor boy was like he was after finding a crock of gold, he was that relieved he hadn't to use his gun.'

Sergeant Driscoll nodded.

'Aye, I can imagine. I don't know would he ever have pulled the trigger if I'd have given the order. Still, there was never a fear of that.'

'He said yourself and Tim O'Halloran had a private whisper and fixed it up between ye. What did you say to him?'

'He says to me an' I says to him. Didn't I know it was only putting on a show he was.'

'Will you stop aggravating me!' Lucy demanded with a touch of petulance. 'It wasn't about the weather ye were talking.'

'Well now, as a matter of fact, woman, it was,' her husband answered with a smile. 'I told him 'twould be a pity to cast a shadow on such a beautiful morning, and that it would be desecrating the Lord's day into the bargain to cause any trouble.'

'And what did he say to that?'

'He said there wasn't a bother on him whether he caused trouble or not. I didn't like that class of an answer, so I said to him, quite stern, don't you know: "Don't be playing the gom with me, Tim O'Halloran, I know you too long for that. Is it a showdown or just a show you're after?"'

Lucy chuckled. 'Ah, God love you, you were never short of the clever word.'

The sergeant modestly shrugged off her praise.

'Sure I knew he was only out to cause a stir and get people talking.'

'That's what you were saying beforehand all right. But Pat said he had hundreds with him, far more than ye could ever have held back. How could you tell he wasn't going to force himself in on you?'

'I'll tell you how I could tell, Lucy,' Sergeant Driscoll confided. 'Didn't he lead the procession in one of his carts, a sort of wagonette affair, fine varnished wings that seemed to flow like a river in the sunshine, yellow paint on the wheel spokes, and a deep belly on her that you could nearly make your bed in if you wanted. Brand new, of course, and if Tim O'Halloran was going to initiate any fighting he wouldn't want to put such a classy conveyance to the risk of damage. So that's why I was sure we'd have no trouble.'

The sergeant didn't mention his momentary fear that O'Halloran might have brought along his new deep-bellied wagon to conceal guns. That had been forgotten in his relief at the peaceful outcome.

Lucy was smiling as she pictured the scene.

'Isn't that just like him!'

'True enough. I praised the contraption, of course. He said he was giving it a run to test it. He'd just finished making it for the Birches of Ballygort, and they're collecting it tomorrow.'

'Isn't it a wonder that a strong Sinn Feiner like himself would do work for them? Sure aren't they Loyalists?'

'And who else would he work for? The man has got to live, and 'tis only that class of people who can give him the big job. I'd say that piece of work would cost them all of twenty-five pounds – if he didn't put on a bit extra for the cause.'

The sergeant took his wife's hand in his and peered into her face.

'Tell me now,' he asked, his voice low and solicitous, 'how are you feeling this morning?'

Lucy puckered her brows and peered back at him, mimicking his look of concern, before her face relented into a smile.

'I'm fine, fine as can be, fine as the lovely weather outside that window and wishing I was out in it. And I'm better now that you're back in one piece. And all the men, too, safe and unharmed.' She paused before adding: 'But I'd be better still if I thought that would be the end of any trouble over at the House.'

'And why shouldn't it be?' the sergeant came back quickly before his wife's softly chastening look pulled him up. He knew that expression – knew it well from the countless times when, over the years, his assurances that their childlessness would surely not last all their lives were gradually seen through as the almost empty formula they had become. Yet Lucy had never openly scoffed at them. To do that would have been to gnaw at the very bond of understanding and affection which held them together, and wouldn't it also be, she thought, a backhanded rebuke of their Holy God's will – perhaps even enough to harden His heart against her permanently? But, though she could utter no word to confound such assurances, neither could she repeat them to herself, and the look in her eyes would usually cut him short.

Now that same look told the sergeant he would be wasting breath to try and pretend to her that he believed there'd be no more from O'Halloran and his Sinn Feiners. The morning's outing wouldn't satisfy those boys.

Sergeant Driscoll got up from the bed and moved over to the window. Through the lace curtains he gazed out on the view. God knows it was a miserable enough sight that met his eyes – the concrete yard at the rear of the barracks, a few bicycles against a wall, his trap, freed of its horse, pointing its shafts up to the sky. His eyes moved to the shed with the winter turf stacked in readiness and beside it another shed which should have been full of coal but which had not yet received its supplies because the Sinn Fein workers on the railway refused to move any trains carrying coal to military or police barracks. It was a dull dumb vista, sure enough, rendered more dispiriting by its deadening familiarity. Even the tiny square of earth Constable Power had succeeded in uncovering in one corner where he had coaxed a meagre quorum of lupins and fuchsia to register nature's presence did little to relieve the monotony.

Worst of all, however, was the picture inside Sergeant Driscoll's head. There was Lucy to worry about; there was the increasing flow of Orders and Directives from the authorities who were growing more and more reluctant to depend on the

37

loyalty of the Royal Irish Constabulary – and with good cause, the sergeant reflected, thinking of his own men's qualms; and there was Tim O'Halloran's campaign against Ambrose Mercer. Without doubt before long there'd be something more unpleasant to contend with from that band than just a noisy demonstration. Lucy knew that, too, and there was no way he could fool her or stop her worrying. But, by God, if anything O'Halloran got up to should cause her to lose this child, too, Sergeant Driscoll swore he'd swing for the man.

'It'll be Andy Doyle's stew and bread pudding today,' Lucy's voice broke in on his thoughts. 'I can smell it halfway up the stairs already.'

'I'm ready for it when he is,' her husband replied, turning back to her. Constable Doyle was the Sunday replacement cook for Julia Hogan, the local woman who came in for the rest of the week to keep the barracks tidy and cook for the men while Lucy was out of action.

'I'm ready myself, too,' Lucy told him.

'I'll bring up yours as soon as he dishes it out, and a bowl of soup with it. You'd like that.'

'I would,' Lucy smiled. 'But don't you be tiring yourself going up and down those stairs. Pat has younger legs. Let him do it. He doesn't mind.'

'Aye, he's a good lad, is Pat Howell.'

Husband and wife avoided each other's eyes, unwilling to acknowledge to each other the warmth of affection they both felt for the young constable. As Sergeant Driscoll clattered heavily down the wooden stairs he guessed that hidden in the depths of his wife's heart was a yearning to mother Pat Howell. He understood that, understood it well. If he wasn't careful, he himself could easily fall into the trap of treating the boy as if he were his own son.

Ambrose Mercer was not a stylish horseman, nor a very compassionate one. His attitude to all living creatures, animal or man, was 'Show them who's boss and they'll respect you'. That this respect was based on fear – was often, indeed, only fear itself – filled him with satisfaction. Physical fear was not an emotion he himself had ever experienced; his apprehensions revolved exclusively about the world of Odron House and his unwavering ambition to become its acknowledged master. Sinn Fein's public show of hostility to his plans would not deter him. Their claim to what was left of the Odron land was nothing new – 'The land for the people' was a catchphrase that was inciting even the beggars in the streets to demand their own plot. Ambrose Mercer took none of it seriously. What were all these agitators but ragged peasants with no power to take the land they coveted, and if they did get it they were too lazy and feckless to farm it properly. But the degree of local support for the Sinn Fein demonstration did surprise him. That was something he hadn't expected, though he didn't imagine it made their threat any more worrying. Indeed, the louder they clamoured, the sooner they'd feel they had done all that was required of them. Oh, they were great actors, the Irish, they liked nothing better than to take the centre of the stage, rave and rant and perform, and then ride home on a tide of self-praise and mutual admiration, usually swelled with gallons of porter. If they had been really serious, would they have enacted such a charade on a Sunday morning, after they had been on their knees praying to their Prince of Peace and that simpering Virgin, and then come along all togged out in their best suits, with a tuneless band, brandishing nothing more lethal than a forest of ash plants? That was the Irish way all right. Typical whiners and hypocrites.

That was what annoyed Ambrose Mercer about the demonstration. If it had been put on only by Tim O'Halloran and Sinn Fein as he had expected, he wouldn't have given it a second thought. How many members could Tim O'Halloran's silly little handful of plotters and play-actors amount to? A dozen? Even twice that? But of course all the hangers-on and coat-tail lickers of the district had taken advantage of the opportunity to come out, mouthing their ridiculous nonsense. There must have been many in that crowd who would doff their hats and show respect to him the very next day – aye, and do business with him, too, if they could – but give them a chance to malign him from behind the safety of a neighbour's back and they'd fight to be first. That really stung him, and when Ambrose Mercer was annoyed or angry his only relief was to take to his horse and ride it hard for mile after mile until its neck and flanks were dripping with sweat, its nostrils flecked with blood, and its headlong gallop reduced to a stumbling walk from sheer exhaustion. Only then would Mercer feel assured of his mastery. Reinstated in his self-esteem, and all his choler blown out of him by the mad ride, he would then lead the horse to a convenient stream where it could slake its parched throat while he cooled his own brow in the rippling waters before sinking back against rock or tree to dream of his future as master of Odron House.

Lately his dreams of that future had taken on a harassing urgency, and Ambrose Mercer was growing impatient. The colonel had been nineteen years dead and, for all his control of Odron House affairs, Mercer saw himself, at forty-one, not really any nearer the status he craved as squire of the demesne.

As he lay, that Sunday afternoon, under a sweeping elm, the shadows thrown across his face by the giant tree might have reflected the twists and turns of his thoughts in their search for a line of action that would hasten events. His dark eyes, usually hard and piercing, had a faraway look as if their gaze was turned inward, and his broad full lips that would curl into a cruel sneer in his dealings with the few crushed tenants still remaining on the Odron lands were pursed in contemplation.

As he saw it, he didn't give a fig for the threat to his own personal safety posed by Sinn Fein's campaign, but it had another danger. If it continued, if it became even more threatening, it could frighten Amelia Odron so much that she might at last be persuaded to give up the estate. What would she do with it? Sell it? He'd nearly have enough to buy it from her out of the money he had hidden away, money he had been carefully and craftily robbing from the estate income since soon after the colonel had died. He knew Amelia would never find out, or even suspect him. He had no trouble convincing her that conditions throughout the whole country had been gradually deteriorating, so the decline in her fortunes had not surprised her. And he had been careful not to be too greedy, always making sure that he left her at least sufficient for her own needs and for those of her daughters – if not, in recent years anyway, for anything in the way of extravagance. But Ambrose Mercer was well aware that that line of thought would lead to a dead end, for he was the last man on earth she would sell Odron House to. He had absolutely no illusions on that score.

There was always old Renfrew of course. He smiled to himself at the thought of the old duffer. Charles Renfrew was their nearest neighbour, with a fine house and a few acres of his own some three miles away. He was a bachelor, the last of a line that could trace its holding in Ireland back to the Cromwellian Plantation. And a big holding it had been, too, until Renfrew, too old or too lazy to continue running it, had sold it back to his tenants under the Land Acts. Sensible enough, perhaps, Mercer had to concede, when you're getting on and alone, and the government stocks he got in return would keep him in comfort for the rest of his life. Trouble was that Charles Renfrew didn't want to stay alone, and that was what worried Ambrose Mercer. For years he had been paying court to Amelia, riding over to the house a few times a week – he was probably there at this very moment to hear about the morning's disturbance – and, though up to now his attentions had shown no sign of winning Amelia's hand, at this stage it might not take much more to persuade her. If she did marry him, one of two things would happen, Mercer reckoned. Renfrew would become squire at Odron, or she would sell up to someone else and go to live with Renfrew in his own home. There was room enough there for Elizabeth and Victoria, too, or she could pack them off across the sea to try their fortune in London's high society.

Either way, a marriage between Amelia Odron and Charles Renfrew was a marriage that would put paid to Ambrose Mercer's ambitions. As he plucked a swaying piece of grass that was tickling his ear and ground it between his teeth, he smiled to himself with quiet satisfaction, nursing the secret knowledge he had that made him confident he could stop such a marriage – at least until he himself was squire of Odron House. Only he and Amelia knew what that secret was, but if anyone else was to learn of it – Renfrew, for instance – what price their marriage then?

The smug look on Ambrose Mercer's features as he reflected on the hold he had over Amelia Odron suddenly faded when he remembered that he was as far himself from the first step towards getting Odron House in his grasp by marrying Elizabeth as her mother was from marrying Charles Renfrew. It didn't worry him at this stage that even if he were installed in Odron House as Elizabeth's husband, there would still be

41

Amelia and Victoria to get rid of. He didn't imagine Amelia Odron would want for long to stay on as his mother-in-law, and he'd not be surprised if she quickly decided to make Charles Renfrew a happy man. That would suit Ambrose nicely – as long as he had Elizabeth wedded first. That would still leave Victoria of course, but perhaps she'd soon find a husband herself. A good marriage settlement – and he'd then be in a position to make one – would surely hasten her search.

But all that was looking too far ahead. First things first, and what was especially galling was that the first step of his plan – to get Elizabeth to say yes – long-term though it had been, was taking all these years to mature. Even more frustrating was the fact that for some time it had made no progress at all, despite promising so much in the beginning. From the night of Elizabeth's deflowering when she was barely seventeen, he had found her an enthusiastic, even a demanding partner. It seemed then that he could easily make her completely dependent on him for the satisfaction she sought. He had thought he had only to bide his time for a few years before she would consent, and consent willingly – nay, eagerly – to be his bride, but he soon discovered that her transformation from a girl into a woman had awakened a sexual appetite that was well-nigh insatiable. It was not long before the young officers who were frequent visitors to Odron House in those years found their weekend stays made deliciously, if exhaustingly, exciting by their hostess's elder daughter. And with the appetite came the wiles – the explanations, excuses and protestations, sometimes even denials – that were constantly employed to assure Ambrose Mercer that he had no real rival. Seethe though he might, he was careful to keep his jealousy and his anger in check, for the stakes he was playing for were too high to be sacrificed by any impatience. He could wait.

So wait he did. But even when there were no longer any virile young officers to be entertained Ambrose Mercer's suit made little progress. Those nights when she brought him to her bed and his strong probing fingers roused her to such savage ecstasy that she would dig her sharp nails into his skin until she drew blood – at such moments she would seem receptive to his repeated proposals, at least not rejecting them out of hand. But once her passion was spent she'd turn such proposals aside, treating them lightly and saying she had time enough yet to worry about marriage. He would not press her then, for to do so would only make her more stubborn. But, knowing as he did the strength of physical desire her body harboured, there was always a risk that while she held him at arm's length someone more high-born and well placed than he might turn up, someone who could match her urge for urge and stroke for stroke, and then where would Ambrose Mercer and all his plans be? That was why he had decided to put it about that they would be married. She hadn't yet faced him with the report – if she did, he'd deny it was his work – but if she did hear the rumour it might bring matters to a head and force her to give his suit more serious consideration. And, however angrily she might react, it would leave him no worse off than he presently was.

It was one thing, however, to have taken action that might stir his fortunes out of the becalmed waters that had imprisoned them for so long, but Ambrose Mercer was too wary a schemer not to have a sharp look-out for any sudden breeze from an unexpected direction that might whip itself into a storm strong enough to dash all his hopes. And Tim O'Halloran and his Sinn Fein might cause just such a breeze. Mercer was cautious enough, too, not to take anything for granted. How sure could he really be that his hold over Amelia Odron, powerful though it was, would be sufficient to stop her marrying Renfrew no matter how frightened she became? She was a woman who had never seen a hand raised against her in her life, and she had two daughters to worry about. Fear for her safety, and theirs, would be a new experience for her, a new emotion she had never faced before. Ambrose Mercer had seen fear undermine even strong men. What might it cause a woman to do, even a woman who knew that any hasty action might result in her awful secret being broadcast far and wide? It could move her to throw caution to the winds and fling herself on the mercy and understanding of the one person from whom she would have wished to preserve her secret – the person who wanted to marry her. And, if that happened, could Ambrose Mercer be absolutely certain that old Renfrew wouldn't play the true-blue Britisher, let bygones be bygones, and take her away from the dangers of Sinn Fein threats? That was always a possibility, and so it had to be reckoned with.

He considered the new factor all the afternoon, lying beneath the tree as the sun still burned down on the scene around him, and his horse, now refreshed, pawed the ground impatiently. At last a glint of triumph began to smoulder in his eyes, and his lips parted in a silent laugh of malign satisfaction. He had worked out a way of setting at rest any fears Amelia Odron might have that would be strong enough to throw her into Renfrew's arms. Granted that Mercer himself was the only man at Odron House who could handle a gun, the few male servants being elderly retainers, and granted it was undeniable that one man alone would not be able to withstand a Sinn Fein attack – but if he were *not* one man alone, if there were others alongside him to protect her, then Amelia would have nothing to worry about. She could feel as safe and secure as ever, and then there'd be no need for her to consider seeking refuge with Charles Renfrew.

Ambrose Mercer sprang to his feet and jumped into the saddle. Elated, he quickly urged his horse into a gallop. He knew just how and where to find that extra protection.

Elizabeth Odron, sitting before her bedroom mirror, feared no attack. She had heard the music of Tim O'Halloran's band that morning and for a moment had been tempted to leave the house, saunter down the drive and peer out the gates to see all the rumpus. And, if the police had been forced into a pitched battle with the demonstrators, that would have been better still. Action, drama, spectacle – these, along with risk, were what gave life excitement for her. Or would do if there were any such action, drama or spectacle to divert her at Odron House. But life there had become boring for her ever since the start of the troubles that were now spreading throughout the country like a forest fire. And, even before that, the level of entertainment mounted at Odron House had been gradually reduced. There was no longer as much money as there used to be, her mother had explained, certainly not enough to pay for unnecessary distractions or festivities. So the balls had been discontinued, the house-parties had become rare – why, this summer there hadn't been even one tennis-party and the grass had been allowed to grow higher than ever before on the court. Worst of all was the isolation. Friends, fearful to trust themselves to the hazard of roads where who knew what terror might lurk in ambush, visited less and less often. And there were no men. The soldiers and young men who in bygone years had dined and wined at their table, the most dashing of whom she would surprise in their room when they stayed overnight, delighting in pleasuring them until dawn forced her back to her own bed – they were no longer available. Now she was reduced to Ambrose Mercer alone and, though she found him a strong and willing lover, variety was what she relished.

As she gazed into her mirror, she unashamedly admired what she saw there. Brilliant green eyes flashing back at her as they surveyed her dark upswept hair, strong cheekbones made more imperious by high-curved nostrils, moistly gleaming full lips. Her glance strayed down to her breasts, almost hungrily straining against her tight bodice. She closed her eyes languorously, all her muscles contracting at the little currents of ecstasy flickering through her body like echoes of the rapturous thrills that sluiced through her under a lover's caressing hands. When she opened her eyes again, she caught sight in the mirror of her maid, Mary Casey, examining her with a fixed stare. Their eyes locked for a moment until the girl turned away to lay out her mistress's dinner-dress.

What had been in that stare, Elizabeth wondered. Was it admiration, jealousy, contempt, or even hatred? Elizabeth never could tell. Mary Casey said little, spoke only when she was spoken to, but there was something unsettling about her. Yet why should there be? She should be glad to have such a good post. If she weren't in Odron House, where else these days could she have got a job? And it had not been Elizabeth's fault or her mother's that Mary Casey's father had been one of their tenants who couldn't pay his rent and had been evicted by Ambrose Mercer. Indeed, it had been Elizabeth's own sister, Victoria, who had persuaded her, despite Mercer's displeasure, to take Mary on. Elizabeth had been glad at the time – it had been growing harder and harder to attract local servants because of all that stupid nationalistic talk – but as the months passed she was often puzzled by the girl, puzzled and worried. Was she as simple and compliant as her silence and easy ways appeared to suggest, or could she be nursing a secret enmity? Elizabeth never knew.

'Did you see that parade this morning, Mary?' she asked now, anxious to find out, if she could, what the girl had thought of the demonstration.

'Is it Tim O'Halloran and his band you mean, Miss Elizabeth?'

'Yes.'

'Ah, no, Miss Elizabeth, sure wasn't I here at the time?'

Elizabeth looked at the maid in the mirror, but the girl's back was turned as she made herself busy at the wardrobe.

'Well, what do you think of it all, Mary? Do you agree with O'Halloran?'

'Ah, miss, that's for men to think about. What would a girl like me want to worry over such a carry-on for?'

What indeed, Elizabeth thought. Except that your father was almost certainly part of the 'carry-on', as no doubt all the evicted tenants in the area were. But Elizabeth didn't pursue the question; there was no point in scratching at old sores.

'If you've finished there, you can go and help Miss Victoria,' she said, pulling the dress over her head. Her sister had no personal maid, preferring to attend to her own needs, but Elizabeth always liked to keep Mary Casey busy and lost no opportunity of pressing her on Victoria when she herself had no use for her.

'I'll see if she's in her room, Miss Elizabeth. She wasn't there a while ago – I saw her in the garden.'

Elizabeth sighed. If Victoria wasn't in the library, she was in the garden. She seemed to spend all her time between the two places. She should get out and about more – not that these days there was anywhere to get out and about to, but she could do with more exercise. The lack of it showed in her complexion. Her thin girlish figure was like a flower pressed between the leaves of a book. Sometimes, when long empty days made Elizabeth fretful and snappish, she regretted that Victoria's interests were so different from her own. But it was a regret she quickly dismissed; anything in the way of a rival under the same roof would have been most inconvenient. Besides, the differences had never affected the bond between them, nor could they persuade Victoria to sit in judgement on her wayward sister.

Elizabeth impatiently drew tight the buckle of her belt. It

annoyed her that she could not tell what Mary Casey might be thinking. If one didn't know what a person was thinking, one could never be sure of mastering them. With men it was different. When men looked at her, she always knew what they were thinking, or she was always able to make them think what she wanted them to. But women weren't like that. They were deeper, more devious, more able to conceal – as she herself was able when necessary.

Sergeant Driscoll stood at the open back door of the barracks, making the most of the balmy night air. Glad though he was to be under his own roof again, he knew he couldn't take anything for granted. Not these days. Gortnahinch might be only a small town and its RIC station only a sub-barracks with nothing like the status of Listowel, fifteen miles away – and certainly not in the ha'penny places with the county headquarters in Tralee – but with Kerry the centre of some of the country's most active Sinn Fein units there was no police barracks that wasn't at hazard. Still, a small one like Gortnahinch had its compensations. The men in his charge had mostly been with him for years and, being only nine in number, they had grown close to one another the way members of a big family do.

He gazed up at the evening sky like a smooth lake of liquid blue, with shoals of salmon pink swimming up from the horizon, betokening more fine summer weather on the way. His pipe was going well, the men had been able to take it easy after the strain and excitement of the morning, and Lucy was in good spirits – 'Holding her own,' the doctor had said. The world seemed a different place when a day that had started out for him so unpromisingly ended up with an arm around his shoulder like an old friend's embrace. He had written up his report, praising his men and the reinforcements from the neighbouring barracks as best he could. They hadn't actually been in action, so he didn't overdo things, and it would have been too obvious to have singled out Pat Howell for special mention. Unfair to the rest, into the bargain. Still, there might be other opportunities. They'd want to come soon, the sergeant told himself, if they were to be of any use, for Constable Howell had spent the afternoon writing letters to contacts in other barracks and he admitted to the sergeant that he was trying to arrange a Police Union meeting in Dublin. It wouldn't be long before the authorities learned of his plans – they had their informants everywhere – and who knew how much rope they'd give the lad before he hanged himself? Certainly their patience couldn't last much longer.

He knocked the dying ash from his pipe against the jamb of the door and put the pipe in his pocket. There was still one thing to be done – write up the daybook and sign it. About to make his way to the dayroom, he heard the phone ring, and waited. Someone would answer it – it would hardly be anything important at that time of night.

'It's for you, Sergeant,' Constable O'Malley's voice called. 'It's Mrs Odron.'

'I'm coming,' he called back. 'No doubt she wants to thank us for this morning.'

It was all of five minutes before Sergeant Driscoll was able to put down the phone and join the rest of the force in the dayroom.

'What's the matter, Sergeant?' O'Malley asked. 'You look as if you're not very pleased with the thanks you got.'

'Oh, no, it's not that at all,' Sergeant Driscoll demurred. 'She thanked us all for what we did – like the lady she is. But there was something else.'

Constable Hogan lowered the book he was reading and glanced up at Sergeant Driscoll. Apart from the sergeant himself, Sean Hogan was the longest-serving constable in the barracks, and his experience and instinct told him that the 'something else' had disturbed the sergeant. His feeling of unrest seemed immediately to convey itself to the other men. They fell silent, and all eyes turned to Sergeant Driscoll.

'Come on, then, Sergeant,' Fahy joked. 'Cough it up, it's only a brick.'

'Unfortunately not a brick, Tom,' Sergeant Driscoll replied heavily, 'not a brick. A bullet. Someone tried to kill Ambrose Mercer.'

There were gasps and whistles at the news. 'Who?' voices asked. 'Is he hurt?' 'Where was it?'

'Easy there, lads,' Constable Hogan intervened. Then, turning to Sergeant Driscoll: 'Was he hit?'

'No. Whoever did it missed him.'

48

'A pity,' muttered a voice in the background.

'He didn't see who it was, then?' Hogan continued.

'He didn't. And there were no witnesses; he was alone at the time. It happened when he was riding back to Odron House. He had been out in the fields all afternoon and was crossing the pasture at the time, so it couldn't have been anyone out hunting. And no one would be poaching at that time.'

'What time, Sergeant?' Pat Howell asked. 'When did it happen?'

'About six o'clock.'

'Six o'clock,' Constable Hogan mused, 'and it's nine-thirty now. Why didn't he report it earlier? Did he explain that?'

'I didn't ask him, Sean. It wasn't himself I was speaking to but Mrs Odron. It seems Mercer only just told her. He hadn't been worried for his own sake and wouldn't have said a word until he thought that whoever shot at him and missed might be bold enough to try for an easier target next time. Like Mrs Odron, or one of the girls.'

'He thinks it was the Sinn Fein boys so?'

'Who else?' Sergeant Driscoll replied, sitting down wearily. The lovely pattern of the day's ending had suddenly cracked, and he'd have the tricky job of mending the crack. 'He thought Mrs Odron should have some protection in case there's another attempt.'

'He doesn't want any protection for himself, then?' Fahy asked.

'He'll have to get it anyway, whether he wants it or not. And the Odron family,' the sergeant said. 'He's not the only steward around with police protection. Browne over at Langan's Hollow has had it for months now. And there's others. So I can't refuse Mrs Odron's request. I'll sleep on it and send someone there in the morning.'

'Just one, Sergeant?' Constable Hogan queried doubtfully.

'Oh, no, one wouldn't be enough. Two at least. It'll be a twenty-four-hour-a-day job. But I can't see how I can spare more than two of you.'

'I'll go if you like,' O'Malley volunteered. A special assignment like that might lead to promotion in due course.

'Thanks, lad, but I'll make my mind up in the morning. And I suppose I'll have to investigate the shooting, too.'

49

'Tim O'Halloran?' Pat Howell suggested.

'I'll have a goster with him anyway,' the sergeant replied. 'See if he can throw any light on the occurrence. Though, even if he can, he'll be too crafty to give anything away.'

Sergeant Driscoll rose heavily and went over to the high desk in the corner where the daybook lay open.

'Isn't it a good job now I followed my own teaching and I didn't sign the book before the day was over? I'd have made a right mess of the page if I did, eh, lads?'

There were nods and grunts of sympathy from the men, but they shared their superior's worry and disappointment. As the sergeant dipped his pen in the ink and started to write, they speculated among themselves about the new development and who would go to Odron House. The younger constables were eager. Life in the Big House was a strange closed world to them, so different from the small farms and villages they had come from. A spell in Odron House would be like a rare holiday. The older men had no such thoughts. What worried them was the pace at which events were moving. This morning the demonstration . . . this evening an attempt to shoot Ambrose Mercer. As like as not, anyone being sent to guard the inhabitants of Odron House might find himself facing more than he expected much sooner than he expected.

Sergeant Driscoll finished what he was writing and put down his pen. But he didn't sign the daybook yet. He looked up at the clock on the wall. Officially the day wasn't over, and he wasn't taking a chance on any more surprises.

3

Tim O'Halloran's workshop wasn't in Gortnahinch itself but almost a mile out the west road, not too far for Sergeant Driscoll to take a leisurely walk there. Leisurely though his pace was, however, the heat was such that he was soon having to run his large white handkerchief around the perspiration gathering inside his collar. He unsnapped the heavy belt from his middle and opened his tunic, appreciating the little eddies of breeze that began to play on his chest. Now and again, like a hen fluttering its wings, he flapped the front of his coat to and fro to encourage the draught.

He smiled ruefully to himself at the irony of the situation: an unwelcome duty was giving him the chance of a welcome break. Sergeant Driscoll liked noting little ironies; they confirmed his view of life as never being a straightforward simple equation but always a mixture of pluses and minuses. Take the business of Ambrose Mercer being shot at. Minus: no need to rehearse the minus in that, it was obvious it meant trouble for him and his men. But plus: it had given him the excuse – the legitimate excuse, he assured himself – to pack Pat Howell off to Odron House on protection duty and so put a stop for a while to his Police Union gallop. Sergeant Driscoll was pleased about that; the lad was certain to run into trouble with the authorities if he were to pursue this idea of a meeting in Dublin, and if anything should happen to put a blight on his career and

51

almost certainly remove him from the barracks the sergeant didn't disguise from himself how sore a blow it would be to him, and to Lucy, too. With luck Odron House would need protection for quite a while, and Pat could be left there for a month or even more before being relieved. That should be enough time for him to cool his heels. He'd hate it of course, being tucked away from things for so long, but he was too loyal a policeman not to accept the sergeant's decision and he'd make the best of it once he saw there was no alternative. Maybe the break might even cause him to lose interest in the idea of a Police Union. Even if that was unlikely, perhaps by the time he came back to barracks so much support would have slipped away that it would be pointless to try to recover the lost ground. You could never tell; stranger things had happened.

'Who's coming with me to Odron House?' he had asked.

Now, *there* was another little plus, the sergeant reflected. He had never thought of trying to put a bit of a snaffle on Tom Fahy as well – probably because it had never occurred to him that a chance would ever arise. And it wasn't that the same man was in any way a thorn in his side. Damn it, no, he couldn't say that of him. He was a good policeman, a fine policeman, even if he had a tendency to be a little irresponsible now and again when out of uniform. But there was no malice in him, nothing like that. Still and all, it would be foolish to pass up the opportunity of tethering him for a while. Besides, he and Pat always hit it off. Pat never got aerated over Fahy's gentle baiting. And gentle it had been from the first day the younger constable had arrived at Gortnahinch station. His shyness had been plain for all to see, and Fahy had immediately taken him under his wing. Of course, Fahy came from a family that had five daughters but no other sons, so perhaps the kindness that lay behind his habitual ebullience spontaneously responded to the opportunity of being guide and mentor to someone he could treat as a young brother. Of course, too, there was the fact that Howell came from Leitrim and Fahy from Sligo, neighbouring counties with the mixture of friendliness and rivalry that grew out of such closeness. The sergeant had no fear that the touch of the playboy in Fahy would lead the younger constable astray; Tom's pleasure-seeking was probably no more than self-indulgent opportunism, the occasional surrender of a lusty young fellow who couldn't restrain himself from sowing the odd handful of wild oats. Sergeant Driscoll wouldn't have wanted a son of his own to behave that way; it wasn't the sort of thing he did himself when he was a young man. But the world had changed since then; the war had altered the pattern, shaken off the dust. And flesh was often weak. Anyway, there was no danger that Pat Howell would kick over the traces. He was out of the old mould, too level-headed and idealistic for any of that sort of carry-on – and also, as it turned out, too caught up in spreading the word about the Police Union to have time for any other distractions. Yes, indeed, they were the perfect team for any joint operation, one good policeman plus another good policeman: no minuses there that the sergeant could see.

It was pluses all around in the countryside, too, he noted as he stepped it out along the narrow road, baked so dry from all the hot weather that his boots disturbed barely a grain of dust. The hay had been saved everywhere, and well saved, too, and the golden cocks, basking in the fields, looked to his straining eyes like rows of giant syrup puddings. Birds warbled in the hedgerows; in the distance a dog barked twice and a man's voice answered it; bees spun their buzzing lassoes about his head and then whisked them away again. The only incongruous sound to be heard was the plod of his footsteps on the hard ground, and when he paused to lean against a bank, take off his cap and have a quiet smoke, nature's music had no discordant rival.

In the few minutes he rested there, the sergeant could have dozed off in the heat and peace of his surroundings. Indeed, for some seconds, perhaps more, he did fall into a bewitched slumber of jumbled dreams in which he heard the long-forgotten echoes of his mother's voice crooning him to sleep. He awoke with a jerk, just in time to catch his pipe as it was slipping from his lips. Puzzled, he shook his head, for the sound of his mother's crooning was still in his ears. He looked around and had a good laugh at himself when he realized that what he had heard was the mooing of some cows in a field behind him where about a dozen chunky Kerrys were moving like so many black dominoes across the green board of their pasture. It was time to set off again. Sergeant Driscoll replaced his cap, shook out his pipe and strode off, whistling softly.

'Ara!' he suddenly chastised himself on recognizing the tune he had unwittingly been whistling: 'A Nation Once Again'. A good song – indeed, a proud song – but certainly not one for him to be airing so near Tim O'Halloran's place. He could just make out a cottage about a hundred yards ahead – was that O'Halloran's at all? Damn the eyesight, he couldn't be sure at such a distance. But as he drew near he recognized the large shedlike structure beside the cottage that he knew was O'Halloran's workshop, and behind it a chimney was smoking away. That would be the smithy of Myles Barratt who, besides shoeing the neighbouring farmers' horses, also made the wheels for O'Halloran's coaches.

The workshop was no more than a large barn, and the sergeant paused for a while at the yard entrance, catching his breath after the walk and surveying the various contraptions that stood there. Not that there was a great deal of finished work in evidence; the wagon that O'Halloran had used for the demonstration stood out, its bright yellow sides boasting its newness. There was a dog-cart, and a market-cart with a heavy list to one side – doubtless a new axle was needed there – and two despondent-looking dung-carts which the sergeant wasn't surprised appeared forlorn, as dung-carts were no longer greatly favoured by the farmers. Tim O'Halloran was nowhere to be seen, but the noise of hammering from inside the shed told the sergeant where to look for him.

He crossed the yard and peered in the open door. O'Halloran had his head bent over a plane, smoothing a wooden plank; beyond him, at the rear of the shed, was the formidable bulk of Myles Barratt, his face cherry-red and glistening as he worked at his furnace. A strange odour tickled the sergeant's nostrils, a fumey burning smell that he guessed came from the piece of ash under O'Halloran's plane. The flare of the match as he relit his pipe to combat the smell with the more palatable aroma of tobacco caught Tim O'Halloran's attention, and he straightened up to see what had caused it.

'Well, well, if it isn't the sergeant himself,' he boomed, shaking wood chippings out of his thick hair and then calling over his shoulder: 'Myles, me boy, we have a visitor. The law, no less.'

Myles Barratt turned his face to the sergeant, his forehead

54

dotted with beads of perspiration and his bald pate looking as if the hot flames he had tended for so many years had burned away all its covering and was now attacking the scalp itself.

'Sergeant Driscoll,' he acknowledged, his voice unexpectedly restrained for a man of such size and in direct contrast to O'Halloran's expansive tones.

'I see the Birches haven't collected their wagon yet, Tim,' Sergeant Driscoll observed. It was as neutral an opening remark as he could conjure up.

'Is it to make me an offer for it you've come all this way, Sergeant?' O'Halloran jested. 'Begob, I didn't realize you were so impressed with it yesterday.'

The sergeant grunted. 'I don't recall being particularly impressed with it yesterday, Tim – or with anything else for that matter.'

Lugubriously O'Halloran licked a forefinger and drew an imaginary downward stroke in the air. 'One up to you, Sergeant,' he conceded. 'I've always held it was an advocate you should have been. You're wasted as a policeman. Sure policemen only apply the law the way a plasterer slaps on a bit of cement and gives the brick a nudge here and there with his trowel to straighten it. Interpreting the law is what you were made for – using it, Sergeant, finding its flaws and injustices. And 'tis many of them it has.'

Sergeant Driscoll refused to rise to the obvious bait. He turned again to the yard, looking out admiringly at the Birches' wagon.

'Not that it isn't a fine piece of work, Tim,' he persisted. ''Tis a credit to you. I'd say that when the gentry see it you'll find a fair bit more custom coming your way.'

'If I do itself,' O'Halloran replied tartly, 'it won't last long.'

'Why is that?'

'Ah sure, that class of conveyance has near had its day, Sergeant. Soon it'll be nothing but the automobile on the road. I wouldn't be surprised – ' he paused, and Sergeant Driscoll detected the curl in his voice that foretold another barb – 'I wouldn't be surprised if I saw yourself behind one of those steering-wheels, as they call them, before long. It's the least your masters could do for such a loyal servant. Wouldn't you say it is, Myles?' he appealed to his companion.

55

'I'd say it is,' Myles Barratt echoed.

'Well, that'd be a bit of progress all right,' the sergeant agreed amicably, 'but you know yourself, Tim, how hard it is to teach an old dog new tricks, so I think I'll be relying on my pony and trap for a while yet. Sure anyway, as long as yourself is around to keep the combination in good fettle, I'll not need to worry. And it doesn't look as if you're likely to be short of material for some time.'

O'Halloran grunted as the sergeant casually examined the well-stocked workshop and its tools. He marvelled at the variety of the latter – saws, lathes, planes, nails, screws, nuts and bolts, a sledgehammer, chisels, a drill, axles and half-axles; and resting against the walls was an ample supply of wood – winter-cut oak still wearing its coat of bark, and plenty of the ash O'Halloran was working on. On the shelves were arrayed the tins of paint, Venetian red alternating with Prussian blue, and pots of dull lead that the sergeant guessed would be used for the undercoats. In Myles Barratt's corner lay bundles of hooping and lengths of iron bars. Myles himself fidgeted about at his furnace but never took his eyes off the fire, on constant watch for 'the heat', the moment when the iron could be properly hammered. The sergeant studied him in fascination as he took up a small stubby heath-broom and sprinkled some water on the flames which seemed to be flaring too freely. He put aside the broom and then worried at the coal with the sharp point of a bright-handled poker until he had excavated from its heart a blazing mass of molten dirt. Scornfully he pushed this away over the edge of the hearth, its glow slowly expiring as it fell on a heap of clinkers already there. Yet still he fed the fire with tiny shovelfuls of coal, half a handful at a time, patting them down over the piece of iron embedded in the flames. Suddenly he drew in his breath in a gasp of triumph as he got his heat. A shower of sparks, like an explosion of tinsel, flew in all directions – up the chimney, against his leather apron – while he threw a pinch of sand into the fire to keep the iron from burning. The sergeant had to turn his face away from the intolerable brightness as the iron began to melt before his eyes and he was forced to take off his cap and wipe his forehead.

Tim O'Halloran had stopped what he was doing to watch

the climax of Myles's operation. The two men were like strange priests joining in some sacred ritual, and in that moment of immolation the sergeant's presence seemed to have been forgotten. He felt a wave of sympathy engulf him, for he knew that O'Halloran's forebodings were not misconceived. Two fine artisans – no, they were more than just artisans or craftsmen – two fine artists who had no alternative but to work away while the shadow of doom loomed over their lives and livelihoods.

'You appear lost in contemplation, Sergeant,' O'Halloran said as he turned to resume his work. 'Or is it a daydream you're having?'

'More a bit of a nightmare you could call it, Tim,' Sergeant Driscoll replied, shaking his head. 'I'm thinking what sort of a world will we have when there's no call for a place like this and work like yours.'

'Oh, I can tell you, Sergeant, I can answer that. Can't you picture it? There'd be no noble broughams on the road, no stylish landaus, no fancy phaetons, no stern governess carts, no jaunty outside-carts, no hardworking dog-carts. And instead of the horse's hoofs clicking out the miles like a clock ticks out time it'll be all noise, ugly noise – engines, horns, hooters, that class of sound.'

'Begob,' Sergeant Driscoll said admiringly, 'if it's an advocate I should have been, it's a poet you should have been. You seem to have it all weighed up like an ode.'

'A lament, dear man, a lament. But sure what use is it to me to be able to see into that particular future when I can't do anything to influence it? Still, there's another future, Sergeant, just as close to me, that I reckon I can do something about. You know well what I mean.'

'I do that,' the sergeant said, putting his cap back on now that the talk had at last turned in a particular direction. 'You mean Odron House, I suppose.'

'I mean Odron House,' O'Halloran repeated firmly. 'No doubt you've heard that that blackguard Mercer is going to marry Elizabeth Odron, and if he does, that land will never come back to the people. You know yourself, Sergeant, what class of a blackguard he is. I'd say he'd even change the name of the place to Mercer House. Mercer House!' O'Halloran finished with a snort, while Myles Barratt, as if to register *his* disgust at the prospect, struck a ringing blow on a piece of iron he had cooling at the edge of the furnace.

'Well now,' Sergeant Driscoll suggested calmly, 'you're taking a lot for granted, and it doesn't do to presume too much these days. In the first place, I wouldn't put much stock in these stories of Ambrose Mercer and Elizabeth Odron becoming man and wife. We have only Mercer's own word on that, and it was yourself classed him as a blackguard.'

Tim O'Halloran raised a hand to silence the sergeant.

'Begging your pardon and not wishing to interrupt you, but it doesn't matter whether it's true or not. Either way that land belongs to the people here.'

'Ah, yes. "The land for the people, the bullock for the road." A fine slogan, Tim, and it's not for me to say there wasn't justice in it. But you know yourself, my good man, that that was the slogan of the Land League and the Land League was half a century ago.'

O'Halloran turned to Myles Barratt. 'Do you hear him, Myles?' he appealed in derision. 'Do you mark the man's words?' Then, turning back to the sergeant: 'I don't need instruction in Irish history any more than the next man. I know well about the Land League.'

'Of course you do, Tim. And you know about the Land Acts, too.'

'I do. Were it not for the Land League, we wouldn't have got the Land Acts. It was agitation that got them for us, Sergeant. If the British government hadn't passed them, they'd have had far worse trouble on their hands. And give the devil his due – I'd be the last to say that those same Acts didn't restore a lot of the land of Ireland to its rightful owners, the Irish people. But remember, Sergeant, under the Acts the landlord wasn't forced to sell the land to his tenants, he wasn't compelled, it was all voluntary.'

'But most of them did sell, Tim.'

'Aye, and why not? Weren't the terms to their advantage? Of course they were, so most of them sold out. Including Colonel Odron. He was one of the best of them. I remember him well. Nor was it for the money he was selling. Not the colonel. He believed in justice – in doing what he knew was right. If he had lived a few years more, there'd not have been one tenant left on the Odron estate who didn't own his own plot. But he died, Sergeant, that was the tragedy of it. He died before he had finished parcelling it all out, and that man Mercer was top dog then. If *he* wasn't there, I have no doubt Mrs Odron would have continued what the colonel had started, but sure she was no match for her steward and his ambition.'

'Was it only ambition, Tim?' Sergeant Driscoll asked. 'After all, if the sales had gone on, Mr Mercer would have been out of a job, wouldn't he?'

'Maybe that was all was worrying him at the start. Maybe not. *I* don't know and *you* don't know. But we both know what he's after now, and it's not only a job. It's the land, Sergeant, what's left of the Odron land. And he's got to be stopped. We can't just do nothing. We have to fight to stop him.'

'Are you telling me I can expect something more than just yesterday's demonstration, then?'

The sergeant stared into Tim O'Halloran's eyes as if the force of his gaze could persuade a straight answer.

'You'd not be expecting me to tell you that now, would you? I said we have to fight, and fight we will. The Irish have always had to fight, but not always for themselves. The shame is how often they've had to fight under the British flag. Indeed, Sergeant, if it weren't for the Irish, Great Britain and its empire mightn't be all that it is.'

'Come on, now, Tim, that's a bit of an exaggeration, isn't it?'

'Is it?' O'Halloran demanded strongly. 'Is it then?' He turned to Myles Barratt and appealed to him. 'Is it an exaggeration, Myles?'

Myles did not reply, as if the suggestion merited only his silent derision, and O'Halloran turned back to the sergeant.

'Let's see now. Let's see if it's an exaggeration. Take all these famous illustrious soldiers, the heroes of Britain. Take the Duke of Wellington, conqueror of the mighty Napoleon, that's an easy one to start with. Where was the Duke of Wellington born, Sergeant?'

'An easy one, aye,' Sergeant Driscoll responded. 'County Meath of course.'

'Is that right, Myles?' Tim O'Halloran called, and with an echoing blow on the bar of iron in his hand Myles Barratt recorded: 'The Duke of Wellington, County Meath.'

59

'Lord Gough, Sergeant?' was O'Halloran's next example.

'Gough? County Limerick?' Sergeant Driscoll essayed.

'Lord Gough – annexed the Punjab for Britain – County Limerick, the sergeant says. Is that right, Myles?'

Myles Barratt struck another blow on the iron. 'Lord Gough, Woodstown, County Limerick,' he intoned.

'General French?' O'Halloran offered.

'That's an easy one. Supreme Commander of the British Expeditionary Force in the Great War. Born in County Roscommon.'

'The Great War, aye,' O'Halloran agreed, 'and South Africa previously. Is Roscommon correct, Myles?'

Another ringing note, another confirmation. 'General French, County Roscommon.'

'Lord Roberts then,' Tim O'Halloran put forward, enjoying his examination of the sergeant's knowledge. Sergeant Driscoll, for his part, didn't want to be bested.

'Earl of Kandahar, Pretoria and Waterford,' he snapped out.

'Waterford the sergeant says, Myles.'

'And Waterford is' – a bang on the iron bar – 'correct. Lord Roberts of Waterford.'

'Here's a harder one then,' O'Halloran posed. 'How about Lord Wolseley?'

Sergeant Driscoll thought for a moment.

'It wouldn't be Dublin itself, would it?'

'Lord Wolseley,' Tim O'Halloran recited. 'Burma, the Crimea, India, China, Canada, Natal, Cyprus, the Transvaal, Egypt. A fair old portion of the British Empire, eh, Sergeant? The sergeant says Dublin for Lord Wolseley – would you agree, Myles?'

Myles Barratt's iron clanged again. 'Lord Wolseley, Golden Bridge House, County Dublin.'

O'Halloran noted the look of pleasure on the sergeant's face. This was a little more than a game now. It was a matter of pride to the two men; what had started as a friendly examination had become a contest.

'How about someone harder, Sergeant?' Tim O'Halloran suggested, a gleam in his eyes. Then, lowering his voice almost to a whisper, he said: 'Sir George White, would you be familiar at all with that boyo?'

60

Sergeant Driscoll stood stolidly. Sir George White? The name meant something to him all right, he was sure of that. But what? He puckered his brow. Finding that the action failed to squeeze out the answer, he took off his cap and scratched his head. No, he couldn't place the man. He said nothing, but kept his cap in his hand, as if to fail the test with it on would in some way reflect on his official position. There was a silence while the two men waited.

'I won't guess,' the sergeant said with dignity. 'Either I know it or I don't, and I don't.'

'Myles?' O'Halloran invited, to save the sergeant the possible insult of having himself supply the answer.

'Defender of Ladysmith,' Myles Barratt said, at which Sergeant Driscoll interjected, 'Of course. I thought he was familiar,' while Myles struck his iron again and went on: 'And born in County Antrim.'

'And there's more,' Tim O'Halloran threatened.

'There is of course,' replied the sergeant, anxious to head him off but also to recover his position. 'There's Lord Kitchener, Kitchener of Khartoum, one of our own, a Kerryman.'

'Aye, a Kerryman, as you say. And all of them fighting for Britain. But what does it mean, Sergeant, to say they were fighting for Britain? I'll tell you what it means. They got decorations and medals and titles and grants for what they did. And what did Britain get? Land. Land. While Irishmen were being deprived of their own land, they were busy winning foreign land for the very tyrant exploiting their own countrymen. Ironic, isn't it, Sergeant?'

The suggestion struck a chord in Sergeant Driscoll's thoughts. There it was again – life's irony. He turned his back on the men and looked out into the yard.

'That's all very well,' he said, 'but they were professional soldiers, acting under orders. *You're* not a soldier, and you, or any friend of yours, have no legal right to any of the land around here.' He turned to face O'Halloran again. 'And if you're foolish enough to try to use force you'll have me to reckon with. I'm giving you fair warning.'

Tim O'Halloran smiled, and then, as if the sergeant had had his full say and now it was his own turn to finish, he went on: 'Land. Land, Sergeant, land. A man is land. It's his element.

He comes from clay, and he goes back to clay. And in between, Sergeant, it's there drawing him. The land needs him, and he needs the land. Our land of Ireland was taken from us, and we'll not rest till we get it back – all of it. You may as well know that, Sergeant. And Mr Ambrose Mercer knows it, too.'

'No doubt he does,' Sergeant Driscoll agreed. 'You told him so clearly yesterday morning. And someone repeated the lesson, only more dangerously, yesterday evening. You wouldn't know anything about that, I suppose?'

Tim O'Halloran put his head on one side and turned to Myles Barratt. Barratt raised an eyebrow, but what it signified the sergeant couldn't guess.

'What is it I wouldn't know anything about, Sergeant?' O'Halloran asked.

'About who fired a shot at Ambrose Mercer and he riding back to the House last evening.'

'Indeed,' O'Halloran mused. 'That wouldn't be what brought you all the way out here now, would it?'

'It might. Then again, it mightn't. It's good to get out from behind the desk for a while. And sure didn't I learn a bit of history at the same time? Sir George White, born in County Antrim. I'll not forget that.'

'Better for you to remember the other things I said, Sergeant, if you'll take my advice.'

'I'll listen to any man's advice, Tim. Listen, mind you, not necessarily take. But I've left you some advice of my own to match it.'

The sergeant turned to go. He knew he'd get no more out of O'Halloran, certainly no more information. But as he bade the men goodbye and started out on his journey back to the barracks something told him that the news of Ambrose Mercer being shot at was no news to them. Something told him very strongly that, even if Tim O'Halloran had not been involved, he had heard all about it before even the sergeant set foot in his yard.

'And where might Mr Mercer be at the moment, ma'am?' Tom Fahy asked.

He and Constable Howell were standing in the drawing-room of Odron House where Amelia Odron had received them

62

immediately they arrived. It was the first time Pat Howell had seen the colonel's widow. On their way out Tom had told him that in recent years she rarely came into Gortnahinch and had been living a life of increasing seclusion. He didn't know what to expect – Fahy's conversation about the Odron family had concentrated on Elizabeth, whom he described as 'a fine filly' – but Mrs Odron's welcome quickly put him at his ease. She was genuinely glad to have their protection – 'relieved' was the word she used; she hadn't slept a wink with worry the previous night. Pat could see she wasn't exaggerating, for under her eyes were tell-tale dark shadows. When she smiled, however, the shadows seemed to disappear, banished by a soft glow that, spilling from the still rich auburn of her hair, shone lustrously in her brown eyes.

She sat down on the edge of an armchair, inviting the constables to sit opposite her on a matching sofa.

Sunshine flooded through the four tall sash windows looking out on the main view, making the men blink as they took in their surroundings. Neither of the two had ever seen such a room in their lives, and Pat Howell was happy to let his companion be their spokesman, while he gazed around in awe. The dark-striped wallpaper bore many portraits and photographs, most of the former being of resplendent bewigged worthies in stiff poses while the latter were mainly of soldiers and military groups. In the middle of the room was a long round-cornered table, its gleaming mahogany surface reflecting in mirror-image the bowl of white roses that had been placed exactly at its dead centre, and the pair of the bowl – but this one boasting red roses – stood on a grand piano that was covered with a drippling lace shawl. Outside the windows the constable could see green lawns, a tennis-court and in the distance a row of sentinel poplars. He wondered if he'd be able to make a hand of tennis at all. Why not, he reflected. He was good at all sports, and if he could wield a hurley to meet a flying *sliotar* he could surely hit a ball over a net with a tennis-racket.

Mrs Odron was telling Fahy that she had no idea where her estate manager was.

'He could be anywhere, Constable. Most days I rarely see anything of him until dinner-time. Sometimes not even then. The estate seems to keep him busy enough. We still have some tenants. And there are the labourers. I suppose they have to be supervised. I don't really know, but I'm sure Mr Mercer can find plenty to do.'

'Yes, I suppose he has a lot of ground to cover,' Fahy put in.

'Oh, indeed. The estate isn't as extensive as it used to be, but one could still get lost in it. Well, *I* nearly could anyway even after all my years here. But, then, I seldom go further than the gardens.'

'So you're not expecting Mr Mercer back before dinner?'

'*I'm* not expecting him back, no. I suppose he might look in for some reason but, even if he does, I'd hardly see him myself. But surely you don't need to find him this minute. Wouldn't dinner-time be soon enough?'

'When would that be?'

'We dine at seven-thirty usually.'

'Will we take a look for him now, Pat?' Tom Fahy suggested, turning to Howell.

'But you haven't been shown your rooms yet, Constable,' Amelia Odron pointed out, as if surprised at their haste.

'Well, perhaps we can get settled in and put our stuff away, Mrs Odron. And then we'll try to find Mr Mercer. Who's in the house at the moment, apart from yourself and the servants?'

'Only my daughters, Elizabeth and Victoria.'

'I don't think you'll be in any danger in the house, not during daylight anyway. Besides, it's Mr Mercer was shot at. And I don't like the idea of him wandering around without protection.'

'That's right,' Pat agreed. 'The sooner we find him, the better.'

'Certainly, if you insist,' Mrs Odron said, rising with the men. 'I'll have someone show you to your rooms.'

She pulled a bell-handle by the fireplace, and an elderly servant appeared dressed in a maid's uniform.

'Margaret, would you show the constables to their rooms. The pink bedroom and the olive one.' She turned back to Fahy. 'I've put you both on the first floor, Constable, in the front so as you'll be able to see the gardens and the driveway at night. In case you hear any suspicious noises.'

The two men followed the maid, picking up their bags from the hall as they went. On each balustrade at the bottom of the stairs was a pedestal on which stood a wooden carved figure, a cavalier and a damsel, smiling at each other across the wide majestic staircase. The top was traversed by a dim panelled corridor, its walls covered with dark oil portraits, which seemed to run along the whole front of the house. Like the stairs it was covered with a heavy green carpet. It struck Tom Fahy that if any interloper managed to gain entry to the house without being seen, he could race up the stairs in a few moments and no one would ever hear him.

'The pink room is this way,' the old maid said, turning right and leading them along the corridor until she stopped at one of the rooms. 'And that's the olive one next to it. There's no difference in them, so ye can take yer pick.'

'And where does Mr Mercer sleep?' Pat Howell asked.

'He's just beyond, next to the olive room.'

Fahy was tempted to enquire what colour Mercer's room was but decided to curb his facetiousness. Just then a door at the end of the corridor opened and Elizabeth Odron appeared. She stood for a moment looking at the group before casually approaching, her long skirt flowing as she walked.

'Good morning,' she greeted. 'Has Sergeant Driscoll sent you to take care of us? I do hope you won't find it too tiresome.' Her words were addressed to both the constables, but it was on Tom Fahy that her eyes lingered.

Pat saw that she was indeed 'a fine filly', though more robust-looking than that description suggested. Her dark hair was swept well back from a broad clear forehead, and her green eyes sparkled brightly as she spoke. Tom Fahy seemed to have forgotten his earlier impatience to get started on locating Ambrose Mercer. He was smiling broadly, telling her it would be a pleasure to watch over her, as if he intended to single out that part of his duty for his personal attention.

'I should have introduced myself,' she said. 'I'm Elizabeth Odron.'

'Oh, I know who you are,' Tom Fahy replied. 'I've seen you now and again in the town.'

Elizabeth smiled, inclining her head as if in acknowledgement of a compliment, for his tone seemed to convey that he had not merely seen her but had taken special notice of her. She was not the least embarrassed that his gaze frequently darted down and up again from her bosom, where the tightly drawn belt around her waist accentuated the contours of her breasts behind a thin silk blouse. Pat Howell found it somewhat disconcerting, and when his companion said, 'My name is Tom Fahy,' adding, 'And this is my colleague, Constable Howell,' he couldn't prevent himself from blushing furiously.

'I hope you'll both be comfortable while you're here. Have you seen your rooms? Are they satisfactory?'

'I was just about to show them, Miss Elizabeth,' the maid intervened.

'You can run along then, Margaret. I'll take care of the men.'

She opened the bedroom door and led the way in.

'This is the pink bedroom. We call all the bedrooms by the colour of their wallpaper; it's much the easiest way of identifying them. Now, which of you will take this room?'

She pirouetted quickly, almost catching Tom whose gaze had been drinking her in. 'Mr Fahy, somehow I don't think pink is quite your colour.'

Tom Fahy was pleased she hadn't addressed him as 'Constable'.

'Do you think it suits Pat better, then?' he asked with a chuckle.

Pat laughed. 'Sure the colour of the walls means nothing to me. Besides, I wouldn't see them in the dark, would I? And I'm usually asleep as soon as my head hits the pillow.'

'You must have a very untroubled mind, Mr Howell. Shall we leave him then, Mr Fahy, and I'll show you your room.'

'The colour doesn't worry *me* any more than it does Pat,' Tom Fahy was saying as they entered the next bedroom.

'Not another untroubled mind surely! My goodness, I'd have thought you policemen have plenty to worry about at the moment. Why, there was an ambush only the other day at Milltown, and that's not all that far away. I read about it in the *Irish Times*.'

'It's a good thirty miles from here.'

'Not that I'm frightened myself by a few Shinners, but my mother gets very upset and she's begged my sister and me not to go out alone.'

'That's sound advice, sure enough. Anyway, Miss Elizabeth, now that Pat and I are here, you've nothing to worry about. You can sleep peacefully at night.'

'I hope you can sleep peacefully, too. At least you'll find the bed quite comfortable.'

She sat on its edge, bouncing up and down a few times to demonstrate its softness. She was smiling up at the constable – provocatively, he thought.

'I'm sure it's better than the barracks anyway,' he commented as he casually sat down next to her and indulged in a few test bounces of his own. His action threw him against her, and he hastened to apologize.

'That's all right, Mr Fahy,' she said, rising. 'I'm not very breakable.'

'No, I'd say you're not,' he replied appraisingly, unable to suppress a more than official interest in Elizabeth Odron. His duties in the past had seldom brought him into contact with 'the quality', and he certainly never had any occasion to pass even the time of day with one of their nubile young women. He wondered if Elizabeth Odron's friendly air, bordering almost on familiarity, could possibly be the normal manner of her class; it was a surprise, without a doubt. Of course, she and Victoria had grown up without a father – and by all accounts the mother hadn't been much help. That would make a bit of a difference all right. And there had been those stories about Elizabeth's high jinks with the soldiers. It looked as if a few weeks at Odron House might not be such a chore after all. The thought filled Tom Fahy with a sudden zest.

'I think we'd better try to locate Mr Mercer,' he said. 'He's the one who was attacked, so the sooner we find him, the better.'

'Do both of you need to go? Who'll be left to protect the rest of us if one of you doesn't stay here?' Elizabeth asked. Her tone was light; one might imagine it carried the hint of an invitation. He decided not to presume too much, too soon.

'Ah, I don't think you have anything to fear,' he laughed. 'They'll not be shooting at you or yours.' And as they were leaving the bedroom he asked: 'Was that your room we saw you come out of?'

'Yes, the one at the end of the corridor. You won't be too far away if I need help, will you?' Once again there was that provocative note.

'And this is Mr Mercer's room next to mine?' Fahy said, stepping out into the corridor.

'Yes. We're all within easy reach of each other. Except my mother and my sister, Victoria. They sleep on the other side of the house.'

Pat Howell was waiting for them at his bedroom door, anxious to begin looking for Ambrose Mercer. 'Would you have any idea where Mr Mercer is now?' he queried.

'None at all, I'm afraid,' Elizabeth replied. 'He's like the Pimpernel. He could be anywhere.'

'Come on then, Pat.' Tom Fahy adopted a businesslike tone that he hoped would make an impression. 'We'd better be off.'

'Oh, you *are* a determined man, Mr Fahy,' Elizabeth chided. 'But I suppose you'll be back for lunch. Has mother told you about meal-times?'

'We'll worry about that when we've found Mr Mercer. Anyway, we know that dinner is at half-seven and we're sure to be back by then.'

'Yes, half-seven, as you say,' she echoed, and this time he was certain she was mischievously mimicking his common usage instead of the more genteel 'seven-thirty'.

'What do you make of that one, Pat?' he asked when the two constables reached the drive. He sounded pleased with himself, as if he already knew what *he* made of Elizabeth Odron.

'I'd say she's a tough customer – a different class of animal altogether from her mother.'

'I think you've struck the nail on the head. There's a bit of the animal in her all right. A bit of a cat – the kind who might be sitting contented in your lap one moment, purring away, and have her claws in you the next.'

'On the way out you were telling me she was a fine filly, now it's a cat she is. There's a mighty difference between the two.'

Tom Fahy gave his friend a playful punch on the shoulder. 'That's just where you're wrong, my son. A woman can be a filly and a cat at the same time. The only one of God's creatures with that capacity, bless her! You want to get to know them a bit more. You just keep an eye on your Uncle Tom!'

Pat Howell ducked his head away in confusion. He was conscious of his own lack of experience with girls. He didn't feel jealous of his friend's confidence but sometimes wished he wasn't so far back down the field himself. Except that if it was Tom's intention to try anything on with Elizabeth Odron, it was a different sort of eye that would need be kept on him. With that Odron girl he might find that he'd bitten off more than he'd be able to chew. Besides, they had a job to do – and it was time to get down to it.

'I suppose we'd better go after Mercer,' he said. 'But it'd be far easier if we knew our way around the estate.'

'It certainly would,' Tom rejoined. 'Maybe we should get Elizabeth to show it to us.' He smiled broadly at the sudden look of alarm on his colleague's face. 'Don't be worried, Pat, I'm only joking,' he added. 'Best thing is for us to split up. There's no point in both of us looking in the same place. I'll take the back beyond the house and you go on ahead. Let whoever finds him stick close to him. And, if you don't find him, come back here at one o'clock.' He gave Pat Howell a broad wink, raised his head haughtily, and in a clipped falsetto voice said: 'Come back at one o'clock, Mr Howell, and you can have your *lunch*.'

'I wonder what you'd get for lunch here?' Pat speculated.

Tom Fahy cast a glance up at the brilliant sky. 'By one o'clock it's not lunch I'll be thinking of but a pint. Howsoever . . . let's get started. Here I come, Ambrose Mercer, here I come.' And he strode off around the side of Odron House and out of sight.

Constable Howell stood for a few moments contemplating. If the weather held, spending a couple of weeks or so in such surroundings would be like a summer holiday in a big hotel – always provided O'Halloran and his boys didn't pay them a visit. Not that Pat thought there was much likelihood of further trouble from that quarter once it got around that there were two policemen on the estate. He put a hand on his holster and felt the hard bulk of the weapon resting inside it. He might hate the idea of having to carry a gun at all, but at least if its presence helped to deter the Shinners he wouldn't complain. Still, he must guard against being over-confident just because he was armed. This was the first job of any importance he had been given by Sergeant Driscoll, and he wouldn't want to let him down. He still wished someone else had been chosen to

69

pair with Tom Fahy. There were others who, like Tom, didn't have anything particularly special to keep them in the barracks, but Pat certainly did. Those letters he had written about the Police Union – there'd be replies to them, and he didn't want to lose any time answering the replies and getting that Dublin meeting arranged. Without a meeting in Dublin to get everyone who was really interested together in one place, he knew that his hopes of reviving enthusiasm for a Police Union stood little chance. Perhaps the sergeant would send any mail out to him; he could easily deal with it while he was at Odron House. But Pat had his doubts on that point; he guessed that one of the reasons he had been sent to Odron House was to stop him from doing anything about the Police Union. The sergeant, of course, would only be out for his own good; Pat knew that. Once Mrs Odron had requested protection, Sergeant Driscoll couldn't refuse her, and Pat wasn't really surprised the opportunity had been taken of moving him out of harm's way. Thank goodness, anyway, that it was Tom Fahy who was chosen as the other half of the act. With Tom around, their stint shouldn't become too boring.

He took some steps down the drive, looking sharply to right and left as if he expected an intruder to pop up out of the ground or from behind a tree. Then he turned and took a few more paces backwards before stopping to survey the front of Odron House. He could identify the four tall drawing-room windows, their glass winking and sparkling under the sun's rays. His gaze moved up to the windows of the first floor, but there were too many there for him to tell which were the rooms he and Tom were to occupy.

How old would Odron House be, he wondered. A hundred years? Two hundred? There had been no fine residences like it that he knew of back home in County Leitrim, but here in Kerry they weren't an unusual sight. Not that he had seen them himself; they were tucked away in their grounds behind the high demesne wall that was the nearest he ever got to them on his patrols. Constable Rafferty knew them all. Buildings and architecture were Aengus's obsession. A Dubliner, he was always boasting of the 'beautiful edifices in the second city of the Empire'. Beautiful Dublin certainly was, though it was more its size that had overwhelmed Pat during the six months' training period he had spent there in the Phoenix Park police depot. Sackville Street, they told him, was the widest thoroughfare in Europe – he could well believe it; and God knows his own home village would have fitted fifty times and more into the Park itself. Ah yes, Aengus would be in his element in Odron House; maybe, if Pat put a word in, the sergeant would send him out for a spell when recalling Tom Fahy or himself.

He walked over the firm grass to see what the side of the house looked like and was surprised to find that one of the first-floor windows there had a well-tended window-box on its sill. It was the only one with such an adornment, and it did help to brighten the otherwise austere exterior. He looked around at the lawns and greenery that filled the view. The early-morning ground mist had completely disappeared, and already there was a tremble of heat haze in the distance. There was no point in going any further down the drive; that led only to the front gates, and he didn't think Mercer was likely to be in that locality. To his right was a small wood – perhaps behind it he'd come upon the pastures and fields where his man might be working or even someone else who had seen Mercer that morning might know where he had gone.

Behind the wood, however, he found not farm land but more gardens, massed with a variety of tall rhododendron and honey-yellow azaleas, and beyond them he could make out someone sitting at the edge of a stream. As he approached he realized that the figure which from a distance had appeared to be a child was in fact a young woman, gazing into the stream with rapt concentration. As she heard him approach she looked round and sprang to her feet.

'Sorry to disturb you, miss,' he said. 'I'm looking for Mr Mercer. Have you seen him?'

She had long fair hair, a strand of which had escaped and was straying in front of her eyes. Quickly she tucked it back in place.

'Oh, you won't find him around here. Are you the policeman Mother got to guard him?'

'I'm one of them. There's another one with me. He's searching for Mr Mercer behind the house.'

'Then I think he'll have more success than you. That's where the farm is. This part is mostly my garden.'

71

'*Your* garden? Then you'd be. . . .'

'I'm Victoria Odron. What's your name?'

'I'm Constable Howell. Pat Howell.'

'Glad to meet you,' she said, putting a hand out for Pat to shake. Taken by surprise, he shot his own hand out, barely touching her, before withdrawing it again.

'Isn't it just a marvellous summer,' she went on, as if their meeting were a social occasion on which one is expected to be affable and polite. 'So un-Irish, this weather. It's a wonderful time for the gardens as well. Everything in bloom. I just love it. Do you have a garden?'

The constable gave a short laugh. 'Garden! There's not much chance for a garden in the barracks.'

'Of course, I forgot that's where you'd be stationed. Do you come from around here?'

'No, I'm here only the past six months. I was born and grew up far away from here, on a small farm in County Leitrim.'

Victoria sat down again and hugged her knees. Pat noticed that she had taken her shoes off and was wearing no stockings. The sight stirred memories of his own childhood. He and his sisters and brothers had gone barefoot most of the time every summer. It wasn't only because of the weather – indeed, that far west it rained in summer almost as much as in winter; it was mainly to save wear and tear on their shoes. With a large family, and feet growing every year, shoes and socks were an expensive item and there wasn't much money to go around. It wasn't until Pat was a good deal older that he had brand-new shoes of his own rather than a pair that had previously been worn by one of his brothers and been mended by his father many times. And socks, too, darned by his mother so often that little of the original stocking remained. But he didn't imagine that Victoria Odron was going barefoot for reasons of economy. He wished he could take off his own heavy regulation boots and toast his feet in the sunshine. Perhaps even go for a paddle in the stream.

'Tell me about it,' she said.

'Oh, there's not much to tell,' he replied, almost stumbling over his words. 'I'm afraid it would only bore you. Besides, I'd better try to find Mr Mercer.'

'The other man has probably found him by now.'

72

'Well, anyway, I'd not want to be disturbing you any further.'

She gazed up at him with a frankly puzzled look. 'Disturbing me? But I wasn't actually doing anything.'

'Well, disturbing your thoughts then.'

'Oh, I have plenty of time to think. It's very quiet here these days. Has been for ages. At least it seems like ages. We never get any visitors now. We used have scores of them – neighbours, friends of mother, friends of Elizabeth. She's my sister—'

'I know. We met her in the house.'

Victoria seemed not to have heard. Head thrown back, she was gazing into the distance. 'We used to have parties and dances and a ball every year.'

'I'm sure you must miss it all,' Pat Howell sympathized. He didn't know what else to say. He should be getting on about his business, but she was so wrapped up in the recollection of her lost world that he felt to leave her without an audience would be unkind as well as rude.

'Not really. I was never that fond of parties.' She leaned back with her hands on the grass. 'I suppose I was a bit too young to enjoy them properly. Elizabeth loved them – all the fun, the games, the dancing, the attention. Especially the attention. Elizabeth loves being the centre of attraction.' There was no note of envy in her voice. Indeed, although Pat knew that Victoria was the younger of the two, she sounded like an older sister being indulgent about the innocent giddiness of a less grown-up sibling.

'Did you ever want to be the centre of attraction yourself?' he asked.

'Oh no. I like to observe other people. They're all so different to talk to. I never have anyone to talk to here. Not nowadays anyway.'

'You have your sister and your mother. Can't you talk to them?'

'We've lived together for so many years that we long ago exhausted all our topics of conversation,' she said with a laugh. 'Besides, mother's main worry at the moment is the Sinn Fein, and Elizabeth is only interested in jewellery and clothes and—' She didn't finish that sentence; instead she looked up suddenly, a new-found enthusiasm in her voice. 'But now you're here. And you said there's another policeman with you. Two new people to talk to. Will you be staying long?'

'I don't really know, Miss. That all depends.'

'And will you talk to me a lot?'

Pat blushed. The directness of the request coupled with its strangeness bewildered him. Could she be that lonely? Once again a vision of his own youth flashed across his mind. His home might have been small but it was always filled with people – brothers, sisters, neighbouring farmers' wives, the farmers themselves in the evenings, and all talking, always talking. He couldn't remember silence or what it was like. And here was this big house and this well-born daughter with no one to talk to at all. It seemed a shame. He was sorry for her. But then he looked sharply at Victoria Odron to see if in some way she might be just making fun of him. Perhaps she was like her sister; Elizabeth's whole air had given him the strongest suspicion that she wasn't really taking Tom and himself very seriously. Perhaps the sisters were two of a kind, but that Victoria had a softer nature than Elizabeth and was more willing, if only for the sake of politeness, to pretend an interest she didn't really feel. Yet he could detect no hint of mockery or insincerity in her voice, no trace of guile in her expression.

'Yes, of course, miss,' he smiled. 'I'll talk to you as much as you like – not that I fancy myself as much of a talker. But I think I'd better be off now. I'm on duty, you know, and it's my first day here, so I shouldn't really be taking it easy.'

He looked down at her. She didn't immediately reply but held him with her eyes. He saw that they were blue, a mirror of the blue skies all around, and their expression was warm, open, hiding nothing.

'Goodbye then, for the moment,' she said eventually.

Her voice was warm, too.

4

THE GORTNAHINCH BRANCH of the Munster and Leinster Bank was grey, staid, suggestive of permanence and rectitude, in no way unconventional in style. Indeed, had it been, it would have looked very much at odds with its surroundings, for it was set in the Square, a cobbled area on three sides of which were gathered most of the town's important shops. The bank's only unusual feature was the five steps up to its heavy metal doors, steps which not only raised it physically above the other earthbound buildings, but also perhaps hinted at a claim to some special distinction in having as its stock-in-trade money rather than base goods.

On Tuesday morning, nearing noon, the Square was a busy place. Horse-drawn vehicles were constantly coming and going, even an occasional motor-car, housewives moved from shop to shop on their errands, children on holiday from school were rolling hoops and playing noisy games of hopscotch. About the only living objects in the Square not on the move – they had been there for quite some time – were a horse between the shafts of a trap outside the bank and the man sitting in the trap. Every few seconds the horse would toss its head and rattle its harness impatiently and the tall figure hunched forward would desultorily flap the reins that sagged between his hands. Sometimes a passer-by would glance at him, touch the peak of his cap and say, 'Mornin', Mr Renfrew,' to be rewarded with a nod and a barely audible 'Good morning to you'. It was clear that Charles Renfrew's thoughts were elsewhere, as indeed they had been for the last ten minutes since he had come out of the bank and resumed his seat in the trap.

Meditatively he pulled at the skin of his neck and readjusted his small bow-tie. An open-necked shirt would have been more comfortable on such a hot day, but when he decided that morning to pay the bank manager a visit, Charles Renfrew felt that some apparel of more dignity, more authority, was required. Not that Dinny Carmody, the manager, would have minded one way or the other. With the bank's customers mostly divided between down-to-earth country businessmen and hard-working farmers, the worn carpet of his office had seen many visitors with mud on their boots. And it wasn't that Carmody's status called for any special deference – not at least from one who had known the manager since he was a junior clerk behind the counter and the size of whose account would, in any event, have been more than enough to excuse a touch of casualness. But, though Charles Renfrew was no longer the owner of a large estate, he felt that he represented a certain style and tradition, that he still had standards to maintain and, heatwave or no heatwave, a visit to the town and the bank was no occasion to let the side down in any way.

Time had dealt kindly with Charles Renfrew. At sixty-two his bearing was as upright and his complexion as healthy as when he was twenty-two. Only now was his dark hair beginning to go silver-grey around the temples and his thick moustache and eyebrows to show tell-tale flecks of white, but behind his heavy spectacles his grey eyes still usually appeared languid and untroubled. His friends often commented that their peaceful expression was the result of his being a bachelor – the reward, many called it, rather than the result; but as the years passed that observation ceased to draw from him its earlier smile of satisfaction. True, he had never yearned for a spouse when he had been a younger man. He had run his large estate himself, had looked after his tenants, and was able to employ as many servants as he required. Of course, his life had not been without its occasional amours, but these romantic affairs had always been taken as they came and forgotten as they went, never preoccupying him, and certainly never threatening to divert him from his business affairs. All this, however, had been before the new Land Acts had gradually made it possible for landlords to break up their large estates without loss to themselves, and when he had eventually taken advantage of the new legislation to sell his tenants the farms they had been working he was left with considerable wealth that Carmody had invested shrewdly for him, twenty acres of land, a large country house – and no more business to fill the idle empty hours. It was then, when he began to realize that he had bought loneliness along with leisure, that Amelia Odron came more and more into his thoughts.

At first he found it difficult to alter his long-held view that she was still Alex Odron's wife, even though she had been a widow for so many years. But his own changed state eventually gave him a fresh perspective, and the respect and affection he had always had for her underwent a transformation into emotions and desires far more personal, far more insistent. In his eyes the woman who before had been attractive was now beautiful, who though she still bore another man's name was in fact unattached, and so with preconceptions banished he was enabled to recognize the true nature of his own feelings. The realization found him completely unprepared. The obvious next step was to propose to her. But to propose to her now, after such a long period when their whole relationship had been one of only close but uncomplicated friendship, would seem . . . ludicrous? offensive? . . . certainly eccentric. The more he thought about it, the more he delayed; and the more he delayed, the more he tried to justify the delay with unconvincing excuses. Amelia Odron was the first woman he had ever really wanted, but because the straitjacket of habit that his long bachelorhood had imposed on his ways could not, he felt, have made him a particularly exciting husband to share the rest of one's life with, he was afraid of being rejected. So when at last he forced himself to propose he was quite certain he had left it too late.

As he had expected, the answer was No, but a 'No' that was accompanied by such an expression of gratitude and so much praise of his own virtues that he felt encouraged to persist. He was careful never to be importunate, never to make his persistence objectionable, but as time passed a new bond was forged.

It was a bond that, because it had grown out of the unimpaired close friendship of a woman and the suitor she had rejected, seemed to allow for a warmer intimacy and an increased sense of privilege than had existed between them before. It kept Charles Renfrew's hopes alive and made him anxious to demonstrate to Amelia that it had some practical advantages, too. If he could show her, without presumption or offence, that he was someone she could lean on and confide in, then surely such an involvement in her life and affairs couldn't but forward his suit. And now, at last, that opportunity was there.

He had gone to Odron House the previous afternoon to take tea with Amelia. Though he called to see her frequently at other times of the week, the Sunday-afternoon visit had been a rarely missed ritual for many years. Now and again the girls, or one of them, might be there, but Ambrose Mercer hardly ever. And very seldom would there be any other callers present, so Charles had come to regard these afternoons as being reserved for him.

The atmosphere on yesterday's visit, however, had been anything but one of contentment, for the main topic of conversation was the morning's demonstration by Tim O'Halloran and his followers. Elizabeth had passed it off as a storm in a teacup, her main regret being that she hadn't been able to witness it herself; Victoria, too, expressed no fear or resentment, and Charles recognized in her quiet acceptance of the situation the same courage and understanding that had been her father's sterling virtues; Amelia had seemed to be holding herself in, perhaps not yet recovered from the shock or not wishing to alarm her children by showing any great concern; only Mercer, against whom the whole protest had been directed, failed to put in an appearance at all. As Charles munched a cucumber sandwich, declined a slice of iced coffee cake and carefully replaced his delicate Worcester cup in its saucer after each sip of tea, he reflected inwardly on the incongruity of the scene. They might have been at a Sunday-afternoon vicarage party in some quiet hamlet deep in the English countryside, but instead they were sitting in a beleaguered mansion in Ireland, a country their armies were thought to have conquered and pacified. Still, the situation might be turned to his advantage, for the morning's threatening parade could not but strengthen his hand.

'Really, Amelia,' he had said as soon as the two girls left them alone, 'these Sinn Fein blackguards can turn very nasty. I don't want to frighten you more than you have been frightened already, my dear, but I feel I must try to make you realize how vulnerable you are here.

'I know, Charles, I do know,' Amelia had agreed, the calm look of her soft brown eyes belying the anxiety in her voice. She was wearing a light summer frock which displayed her still youthful figure to full advantage, and her hair was an auburn arch rising from the yellow chiffon scarf around her neck. Charles thought she had never looked more attractive; he had to make full use of his opportunity.

'But if you know, then surely you must do something about it. After all, it's not only yourself you have to worry about; there's Elizabeth and Victoria, too. Again, my dear, I don't want to alarm you unduly, but there's no doubt that things are going to get worse rather than better. It's the same throughout the country. You have only to read the newspapers.'

'You're right, Charles, of course you're right. But what can I do?' The note of anxiety had sharpened into one of near-frustration, as if she knew what his reply would be and was almost ashamed that yet another rejection, even in the face of the new danger, would appear unreasonably stubborn.

'Oh, dear Amelia, you *must* know the answer to that. Sell up the rest of the estate and marry me.'

'No, I can't,' she replied quickly, turning her head away to look out the window at the tall elms in the distance. She kept her eyes firmly fixed on the view, and Charles glanced sharply at her. 'I can't,' she had said. He was sure she had never said that before. It had always been a grateful smile and 'Thank you, Charles, but I don't really think so,' or some such polite refusal. But this was different – not only in form but in intonation, too. She would if she could, but something was preventing her. Surely he wasn't just imagining that. Surely that was the message behind her words.

'Why not? Why ever not?' he persisted with more force than he had used on previous occasions. 'Is it because of the girls? They could come and live with us. I don't have to tell you that. You know I've said so all along. There's plenty of room at Gort Wood.' He paused, and when Amelia shook her head as she always had done in the past in response to that suggestion he rushed on: 'Maybe you'd prefer to hold on to Odron House in case either of the girls should want to come back and live here when they get married. If so, I'd be more than willing to pay for the upkeep in the mean time. It wouldn't matter how long it might take.'

'No, Charles, I could never allow you to do that.'

'Oh, nonsense,' he replied almost impatiently, sensing that he was at last making some headway. Alex, when he had been alive, had never shilly-shallied about any project once his mind was made up; Charles resolved to press on.

'You must know that I'm very well off – more money than I'll ever be able to spend. But, if it would make you happier to pay for the upkeep of Odron House yourself, well and good. Presumably you have a fair income from the government stocks Alex got when he sold off some of the farms, and you'd have more if you got rid of the rest of them. I don't mean to pry, my dear, but no doubt you've been investing the income from the estate since Alex died. In all these years there must have been a tidy sum left after the normal running expenses.'

Amelia raised her shoulders and then let them fall into a despondent gesture.

'When Alex . . . after he died. . . . I'm afraid I wasn't taking much notice. I presumed everything was continuing as it had before – with the estate, I mean. But it seems I was mistaken, and for quite some time it's all been rather going downhill.'

'Indeed?' Charles was surprised at this information.

'Oh, yes. What's been coming in in the past few years has hardly covered expenses. You must have noticed, Charles.'

'Noticed what?'

'Why, how much has changed. At Odron House, I mean. You know how we used to entertain: parties, dances – oh, the usual social round. I wasn't greatly interested in all that for myself, but I thought that with the girls growing up. . . .'

Charles shook his head in annoyance at his own obtuseness and lack of observation.

'It never struck me. I suppose it must have crossed my mind that life here wasn't as gay as it used to be, but I never attached any significance to it. And for the past few years I put it all down to the increasing troubles in the country. Most of our

80

sort, you know, have been affected by all the fighting and hatred and those Sinn Fein outrages, so naturally we've been inclined to lie low, so to speak. I suppose I presumed that was the reason you had dropped all those parties and weekends.'

'No, it wasn't only that,' Amelia said. 'I explained to the girls. I told them we just couldn't afford it any more.'

Charles's eyebrows came together, and his brow creased in puzzlement. He leaned forward in his chair.

'But that doesn't make sense, Amelia. It's a while since I sold my estate, but I've kept in touch and I can tell you that farming has been a profitable business in Ireland in recent years. There may have been the odd patch but, my goodness, who do you think fed Britain during the war? If your land wasn't producing a handsome profit, I'd be astounded. Has Mercer been mismanaging it?'

It was at that point that Amelia had suddenly appeared to find the trend of the conversation embarrassing, perhaps even distressing. Certainly there was a clear plea in her voice as she appealed to him: 'Please, don't let's talk about it any more, Charles. It doesn't really matter. I'm sure things will pick up.'

But to him it did matter. This, he felt, was the opportunity he had been waiting for, the chance to become more involved in Amelia's life, to induce her to turn to him for guidance. And now that such an opportunity had arisen he wasn't going to let it go a-begging. He had always taken it for granted that as far as the running of the estate was concerned Amelia could have complete confidence in Ambrose Mercer. After all, Mercer's reputation as a thoroughly competent manager had never been questioned. Yet Charles had sensed in Amelia's refusal to let him pursue that point not only embarrassment but also – could it be? – something she wished to hide.

At home after his visit, he had spent the whole evening turning the situation over in his mind. The fact that Amelia had now revealed as much as she did when throughout the years she had given no hint of her difficulties showed how serious they must be. But if he tried to force her to reopen the discussion such unwelcome pressure might lose him all his newly won ground. That was something he couldn't risk. Yet he was convinced that his query about Mercer's possible mis-management had been the turning-point of their conversation.

81

And he had thrown it out quite without premeditation. He hadn't for a moment thought there could be anything in it. But why had Amelia refused to discuss it? Was it only because his question was one that, in her ignorance of estate management, she couldn't really answer? Perhaps. Yet, if it was only that, she would have said so. Again he had the feeling that there was something more to it. As she had pointed out, the scale of entertainment at Odron House had been reduced almost to nothing in the past few years, so even if money had been very short before then, all that economizing should have gone a fair way to restoring her fortunes. But according to her it hadn't. And Charles was sure Amelia was above suspicion herself. He couldn't possibly believe that her story had been a concoction, that her straitened circumstances had come about because she was frittering the profits away. On what? Clothes? If so, she never wore them. Jewellery? Likewise. The stock market? Nonsense, Amelia was no gambler. Then what? If she was hiding something – not any indiscretions of her own, but suspicions about someone else's action . . . suspicions she couldn't prove. . . . That would account for her reluctance to pursue the question.

When Charles Renfrew awoke the next morning his mind was clear. He didn't like Ambrose Mercer, but despite his uncouth ways, his hard-heartedness, his inhumanity – indeed, despite his inability to lay claim to a single redeeming virtue – it was at least generally agreed that he knew his job. And Charles had no doubt that he did. He recalled that Alex had always told him how bright Mercer was – no, *sharp*, that was the word he used – how keen he was to find out every little detail about the running of the estate, how quickly he picked up everything that was taught him. Alex had been quite proud of his protégé, quietly pleased with himself that his judgement of young Mercer's capabilities was being proved correct. Perhaps the youth's enthusiasm and aptitude blinded Alex to the flaws in his character, flaws that quickly turned him into a feared and hated taskmaster once he had been given a free hand. But it might not have been Alex's fault: the flaws may not have been evident then. Or perhaps even at that fairly tender age Mercer was calculating enough to pretend subservience and servility until he had learned all he wanted to know. And learn it he certainly did. In which case, the estate profit should not have declined as disastrously as Amelia had indicated. In which case. . . .

The more he thought about it, the more certain Charles became that the obvious conclusion, no matter how unbelievable it might appear at first, had to be correct. In his book one and one always made two; a lifetime spent managing his own estate had taught him that he could always rely on that equation. A good estate manager plus almost two decades managing a large estate – even if there had been more bad years than good, and Charles Renfrew knew that it had been the other way round – the answer should have been wealth, considerable wealth. Yet it seemed the answer had been the opposite. So where had the money gone? Mercer couldn't have got through it all. His habits were known, and there had never been any stories of dissipation or philandering or anything like throwing money around. Far from it; when he went on his drinking bouts in the local public houses, he didn't buy for anyone and no one bought for him. But, if Charles was right, there had to be a lot of money somewhere. A bank? Yes, that was the only place it could be. There was only one in Gortnahinch, and the Renfrew account had always been held there so Charles was a highly valued customer. Would he be valued highly enough to be able to winkle some information out of the manager, Dinny Carmody, without actually forcing him to offend against his code of professional ethics? Could he manage to make him reveal the extent of another client's financial position? It was a long shot, but he could try. It was at least worth a chance if it might help Amelia.

The information he was seeking proved far easier to obtain than he had expected. Immediately he entered Carmody's office and the usual exchange of pleasantries had taken place, the manager had commented: 'A bad business that, last evening, Mr Renfrew.'

'Last evening? What business was that, Carmody?'

'Why, over at Odron House. Didn't you hear of it?' His small eyes shone at the prospect of being able to tell Charles Renfrew something about Odron House that he didn't already know.

'I suppose you mean that demonstration by Sinn Fein. But that was in the morning,' Charles pointed out, surprised at the

83

inaccuracy of Carmody's knowledge. He could usually be relied on to be absolutely up-to-date and correct in his information.

'Oh, no, not that.' The manager sat forward in pleasurable anticipation. 'I mean what happened later on. The shooting.'

'Shooting? What shooting?'

Charles stiffened in his chair. Carmody's habit of putting the tips of his fingers together when he had something to tell, like one of his ruddy priests imparting a blessing, was particularly irritating.

'Sure it's all round the town. I thought you'd have heard by now.'

'What, man?' Charles demanded, angry at the way Carmody was doling out his news and prolonging the suspense. 'What are you talking about?'

The manager, taken aback by his unexpected agitation, was sufficiently shaken to tell his tale without further ado. The news shocked Charles. That someone – presumably one of the Sinn Fein gang, probably over-excited by the morning demonstration and quite likely with a few pints inside him – had taken a pot-shot at Ambrose Mercer did not stir in him any great sympathy for the steward, but the effect it must have had on Amelia made his concern even more urgent than before. Things had become really dangerous so much sooner than she or he could have anticipated.

Carmody had chattered on, deploring the incident, uttering all the conventional and diplomatic clichés – 'a blessing from above that the shot missed and Mr Mercer was unharmed'. That gave Charles his opportunity.

'Yes, indeed, Carmody, as you say, a blessing. A relief, too, no doubt, for you.'

'For me?' the manager asked, puzzled. 'Why for me, Mr Renfrew?'

'Well, I suppose it would have meant one client less for you, wouldn't it? And not your smallest client, either, I dare say.'

Carmody shook his head.

'Indeed, no. Mr Mercer has no account here, and never had, either.'

Charles was completely nonplussed. He had convinced himself that Mercer was a scoundrel and that he would have built up a very large balance at the bank with the money he must have been stealing from Amelia down through the years. To learn that he hadn't even an account there was totally bewildering.

After he left the bank Charles tried to collect his thoughts. The utter failure of his expedition into Gortnahinch was a rueful disappointment; for, apart from coming up against a blank wall as far as information about Mercer was concerned, there was the alarming news of the shooting at Odron House. His first instinct was to go out there immediately and see if he could be of any help. But, if Amelia had needed him, she would have phoned. She would certainly have reported the matter to the RIC, and they'd probably be at the House already. They'd be making their investigations, no doubt. They'd be looking for Mercer's assailant. That would be their quarry. But Mercer himself was *his* quarry. He wouldn't let himself be distracted from that conclusion. And he wasn't going to let himself be stymied by his initial setback.

For some time he sat in his trap in the Square, considering his next move. Some of the townspeople turned to look back at him in surprise after they passed. A few shopkeepers came to their doors to observe him, pretending they were looking at something else, and then saluted him in embarrassment when he returned their stare. The puzzled face of a housewife appeared behind her lace-curtained window every few seconds, checking on whether he was still there. He paid them no attention.

At last he came to a decision. Back to first principles: one and one still made two. His reasoning still seemed to him to stand up: (*a*) Mercer had to be guilty; (*b*) if that was so, there had to be money salted away; (*c*) if the money wasn't in this bank, it must be in another one. Mercer wouldn't want anyone in Gortnahinch to know his business. Charles was surprised at himself for not having thought of that before. It made things more difficult for him, of course; he wasn't in a position to make enquiries in any other bank in the country. But it gave an impetus to the germ of an idea that had been at the back of his mind from the first moment he began to suspect Mercer of duplicity: Tim O'Halloran was the man to consult. If he were to take O'Halloran into his confidence, tell him of his suspi-

85

cions, O'Halloran could do the job for him. He was bound to have Sinn Fein supporters in the banks – everyone knew that the movement had a massive membership not only among the labouring and tenant classes but also in the RIC, the Post Office and every section of the country's commercial life. If Mercer had an account in any bank in the country, O'Halloran would be able to find out.

The idea appealed to Charles. It was neat and effective, and it would kill two birds with the one stone, for while O'Halloran was making his enquiries, presumably he would suspend any hostile activities at Odron House. He might even be much happier to show Mercer up and bring him to book in a court of law than to have to put an end to him by violent means.

'Chuck, chuck,' Charles called to his pony as he shook the reins. 'Giddy yap.' He turned him in his tracks, pointed him in the direction of O'Halloran's workshop, and set off at a trot.

Elizabeth extended her arm and held her hand up straight, moving it from side to side to admire the jewel from different angles. She rose from her dressing-table and stood in front of the windows, holding her hand up once again to take pleasure in the effect of the light playing on the sapphire ring. Its shade of blue rivalled that of the sky. She looked from one to the other. The blue of the sky appeared to be not so much a colour as the impression created by clear, empty, infinite space, while that of the jewel was like a glowing heart in the depths of the stone, a heart that in its repeated pulsing diffused the warm blue rays throughout the jewel's surface.

The ring had been a present from Ambrose Mercer for her birthday earlier that year. The only present he had ever given her. And she knew she would not have got even that if she hadn't shamed him into it by complaining that he never gave her anything. He really hadn't any alternative if he wanted to keep alive his hopes of marrying her. Her mother hadn't been pleased, however. Didn't think it seemly that their estate manager – 'He *is*, after all, an employee, Elizabeth' – should be giving her daughter expensive jewellery, birthday present or not. For a while Elizabeth had wondered whether her mother suspected anything. Did she fear, perhaps, that there might be some special significance in Mercer's choice of a ring rather than some other more impersonal or conventional birthday token? Oh, if she had known! What ructions it would have caused! Elizabeth had told her that Ambrose said she could regard the ring as an engagement present if she wished. Amelia had grown quite agitated at that, but Elizabeth had passed it off as a joke. It was typical of his meanness – an engagement and birthday present all in one. Not that she was interested in the suggestion anyway. She had made it quite clear to him already, time after time, that she had no mind to get married so soon. Admittedly she had been making the same excuse for years. But, for goodness' sake, wasn't she still young enough for it to be a convincing excuse? Perhaps it was his own age that was beginning to worry him? Hardly. He was as strong and as virile as ever. But as unimaginative, too. It hadn't mattered so much in earlier years when there had been those wonderful soldiers to provide variety, all so fresh, so different in their ways and wants. But now going to bed with Ambrose had grown stale. It had become predictable and dull. Well, no, not exactly dull, not when it came to it; his appetite was still almost that of an animal and usually succeeded in leaving her drained and happily exhausted. But the thrill of anticipation was gone, the special excitement of meeting a new young man, sizing him up, wondering what his reaction would be when she surprised him in his room. She could usually sense beforehand whether he was experienced or not and how warm a welcome she would get. That was what she had been missing lately, that tingle in her blood that grew hourly throughout the day until by the time evening came she was conscious of her body's readiness like a pain in her entrails. She felt the tingle now; she felt it and felt the first luxurious wave course through her. She was certain that policeman would want her. He'd be a new experience; she had never had one of the natives before. Would he say his prayers beforehand, or perhaps bless himself? They were so pious, the Irish. One couldn't tell. Would he be rough? She'd tame him if he was. She'd enjoy that.

She took the ring off and set it down on the dressing-table. Yes, it *was* beautiful, but if it had taken so long to get that much out of Ambrose what likelihood was there that his sudden generosity would be maintained? She had put it to him quite bluntly at the time.

'What could you give me, if we were married, that you're not giving me already?' she had asked coquettishly.

They had been lying in her bed, the house silent, the birthday celebrations well over.

'More presents,' he had answered, but so matter-of-factly that it was obvious he wasn't disposed to take her question seriously. In revenge she had put her hand between his legs and given it a sudden sharp twist.

'Christ, woman,' he had sworn, pulling himself away in pain, 'have you got that bloody ring on in bed?'

The pain had not lasted. In fact his anger at her savagery had only made him look for his own revenge, and he had driven into her with a force that had made her gasp. That was certainly one occasion when a sapphire had had the opposite of its legendary effect. Victoria had told her about it the next day, when together they had been admiring the ring.

'Did you know that cardinals of the Catholic Church have to wear a sapphire on their right hand?' she had said.

'Did I? Yes, I believe I did. Isn't there some ritual when a Catholic meets a cardinal? It's the form to kneel and kiss the ring, isn't it?'

'Yes, but there's more to it than that,' Victoria had continued with a half-smile. 'Because the sapphire is blue, like the sky, it's supposed to turn a man's thoughts to heavenly things and so control his sexual appetite. Presumably that's why cardinals have to wear it.'

Elizabeth had burst into laughter.

'Well, I can assure you, little sister, that it hadn't any such effect on Ambrose.'

'Yes, but *he* wasn't wearing it, was he?'

'That's right, he wasn't. *I* was. And I didn't notice that it had any effect on me, either, for your information.'

'I wouldn't expect it to,' Victoria had rejoined. 'Not on you. Nothing would.'

'Am I beyond redemption then?'

Victoria sighed. She had long since given up trying to reform Elizabeth, recognizing early on that her sister was as powerless to reject her nature's demands as a tree is to hold its branches still in a storm. She could only hope that that particular storm would abate before Elizabeth destroyed herself completely, or that someone suitable – certainly not Ambrose Mercer – would carry her off and marry her before she got into any trouble. In the meantime, Victoria took upon herself the duty of protecting her sister from discovery by their mother.

Elizabeth knew she could rely on her sister and was glad she did not have to hold anything back from her. It would have been hard to, anyway, thrown so much together as they frequently were. When they had been very young, the five years between them had been just enough for Elizabeth to regard Victoria as a baby and to 'mother' her. When they were growing up, Victoria had been the very opposite of Elizabeth, serious and studious. Everything interested her, and their father's library fed her appetite for knowledge. Elizabeth remembered how she was always coming to her with snippets of curious information – 'Elizabeth, did you know that . . .?' or 'Would you ever believe . . .?' – or how often, when a particular subject might crop up in conversation, Victoria would prove to have a quite unexpected familiarity with it. Elizabeth grew to admire and respect her sister.

It seemed natural to them to have no secrets from each other – except for Elizabeth's sexual initiation and her immediate surrender to the bodily craving it stimulated. Victoria was much too young at the time to be made privy to such grown-up womanly activities, and indeed that was the only period in Elizabeth's life when the age gap between herself and her sister interposed a barrier between them. But she had reckoned without Victoria's percipience and her familiarity, if only secondhand through her constant reading, with the temptations of the flesh. When eventually her need to tell someone of her quite stunning discovery made the secret no longer containable, she found that Victoria already knew, or guessed, what was going on, both with the visiting soldiers and with Ambrose Mercer. It shouldn't have surprised her, for at that time Victoria's room was next to hers and she was awake into the small hours every night, reading. For a while Victoria did preach the virtues of self-denial, but before long she had to admit that she had never seen Elizabeth as one who could refuse the apple. From then on her concern was to protect her sister, moving her room to the West corridor, where their mother slept, so that she could be on hand to divert Amelia if for any reason she should find it necessary to set out for Elizabeth's room some night when her sister was not alone. It had, at the time, occurred to Elizabeth that Victoria's action might have been a sign of her disapproval but, to her relief, Victoria ridiculed such a suggestion.

'No, Elizabeth, you don't understand, do you? I don't regard you as evil. You, evil!' She laughed at the idea.

'Sick then? Or even mad?'

'Oh, don't be melodramatic.'

'Well, just a bit weak-headed perhaps,' Elizabeth suggested, feeling, now she was reassured that Victoria didn't look upon her either as a monster or as someone diseased, that she could be a bit frivolous.

'Weak, yes,' Victoria agreed, 'but not in your head.'

Elizabeth gave a surprised look.

'You're not suggesting the weakness is rather lower down in my body, are you? It's not like you to make that kind of joke, sister.'

Victoria blushed hotly. 'No, of course not.'

'I'm only teasing,' Elizabeth consoled her.

'Well, don't.' Victoria's view of love made her recoil from any suggestion of prurience or what she thought of as 'dirty talk'. Sexual indulgence for the sole sake of gratification held no attraction for her, but seeing it ensnare her own sister for whom she felt so much love had made her face it realistically and try to understand it. She thought she did understand it, as far as Elizabeth was concerned.

'I don't think you're in any way weak-minded,' she explained. 'Rather the opposite, in fact. What I mean is that the weakness is in your nature, so that if there's something you want you're strong-willed enough to take it, no matter if you're not entitled to it or if it will harm you – or harm others.'

'You just mean I'm plain selfish. Isn't that so?' Elizabeth asked with a patient sigh.

'Well, you can't help yourself, can you? Remember the strawberries and cream?'

'Oh, my goodness, Victoria,' Elizabeth protested with some amusement, 'you're not still on about that after so many years! We were only children then.'

'Quite,' Victoria agreed. 'That's my point. You had had

90

your strawberries and cream; what was left was for me. You wanted them, and I wasn't there. So you took them. You were weak enough to want them, as you put it. It's only because it was something that happened when we *were* children that I used it as an example. "The child is father to the man."'

'I beg your pardon?'

'It's a quotation.'

Elizabeth took Victoria in her arms and hugged her. 'Oh, my clever little sister. Aren't I lucky to have a sister who knows so much and who is so pure and kind and loving and understanding and protective!'

Victoria pushed her off, good-naturedly.

'Oh, it's not so much you I want to protect. I can't protect you, can I? Because I can't make you stop. It's Mother I'm worried about. She's the one who needs protection.'

'Mother?'

'Of course. If she finds out, she's the one who will suffer, not you. She's the one who'd be hurt, not you. After all, it hasn't worried you that *I* know, has it?'

'But that's different. You're my sister – and you understand me. As you've explained.'

For a while after that Elizabeth *had* worried about Amelia, and about their relationship. Was there one? Elizabeth could not fathom her mother, had never been able to. She couldn't even remember ever having a mother, the sort of mother she presumed other girls had. Amelia had sometimes played with her and Victoria when they were both children, had sometimes picnicked with them in the grounds, had sometimes paid them visits in the nursery. But Elizabeth couldn't put her hand on her heart and swear that she actually remembered enjoying those occasions. Not, at any rate, while her mother was there. In Amelia's presence there was more formality than fun at such times, and if Elizabeth had learned one thing since then it was that formality and fun did not go together. But her mother's participation had always seemed to be dictated more by duty than by desire, as if her thoughts were elsewhere. And she had always been so correct – she never put on old creased clothes so that one could wrestle and tumble with her, she never romped around, her hair never fell out of place.

Nor could Elizabeth recall that later years brought any

change in the pattern. She was never encouraged to share a growing girl's confidences with her mother, she and Victoria were told nothing about Amelia's childhood and past, they learned no more than the barest details about their father. It seemed that silence was Amelia's preferred element. Elizabeth wondered what happened when Charles Renfrew was alone with her through those long Sunday afternoons. Did old Renfrew regale her with tales of his own adventures? Unlikely. Did he talk at all? If so, it must have been a monologue. Or perhaps they both sat in silence, he boring her, she boring him. But then he wouldn't have kept coming, would he? They couldn't possibly be. . . . Elizabeth burst into laughter when that outrageous idea occurred to her. Not stuffy old Renfrew surely. And not Amelia, just as surely. The whole impression her mother seemed to convey was of a woman under some sort of cloud – regret, depression, ennui? She didn't know and, in the absence of any clue from Amelia herself, it did not occur to her that her mother's withdrawal might have been induced by loneliness.

With Victoria no longer occupying the bedroom next door to hers, Elizabeth lost all feelings of constraint. She was able to take advantage of every opportunity for varied sexual experience that arose, and if no one new was at hand there was always Ambrose. His anger at the way she pressed her favours on other men was not something that caused her the slightest worry. In any event, he was unable to express it too forcefully for fear of losing whatever hold he had on her affections. He had to swallow his bitterness, take what he could get of her, and console himself with the thought that at least he was on the premises; in his hands he held the future of Odron House, while the others were birds of passage who would be replaced by their successors until Elizabeth tired of the whole process and fell back on him. And Elizabeth, always so sure in her reading of men's minds – and particularly of Ambrose Mercer's obvious ambitions – craftily kept his annoyance within bounds and his subservience constant with assurances that while one was young and strong was the time to take one's pleasure; her turn to settle down would come soon enough. All right, Ambrose consoled himself, give her a few more years and his claim would come into its own. He would wait and plan and go to her bed whenever she called. Which was exactly what Elizabeth had worked out as the way to handle her mother's estate manager.

For Ambrose Mercer the termination of the stream of male visitors, military and otherwise, to Odron House along with the end of the supporting parties was an unexpected but welcome result of the countryside troubles caused by the increased Sinn Fein aggression. It removed all his casual rivals and literally threw Elizabeth more into his arms. To him it was like that first year when she was learning from him the delights of love and became petulant whenever she had to miss her almost nightly lesson.

Elizabeth, however, had no such reason to welcome such developments. Ambrose was no longer enough. She needed the variety she had become so used to. Without it she felt the days and weeks dragging. She felt she was being starved. The arrival of Constable Tom Fahy was the most exciting thing that had happened in months, much more exciting than the noisy Sinn Fein demonstration had been. He was a fine figure of a man and he had that look in his eye. She was certain he had. She hadn't spent years sizing up a man's possibilities as a bedmate for nothing. The way he spoke, the way he looked, the way he smiled – it all told her. And the sudden urge in her blood, the clamour that had been absent for so long, that confirmed it. Constable Fahy was for her. Victoria would have to be on guard again – just in case. She wondered for a moment how her sister would take the news. But why should she mind? She never had before. Perhaps it would be as well to alert her without delay. Besides, the anticipation was too exciting for her to keep to herself a moment longer than necessary.

She looked into the library and was quite glad to find it empty. That meant that Victoria was almost certainly somewhere in the grounds – the best place for her to be in such wonderful weather.

She tried her sister's haunts – the stream, the applehouse, the greenhouse – eventually finding her in the stable-yard. Victoria had led the colt out of its box and, brush in hand, was patiently grooming it, embossing a series of half-circles on its gleaming quarters.

'What in the world are you up to? Surely you're not going out

93

riding in a skirt.' Elizabeth didn't doubt that Victoria could take it into her head to go out riding in a skirt rather than in her jodhpurs – bareback, too – but she knew, too, that Victoria's preferred relaxations were seldom so strenuous.

'Don't you think he looks marvellous, Elizabeth?'

'Yes, he does. But why the sudden interest and attention?'

Indeed, the colt did look a picture. His intelligent head was held high in appreciation of Victoria's touch on his skin, much as the farmyard cats would stretch out their necks and close their eyes in ecstasy if anyone stroked them under the chin. His whorled nostrils swelled in and out, and his bold eye stared hugely in concentrated pleasure. Elizabeth patted his neck, and he turned his head to nuzzle her.

'It's a shame we don't show him off more,' Victoria said. 'We should exhibit him at the annual show. I shouldn't be surprised if he won a ribbon.'

'Just at the moment the local show mightn't be the best place to exhibit him – or ourselves, for that matter.'

'Oh, nonsense, Elizabeth. I think we should take part. We always did, years ago. I mean Father did. With plenty of success, too.'

'Father! What brought that up all of a sudden?'

'I found some old diaries of his, in the library. Not personal diaries, just various records of places he went to, special events, things like that. Just a record really. But it did tell me how much he was involved in local affairs. It's a pity it all seems to have been lost.'

'Yes, perhaps it is,' Elizabeth agreed, thinking more of the attractions a revived social scene might bring. But all that was speculation, and in the future if it were to come about at all. Her Constable Fahy was here and now.

'I've been looking for you, Vicky, to tell you about the policemen. Two of them have come – to give us protection from the Shinners.'

'I know. I met one of them.' Victoria was not excited. She seemed more interested in completing the grooming process than in the new arrivals.

'Oh, which one did you meet?'

'Howell he said his name is. Pat Howell. He's nice. Shy, but nice. I liked him.'

94

'Oh, that one. A boy more than a man, I'd say. But you didn't meet the other one. Now, he *is* a man.'

Victoria's arm holding the grooming-brush was arrested in mid-stroke. She couldn't but note the excitement in her sister's voice. She straightened and looked squarely at Elizabeth.

'You must be mad,' she protested. 'I know what you're up to. But he's a policeman, Elizabeth.'

'Oh, don't be a snob!'

'Stop it,' Victoria insisted, but more in resignation than in anger, as if she already recognized that nothing would deflect Elizabeth once she was aroused. 'You know well what I mean. I mean that you could get into trouble making passes at a policeman.'

'Victoria, my dear,' Elizabeth told her sister mock-patronizingly, 'a policeman is only a man with a uniform on. Take the uniform off him and what have you? A man, the same as all men. I suppose Mother will expect them to have their meals in the kitchen. I shall have to persuade her that they must eat with us. After all, how can they protect us properly if they're not allowed to stay near us?'

'Oh, of course,' Victoria said with heavy sarcasm. 'The fact that you'd want every possible chance to work your wiles wouldn't have anything to do with it, would it? Really, Elizabeth, you are quite shameless – and quite mad.'

Victoria knew there was no point in arguing. She could only hope that the constable would reject Elizabeth's blandishments without fuss. She'd have to watch her sister carefully. A member of the Royal Irish Constabulary was different from all Elizabeth's other men. Out of uniform he might or might not be the same, but that particular uniform was special. Elizabeth might easily land herself – and the family – in a lot of embarrassment, or even worse.

Victoria took the colt's leading-rein and flicked it to show that the grooming was at an end. The horse neighed and demonstrated on what good terms it was with itself by rearing up on its hind legs with a loud commotion. Elizabeth stared up at it pawing the air – at its thrashing hoofs, its floating mane, the swelling veins of its belly, and its potent sex like a gun between its legs.

She turned away to find her mother, anxious to lose no time

in putting her plan into effect. As she expected, Amelia's initial reaction was not very favourable, but her misgivings melted away when she saw the logic of Elizabeth's argument that banishing the constables to the kitchen every time the family was at table was not the best way of getting the protection Amelia herself had requested.

'Yes, of course you're right,' Amelia finally agreed. 'These aren't very normal times, are they, and our safety must be our first consideration.'

'After all, Ambrose has been eating with us for years,' Elizabeth pointed out, 'so why shouldn't they, too.'

Safety was indeed uppermost in Amelia's mind, but the fact that Ambrose Mercer would be very unlikely to welcome the idea of having the policemen share their table gave her particular satisfaction. His presence at family meals was a privilege she had been unable to resist; now, at last, he would see that he wasn't so special after all.

'Begob, Myles, but aren't we very popular all of a sudden! We're getting nothing but the best out to see us today – first the law and now the quality.'

O'Halloran and Myles Barratt were perched on the wall near their workshop from where they had a clear view of the road in both directions. They had discarded their heavy leather aprons, and with shirts unbuttoned and sleeves rolled up were enjoying the sun while they ate their lunch of sandwiches and strong tea.

Myles's snort was the only acknowledgement he made that he, too, had taken note of the fact that Charles Renfrew's trap, having come level with them, had slowed to a halt. As Renfrew jumped down and saluted, O'Halloran greeted him with: 'I doubt now, Mr Renfrew, that you've come to share our elegant lunch, and from where I'm sitting I can't see anything wrong with that conveyance of yours. Not that there should be; for, as you well know, when I make them, I make them right. So would it be a new trap you require by any chance?'

'No, O'Halloran,' Charles answered, leaning his back against the wall beside the men and wiping his brow with a large silk handkerchief that he pulled from his sleeve at the wrist. 'I'd have no use for a second trap and, as you say, the one I have is serving me well.'

'In that case, Myles,' O'Halloran said, turning to his friend, 'I must deduce that our visitor isn't here on business.'

'Well, I am, as a matter of fact,' Renfrew informed him. 'But it's rather private.'

'Do you mean personal?'

'Um, not exactly, no, not exactly personal.'

'What would it be to do with, Mr Renfrew?'

'Well, it's about Ambrose Mercer and yesterday's goings-on.'

O'Halloran gave a bellow of laughter and slapped his knee.

'Myles,' he addressed his friend, 'if you know your ancient history, you'll have heard of the oracle at Delphi.'

'Maybe I have,' Myles Barratt rejoined quietly, his cautious tone pitched to convey the suggestion that he probably had known at one time but that was a long while ago. He waved a wasp away from his sandwich and waited for enlightenment.

'I'm thinking,' Tim O'Halloran declared, 'that the people in this part of the world must regard me as if I was some class of oracle. Would you believe it, Mr Renfrew, that you're the second person who's made a special journey out here this morning to question me about what happened yesterday? The second person, and the day not half-over yet! I wouldn't be surprised if Ambrose Mercer himself was already around the corner, waiting his turn.'

Charles Renfrew laughed. 'Well, if he is, I didn't pass him on the way. But who's been out to you already about it?'

'Sergeant Driscoll was here bright and early. Though maybe not so early, and not so bright, either, for he seems to think I put up someone to take that pot-shot at Mercer.' He laughed again, and Myles Barratt's soft chuckle was like a distant echo.

'Well, I didn't come here to ask you any questions about that or to find out who tried to shoot him,' Charles said. 'It's none of my business, but obviously whoever did it wanted to get rid of him.'

'I suppose there'd be some who'd be saved a deal of trouble if he was out of the way,' O'Halloran observed in a casual tone of voice.

Myles Barratt nodded his agreement, and the two of them

continued at their lunch, content to wait for Charles Renfrew to state his business in his own time. Charles, for his part, saw no point in beating about the bush. If, as he believed, Tim O'Halloran was a man of action, the best thing was to come to the point without delay.

'To tell you the truth, O'Halloran,' he said, 'it would save *me*, too, a lot of trouble if Mercer was out of the way.'

'Oh?' O'Halloran's head jerked back in surprise, and Charles was quick to explain.

'I don't mean to suggest that I want him killed. Good Lord, man, I don't hold with murder. But I have my own private reasons to want to see the back of that party.'

O'Halloran nodded. 'I think I understand your drift,' he said, and the studied emphasis clearly conveyed that he had a fair idea of why Ambrose Mercer was an obstacle to Charles as well as to Sinn Fein. Charles had never spoken to anyone of his desire to marry Amelia, and he was sure that she had never revealed his proposals, but somehow these local people seemed to be aware of everything that went on in Odron House.

'Look here, O'Halloran,' he said bluntly, 'I think it may be possible to get rid of Mercer without any violence at all. But it will need your help, and if you can manage it, then I'm fairly sure I can see that the rest of the Odron estate goes back to its remaining tenants. I can't promise it, but at least you have my word I'd do all I can in that direction.'

Tim O'Halloran turned to look at Myles Barratt. The latter drained the last drop of tea from his mug and shook it out. O'Halloran had already placed his own mug beside him on the wall. Now he moved it out of the way to make room for Charles to draw nearer.

'We're listening, Mr Renfrew. We're with you so far.'

Charles proceeded to tell the two men about the state of the Odron fortunes and his suspicions of Mercer's part in the decline. When he had finished, Tim O'Halloran thought for a moment. 'If Dinny Carmody says there's no account in his bank,' he muttered, 'then you can believe that.'

'Of course,' Charles agreed. 'I've known him and dealt with him since before he was made manager. He wouldn't lie. Besides, why should he?'

'He's a heavy drinker, is Mercer,' O'Halloran stated. 'Could the money have gone there? If, that is, you're right about him taking it.'

'But we're talking about thousands of pounds,' Charles pointed out, 'many thousands. He couldn't have given the publicans that much unless he's been drunk from morning till night every day of his life. A heavy drinker, certainly, but an out-and-out drunkard?'

'It's not that then,' O'Halloran agreed, 'for heavy drinker though he is, it's well known he's mostly a one-night-a-week man. Friday night is his – he patronizes O'Brien's down by the well as a rule, but he's been seen in other places now and again.'

'I can see you've been keeping tabs on him,' Charles commented. 'I'd say you'd not have much trouble finding out if he's got the money in some other bank somewhere. I suppose Tralee is the most likely place.'

O'Halloran did not confirm or deny the suggestion. All he said was: 'And if he hasn't?'

Charles considered the possibility. If there wasn't an account somewhere, it would certainly be a blow to his theory. But then his mind sprang back to the equation on which the theory was based.

'The money must be somewhere, O'Halloran,' he insisted. 'If it's not in a bank, then he's hidden it.'

Tim O'Halloran turned once again to Myles Barratt. The two men stared at each other as if in silent communication. Finally Myles looked up at the sky, then took his mug and slid his heavy body down off the wall. Charles irrelevantly wondered how he had ever managed to lift himself on to it, until he noticed one stone halfway down jutting out like a step from the other bricks. O'Halloran, too, prepared to move back to work.

'Give me a while, Mr Renfrew,' he said decisively. 'Come back in a week and we'll have another talk.'

'And in the meantime?' Charles asked.

O'Halloran looked up at the sky just as Myles had done, then he looked back at his visitor with the suggestion of a smile on his face.

'Ah,' he replied lightly, 'have no fear. I'd say the weather will hold until then.'

That was good enough for Charles.

5

ONE BY ONE Sergeant Driscoll opened the drawers in his desk. He stared for some moments at the accumulation of paper in each drawer, then abruptly banged it shut in frustration. It was an unrewarding routine, but one he always fell prey to when he was worried – a search for some document he had not fully studied or any piece of unfinished work on which he could concentrate and so for at least a while banish from his mind whatever was disturbing him. He never did find anything, nor did he expect to. He knew to the last scrap of paper the contents of every drawer; given time enough and reason enough he could have made a list of the lot: Acts of Parliament about everything under the sun from poaching to unlighted vehicles at night, dog licences, drinking hours, hawkers, tillage census, and even chimney-sweeps; discarded Great War recruitment posters for almost every regiment in the British army; the large wall-map of the war front, now folded up and kept as a memento, that had adorned the barracks wall with its ranks of little red buttons adjusted daily to mark territory lost or gained; old copies of *Hue-and-Cry or The Police Gazette*; even circulars about the Police Union that from time to time Pat Howell would quietly leave on his desk; and assorted Orders, Instructions and Directives from the Divisional Inspector's office – there seemed no end to the size and variety of the accumulation.

Across the corridor the constables in the day-room, conscious of their sergeant's distress, were as quiet as mice. Two of the younger ones, Andy Doyle and Francie O'Leary, were bent over the latest Acts in case the County Inspector decided to test their knowledge of them on his next visit; Denis O'Sullivan was writing a letter home; Sean Hogan was reading the recently published *The Graves of Kilmorna*, by his favourite author, Canon Sheehan; and Constables Power, Rafferty and O'Malley were sitting at a table in the corner, tunics open, playing nap. Whenever Mick O'Malley was forgetful enough to put a card down on the table's surface with a snapping sound, his companions threw him a slightly sharp look as if chastising him for being so noisy, and at the commencement of each game the players took great care to make their bids *sotto voce*.

Concentration, however, was only fitful. Like Sergeant Driscoll everyone was waiting for Dr Harvey, who was upstairs examining the sergeant's wife, to come down with his report. Lucy had not had a good night, and early in the morning Sergeant Driscoll sent for the doctor. He hadn't said much, except that herself was upset, but they all knew that what he feared at this stage was yet another still-birth.

Certainly Lucy's sudden bad turn was what was uppermost in the sergeant's mind. If the worst came to the worst – if the doctor's news was bad – they'd have a harrowing period ahead of them. He'd need all his mental and spiritual reserves to carry them through. But just at that moment reserves of any kind were at a low ebb. Bad enough to have O'Halloran and his boys to cope with; bad enough to have had to send Fahy and Howell to Odron House and be two men short; it wasn't even any consolation that Fahy hadn't phoned him on the previous evening – he presumed there was nothing special to report, for knowing the local postmistress's habit of listening in to calls, he had instructed Fahy not to phone the barracks unless he had to and then to be as brief and cryptic as possible. Nevertheless he couldn't help wondering how the two men were getting on. And now, on top of all these worries, there was this latest Order from Divisional Commissioner Smyth's office in Cork – an Order the sergeant didn't like one bit. God knows he couldn't claim it was all that much of a surprise. He had been aware for some time of the authorities' policy for the military to take over

101

selected police stations, dispersing most of the complement of constables to unimportant outlying billets. Any RIC barracks that was suspect was put on the list, any barracks where it was thought the men mightn't be as keen as the Crown would like on tracking down proscribed Sinn Feiners, and Sergeant Driscoll had no doubt that Constable Howell's Police Union activities would automatically have brought his barracks under suspicion. He had tried not to let the knowledge colour his attitude to Howell or affect their relationship, and he had not spoken to him or to the other men about the danger that might face them. He didn't see that there was anything to gain in upsetting them sooner than might be necessary; and, indeed, because he *had* kept his counsel, no one appeared to have given the possibility of being taken over by the military a moment's thought.

Sergeant Driscoll sat back behind his desk and slowly filled his pipe. He lit a match, holding it for a moment, squeezing his eyes shut until a twinge of indigestion had passed. Then he put the flame to the tobacco and sucked strongly. No need to panic. If the military hadn't taken over by now, like as not they never would. There was no special significance in the Divisional Inspector's Order landing on his desk that morning. It was a general Order that would have been sent as a matter of course to every police barracks in the country, good or bad, loyal or suspect.

The pipe wasn't giving him its accustomed satisfaction and he laid it aside, eyeing it beadily as if it was somehow at fault. But he knew it was the shock of all the disturbing events that was spoiling its taste. And the shock would account for the bout of indigestion, too. It was all very well to try to reassure himself but, general or not, there was the Order in front of him, in black and white, and every time he looked at it a wave of cold terror swept through him. He thought of the effect it would have on his whole life if Gortnahinch should become a military post – 'a combined Military and Police Station' was how the Order put it. Paragraph three: that was the bugger. He read it again for the umpteenth time. 'The number of police at combined Military and Police Stations will be reduced to a minimum. At out-stations three will be sufficient.' (He had heard that in some places even two had been considered enough.) 'The men left at these stations will be the men with the best local knowledge and will act as guides to the military. At least one must be a Sergeant or Head Constable. The other police will be used to strengthen the weak stations.'

At least one must be a Sergeant or Head Constable, that was what stood out. He wasn't lulled by its guarantee that his position was safe, that he wouldn't be moved – he'd be better off if it was otherwise. For what it really meant was that, as the sergeant left in the barracks, he'd be the one to act as a guide to the military. If Gortnahinch was taken over, he'd be expected to turn informer, to reveal who was and who wasn't a member of Sinn Fein, to point out houses he knew were meeting-places, to deliver into the hands of the British forces neighbours and friends he had known all his life, whose only crime was that they had supported the cause of freedom for their own country. If he didn't co-operate, he'd be dismissed without any pension, and then what would he and Lucy do? How could they live? *Where* could they live? And if they should have a child. . . . It might be better if there was no child after all.

He shuddered violently, conscience-stricken at having almost wished a further misfortune on his wife. He put his head in his hands and closed his eyes. All his life he had been conscientious and loyal, and now, so late, so unexpectedly, came the bitterest of ironies, the possibility of having to pit his whole future against total loss of self-respect. That was what he'd be faced with. Perhaps even worse, for if he stayed and did the Crown's bidding he'd be a marked man, looking over his shoulder everywhere he'd go for fear of the assassin's bullet.

For some minutes Sergeant Driscoll remained motionless, trying to regain his self-control. Gradually the feeling of desperation ebbed, and he found his lips moving in a silent prayer until the image of an overrun police station and of himself as a virtual hostage faded.

'God be good, it won't come to that,' he muttered. It was silly to get into such a lather at this stage – as if the worst had already happened. It was because of Lucy, yes, because of the bad turn she had taken; that was what had him on edge, ready to believe anything. And the tension of waiting for the doctor to come downstairs hadn't helped, either.

Sergeant Driscoll straightened in his chair. Cool, boyo, stay cool and calm. This latest Order now – he'd give it no more relevance than he'd given most of the other Orders that had plagued him throughout the years. There was plenty of room in the wastepaper-basket for it. No, even that would be special treatment. He opened a drawer in his desk, carefully buried the Order under a bundle of old reports, then shut the drawer with a bang. Satisfied, he sat back and once more lit his pipe.

Within a minute he heard Dr Harvey leave the bedroom and start to come downstairs. The sergeant rose, mentally bracing himself for the doctor's report. He put his smoking pipe into a bowl on the desk and went to the door to meet him.

'Well?' He managed to keep his voice calm and natural, but it was impossible to stop what seemed to be all the breath in his body gathering into one huge lump and trying to force its way out through his very breastbone.

The doctor's elderly stooped figure, neat and professional in its correct black coat and wing collar, brushed past into the sergeant's office. Dr Harvey prided himself on the accuracy of his diagnoses, not only of people's afflictions but also of how best to tell them and their kith and kin whatever it was necessary to tell them, be it good news or bad. He had attended Lucy Driscoll all her married life and had judged very early on that the right way to handle her husband was to be brief, blunt and to the point.

'Well, John.' He turned to face the sergeant, who had re-entered his office and closed the door behind him. 'Basically there's no change. A slight rise in blood pressure, that's what made her so restless during the night but that's nothing out of the way. Sure you have no more to worry about than you had last time I saw Lucy. But no less, either. Bear that in mind.' He motioned the sergeant to resume his seat and waited until he did so before continuing. 'The fact is, quite simply, that she's nearing to her time.' He gave a positive jerk of his head and added lightly: 'She should go into labour within a week – maybe sooner. But we don't want to be caught on the hop, so it might be safer to move her tonight to the hospital in Listowel.'

'Hospital, is that it?' Sergeant Driscoll repeated somewhat doubtfully. Women didn't go into hospital to have a baby unless they were in a bad way.

'Don't sound so cast down about it, John. You should be

104

pleased. It's the last lap, man. And for a woman with her history it's the wisest course. She'll get the best of attention there – plenty of help right on the spot. I'm in and out myself almost every day, so I can keep an eye on her, too.'

'Sounds as if that's the best plan so,' the sergeant said, relief flooding through him. If Dr Harvey thought it was time to move Lucy to hospital so as to give her the best chance of having her baby, that's exactly what it was. And Listowel was only a stone's throw away. He could make time to get in to see her himself almost every day.

'Leave all the arrangements to me, John. I'll send an ambulance and a nurse out tonight. I've told herself and I think she's easier in her mind now.'

'Me, too,' the sergeant responded. 'At first I thought it was the old story once again. But with God's help perhaps it will be all right this time.'

'With God's help.'

'Aye, with God's help,' Sergeant Driscoll repeated, 'and yourself to assist. I'm very grateful.'

Dr Harvey raised a hand in acknowledgement.

'Put the pipe back in your mouth and sit down at your desk. Work is the best cure for worry,' was his parting advice. At the door he turned to add: 'It's the cheapest prescription I can give you, John, but it's the best for all that.'

'If you're so tired, why don't you go to bed?' Pat Howell said. He was in bed himself, sitting up, hands crossed behind his head, revelling in the luxury of his surroundings. Tom Fahy sat on the edge of the bed, yawning, his blue and white striped pyjamas straining across his broad chest.

'I'll go soon,' he said. 'I'd be gone already but that I know I'll be awake for hours, just as I was last night.'

'What kept you awake? You weren't expecting trouble, were you?'

'Trouble? Sure what trouble should I expect?'

'Well, Ambrose Mercer,' Pat Howell suggested. 'I mean, if whoever shot at him decided to try again, he could be hanging around at night. You'd never know.'

'That's just it, Pat: you'd never know.'

'What do you mean by that?' Pat Howell cocked his head to

one side and looked sharply at his colleague. He knew him well enough to sense that there was something behind his comment. 'Come on, cough it up. It's only a brick, as you say yourself.'

'You haven't had much conversation with Mercer, have you?' Tom Fahy asked, not yet ready to come to the point.

'Much?' Howell protested. 'I haven't had any. Sure it's you who's been keeping tabs on him ever since you found him yesterday.'

'You're welcome to him if you want. But he's a crafty customer, and he has the stamina of a rhinoceros. No wonder I'm whacked out after being in the fields with him all day.'

'Well, I'll take over for you tomorrow if you like. You've only to say the word.' Pat Howell drew his knees up under the covers and leaned forward eagerly, hoping to be given a turn at what seemed the more exciting part of their assignment at Odron House. But to his surprise his friend declined the offer.

'No, I'll stay with him a while longer. I want to find out more about him.'

'What do you mean? You're not getting to like him, are you?'

'No one could like that boyo,' Fahy replied, stretching a long hand over his shoulder and in under the collar of his pyjama jacket to scratch his back. 'I certainly don't like him, and he doesn't like me, either. You heard the way he was trying to needle me at dinner tonight. He says I'm in the way and a nuisance. And of course his opinion of the Irish is well known. He's never made a secret of it.'

Fahy rose from the side of the bed and went to peer out the bedroom window across which had been drawn a heavy embroidered curtain. Satisfied with what he saw, he returned and sat on the bed once more, this time at its end, facing Pat Howell.

'It doesn't make watching him any easier,' the latter said, 'if the two of you don't get on.'

'Ah, come on, man, you didn't expect me to get on with him, did you? Sure you know his reputation.'

'I suppose you're right,' Howell agreed. There was silence for a moment as he studied his friend's enigmatic look, certain now that he had more information to impart. Then suddenly something occurred to him, and he said: 'You know, it's queer that he should say you're in the way. Sure wasn't it himself that brought us here?'

Tom Fahy's face broke into a smile, and he gave a little cackle of satisfaction.

'I wondered if that would occur to you, Pat. It seemed strange to me, too. And it's not the only thing. I questioned him as much as I could about the shooting and I'm as wise now as I was before.'

'Why? Wouldn't he satisfy you?'

'Wouldn't? It was more that he couldn't. He was very vague about it. Got nasty when I pressed him. I asked him to show me where it happened, but he said he hadn't the time to take me there and anyway that it didn't matter where he was shot at.'

'So?'

'Well, to be honest, I got the distinct impression that not only was he annoyed at having me on his tail, but he was surprised into the bargain.'

Pat Howell lowered his hands from behind his head and laid them on the coverlet.

'I don't get you,' he appealed.

'Well, it seems he thought we'd both stay in the house all the time, to protect Mrs Odron and the girls.'

'But, dammit, it was *he* was shot at,' Pat Howell protested.

Fahy stood up and was silent for a moment. Then slowly, a note of doubt in his voice, he said: 'Was it? I wonder.'

'What do you mean, Tom?' Howell asked, jerking himself upright off the pillow which he had arranged to cushion his back. 'What are you saying? If it wasn't Mercer was shot at, then who was it? Who else was about at the time?'

'No one, as far as we know.'

'Then it must have been Mercer.'

'Yes,' Fahy agreed. 'If there was anyone shot at at all.'

Pat Howell's mouth fell open in surprise, but before he could pursue Fahy's startling suggestion his colleague's demeanour changed completely.

'Ah, what matter?' he laughed lightly, then stretched his arms out as another huge yawn overtook him. 'About the only bloody time I can be off duty in this place is when I'm in bed—'

'If O'Halloran's boys pay us a visit in the night,' Howell interrupted, 'you'll be back on duty damned quick.' And he laughed.

'That's no joke, boy. I'd better be getting my head down, just in case. I'll see you at breakfast.'

'Pleasant dreams,' Pat Howell said tauntingly. 'If you hear Mercer walking about in the night, don't bother getting up to follow him. He'll probably be only going to the jakes.'

'God save your ignorance, young Howell,' Fahy remarked at the door. 'Have a good look under the bed, boy.'

He left the room, and Pat Howell immediately ducked his head down over the side of the bed and lifted the coverlet out of the way. To his amazement, there, almost under his nose, was a large china chamberpot adorned with a smiling pink rose transfer. He let his breath out with a whistle and pulled himself back into his bed. 'Bejay,' he said quietly, 'it's just like Fahy to know about that. He's up to every trick.'

As if to confirm his thought, the bedroom door opened slightly and Tom Fahy poked his grinning face around it.

'A good policeman', he admonished, 'should always look under the bed.'

He was gone before Pat Howell could lay his hands on anything to throw at him.

He stood for a while outside the door, delighted with himself at having caught out his colleague. He was about to go into his room when a door at the end of the corridor opened and Elizabeth Odron stepped out. Standing as he was in his highly unflattering pyjamas, he blushed scarlet, but even in his discomfiture he noted how smart she looked in a jade dressing-gown, knotted tightly at the waist, with the end of her light-green nightdress showing. Fahy turned quickly to escape her gaze and avoid further embarrassment but, quick as he was, Elizabeth was at his door before he could get it closed.

'Were you looking for anything?' she asked. 'You weren't disturbed? By any unusual noises, I mean.'

'No, no, Miss Elizabeth, I was just in with Pat – Constable Howell. Comparing notes, you might say. I hope we didn't wake you up.'

Elizabeth ushered him into his room and closed the door behind her.

'Comparing notes?' she said brightly. 'Oh, do tell me what that means. I didn't think you could have made many notes in the two days you've been here. Do tell me, won't you?'

'There's nothing to tell, Miss Elizabeth. And it's late anyway. I have to be up early in the morning to keep pace with Mr Mercer.'

'Oh, don't be such an old stick, Tom,' she said, refusing to take seriously his attempt to put her off. 'You're not really an old stick, though goodness knows those pyjamas of yours went out with the Boer War.' Fahy blushed again, but there was no stopping her. 'You can't fool me. You haven't got your uniform on now, so there's no need to be stuffy, is there, Tom? You see, I'm calling you Tom – I can't keep calling you Constable – and it's about time you started calling me Elizabeth. How are you getting on with Ambrose? What do you think of him? Go on back to bed. I'll sit here and you can tell me.'

She went to his bed, drew back the covers for him and unselfconsciously sat on one side of it, crooking one leg over the other so that the lower half of her dressing-gown fell open. Constable Fahy, left stranded in the middle of the room, contemplated her as she smiled archly up at him.

'I'll tell you what I think, Miss Elizabeth. I think that if you're not careful you'll be waking Mr Mercer and that might take a bit of explaining.' He was also thinking that if Mercer's boast of his intention to marry Elizabeth was true he could turn very angry.

'Mr Mercer has no rights over me,' she retorted calmly – an answer, Fahy thought, that seemed to cast doubts on any proposed marriage.

'Maybe he has none over you. But he has over me, in a manner of speaking anyway. If he reported to Sergeant Driscoll that you were in my bedroom, and both of us in our night attire, I wouldn't be here much longer.'

'Oh, I wouldn't like that. I'd be most disappointed if you had to leave so quickly.' Was she making fun of him, Tom Fahy wondered. 'But you needn't worry. Ambrose won't wake up, he's a very heavy sleeper.'

And no doubt you're the one who'd know, the constable said to himself, remembering the stories about the two of them. But there was obviously no way of budging her short of using force, and if he tried that and she kicked up a row he'd be in trouble anyway. He eyed her as steadily as he could, and she looked straight back at him. He was beginning to have strange, almost alarming suspicions. Was she just an over-friendly, over-indulged young lady with a streak of mischievousness, or was she an outrageous flirt? Or worse? He wasn't the man to look a gift horse in the mouth – especially such an attractive one – but, though she had caught him out of uniform, that didn't mean that he was off duty; technically he was on duty all the time he was at Odron House. In any event, she had the upper hand for the moment and there seemed to be no alternative but to play along with her. Suddenly he realized that his tiredness had gone.

'You'll catch cold standing out there like that, Tom,' she urged as if to help him make up his mind. 'You'll be much warmer in bed.'

'Fair enough, Elizabeth,' he said, getting into the bed and pulling the covers over his legs.

'That's better, you called me Elizabeth.' She turned to lift the pillow and prop it up as a support behind his head. As she bent over him, her body came close to his face, so close that her chest, bare where her nightdress hung loosely, brushed his nose. To his surprise her skin was faintly scented. It gave him a feeling of relaxation mixed with the stirrings of desire, and only for a brief moment did his mind concern itself with the curious phenomenon of a girl putting scent on herself before going to bed.

'Your nose is cold,' she said as she drew back and settled herself on the bed, half-turned to him, almost in the posture, it occurred to him, of one riding side-saddle. He imagined she was damned good on a horse. Her class usually was. And there'd be no old-fashioned side-saddle with her, either; she'd want her legs firmly around its belly so that it would know who was boss.

'I hope the rest of you isn't as cold as your nose,' she teased with a smile. 'If it is, I'll have to get you another blanket. But the linen cupboard is all the way downstairs.'

'Ah, there's no need for that. I'm not a bit cold,' Tom Fahy assured her.

'I'd be surprised if you were. A big strong man like you must have plenty of hot-blooded energy.'

Again he sensed a mocking note but he ignored it, determined to keep his wits about him. If she was just playing

110

games, he didn't mind going along with her for a while.

'True enough for you, Elizabeth, I don't think I'm lacking in that department. But if it's hot-blooded energy you're talking about, there's no one to beat that fellow Mercer. He's got enough for a herd of elephants.'

'Oh, really,' Elizabeth complained testily, 'can't you forget Ambrose Mercer? You've been out with him all day. Surely you don't need to think of him when you're in bed.'

'And why wouldn't I? Isn't it my job to see that no one kills him?'

'I don't think Ambrose will let himself be killed that easily.'

'Bedad, then, he wouldn't know much about it if it was a bullet in the back he got.'

Elizabeth threw her head back, as if with the action throwing aside the whole topic. She pressed a hand on the bedclothes where Tom's legs were, and said pleadingly: 'Please, can't we just forget him? Remember, you have others to worry about, too: my mother and Victoria and me. My mother and Victoria are safely tucked up in bed, so that leaves only me.'

'And that's where you should be,' he told her, looking at her as cheekily as he could, but still holding back, deciding that if either of them was to make a move he'd feel more confident if the first open hint came from her. It wasn't his way to let the girl make the running, but he'd never found himself in quite this sort of situation before, and certainly never with someone of Elizabeth Odron's class.

'I have the whole night before me to go to bed if I want. Really, we spend too much time asleep. The whole world does. One-third of our lifetime.'

Her hand began to press harder on his thigh, and he felt it move up higher as she leaned forward. 'Besides,' she added, 'if you're so keen I should be in bed, who don't you move over and make room for me?'

Quick as a flash Tom Fahy came back: 'Well, if I did that, you'd have the law on your side, but 'tis a sure thing that I wouldn't have it on mine.'

'Oh, aren't we the witty boy!' Elizabeth replied.

'The life and soul of any party,' Tom Fahy joked, anxious to keep the exchange on a light-hearted level for the moment. Not that he would object to a little dalliance with her – even more

111

than that if he was quite sure that there'd be no repercussions – but he wished he had some more time to think about it. A stolen kiss or a quick cuddle in a dark corner at a party or a dance was a harmless innocent diversion, a passing opportunity that was part of the fun and spirit of the occasion, and was over and forgotten with him off and away to the next one before the night, or even the hour, was out. But this was something different altogether. Miss Elizabeth Odron was obviously all that her reputation reported her to be, and as he contemplated her lively enticing expression and thinly covered body and felt her hand edge ever higher on his thigh he told himself: God, there'd be eating and drinking in her. But it'd be a much more dangerous escapade than he had ever been involved in before. If it got out, there was Ambrose Mercer to reckon with and, worse, there was his career in the force. And he'd be in Odron House for at least a month. His head swam at the prospect of all the nights that could be stretching ahead with such a woman ready, willing and able, but then it also struck him that it was a long time to be trapped if for any reason he wanted to put an end to proceedings before he was due to go back to barracks.

'Well, you're not exactly being the life and soul of the party just now, are you?' she teased, leaning forward and slowly moving her head from side to side so that her hair was brushing his face. The scent from her body assailed him, and he had to close his eyes with sheer languour. What had he been thinking? That he'd be trapped in Odron House with her for a month or more. But look at him now, really literally, physically trapped by her. And in bed in his pyjamas, and her gown almost open so that the swell of her bosom was tantalizingly close.

Suddenly she took his hand and before he could check her she had pushed it down inside her nightdress. She held it there and pressed her face to his cheek, licking the lobe of his ear. Almost involuntarily his thumb sought out her nipple. Hard and aroused, its point was almost sharp. He stroked it and was rewarded with a frantic intake of breath.

'Let me in with you,' she whispered, but he had his other arm around her now, trapping *her* against him, and wouldn't let her go.

'There's no rush,' he whispered back. 'Wait a while.' This

112

was pleasure enough for him for the moment, and he wasn't sure that he wanted things to go much further on this first encounter.

Elizabeth, however, had other ideas, and when she found he was too strong for her to be able to escape his imprisoning embrace she quickly plunged her free hand down under the blankets to alight on the soft truss of sex between his legs. His body gave a spasmodic jerk at the contact, but otherwise he remained motionless. Slowly and deliberately she firmed her fingers around his organs, opening and closing her fist until she heard his sudden gasp and felt the response against her palm.

'Nice?' she whispered, but to her surprise his answer was to put his own hand down and grab her wrist in an effort to pull her away.

'I'll squeeze,' she warned. 'Hard.'

'No, you won't,' he said.

'Why not?'

'Well, you wouldn't want to injure me there now, would you, and maybe put me out of action for the next few nights?'

She looked at him strangely, nonplussed by his reply.

'Does that mean you're rejecting me?'

'Just for tonight, Elizabeth. Just for tonight.'

'But why not tonight?' she asked.

He took his hand from off hers, wrapped it around her shoulder and kissed her. She responded by taking her own hand from under the bedclothes and embracing him. He let her hold his lips as long as she liked, and when she drew away he said: 'To answer your question: let's say I'm a slow but steady worker. The law, you know, it always proceeds step by step. Besides, if we stop now, look at the pleasure I'll have tonight anyway just thinking about the pleasures we both can have on other nights. Tomorrow night maybe.'

She laughed into his face.

'You're certainly a cheeky one,' she said. 'What makes you so sure that if you send me away tonight I'll give you another chance tomorrow night? Or any other night for that matter.'

But Tom Fahy had little doubt that Elizabeth Odron would be knocking on his door again. She was too keen and hot-blooded to keep away, especially as Ambrose Mercer would have been the only sparring partner she'd have had for some time and she must be rarin' for someone new. She'd need little encouragement.

'Ah, sure,' he said, putting his arm under her and lifting her off the bed, 'that'll be up to yourself.'

She stood by the bedside, looking down at him, her expression one of puzzled amusement.

'I must say you're a cool one, Constable Fahy.'

He looked back at her, a slow grin breaking over his features.

'Well, meaning no offence now, Miss Odron, but I can't say the same for you – if you get my drift.'

She made no answer to that but bent down and gave him a soft motherly kiss on the forehead.

'See you tomorrow,' she murmured.

'With God's help,' he answered.

She turned and left the room, closing the door quietly behind her.

'Sweet Jesus!' Tom Fahy gasped. Elizabeth Odron was a completely new experience for him. Yes, she'd be back again, he was certain of that. But what he wasn't certain of was whether the prospect delighted him or frightened him.

'Sweet suffering Jesus!' he whispered again to himself as he readjusted his pillow and settled back in the bed to think.

6

On Wednesday morning the weather broke.

At breakfast neither Elizabeth nor Victoria could conceal their disappointment as they contemplated the streaming windows, but Mrs Odron seemed unconcerned. As Pat Howell filled a second cup of tea and overcame his shyness to take a third slice of hot buttered toast, it struck him that the rain might have been falling in another country for all the effect the weather's vagaries appeared to have on her. Since he and Tom Fahy had arrived she had spent most of the time in her room, and they had seen her only at meals. She was a pleasant attentive hostess on these occasions, but behind the easy and gracious manner Pat sensed a preoccupation, as if her mind was on other matters.

'I rarely go out, Constable,' she was explaining, 'so it really makes little difference to me whether it's wet or dry. Of course for those who have to be out and about it must be quite a nuisance. People like yourself, out on patrol in the rain, it must be quite wretched for you.'

''Tisn't very pleasant, sure enough, Mrs Odron,' he replied, 'but I don't mind if I have my waterproofs on. The sergeant in my first barracks had his own way with that sort of situation. When it was time for his patrol, he'd get dressed up and then he'd go a few yards up the road and come back immediately, saying: "Better wait till the shower passes." Of course if it was

115

over in a minute or an hour made no difference, for he wouldn't go out again. Technically, you see, he'd been out on patrol, so his conscience was satisfied.'

'Hardly a very comforting story,' Elizabeth commented tartly. 'I hope that's not the way you behave in Gortnahinch station.'

'Oh, we'd never get away with anything like that here. Sergeant Driscoll would soon have us on the carpet.'

Elizabeth made a grumpy disdainful sound and turned once again to the window.

'Really, Elizabeth, you can't complain,' Victoria protested. 'We've had wonderful weather so far.' She gave Pat a bleak smile, clearly making an effort to raise everyone's spirits. His own were unaffected by sudden changes in the weather. Having been brought up on a farm, he had learned to be sanguine about the elements. Bless the sun or curse the storm they might, but rain or shine never left them at a loose end. For Elizabeth and Victoria, however, he knew it must be very different. He wondered what it was like for these two girls when the weather closed in, as it so often must in this part of the country. Living in a mansion, waited on hand and foot, just three women who were seeing each other every day of their lives, cooped up together – what did they find to do? In the two days he had already been at Odron House, Elizabeth had spent one day out riding and the other in Gortnahinch, ignoring his advice that it might not be safe for her to go out alone; and since his arrangement with Tom Fahy had been that he should keep as close to as many of the family as he could he had, at Victoria's insistence, spent mornings and afternoons in the gardens, keeping her company and willingly submitting to her demand that he fulfil his promise to talk to her.

'Yesterday's weather isn't much help today, is it?' Elizabeth snapped at her sister. 'That's the end of our summer no doubt.'

'I wouldn't be too sure, you know,' Pat said. It wasn't meant as an empty formula to cheer her up. He was able to remember high-summer heatwaves such as the one they had been experiencing – not that many, but they had occurred – when a single day's rain did not necessarily mean the end of the good spell but was simply a respite before the skies cleared again and the sun returned. Of course from where he was sitting at the table it

116

was impossible for him to tell if this was just such a break; he'd need to be out in the fields to feel the wind and read the sky, and even then, unlike his father, he might make a wrong prediction. So he wasn't surprised when Victoria wrinkled her nose and said: 'Oh, you're just saying that. You *are* just saying it, aren't you?'

'No, I'm not,' he defended himself.

But that wasn't good enough for Elizabeth.

'Well, if you mean it, how can you tell?' she asked, her voice betraying a hard edge. Pat Howell already had seen how different she was from her sister, more practical, more materialistic, more impatient of anything that smacked of speculation. She could, he judged, be tough and ruthless for her own ends. He greatly preferred Victoria. She was glad of his company and she put him at his ease. He'd never have got on with Elizabeth; he wouldn't have had the slightest idea what to talk to her about.

She was looking intently at him now, waiting for his reply, showing him that she wasn't going to let him get away with anything, even with what might have been only a polite piece of smalltalk.

'Come on, Constable,' she insisted, 'is it or isn't it going to rain all day?'

He was stung by the mocking tone, and the form of address confirmed that she was engaged in her favourite game of baiting people.

Victoria had also caught the note of challenge and she threw Pat a look of concern.

He rose, pushed his chair back from the table and made for the door.

'Where are you off to?' she asked anxiously.

'I think Constable Howell must be beating a hasty retreat,' Elizabeth taunted. 'Or else he's had enough breakfast and doesn't like the idea of having to eat his words as well.'

'Elizabeth!' Mrs Odron rebuked sharply, remembering her role. 'Constable Howell is a guest in our house, and he is, after all, here for our protection. I do think you might spare him such remarks.'

'Oh, it's all right, Mrs Odron,' Pat put in. 'Anyway I'm only going to the door to have a look at the sky.'

117

Once outside, he found the rain falling steadily, sudden wind-gusts driving it in on him so that he had to turn up his tunic collar. His first thought was one of sympathy for Tom Fahy. Poor Tom! He had been up and gone almost two hours before, doggedly keeping to his task of staying close to Ambrose Mercer. That man Mercer was like a ball and chain tied to Tom's ankle, though Tom had told him that Mercer still considered it to be the other way round. And he certainly had no intention of hiding his annoyance; at dinner the previous evening, even though by then he had had what he called a bodyguard for less than two days, he had tried to persuade Tom that he'd never have the stamina to keep up. But Pat knew that that sort of taunt would be akin to a challenge to the likes of Tom Fahy. And Elizabeth Odron's intervention had only made Mercer angry and lessened the chances of dissuading Tom.

'Ambrose, you've been too long the only man around here,' she had said, 'so you think no one else can match you. I'm sure there's nothing you can do that Tom can't.' Her voice was light – deceptively light, Pat had thought, and he felt her comment was far more than a piece of friendly banter. Certainly Mercer's reaction was surprising; that he was a choleric individual with a short temper they all knew, but his anger at Elizabeth seemed more extreme than was necessary, as if he found something in her remark that was almost a personal betrayal. It was with obvious difficulty that he had restrained himself.

'I've been here a long time and here I'm going to stay,' he rasped. 'That's one thing Mr Precious Constable Fahy can't do. I don't need any nursemaid. I'm not afraid of any Shinners. Loudmouths and windbags all of them.'

'But it was you yourself who suggested getting police protection,' Elizabeth pointed out.

Mercer laughed. 'It wasn't for me I suggested it. It was for you and your sister and mother.'

'That's quite true,' Amelia had intervened. 'Ambrose felt we needed police here in case the house should be attacked.' She gave a shudder and added: 'You know there've been many houses just like ours burned to the ground. I'm almost afraid to open the *Irish Times* any day for fear of reading about another burning. Oh, it's really awful! How much longer do you think it'll go on, Constable?' she asked Tom.

'What would he know about it?' Mercer had snorted. 'Anyway, the police are probably in league with the rebels.'

The accusation was greeted with shocked exclamations from Amelia and Victoria, while Elizabeth smiled at Tom Fahy as if encouraging him to reply.

Pat remembered how calm his colleague had remained.

'Speaking for myself, Mr Mercer, and for the rest of us in Gortnahinch barracks,' he had said, 'we took an oath of duty and loyalty, and though there may be some among us now – I won't deny it – who may regret that oath, we are men of our word. *I'm* certainly not in league with Sinn Fein. If I was, sure couldn't I easily shoot you while we're out in the fields and say it was one of the Sinn Fein boys! After all, there weren't any witnesses, were there, when someone took a pot-shot at you on Sunday, so it wouldn't be difficult for me to find an opportunity when no one was around.'

'You wouldn't have the nerve,' Mercer had replied with as much derision as he could.

'Oh, Ambrose, Ambrose,' Elizabeth kept on mockingly, 'that sort of remark is just what might make Tom lose patience with you.'

'I don't care a damn for Tom or his patience,' he growled, leaning heavily on Tom's name, obviously furious that Elizabeth was on familiar terms with him but anxious, nevertheless, to try to conceal his jealousy.

Pat Howell had kept silent during the exchange which was ended by Mercer rising from the table and saying: 'By the time I've finished with the constable, he'll be sorry he didn't stay in the house looking after the women.' He went to the door, then turned to Tom, adding, with a note almost of triumph: 'I'll be making an early start tomorrow. Six-thirty. So better get a good night's sleep if you're thinking of coming along. And be prepared to stay out all day.'

Pat had heard the men leave by seven o'clock, their steps crunching on the gravel of the front drive as they made their way around to the stables at the back of the house, Brutus yapping excitedly at the prospect of an outing. Even then the rain had been pelting at his window and he felt almost ashamed at the easy part he had drawn in their Odron House assignment. But, then, he hadn't actually drawn it – Tom had

119

insisted that it was better for the same man to shadow Mercer all the time. It was almost as if he suspected him of something, or even was deliberately trying to provoke him. Whatever Tom was up to – if he was up to anything at all – he'd have his reasons. And, sorry though Pat felt for him, he was glad he was able to savour the extra comfort the break in the weather seemed to add to the warmth of his bed, and especially glad that, weather apart, he was the one to be left in Odron House. Being there all day really was like a holiday: lying in bed at dawn, knowing he had what amounted to another day off. And his fears that he might be bored hadn't materialized at all. Indeed, it was very much the opposite with Victoria Odron as his constant companion. But was it simply because she *had* been his constant companion for two days that he was beginning to feel close to her in a way he had never felt with any other girl, or was it . . . what? He didn't know, but it was strangely exciting to snuggle down in the bed, listening to the rain belting down, and be able to look forward to another day at her side.

Now he looked up at the skies and tried to gauge what the weather would do. He had to run down the drive for some yards so as to bring into vision more of the sky behind the house. The slant of the rain and the movement of the tall cypress-trees near the tennis-court measured the strength of the wind for him. He shivered slightly and turned up the collar of his tunic, but his involuntary action was not caused by any feeling of cold, only by the misery of getting wet. In fact the air, he noted, was quite warm. That was promising. He wished his father was around to consult; he'd like to be able to go back to the ladies with an opinion on the weather that was firm, authoritative – and encouraging. In fact already an opinion was forming in his mind, and an encouraging one, too, but he wasn't very sure how much reliance he could place on it. It would be a pity to make a fool of himself; if he was wrong, Elizabeth would certainly not let him forget it and he might look a bit of a gom in front of Victoria after marching out so confidently to read the signs. As he took a last look around, he wondered what his father would be doing at that moment at home on their tiny farm in Leitrim. He wouldn't be out holding a finger to the wind anyway; he'd have done that hours ago. That's if it was raining up there at all. It probably was; it did most of the time.

Back in the breakfast room he found that Elizabeth had already left – obviously she didn't believe that his weather forecast would be worth waiting for.

'You're drenched!' Victoria exclaimed immediately she saw how wet he had become. 'Dry yourself with this,' she said, pressing her handkerchief into his hand. 'I have another.'

Pat was embarrassed by her concern and attention, and Mrs Odron laughed.

'That isn't going to be much help, Victoria. Let the constable go up to his room and dry his head with a towel. We don't want him getting a cold on our behalf and having to take to his bed.'

'Yes, I'll go up so,' he said. 'I won't be a minute.'

'And when you come down you can tell us what the weather is going to do,' Amelia added.

'Oh, I can tell you that now,' Pat answered. 'That rain is down for a while, most of the day anyway.' And before Victoria could show her disappointment he added: 'But the sun will be back tomorrow.'

'Promise?' she said, smiling.

Pat hesitated. 'Yes, I promise,' he replied, wishing fervently that he had his father behind him to back his prediction.

Sergeant Driscoll made his way towards the screen in the corner, behind which the Sister had told him was his wife's bed. It was the afternoon visiting hour; all the women were awake and sitting up in their beds, having had dinner. Some had their newborn babies in their arms, trying to quieten their cries; others cast fond glances into the cots by their bedside and stretched out a hand to adjust the coverlet or smooth down the sheet next to the child's softly breathing nostrils; most had visitors – mothers, husbands, siblings of all ages and sizes, sitting or standing around, admiring the new offspring. All was noise: laughter, chatter, the high voices of youngsters' questions, the stern admonitions of elders, the clanking of tins and bottles. But despite all the hubbub Sergeant Driscoll tiptoed, the creaking of his boots turning his face red with embarrassment. Some visitors, noting his uniform, lowered their voices or even fell silent as if he was about to chastise them for breaching the peace, and then when he passed they followed his progress towards the screened-off corner.

121

The sergeant peered around the screen, fearful of finding Lucy stretched out in some distress. Why else should there be a screen at all if it was not because all was not well? But he found her sitting up jauntily, her face all smiles as she said: 'Wisha, John, isn't it just the size of you! If I'd never known you were coming, wouldn't I have recognized the tune of these boots of yours from miles away? Didn't Mrs Hogan polish them at all for you this day?'

'Sure you know she did. Mrs Hogan isn't the one to neglect us now, is she?' the sergeant replied, his heart much lighter at finding Lucy bright and well. 'Anyway,' he added with a little laugh, ''tis not polish these boots need to silence them but a drop of oil.' He took a seat beside the bed and settled his cap on his knee before asking: 'For what have you a screen around you? It put the heart across me when I saw it. I thought it was the way something was wrong.'

'Divil a bit is wrong with me,' Lucy assured him, putting a hand on his and giving it a comforting squeeze. 'The screen is there since this morning when Dr Harvey looked in. I told the Sister to leave it; I felt a bit shy with the other women here. I'm not used to them yet.'

'You, shy!' the sergeant exclaimed. 'I've never known you shy of other women in your life. Sure women's chatter was ever your favourite diversion.'

'Ah, what would you know about it? And it's little chance I get for chatter with women or any other mortals in that barracks of yours,' Lucy threw back at him, tossing her head in mock annoyance. But the confusion of her gesture was sufficient to appraise the sergeant of his gaffe and make him realize that it was not the other women his wife didn't want to see, but the babies they so lovingly and proudly cosseted.

'I'd have come to see you sooner,' he explained, 'but it's busy enough in the barracks these days with three men out.'

'Three? Who's out besides Tom Fahy and Pat? Is one of the men gone sick?'

'Ah, not at all. It's just young Francie has a day's leave.'

'He didn't pick the best of the weather for it, then,' Lucy said, looking out the window beside her.

'Ah, that won't last,' her husband assured her, following her gaze. 'You have a nice view from here.'

'I have that,' Lucy said. 'Better than the one from my own bedroom window.'

Sergeant Driscoll grunted his agreement. He looked out on the hospital grounds. The light rain seemed to wash brighter than ever the green of the grass, making the well-kept lawns stand out from the dark pathways between them. Every now and again one of the nursing Sisters would hurry along to or from the hospital building, an umbrella held in one hand and the long skirt of her nun's habit held up in the other for fear it might brush the ground.

The sergeant turned to his wife, almost fearful to ask the question uppermost in his mind.

'You haven't told me what Dr Harvey said,' he commented as casually as he could so as to hide his anxiety.

'Sure you didn't ask me, so I thought you weren't interested and that it was only to see the other women you had come,' Lucy joked. 'Can't you tell there's nothing much wrong with me?'

Sergeant Driscoll didn't reply, but the warmth of the look he gave his wife was his answer. His heart began to rise with hope. Lucy was looking better – looking happier – than she had done for some months.

'But did he not say anything?' he had to persist.

This was the first time in all their married life that they had been separated, and he couldn't believe that while they were apart something important hadn't taken place or been said that he should know about. The strain in his features showed his anxiety, and Lucy half-turned in the bed so that she was able to take both his hands in hers. She squeezed his fingers, lifting and then letting fall his hands, like two young sweet-hearts signalling their love with touch and movement rather than with words.

'Set your mind at rest, man dear. I'll tell you what he said. "So far, so good, missus, so far, so good." Those were his very words.'

Sergeant Driscoll nodded, containing his relief and joy. But still he wasn't satisfied.

'Is that all?' he asked. 'Did he say anything else?'

Lucy smiled, as if keeping the best bit to herself for as long as possible.

'He said I'm near my time. Very near. It could be any day now.' And then, seeing the excitement start to rise in her husband's eyes, she gave his hands a warning squeeze and added: 'But don't be getting all up in the air about it. We've had this before.'

Sergeant Driscoll nodded and looked away, trying to conceal the turmoil in his mind at the clash of fear and hope – fear that it would all end in yet another still-birth, hope that, no, this time would be different.

'Well, anyway, 'tis in the hands of the Lord it is,' his wife reminded him, but he could tell from the misting of her eyes that she, too, was sharing the same emotions. 'You go off now,' she added. 'You have your work and the men to worry about. You don't need to worry about me. I'm grand here, and the Sister will telephone you the moment there's any news. So be off with you.'

Sergeant Driscoll rose, dropping his cap so that he had to stoop to pick it up. He straightened, hesitated, then bent again to kiss his wife.

She gave him a special smile. 'Didn't the screen come in handy after all! You'd never have kissed me with all the others looking on if it hadn't been there.'

She was right of course, he admitted to himself.

'I'll come in again tomorrow – or, if I can't, one of the men will be over,' he said.

Lucy nodded and then shooed him off. He turned and creaked his way towards the door. The other patients and their visitors lowered their voices as he passed and gave him vague salutes. He noticed – what he had missed on the way in – the sweets and chocolates and flowers the visitors had brought. My God, he thought, and me coming in with one arm as long as the other. Well, amn't I the right gom!

Constable Fahy shook the drips from off the peak of his cap and grimaced to himself. He remembered the last time he had sat under a tree eating a sandwich. It had been summer then, too, but it hadn't been raining, as it was now, and his companion had been a most pleasant acquaintance of the opposite sex, not a hostile, uncommunicative and thoroughly rough-grained individual such as Ambrose Mercer. Selfish, too! They had

124

spent a long morning alternately riding in the open horse and trap through the unrelenting downpour or trudging through fields where Mercer could check on cattle or pigs, or sometimes, when he got the chance, upbraid a labourer for sheltering from a drop of rain, and now here they were, sitting on waterproofs under a tree eating their lunch. Though the tree was large and leafy, it still couldn't keep them completely protected, and the lunch, for Tom Fahy anyway, left something to be desired. That something was a bottle of stout; Mercer had four of them, but he must have got them from a stock of his own, for there had been none in the kitchen of Odron House, where all the kitchen maid could offer the constable to go with his packet of sandwiches was tea or milk. He had accepted the milk, for he had to have something to drink, but he swore to himself that anyone with an ounce of humanity and four bottles of stout having lunch under a dripping tree beside a fully grown male whose only beverage was a harmless drop of milk would have offered him at least one of the bottles.

He certainly would have if he had been an Irishman. Or even if he had been any other Englishman except Ambrose Mercer. But, then, it had been clear to Fahy that Mercer was determined to make life as difficult and as miserable for him as he could. And miserable it certainly had been that morning! Mercer would stride along, picking the most difficult paths he could, his gumboots taking him easily and comfortably through mud and over rough stones, while Fahy stumbled behind him, his policeman's boots squelching and slipping as he determinedly kept pace and tried to avoid being tripped up by one of Brutus' unpredictable sorties. Thank goodness, he told himself, the weather had been so fine up to now or else some of that ground would have had him sinking up to his oxters. But he wasn't going to give in, or even by the slightest sign shown any weakness. He'd stick to the bugger through thick and thin! And not only for his own satisfaction, but also because there was some tiny serpent in his mind whispering to him that Ambrose Mercer wasn't only a roughhewn, uncouth, flinty bastard but that there was something, if not downright evil, at least sinister about him, and that if only he could be sufficiently roused to the point where he'd lose his temper he might say something that would confirm all Tom Fahy's suspicions about his story of being shot at.

But, even if Mercer wouldn't share his lunch with anyone, Tom could share *his*. He extracted a bit of meat from one of his sandwiches and fed it to Brutus. The dog was sitting on its haunches between the two men, eyeing the rain as if it couldn't believe the change in the weather after so many dry hot days. It grabbed the meat from Fahy's hand and masticated it eagerly. The constable tore off another piece and made to give it to the dog.

'Stop feeding that brute,' Mercer rasped. 'He's my bloody hound, and I'll feed him myself when it suits me.'

Brutus looked from one to the other. He seemed to recognize the authoritative tone of his master's voice and to fear it, but the piece of meat he had eaten had sharpened his appetite for the further tit-bit being offered, and after a moment's hesitation his head shot forward, teeth snapping to clutch the meat.

'I told you, Fahy, leave the bloody dog alone,' Mercer raged. He lashed out with his boot at Brutus, catching him a painful blow in the ribs. The dog yelped and sprang up, still holding the food in its grip, and it quickly moved around to the policeman's other side, away from its master, to continue chewing.

'You're a right animal yourself, Mercer,' Fahy said coolly.

'Never you mind what I am,' came the angry reply. 'It's none of your business. And another thing: it's *Mr* Mercer to you. Remember that.'

Fahy laughed. 'Ah, sure I don't mind calling you Mr Mercer back at the house, or when anyone is around, but plain Mercer will do for me out here. After all, there's no one to hear me, is there? So, if you want to go complaining to anyone that I was being disrespectful, you wouldn't be able to prove it, would you? No witnesses, you see.' Tom Fahy paused before almost off-handedly adding: 'Just as there were no witnesses to your story about last Sunday.'

The constable deliberately refrained from looking to see Ambrose Mercer's reaction to that remark. He put the bottle of milk to his lips, throwing his head back to empty its last drops while surreptitiously, with his other hand, pushing another bit of meat towards Brutus' jaws. Mercer's reaction, however, was swift and irate.

126

'What the hell do you mean? Are you calling me a liar?' he shouted in fury.

The blood rushed to his face and he jumped to his feet, towering aggressively over the constable. Tom Fahy looked up at him, quite unperturbed – indeed, secretly delighted to have struck such fire from his adversary.

From his higher vantage-point Mercer suddenly saw his dog still being fed and he cursed viciously, kicking at the remains of the meat and grinding it into the earth. Brutus whimpered and slunk back on his belly.

'I've told you once,' Mercer raved, 'leave that blasted dog alone.'

'Have you ever heard the saying,' Tom Fahy asked mildly, ' "A dog is a man's best friend"? A pity the reverse isn't always true. You're certainly not that dog's best friend, are you, Mercer?'

Ambrose Mercer glowered down. His fists clenched and unclenched, but then, regaining control of himself, he resumed his seat.

'That dog is mine and I'll treat it any way I please,' he declared.

'You think authority is the greatest thing in the world, don't you?' Tom Fahy said, delighted with Mercer's reaction to his baiting and anxious to keep the conversation on a personal level. 'You like throwing your weight about, especially at anyone or anything that can't answer back.'

Ambrose Mercer was silent for a moment. Then, without turning to look at the constable, he said slowly and forcefully: 'People like you just make me sick. Authority? You're a right one to talk. What the hell do you and your cronies do but throw your weight around? Of course it's easy for you. You have the law on your side. I wonder how smart you'd be without that uniform to protect you. Or I wonder how much of an impression you'd make without it. It's not you the people obey, you know, Mr Constable Fahy, it's only the bloody uniform. "Yes, sir" and "No, sir" and "Sir, if you please" is just all kowtowing to your brass buttons and the threat of clapping them into a cell,' he finished with a snort.

'And why exactly do people obey *you*?' Fahy asked.

'Because they recognize someone better and stronger than

127

themselves,' Mercer declared. 'That's real authority, not the fake stuff of a uniform or a warrant or a summons.'

'And the real stuff is what you have so?'

'I have it. I've earned it,' Mercer said, and then, quite venomously: 'I've suffered for it. I wasn't born on a farm like most of you fellows. Food when you were hungry and as like or not allowed go your own way when you were growing up. Do you know where I was born, Fahy?'

'How would I know where you were born? Of course I don't.'

'No, of course you don't. Well, neither do I. All I know is that I grew up in an orphanage. That's where I learned about authority. No kisses and cuddles there. The rod, and bread and water, Fahy. I'm glad now, glad, because it toughened me. And as soon as I could I joined the Army. And that toughened me more. That's how I learned about authority. I learned that if you want to get anywhere you have to have authority.'

'Do you believe in God, Mercer?' Tom Fahy asked.

Ambrose Mercer turned on the constable a look of amazement.

'What sort of a daft question is that?'

'Oh, it's not so daft. You see, God has authority, over all the world, over all the people. But He has compassion, too. Your authority is based on fear, isn't it?'

Mercer laughed. 'You Irish are riddled with it, aren't you? This mealy-mouthed religious twaddle. You're all the same.'

'If you call mixing authority with compassion "mealy-mouthed religious twaddle", then there's more than us has it. Yes, and practised it, too. Your old master, Colonel Odron, the Lord have mercy on his soul. He had authority – more than you have, because he owned the Odron estate and you're only its manager. But look how he used his authority. But I don't suppose you approve of that, eh?'

'A lot you know about Colonel Odron!' Mercer said derisively. 'I don't believe you ever saw the man in your life, not to mind speaking to him. You'd only have been a child then.'

'Oh, I wasn't even here at the time, I agree,' Tom Fahy conceded. 'I was only a youngster, still at home up in Sligo. But I didn't need to know him. I've heard plenty about him from people who did know him. And I heard how he bought you out

128

of the Army and gave you a home here. You talk about the hardship of being brought up in an orphanage. Where do you think you'd have been if it wasn't for the colonel? A one-stripe corporal is about the highest your sort would have risen in the Army, sleeping in barracks huts instead of in the fine soft bed you have in Odron House. That's what the colonel did for you, Mercer.'

Ambrose Mercer looked at Tom Fahy and laughed. It was a harsh laugh, full of disdain and sarcasm.

'So that's what the brave and noble Colonel Odron did for me, was it? For me! You're a right fool, Fahy. Not that you're to blame, I suppose. You take your cue from all the rest of the gentry and masters around here – all the ones in authority. And so you automatically side with your kind.' He paused a moment, then in hard measured tones continued: 'Let me tell you something, laddie. What Colonel Odron did wasn't for me. Oh, no! It was for himself. I was his batman in the Army, and you know what a batman is. Just a servant. A plain, unimportant, put-upon servant who had to polish his buttons, pull off his boots, make his tea, run his errands, do everything he asked. Asked? No, commanded. Because, remember, it was the great British Army where an officer was God Almighty and other ranks had to crawl on their bellies if that's what the officer wanted. So if a batman wanted to stay out of trouble he made sure to jump to it when told. And I jumped, Fahy, I jumped often and high. I was a good batman. I made sure I was. And that's what Odron didn't want to lose when he left the Army. More fool he'd be! He had a ready-made servant who knew all his little ways and who, in gratitude for being given a home in a bloody awful country, he thought should serve him for ever and continue to make his life in Odron House as easy as it was in the Army. So don't make any mistake about it, that's why I'm here now. It was for himself your precious colonel brought me over here, not because of any love for me. Just bad luck on the bugger that I'm sitting here now on top and he's under the sod – six feet under.'

'Well, aren't you the right sardonic ungrateful bastard!' Tom Fahy exploded. 'And twisted, too. You see everyone as an enemy, to be kicked around if you get half a chance. It's no wonder if there's nobody around here who has a good word to

129

say for you. God knows it's hard for me to say that to any man, but it's no harm to let you know it – if you don't know it already.'

Mercer stood up and shook crumbs off his lap.

'Whether I know it or not doesn't matter because I don't give a damn. To tell the truth, I prefer it like that. It's the best way to get what you want because people know they can't mess you about, or if they try to do you down it's at their own peril.'

Tom Fahy rose, too, and faced Mercer, intent on a last effort to provoke him further before they moved off.

'And you intend to get what you want or die in the attempt, don't you, Mercer, no matter who you have to hurt on the way?'

Mercer's eyes flashed, and his lips parted in a smile of relish.

'Hurt? They don't know yet what being hurt is like. Just wait. When I'm—'

He snapped his mouth shut, biting off the rest of his words.

'When you're what, Mercer? When you're what?' Tom persisted.

'Get up there, Brutus, you lazy bugger,' he snapped at his dog, ignoring the question. 'All I've got to say to you, Constable Fahy, is that you have quite a few miles more to cover this afternoon, so you'd better save your breath. You'll need it all.'

He strode off, turning only to whistle at the dog. Brutus, however, waited until the constable moved and fell in behind him. Tom Fahy shrugged and sighed. He was happy enough with the way the conversation had gone. He hadn't learned anything new, but there was still time. What made him distinctly unhappy, however, was the fact that Mercer was determined to have him trudging around for the rest of the day and the rain still falling. He sighed again as he followed his quarry. Lucky Pat Howell – no doubt he was indoors all the time, dry, warm, well fed and contented.

Tom Fahy was right – Pat Howell was well contented with the day's progress. He hadn't put his nose out the door since his brief after-breakfast expedition to read the skies, so he had kept bone-dry; lunch was a royal feast compared with Fahy's sandwiches and milk, so he had no hunger pangs to worry him; and he wasn't merely warm – he was extremely hot, for Vic-

130

toria had insisted on lighting the library fire quite soon after breakfast.

'But it's the middle of summer,' he had protested.

'Oh, don't be so conventional,' she laughed. 'Just because it's the middle of summer doesn't mean it's against the law to have a fire. We're obviously going to be in all day, the rain makes everything dismal, and just sitting around we can get quite chilly. At least *I* can, but *you* don't have to stay with me. I don't think anything will happen to me here, so you can't be accused of deserting your post if you should leave me alone.'

She was attending to the fire as she spoke, with her back to Pat, and he wondered whether she might be teasing him. In his brief contacts with Elizabeth while he had been at Odron House he had seen how given she was to teasing – Victoria was her sister, so maybe they had that leaning in common. But that, he felt, was unjust to Victoria; her teasing was pure light-heartedness, while her sister's frequently was not without an ulterior motive, sometimes even malicious. And though *he* might be conventional, as she had suggested, *she* certainly wasn't. Perhaps it was her craving for someone to talk to, or the fact that all her life she had been free to follow her own ideas and inclinations, but she appeared to take people very much as she found them. At least that was how she took Pat, and he was glad of it because he didn't really want to leave her alone. He told himself that it was his job to stay as close to her as possible. He was there to protect the Odron family, but there was no question of sitting with Mrs Odron, who seemed to spend most of her day closeted in her room, and Elizabeth was the last person in the world who appeared to need – or, indeed, would submit to – his 'protection'. Besides, even if he had been able to keep track of her, he wouldn't relish being made the butt of her sarcasm. So the best way he could fulfil his assignment was to watch over Victoria – and he was realistic enough to admit to himself that that was just what he wanted to do. She had kept him with her virtually since the moment they had met in the garden and she seemed genuinely to like his company. They chatted continuously like two young people discovering, to their surprise, another of their own kind – comparing likes, dislikes, hopes, fears – testing each other out step by step from instant attraction towards something closer that as yet neither

131

of them could recognize. Whenever a silence fell between them, which wasn't often, Victoria would remind him, clearly enjoying the opportunity to tease: 'Come on, Pat, say something. You promised to talk to me. Surely you're not going to break your word.'

The first time she had said that, Pat Howell hadn't immediately realized that she was only making fun of him, and he indignantly denied that he would ever be capable of breaking a promise. She had looked at him sharply, taken unawares by his naïvety, and seeing beneath it the core of humanity and integrity that shaped all his responses. She had involuntarily touched his hand to emphasize her assurance that she hadn't been serious – and he had smiled and blushed for his own gullibility. The exchange had become a sort of code between them, so that whenever she subsequently found a chance of using that code he remembered the first time and knew that the teasing reminder was her way of saying that she liked their conversation and liked him, too. For the same reason he wished he was able to tease her back, but he did not have the right phrase or tone and so could only accede to her request and talk seriously.

As soon as she had the fire going satisfactorily she had pulled up the long stool close to it and sat down at one end, making obvious her invitation to him to sit beside her. When he did so, she leaned back, clasping her hands around her knees in one of her favourite poses, and said: 'Well, now, what shall we talk about? Are you missing the barracks, feeling lonely away from your friends?'

Pat shook his head. 'No, I'm certainly not lonely.'

'That's nice to know. It means you're not bored here.'

'Not a bit. But. . . .'

He paused. It was true he wasn't lonely, but though he wasn't missing the barracks either, he was very worried that his absence meant he was unable to see what replies he might be getting to his letters about a meeting of Police Union supporters in Dublin. Probably there weren't any replies yet – he had posted his letters only on Sunday – and surely the sergeant wouldn't hold on to them until this Odron House assignment was over or someone else relieved him. That could be weeks off yet, and if he didn't deal with any replies before then his whole plan could fall through.

'But what?' Victoria questioned. 'Is there something worrying you?'

'Yes, there is,' Pat said. He didn't see any harm in telling her about the Police Union. It was something to talk about, and he knew he could trust her. And, besides, he found it helped him to have a sympathetic listener instead of keeping his worry bottled up inside him.

She agreed it was unlikely there'd be any replies yet. That was some consolation.

'But when they do come I won't be there to get them,' he pointed out morosely.

'Oh, cheer up,' Victoria cajoled him. 'Look, I'll tell you what we'll do. If you're right about the weather and it's fine tomorrow, we can cycle in together to collect any letters for you.'

Pat brightened for a moment at this suggestion, but then a look of doubt came into his eyes.

'I don't know if I can do that. I don't think the sergeant would be very pleased to see me turn up at the barracks suddenly when I'm supposed to be here.'

'You're not very bright, are you?' Victoria teased. 'Supposing I just happened to be going into the town myself. Your sergeant might be very angry if I went alone, without any protection. I know Elizabeth wouldn't think twice about doing so, but that's different. And with your colleague minding Ambrose it's impossible to watch over all of us at the same time.'

'Yes, you're quite right,' Pat put in enthusiastically.

'That's fixed, then. All we need is a fine day. I like looking out at the rain, but I don't fancy cycling in it, do you?'

'No, I certainly don't,' Pat agreed, and during the course of the morning he went over to the window many times to cast anxious glances at the skies in the hope that his weather prediction would not let him down.

By mid-afternoon the rain was down to a light persistent drizzle. Implacable and soundless, and as thin as gauze, there were moments when it deceived Amelia into thinking it had stopped, and then she would stare out her bedroom window, concentrating her gaze on the nearest tree in the garden below. Against the moving leafy background the rain was again

133

discernible; against the sky nothing could be seen. But at least when she looked at the sky it wasn't all as grey as it had been, so perhaps the young policeman's forecast would be fulfilled. She hoped so, for Victoria's champion would then be vindicated. She didn't think either of them yet saw Constable Howell in these terms, but to her it had been clear at breakfast that each was unconsciously reaching out to the other. And when they'd opened their eyes next morning and find the sun shining again – if, indeed, the fine weather should return – Victoria would be full of admiration for the policeman's knowledge, and he would take it as a feather in his cap that he hadn't let her down.

The sight of uniformed men in the house again, and the recognition that Victoria was attracted to one of them and he to her, reminded Amelia poignantly of Alex and herself. But, feeling strangely disturbed, she turned away from the window. It wasn't the past that disturbed her; day by day, for so many years, its changelessness had been her refuge, and she had haunted it willingly – the living haunted the dead. Except that she hadn't been living. She could see that now. Victoria's attraction to Constable Howell had set off in her again life's old alarm. Like the rain outside the window, which with the empty sky behind it had seemed invisible, but against the lush green branches had been given form, so it was with her. Trapped in the void of memory she was bereft both of past and present, an invisible cipher; only by stepping into the quick of the present could she once again have shape and substance. It was the present that had come to haunt her now, not the past; the present, beginning, unbidden, to make her part of its pattern.

The sudden realization induced a stab of panic. Was she ready for such a transformation? For so long the past had been her world, her paradise and consolation, her prison and punishment. Was it time now to shake it off?

She looked around. She had kept everything unchanged since Alex died – the dove-grey wallpaper with its flowered pattern, her embroidered dream-mansion on the wall opposite the bed, and the bed itself. She tried to take her eyes from the bed, fearful that it would remind her not of her joy, but of her shame, of that one betrayal she could never redeem, never forget. She covered her face with her hands in an effort to shut out all sight, but in the darkness of her head some devil-operated magic lantern cranked on. She thought of Alex's letters tied in a bundle in her drawer, the letters he had written her during the four years before he returned to settle down in Odron House. They would be her antidote. She knew them by heart, the words he used to express his need of her, the phrases that made her limbs melt with their graphic description of how he would love her. These were the scenes to replay – two figures on the bed, she and Alex knowing each other, arms and legs entwined, bodies straining towards communion. Yet, try as she might, these images were beyond her command. She opened her eyes, hoping that all she would see was the here, the now. But what she saw twisted her features into a mask of horror. For the bed was not empty. Two figures still writhed on it in a contorted embrace, but the figure beside her was no longer her lithe-limbed smooth-skinned husband; it had assumed the outline and lineaments of Ambrose Mercer. The fingers that had so slowly, so thrillingly moved over her from breast to thigh, pausing to draw a shiver of response from each special place, were not the elegant fingers she had noted when she first met her soldier at that fateful gymkhana. They had thickened and hardened into the grasping animal fingers of the rough orphan her Alex had saved and succoured, and who, with his saviour dead and buried, had sought to put himself in his place. How could she have been so mad! Had she been so relieved to have all the worries of running the estate taken off her shoulders and so reassured by his almost daily confident reports that she allowed her sense of gratitude to unbalance her? Had she been so blinded by his constant solicitude that she began to look on him as a friend and forget he was an employee? Had his youth, his virility, fed the hunger of her body, so cruelly deprived of what it had grown to crave, so that somehow, perhaps unwittingly, she had shown him some encouragement? How else could she have succumbed, even once, besmirching and putting at such hazard Alex's name and reputation for a few brief moments of brute carnality?

'No! No!' she cried.

She rushed to the bed, tore off the counterpane and savagely trampled it on the floor. The past was dead and done. It had been her gaoler for twenty years; she would be a willing prisoner no more. She looked at the needlework on the wall.

135

Cloth and thread, 'a good piece of work . . . artistic' as her mother had commented, but still no more than cloth and thread and a young girl's romantic dreams. Deliberately she took it down, fetched a scissors from her dressing-table, and calmly, methodically, commenced to unpick it colour by colour, piece by piece.

By dinner-time the weather had improved considerably. The rain had at last ceased, and every now and again a gap in the gradually clearing clouds allowed the sun to shine in on the long table, glinting on the dishes and silverware, and adding to Constable Fahy's appreciation of the food after the rigours and privations of his long day out. As he raised his head from his soup a sudden flash of sunlight burst through the windows, making him blink with its strength.

'Better late than never, I suppose,' he commiserated with himself. 'The sun, I mean. Still, a pity that rain couldn't have come at night instead of in the day.'

'Ah, you're a pansy-boy,' Mercer said. 'I suppose when it's raining all you policemen just sit in the barracks so as not to get your feet wet.'

Victoria, alive to the barb in Mercer's comment, feared that Elizabeth might retail Pat's breakfast-time story of how wet-weather patrols were circumvented in his first station and so lend the taunt some substance.

'Well, tomorrow is going to be fine again anyway,' she said in an effort to deflect the conversation.

'Yes,' Amelia added, 'it does seem so.'

'You ladies sound very confident,' Tom Fahy joked. 'Do you know something about the weather that the rest of us don't?'

'Oh, we're not just guessing,' Amelia assured him, with a bright smile at Pat. 'Constable Howell said the heatwave would return tomorrow and it looks as if he's right, doesn't it?'

'Ah, the bould Pat, of course,' Fahy laughed. 'I forgot that where he comes from they make the weather up there. Right, Constable?'

Pat did not reply, but Mercer interjected: 'Just as well. I have to go to Tralee tomorrow, to the fair, and trade is not good there when it's wet. No doubt I'll have the pleasure of your company, Fahy?' he added sarcastically.

'And mine,' Elizabeth put in eagerly. 'I haven't been into Tralee for months. But with Constable Fahy to protect me I should be safe enough.' And, as if to annoy Ambrose Mercer, she turned to Tom and asked, almost coyly: 'I won't be in the way, will I?'

'Not a bit of it,' Tom Fahy replied, while at the same time Mercer's surly 'You'd be better off staying here' made Elizabeth retort: 'Oh, if you don't want me, I'm sure Tom does. Don't you, Tom?'

Fahy looked up and saw the the ire rising in Mercer's eyes. Great, he thought to himself, get him on the run again.

'Any time, Elizabeth, me girl, any time,' he replied familiarly, taking full advantage of her obvious encouragement, malicious though it may have been.

'Perhaps you would try to get something for me in Tralee, Elizabeth? Some thread,' Amelia said.

'Thread? But there must be plenty of thread in Gortnahinch,' Elizabeth answered in surprise.

'Oh, not the kind of thread *I* mean. It's special thread for embroidery. I'll write it down for you before I go to bed tonight. I'm sure Cominsky's in Bridge Street would have it. I haven't been there for a long time, but I don't imagine they've changed much.'

'Certainly, Mother,' Elizabeth said, hiding her surprise. Amelia hadn't done any embroidery for many years, possibly not since. . . . What could have sparked off her sudden revival of interest? My, my, she thought, things were happening at Odron House. Demonstrations, bullets, resident policemen, and now a busy mother. Times were getting interesting again.

The same thought was running through Tim O'Halloran's mind at about the same time. Things were certainly getting interesting: his latest information was that Ambrose Mercer had no bank account in Tralee. Which was just what he expected to hear. And, if he hadn't one in Tralee, he certainly wouldn't have one any further afield. O'Halloran was confident of that. But the news in no way weakened his inclination to agree with Charles Renfrew's suspicions about Mercer. The facts were plain and led to only one conclusion: Renfrew's conclusion. So Mercer must have money hidden away somewhere. A lot of money. Buried in a field? Perhaps. But inconvenient. And a man of Mercer's ilk would surely prefer to have his hoard as near to hand as possible. That way there was less danger of anyone stumbling on it, and that way he could remove it himself at a moment's notice if it became necessary. Now, where might such a place be, O'Halloran asked himself. There was only one. The sort of place where secret private possessions were often hidden – deeds, wills, jewellery, even a gun or two if it came to it, and money. Most certainly money.

So Tim O'Halloran was striding to Ger Casey's cottage where he knew he'd find Ger's brother who had been evicted by Mercer and who could be relied on to get a message to his daughter, Mary Casey, who worked at Odron House and who'd be more than willing to help and who would surely be able to find an opportunity. . . . It was like the old nursery rhyme, 'The House That Jack Built'.

'Aieee,' O'Halloran cried to the lightening skies. 'This is the dog that worried the cat that killed the rat that ate the malt that lay in the house that Colonel Odron built.'

His delighted laughter rang out over the deserted roads and fields.

7

Mary Casey poured herself another cup of tea.

She loved the summer-morning breakfasts at Odron House when sunlight flooded into the large kitchen, glinting on the scores of pewter jugs and vessels arranged on the shelves, making the brass hinges of the big ovens sparkle like the burning coal in the range, and warming the stone floor that the housemaid, Eileen O'Brien, kept spotlessly clean. Normally Eileen's bubbling young spirits matched the surrounding glow, but this morning the poor girl, smothered under a heavy cold, was as quiet as a mouse. It's an ill wind, Mary thought to herself, for Eileen's misfortune might well give her just the opportunity she needed. She had been surprised to see her father outside the back door the previous night, looking for her, and even more surprised at what prompted his visit, but if she could do anything to pay back Ambrose Mercer for his treatment of her family she was more than willing.

'Will you be having another cup, Cook?' she asked the buxom silver-haired woman opposite her.

'Wisha, why not?' Cook replied. 'I can take my ease for the morning.'

'We all can,' Mary said. 'You, too, Eileen. And I'm sure you're not sorry, with that cold you have.'

The housemaid shrugged and nodded. Mary pushed the teapot over to her, but as she started to refill her cup the rising steam tickled her nose. She put the pot down with a bang and sneezed twice rapidly.

' 'Tis worse you're getting, girl,' Cook observed with a disapproving shake of her head. 'A day in bed wouldn't do you any harm.'

'Ah, how could I stay in bed? Haven't I the rooms to do?'

'I'll do them for you, Eileen,' Mary Casey offered. 'Miss Elizabeth is gone off to Tralee with Mr Mercer and one of the policemen. And Miss Victoria said she'd be going into Gortnahinch soon with the other one and they wouldn't be back until lunch. So I'll have little to keep me busy.'

'That's a dacent offer,' Cook commented. 'I'd grab it if I were you.'

'Ach, 'tis only a summer cold I have,' the housemaid replied as she took a handkerchief from her apron pocket and dabbed at her nose. 'I'll be able enough.'

'Whatever you like,' Mary said, affecting indifference. 'But the offer is there if you want it. 'Tis too conscientious you are, and you'll get no thanks for it.'

She decided not to press the matter further at that stage. Eileen, she knew, liked to make up her own mind and so her first response to advice was often discouraging. She remembered with a smile the time the girl had been going out to a dance at the crossroads wearing colours that, as Cook said, made her look like 'six of one and half-dozen of the other', and had dismissed Mary's suggestion that she should change into something less likely to draw ribald comments from the men. But she wasn't gone ten minutes when she returned and asked Mary for a loan of a white blouse.

'It's great all the same,' she said now between snuffles and sips at her cup of tea, 'to have them all out of the house for the day. Except the missus, of course, and she's no trouble.'

'It is indeed,' Mary agreed. 'And the two policemen as well. The good-looking one is with Mr Mercer all the time, and Miss Victoria keeps the young one busy, so at least they're not under your feet.'

'That's all very well for the pair of you,' Cook complained, 'but I have two extra mouths to feed. And men into the bargain. I declare to God but that one – the one you called good-looking – he's got an appetite like a horse. I boiled six

140

extra spuds last evening and, would you believe it, didn't he polish them off!'

'All by himself?' Eileen asked.

'Well, I'd swear he had the most of them.'

'I suppose it's all the fresh air and the walking he has to do to keep up with Mr Mercer gives him the appetite. And besides, they're probably half-starved in that police barracks. Sure look at the young one – there's not a pick on him.'

'I don't know is there something between him and Miss Victoria?' Mary suggested.

'You know,' Cook echoed immediately, busy-voiced now at the hint of a romance, 'I thought the same myself. You two aren't here long enough, so you wouldn't know Miss Victoria as well as I do, and I can tell you she's a much brighter girl since he arrived.'

'Ah, but it couldn't come to anything . . .' Eileen began to say when her voice broke off as a fit of coughing overtook her.

'My God, girl, you're for the fever hospital for sure,' Cook warned, rising to wash her cup at the sink.

It was the signal that breakfast was over, and as both the other girls got up from the table a violent shiver gripped the young housemaid's body. Turning from the sink, Cook saw the spasm and tossed her head.

'Ah, well,' she said in a take-it-or-leave-it-tone, 'definitely the fever ward, young lady, if you don't look after yourself.'

'Well, she's heard my offer,' Mary Casey observed lightly, as if she hadn't much expectation that Eileen would accept. 'A body can't do more than offer.'

The housemaid sat down again. 'I'm feeling a bit dizzy. Perhaps I'll go back to bed after all. Do you think I should?'

'Wisha, isn't that what we've been telling you since you got up?' Cook declared. 'Wait till I get a jar for you.'

She opened a cupboard and took out a stone hot-water jar which she proceeded to fill from a boiling kettle.

'Now, take this and off with you. Keep well covered and I'll bring you up some hot gruel later.'

'And don't be thinking of anything,' Mary added. 'I'll do the rooms for you. Sure what extra is it? And I'll be glad of something to keep me busy while Miss Elizabeth is away.'

As the housemaid shuffled off, hugging the stone jar to her

141

bosom, Mary Casey felt well satisfied. With the house virtually empty and Eileen in bed, things couldn't have worked out better.

'Come on, Lazybones, it's time to get started,' Victoria called as she stood on the front steps of Odron House. Pat Howell joined her and looked up at the sky. Yesterday's blanket of grey had completely disappeared, and the sun was back in all its glory.

'Well, is it warm enough for you yet? It's nearly eleven o'clock already. Half the morning is gone.'

'Sure where's the hurry?' the constable shrugged. 'We've only a couple of miles to go, I won't be no more than five minutes in the barracks and we'll be back in time for lunch. Isn't that what you want?'

They mounted their bicycles and pedalled down the drive, turning into the silent empty road that led to Gortnahinch.

'Oh, it's heavenly!' Victoria exclaimed. 'What a wonderful summer we've been having. Listen! Just listen!'

'Listen to what?' Pat said. 'I can't hear anything.'

'The bicycle wheels, listen to the bicycle wheels. The sound they make as they go round. Isn't it like the sound of the wind in the trees?'

'My God!' the constable laughed. 'That's something I never heard said before. It doesn't sound like anything much to me.'

'Oh, you have no music in your soul,' Victoria retorted.

'I have so,' Pat Howell protested, carefully steering between frequent pot-holes. 'Would you believe I won medals for Irish dancing when I was a boy? How do you think I'd have done that if I hadn't an ear for the music?'

Victoria's machine wobbled dangerously as her laughter at the thought of Pat step-dancing shook the handlebars.

'I don't believe you.'

''Tis no lie,' Pat declared vehemently. 'I'll soon show you.'

He pulled his bicycle up sharply, jumped off and carelessly let it spin into the ditch. Victoria, taken by surprise, carried on for some distance before slowing and wheeling her machine around to return to where Pat stood in the middle of the road, hands stiff at his sides and eyes staring glassily ahead of him.

'Of course I'm a bit rusty – I haven't done this since I was a nipper. And without music to give me the beat it isn't easy.'

'No need for excuses,' Victoria cajoled. 'I can whistle quite well.'

'But you wouldn't know an Irish jig.'

'I know "The Sailor's Hornpipe". Wouldn't that do?' And she immediately launched into the tune, her surprisingly sharp whistle negotiating the twists and turns of the melody with strict rhythm and accurate pitch.

Pat's fixed gaze relaxed for a moment as his head nodded in accompaniment. Satisfied with what he heard, he refixed his features into a mask of stern concentration, waiting for an entry-point, and then, arms and the upper half of his body rigid, his legs began to dance.

Up and down his thighs raced, their movements short and crisp, legs thrown forward and then jerked back as if on springs, while the toes of his boots sometimes flicked at the air as if trying to connect with a nonexistent ball, at other times delicately rapped the ground behind him. His mouth was closed tightly, the breath pumping from his nostrils with the unaccustomed exertion. His body deviated neither backwards, forwards, nor sideways, but kept jigging over the one spot in the road as if held there by some underground magnet. Soon clouds of dust began to rise around his flying legs.

Suddenly, in the middle of the exhibition, he collapsed like a punctured balloon. Overcome both with breathlessness and a fit of laughter that was just as taxing as the bout of step-dancing had been, he bent over and sank to the ground in a spluttering heap. The sight was too much for Victoria. Throwing her bicycle down, she tottered over to him, her body shaking. He was sitting in the road, tears rolling from his eyes, unable to restrain his laughter. Victoria tried to say something but, too overcome herself even to remain standing, she sank down beside him, her head on his shoulders, and the two of them rocked back and forth until eventually the fit died out in hiccuping whimpers.

Victoria took a lace-edged handkerchief from her sleeve and dabbed at her eyes. She put a finger on Pat's chin, tenderly turned his face towards her and softly wiped the wet runnels that the tears had left on his cheeks. They looked at each other for a moment, but then Pat quickly turned away in confusion.

'You'll be destroyed sitting down there in the road,' he said to cover his embarrassment. 'And if anyone should come along. . . .'

'Is that all that worries you?' Victoria asked.

'It's you I'm worried for. Come on, I'll help you up.'

He rose himself, putting his hands on her waist and lifting her to her feet. Before he could remove his hands Victoria put her own over them, holding them there. But again Pat turned aside, pulling himself away and going to retrieve his bicycle.

'We'd better be getting on,' he said, 'and not be standing here like two amadhauns.'

'I know what that word means. It's the Gaelic for "fools". When I was a child I heard the men on the estate say it. They told me what it meant. They used it a lot.'

'I'd say that's not the only word they used,' Pat commented as he and Victoria remounted their bicycles and started to pedal once again. 'But I hope they didn't teach you any worse ones.'

'Oh, I know quite a few Gaelic words,' Victoria told him.

'From the men on the estate?'

'No, from books in the library at home. My father's books. I often take them down and read them. He must have been very interested in Ireland; he had a lot of books about it.'

'Do you remember him at all?'

'Oh, no, I couldn't remember him. I was only one when he died. And Mother hardly ever mentioned him when Elizabeth and I were growing up. But the tenants on the estate did. I used to talk to them about him. They liked him a lot; he got on very well with them. They told me that when he died six of them carried his coffin all the way to the church.'

'What about when he was born? Did they have a celebration then?' Pat asked.

'I don't know. Was that usual?'

'In some parts of the country it was. My father told me that he heard of it when he was young. When the lord of the manor had a son, there was great dancing and drinking by all the tenants. They kissed the baby's hands, and old women came from miles around prophesying about all the good times he'd bring them, and spitting on him.'

'Spitting on him?' Victoria echoed in amazement.

'Yes. It was an old custom, meant to bring him luck. Oh, it was a great time, by all accounts. Nothing like it now. Judging by last Sunday's to-do there's no love lost between the people around here and your family.'

'Oh, no, you're wrong,' Victoria hastily put in. 'I'm sure you're wrong. I'm sure they have nothing against us. It's Ambrose Mercer they hate.'

'Do *you* hate him?'

Victoria shrugged. 'Sometimes I do.'

'Sometimes? Why sometimes?'

She shrugged again, avoiding giving Pat a direct reply.

'Well, you'll soon be having him as a brother-in-law, won't you?' he said.

Victoria's bicycle swerved dangerously as she sharply turned her head.

'Whatever do you mean?'

'Isn't he going to marry your sister? The story is around the village. I'm told he's been boasting of it for the past few weeks.'

Victoria pulled up hastily, and Pat had to brake suddenly. He turned to see her standing in the middle of the road, the bicycle still between her legs, a look of utter stupefaction on her face.

'Marry Elizabeth! But that's utter nonsense. Oh, I know she leads him on. She always has done. That's . . . well, that's the way she is with men. But she'd never marry such a . . . such a . . .'

She remounted her bicycle, too surprised and angry to find words strong enough to express her feelings.

'Such a what?' Pat persisted.

'Well, such a liar, for one thing,' Victoria declared decisively. 'I can't imagine what he's up to, spreading such a story. I don't think Mother or Elizabeth would be very pleased if they heard it. You won't say it, will you?'

'Me! It's none of my business. I'll certainly not mention it.'

They breasted a hill and came in sight of Gortnahinch. Approaching them was a procession of carts loaded with milk-churns. Most of them had young girls holding the reins on the way back from the creamery where they had delivered that morning's supply of milk. They jogged along at an easy pace, each girl dressed in a shawl over apron or frock, in no great hurry to get back to their chores, and as they passed they called out cheery greetings or raised a hand in salute.

Almost immediately Pat and Victoria were in the street leading to the Square and they pulled up outside the police station. With the sun playing on it, the squat grey building looked quite inoffensive, the gilded emblem of the crown over the door glinting merrily, the door itself wide open, and Saucy, the cat, asleep on a window-ledge, taking full advantage of the summer weather.

'I'll only be a minute,' Pat said. 'Just to see if there are any letters for me and have a few words with the sergeant. I suppose he'll want to know how we're getting on at Odron House.'

As he entered the barracks, Victoria leaned her bicycle against the wall and softly ran her finger along Saucy's head. The cat's ears twitched, but it was too comfortable even to open an eye.

Greetings and jocular remarks met Constable Howell when he entered the dayroom.

'The wee one is back,' one of his colleagues shouted. 'How are you enjoying your country holiday?'

'Does the butler lay out your uniform every morning for you, Pat?' Francie O'Leary asked.

'Maybe he tries to dress your lordship as well,' Constable Doyle added.

'And how is Tom getting on?' Sean Hogan enquired. 'Did you leave him minding the shop?'

'It's more than the shop he's minding,' Pat replied. 'The poor fellow is walked off his feet. He must have lost stones already tramping half the countryside trying to keep up with Ambrose Mercer. I offered to take over from him, but he wouldn't have it.'

'Ah, sure you were always the lucky one,' joked O'Malley. 'If your bread fell on the ground, it would land butter side up. What brought you back anyway? Were you getting lonely for us?'

Suddenly there was a low whistle from Andy Doyle, who had strolled to the window. 'Begob, boys, he's brought company with him, too. Miss Victoria Odron, no less. That's her outside, isn't it, Pat?'

146

'It is,' Pat Howell agreed, 'but what of it? Tom is gone into the fair in Tralee to keep an eye on Mercer, and the other sister is with them, so if I'm supposed to be protecting Victoria I had to bring her here with me, hadn't I? And it was her idea to come in anyway.'

'Aha,' Denis O'Sullivan said with relish, 'so it's *Victoria*, is it? Not Miss Odron or even Miss Victoria? Aren't you the cute one?'

A ribald cheer went up, and the noise brought Sergeant Driscoll from his office.

'Constable Howell, no less,' he exclaimed. 'I wasn't expecting you. Was there something special brought you in?'

'Yes, Sergeant, sort of special.'

'Come inside, then.'

Sergeant Driscoll led the way back to his office and closed the door. He turned immediately and took the constable's hand, pressing it in his own.

'I'm glad to see you, Pat. There's nothing wrong, is there? Out at Odron House, I mean. What about Tom? Where's he now?'

The sergeant sat back behind his desk, contemplatively stroking the blotter before him as he listened to Constable Howell's brief outline of the progress of their assignment at Odron House.

'So there's really nothing to report,' he said as Pat finished. 'Well, I suppose that's better than if you *had* something to report – something bad, I mean.'

'How long will we need to be out there, Sergeant?' the constable enquired. What he really wanted to know was whether there were any letters for him, but he felt it would be better to work up to the question. Despite his anxiety, he didn't want it to look as if his mind was more on his Police Union hopes than on his Odron House duties.

'Oh, isn't it keen you are to come back, my lad! Sure you've been there only a few days yet. What's your rush? Aren't you happy having a soft bed to sleep in and the best of food on your plate, eh?'

Pat shrugged and then smiled good-naturedly as he saw the mischievous glint in the sergeant's eye.

'Are you off back to Odron House now?' Sergeant Driscoll asked.

'I suppose so,' Pat replied. 'Eh . . .' He hesitated.

Sergeant Driscoll grunted. Then he opened a drawer in his desk and took out two envelopes.

'These came for you. I was going to send them out but I thought I'd wait a few days to see if there were any more coming in. I suppose they're replies to those letters you were writing last Sunday.' He sighed, then added, 'Ah well . . .' and Pat sensed that the few words were meant to convey, yet again, a friendly warning. He blushed as he stuffed the letters into his pocket, saying: 'I'll take them with me. I'll just hop upstairs to see Mrs Driscoll before I go. How is she?'

'Holding her own well,' the sergeant told him, pleasure in his voice, 'but you'll not find her upstairs. Doctor Harvey moved her to the hospital in Listowel a few days ago. Oh, nothing to worry about,' he hastened to add at the look of alarm that appeared on the constable's face. 'Just so as she could get constant attention and have everything ready the moment . . .' He paused. 'Say a prayer for her, Pat, won't you? She'll need all the prayers she can get now. Doctor Harvey says that all being well it might happen in the next week.'

'Don't worry yourself, Sergeant,' Pat assured him. 'It'll be all right this time with the help of God. She's well in herself, you say?'

'Oh, she is. I haven't seen her today, but she was fine yesterday.'

'Couldn't I go out and see her now?' Pat asked eagerly. 'Sure by the time I have a chance of seeing her again, she'll probably be a mother. Is it all right if I go?'

'Of course it is, lad. And she'll be glad to see you, too. She asked me how you were getting on. You can tell her I'll be in to see her tonight.'

'I can take Miss Victoria with me, I suppose.'

'You could if she's willing. Would she mind going?'

'Mind, Sergeant?' Pat replied. 'Not that girl. She may be gentry, but there's no side on her at all. She's no different from you or me.'

Sergeant Driscoll was amused by Pat's enthusiasm but he made no comment on it. 'Well,' he admitted, 'it'd be nice for the missus to have a woman visit her – it's been only men so far.'

'We'll go then. Sure it's a lovely day; the spin out there will be no trouble at all.'

Victoria welcomed the invitation to visit the sergeant's wife. Visiting the sick was an activity that figured largely in many of the novels she had read, but the opportunity to do so had very rarely occurred to her. She remembered that once, when she was a child, she had been taken by a family servant to the cottage of one of the tenants who had a young girl of about ten seriously ill. She could recall the low barnlike little cottage with a small stack of turf against one wall, its two crowded rooms in which everything seemed to be awry. The picture in her mind was one of stark cheerless gloom, barefoot children playing on the floor and constantly being hushed by their mother, and on a battered mattress in a corner a little girl lay with her eyes closed. A flickering candle stood in its own grease on a piece of tin by her head, and her brow was wet with fever. 'What's wrong with her?' Victoria had asked, receiving in reply only a muttered doleful 'Ah, God help her, the creature, 'tisn't far she is now from the good Lord and His Holy Mother'. Victoria had taken that to mean that the little girl was near death, and for days afterwards she had begged mercy for her in her prayers. When a week later she learned from the same servant that the child had made a rapid recovery and was romping around with her brothers and sisters, Victoria felt a thrill of pride and self-congratulation, certain not merely that her own prayers had saved the child's life but also that her sagacity in addressing them not to her usual 'Jesus, meek and mild' but to 'the good Lord and His Holy Mother' had been the deciding factor.

'What's wrong with Mrs Driscoll?' she asked Pat. 'I hope she isn't too ill.'

'She's going to have a baby,' Pat told her, a blush creeping up his cheeks.

'But women don't go into hospital to have a baby. I thought they have babies at home.'

With some embarrassment Pat explained about Lucy's history of miscarriages and still-births. 'It's because of them that she's been moved, the sergeant said.'

'Shouldn't we get something for her?' Victoria suggested. 'Some sort of present. I'm sure it's usual to bring a present when you're visiting a patient in hospital.'

Pat Howell was momentarily nonplussed. Then he suddenly sprang into action.

'Wait a moment,' he said, running back into the police station. He reappeared almost immediately, a cat-basket under his arm, and scooping Saucy off her comfortable ledge before she could even open her eyes he secured her in it.

'Lucy will be delighted to see her. She loves that cat.'

'But that's not a present,' Victoria protested. 'We can't leave her there. I doubt even that we'd be allowed to bring a cat into a hospital.'

'Sure what harm could it be? They'd never know. We can say there's fruit and things in the basket.' Pat's broad smile of glee won Victoria's acceptance.

'All right, then. But have you any money?'

'What for?'

'Oh just a shilling or two. At least if we put some fruit and chocolate and a bottle of lemonade into the basket with the cat we won't really be lying, and we can have a picnic on the way back. I'd like that. Would you?'

As Pat looked into her soft eyes, the idea of a picnic with Victoria really took his fancy. Eagerly he jumped onto his bicycle, looking forward at least as much to the picnic as to visiting Mrs Driscoll.

The hospital, when they came on it, was anything but a cheerful sight. Ancient and dilapidated, its exterior had clearly been neglected for many years. Its long and low two storeys contained a succession of gaunt windows that, despite the temporary reflection of the sun's rays, were like so many old unhealed scars. The hospital grounds, however, although not very extensive, were by contrast extremely well kept, and the neatly trimmed grass plots with their beds and banks of brightly nodding flowers drew appreciative glances from Victoria.

'At least the patients have a nice view to cheer them up,' she said.

'If they're lucky enough not to be at the back,' Pat argued, suddenly daunted. He had never been in a hospital, couldn't even remember the last time he had been ill, and the realization that this grim building housed so many sick people momentarily dampened his spirits. To be deprived of health and

150

strength, to be stuck in bed all day unable to enjoy the fresh air and sunshine, to be separated from your friends and loved ones – he shuddered at the thought.

As they reached the main door he suddenly remembered the cat-basket and craftily he pushed it into Victoria's arms, saying: 'You'd better take this in. If it's supposed to be a present, they'd expect the girl to be bringing it rather than the man.'

Victoria had little chance to demur. 'Cad!' she hissed at him in pretended annoyance, thinking that in his policeman's uniform no one would have been likely to question the nature or contents of anything he might be carrying.

Inside he stopped a nun to ask where they'd find Mrs Driscoll. 'The sergeant's missus,' he offered as additional identification when the nun seemed not to recognize the name.

'She's going to have a baby,' Victoria put in, anxious to get away and find Mrs Driscoll before Saucy got angry in her basket and started to miaow.

'Ah, sure I know her now. She's not long here,' the nun exclaimed, her face lighting up with pleasure at the idea of a birth. 'That'll be the Little Flower Ward. Go to the end of this corridor and you'll come on it on your left. You can't miss it.' Her lilting Cork accent almost sang the information as she added: 'It's not visiting time now but sure' – and she touched Pat's sleeve – 'they'll not mind, seeing it's a policeman you are.'

Immediately the nun's back was turned Victoria thrust the basket back at him, with 'You take it now. You heard her say it's all right – "seeing it's a policeman you are".' Pat, used at last to her teasing, grimaced but made no objection.

At the entrance to the Little Flower Ward they paused, Victoria taking in the sight of so many patients, their beds facing each other in two rows, some sleeping or dozing, a few with cots alongside in which babies slumbered, and one or two hidden from view behind screens. Pat's eyes darted around anxiously, trying to locate Lucy. Could she be behind one of the screens, he wondered, as he failed to recognize her. He could hardly dare look behind them; even a policeman wouldn't be allowed such licence.

151

'Which one is Mrs Driscoll?' Victoria whispered.

He shook his head, wishing one of the nuns was around. They'd know which bed was hers, surely.

Suddenly, as he was moving the basket from one hand to the other, the lid burst open and Saucy sprang out, tail flaring. 'Jesus,' Pat swore, trying to cross himself in contrition and grab the cat at the same time. But with a squeal Saucy eluded his grasp, turned for a moment to glare at him balefully, and then sped up the ward. The patients who weren't asleep looked on with a mixture of amazement and glee as Pat immediately started to give chase, but before he had taken more than a few heavy-booted steps that echoed off the wooden floor Saucy had jumped on to one of the beds where its occupant had been sitting up, head tilted back against the pillow and eyes closed in rest. The soft shock of the cat landing on the counterpane made her open her eyes. For a moment their look was one of complete bewilderment, and then, as Saucy made a little miaow of greeting, recognition dawned.

'Wisha, Saucy, *a stór*, where in the name of heaven did you spring from?'

'I'll be damned,' Pat exclaimed. Now that the woman had her head down he could see it was Mrs Driscoll. He hurried to her bedside, Victoria on his heels. Lucy's eyes lit up.

'God love you, Pat, I thought when I saw Saucy it was the way she had come in all by herself.'

'I guessed you'd be missing her, Mrs D., so we brought her along in the basket. But she's a divil, isn't she, making a burst like that?' The 'divil' in question was contentedly perched beside Mrs Driscoll, having her head stroked and purring in appreciation.

'And the young lady is Miss Odron, isn't it?'

'Yes, Victoria Odron,' Pat said.

'Ah, don't I know her well to see, all her life.'

'I hope you don't mind my coming, Mrs Driscoll.'

'Mind, girl, why should I mind? It's lonely enough here. You're very welcome indeed.'

'I brought her with me from Odron House,' Pat explained. 'Tom Fahy and myself are out there on protection duty.'

'Don't I know that,' Lucy said, turning to Victoria. 'I hope he's taking good care of you now.'

'Oh, he is, Mrs Driscoll. He never leaves my side.'

Lucy threw the girl a sharp look, and the knowledge immediately broke on her. That girl is in love with Pat Howell, she thought. It wasn't only the tone of Victoria's reply; it wasn't even Lucy's womanly intuition that made her certain. It was the glow that, invisible to others, Lucy saw irradiating the girl's whole presence, the glow she remembered feeling herself in her young days whenever John was nearby and which still could suffuse her with a quick warmth on his return after being away.

Victoria's words had made Pat blush with embarrassment but not, Lucy guessed, with an answering love. Not yet anyway. Pat, she knew, would take time to awaken. All the barriers between them would be enough to conceal from him the true nature of his own feelings, though they couldn't smother the disturbance these feelings were causing. His blushes told her that much. She knew, too, that it would need something sudden, something strange and powerful, to sweep away these barriers so that he could see what he was being offered and reach out to take it. Lucy was certain that was the way it would have to be, if it were to be at all.

'Draw up a chair, let ye, and sit down,' she insisted. 'Now that you're here, you'll stay a while.'

Pat bent to lift a chair from the wall for Victoria, but the sudden movement startled Saucy. No doubt fearing that she was going to be snatched up and imprisoned in the basket a second time, she leapt off the bed and scampered down the ward.

'Oh my God!' Pat shouted, giving chase, not restrained this time by the dreadful racket his boots were making on the floor. But the noise was too much for the patients who had been sleeping, and aroused from their slumbers to see a uniformed member of the RIC careering around the ward, they thought some criminal had broken in or that the hospital was being attacked by Sinn Fein. Only the laughter and joyous shrieks of their companions who had seen the cat's mad dash told them that they were in no danger and stopped them from frantically ringing their bells to bring the nuns on the scene. Worse, however, was to come, for the general hubbub woke the babies in the ward, and their combined squawking and howling, adding to the din, in a moment transformed what had been a place of idyllic peace into bedlam.

Saucy, desperate to escape Pat's alternating clutches and blandishments, had taken refuge under one of the beds, whereupon Pat stationed himself on one side and motioned Victoria to guard the other, hoping that way to trap Saucy. Both of them went on their knees to peer under the bed in an attempt to attract the now thoroughly unco-operative animal. Above them, the bed's occupant, a large woman with puffy cheeks who had clutched her sheet up under her chin in an unavailing effort to hide her capacious bosom from male eyes, quickly became outraged at the indignity. Policeman or no policeman, he wasn't going to go peering under *her* bed. She looked around for a weapon, grabbed a newspaper from the table beside her, and started to batter Pat's head with scything blows and vigorous side-swipes, egged on now by the raucous encouragement of some of the patients who found the escapade the only bit of light relief they had had since their arrival in the ward. Not so, however, the two mothers trying to pacify their squalling babies, nor one petrified patient near the door who was whimpering with alarm. Turning her head from side to side in search of assistance, she caught sight of the bell beside her, and with the desperation of a shipwrecked sailor clutching at a floating spar she grabbed it and shook it madly. The uproar was by now complete. Even without the frantic pealing of the bell it would surely have penetrated to every corner of the hospital and brought someone at a rush to investigate. It did.

An old nun appeared, bent and cowled like a witch, hobbling along with the aid of a stick. Behind her was a young acolyte, having to hurry to keep up with the old nun, whose stick, wielded like a paddle, helped to propel her at a much faster pace than her ancient limbs would otherwise have been able to generate.

'What's all the row, in the name of the Lord?' she demanded angrily, brought up short at the sight of a policeman and a young woman on their knees on either side of a bed while the bed's occupant was threshing ineffectually at the policeman's head, her weapon having disintegrated into separate sheets of newspaper that were floating down to litter the highly polished floor.

154

'A cat, Sister Benedict, a cat!' the patient was squealing. 'There's a cat under my bed!'

Sister Benedict turned to the young nurse and with a peremptory gesture directed her to investigate. 'Let you take a look, Sister Vincent. Quick now.'

The young nun knelt and pushed her head forward. At first she could make out nothing in the darkness, for Saucy was by then stretched along the skirting as far back as she could get from any attempt at capture.

'Well, Sister? You're not saying your prayers down there, are you? Do you see a cat or not?'

'It's there for sure, Sister, I saw it,' one of the other patients sang out, corroboration speedily following from two more patients. Lucy didn't know whether to laugh or cry. She wasn't afraid for Saucy, but she knew how scarifying Sister Benedict's tongue could be if she discovered that Pat Howell was responsible for all the uproar.

'I see it now, I see it, Sister,' Sister Vincent confirmed as Saucy turned her head and the fire in her eyes pinpointed her. 'It's a cat all right, a lovely cat.'

'Get up, you silly goose. There's nothing lovely about a cat in a hospital. Is it a seizure you want some of your patients to have with all the fuss and fright? Well, don't stand there like an amadhaun. Get the cat out. We can't leave it there.'

Sister Vincent rose smartly to her feet, followed somewhat shamefacedly by Pat and Victoria. Pat didn't see how they could recover the cat except by scrabbling for it under the bed and risking painful scratches, but he feared that if he opened his mouth he might reveal himself as the one to blame for all the hullabaloo. The young nun, however, had an answer to the problem. Looking around her sharply, she assured Sister Benedict, whose stick was quivering in her hand like a divining-rod over a hidden stream: 'I'll get her out, the poor creature.' She went to the bedside of one of the patients, poured some milk from a glass standing on the bedside table into a saucer, and swiftly and smoothly returned. Lowering the saucer carefully, she placed it on the ground and began cooing and pish-pishing to the still beleaguered cat.

'Let's all move away now,' she implored. 'If we stay here, she'll be too frightened to come out, don't you know?'

Dutifully everyone trooped to the end of the bed, Sister Benedict delivering herself first of a loudly distrusting snort. All the patients leaned forward in their beds, trying to see as much as they could. The crying of the babies had subsided, and the sergeant's wife kept her peace, too, though greatly tempted to call Saucy, for she knew the cat would recognize her voice. But to utter the animal's name was to give the game away and bring down the wrath of the feared Sister Benedict on Pat Howell and his young lady.

For a minute there was silence in the ward as everyone awaited Saucy's appearance like an audience when the lights have been lowered in the theatre and all eyes are fixed on the stage for the first glimpse of the play's star. A baby made a noisy sucking sound which was immediately stifled by the mother adjusting the bottle.

Suddenly a noticeable craning forward of the women in the beds nearest the focus of interest told those who had no view of the arena that something might be happening. Tentatively a little brown face appeared from under the side of the bed – the star taking a surreptitious look around the curtain to gauge the mood of the audience. Satisfied of its reception, it turned its attention towards the spotlight of the saucer of milk, strutted up to it and, after two investigative sniffs, stretched forward and drank with gusto.

'Isn't it a dote!' the young nun crooned, almost as if it was a newborn baby she had just delivered.

'Dote or not, it's got no business in here,' Sister Benedict croaked.

Her stricture was enough to make Pat Howell leap into action. With a quick step forward he picked up Saucy in one hand, threw open the lid of the basket and dumped her inside, firmly closing the lid again.

'There you are now,' he announced in triumph as he turned to address Sister Benedict. 'She's safe in there till I'm going. I'll stay just a few minutes with Mrs Driscoll. I'll see the cat doesn't get out till we're clear of the hospital. Isn't it great I happened to have a basket handy?' he finished slyly.

Sister Benedict turned her wizened face up to examine his innocent expression. One of her hairy grey eyebrows raised itself a fraction above the other. It may have been an indication of some doubt in her mind or it may have been in order to see him better.

'Humph!' she snorted, adding, with not a trace of levity in her voice: 'I suppose you'll expect to get promoted for that arrest.' And she stumped her faintly zig-zag course towards the door, attended closely by Sister Vincent, smiling with pride at having dealt so cleverly and efficiently with the crisis.

Peace was restored to the Little Flower Ward.

'Aren't you a right terror, Pat?' Mrs Driscoll scolded him affectionately when he and Victoria returned to her bedside. 'Whatever made you bring Saucy at all?'

'Didn't I tell you! I thought it was the way you might be lonely for her.'

Lucy turned to Victoria. 'Little does he know what makes a woman lonely, Miss Odron. Still, it was considerate of him, I must say that. He's a good lad, is our Pat.'

The constable looked elsewhere to hid his embarrassment. Victoria smiled and nodded at Lucy, as if to let her know that she was well aware of Pat Howell's virtues.

Mary Casey closed the door softly behind her. The room she found herself in was the same size as Miss Elizabeth's next door to it, though larger than Miss Victoria's on the other side of the house. But the difference between it and Miss Elizabeth's room made her nose wrinkle in disapproval. What struck her immediately was the spareness of the furniture and the dullness of the walls. The wallpaper, she could see, had originally been yellow and must at one time have surrounded the room's occupant with an atmosphere of warmth even on the gloomiest day, but now it had paled to a wan ash. In a corner was a single bed, its blankets disarranged, with large dirty stains disfiguring the wall behind it and along its side. It reminded the girl of the poorhouse where as a child she had visited her grandmother; the memory made her shudder and look away.

Beside the bed was a marble-topped table on which stood a basin and ewer. She went over and peered into the mould-spotted mirror that hung from a nail above it.

'Lord o' mercy!' she whispered as she saw her own reflection. Was it the mirror of her nervousness that made her look so

157

white? She knew she had nothing to fear: Ambrose Mercer was off for the day, the two girls out also and the policemen with them, so only Mrs Odron was left – and what would bring her to Mr Mercer's room? She couldn't think of anyone else who'd have any reason to come in but, if by chance someone should, she had her explanation pat: she was doing the room today for poor Eileen who had a terrible cold and had taken to her bed. She nodded to herself in the mirror; it must surely be excitement that had made her lose her natural colour – the excitement of being part of a secret plot and of knowing how much depended on its success. She felt thrilled at being important, but it was important, too, to keep her head.

She moved away from the bed. Making it up could be left until last, because if by chance anyone *did* happen to come in and show signs of wanting to stay or even call her away to some other task she could get rid of them by saying she still hadn't finished her work in the room.

She looked around, asking herself where would she hide anything precious if it were her room. In one of the pieces of furniture was the most obvious place. There was a wardrobe, a chest of drawers, a table, a hard chair, and an old armchair that had seen better days. God knows, she didn't have anything more in her own room, but at least she made it look cheerful and welcoming. Still, what could a body expect from a man like Ambrose Mercer? From the little she had seen of him herself, and from what she had heard about him from others, he wasn't the type to care much about comfort or nice surroundings. Signs on! The assortment of articles lying haphazardly in the corners would have told a blind man that it was out in the fields Mercer spent most of his time. There were two pairs of wellington boots, unpolished but reasonably scraped clean of mud; many pairs of riding boots – though some, Mary noted, weren't pairs at all but odd boots; some old dog-collars, their leather frayed from use; a couple of riding crops; a whip, and a second one thrown on the bed.

From a hook in the back of the door hung an ancient, almost rotting kit-bag with what looked like a small label stuck to it. She went over and tried to read it. The writing was very faded – a line of letters, a longer line behind it and then some numbers. 'Well, would you believe!' she exclaimed to herself. This must

158

have been his kit-bag when he was batman to the colonel. But that was twenty years ago and more, in the British Army. 'Well, would you believe it!' she repeated, aghast at the idea that he'd have kept it hanging up there for so long – a dirty useless old bag that from the way it sagged on its hook was clearly empty. She remembered the story they had told her in the kitchen, that he had grown up in an orphanage. An orphanage, she guessed, was just the place to turn a boy into a bully if he was that way inclined. And the Army afterwards – wouldn't that make him worse! Make him hard and cruel, just like Ambrose Mercer was, a tyrant who ground a man under his heel when he had him down. And who'd take the last crust of bread from his mouth, too. Oh, he'd be well capable of getting up to no good, thieving and stealing, and hiding away his loot so that no one would ever find him out. That was what her father had said Tim O'Halloran suspected. If that was the case, and if it was in this room that the money was hidden, Mary Casey was determined to find it. 'Find it if it's there, girl,' he had charged her. 'And, if you find it, don't touch it. Just come and tell me.'

She backed herself against a wall and took stock. Where would it be now, if it was here at all? The drawers? She went and pulled at one. It came open immediately. There seemed little in it except gansies and men's things. She didn't want to touch the articles; anyway there wouldn't be room under them for a lot of money. It was the same with the other two drawers; indeed, the bottom one was quite empty.

The wardrobe had only coats and cloaks in it. She pushed them aside to make sure there was nothing lying in its dark corners. Then she looked up and wondered. It was a very deep wardrobe. If it was a hiding-place he was after, there could be something on top of it pushed back against the wall, safely out of sight.

She carried the chair over from the table and placed it down in front of the wardrobe. Her flesh tingled with anticipation as she lifted her skirts and climbed up. Wouldn't it be great to find his hoard first shot! She was just tall enough to see over the top. There *was* a box there – a cardboard box. With difficulty she stretched her arms towards it, not caring that her sleeves were dragging in the layers of dust that appeared to have accumulated there, but it remained still just out of reach. Grunting with the effort, she pressed against the wardrobe door, straining forward on one side so that the fingers of her right hand just managed to scrabble at a corner of the box and ease it ever so slightly towards her. Changing her position she stretched her left hand over the top of the wardrobe, pushing and coaxing until she was able to move the other side of the box a little from the wall. Then, alternately using right and left hand, she eventually manoeuvred it far enough forward to get both hands on it and lift it down. Dust floated up in a cloud, filling her nostrils and making her sneeze violently. But she kept her grip until she was able to step off the chair and put the box on the floor. Flushed with the exertion, she took a deep breath, made a quick sign of the Cross, and took off the lid. Amazement spread over her face as she contemplated its contents. Inside was a gleaming, polished, elegant top-hat!

Rubbing her fingers down her apron to clean them, she carefully lifted out the hat and stared at it. What in the world was Ambrose Mercer doing with a top-hat? And hidden away where no one would ever see. To judge from the amount of dust that the box had gathered, he hadn't looked at it himself for a very long time. Turning the hat this way and that in her hands, she suddenly saw a label on its inner band. She couldn't quite make it out – it was so faded – but it seemed to be the name of the outfitters where it had been bought. Clear enough underneath it, however, was the address – Sackville Street, Dublin; and below that, in indelible ink letters, was printed 'Colonel H. A. O. G. Odron'. The colonel's top-hat! How did Mercer happen to have it? Had he stolen it? Had the colonel given it to him? What was he keeping it for at all? Mary Casey shook herself, roused her thoughts, and put the hat back where she had found it. It was a strange article to come upon in Ambrose Mercer's room, but it wasn't what she was looking for.

Then she remembered the old kitchen knife she had slipped into her apron pocket before coming up. Her father had told her to take some implement with her in case she had to prise up one of the floorboards. She examined the floor, daunted at the prospect of going that far. The bare boards were covered by a square of old linoleum that left a few feet margin all round the room between its edge and the wall. One corner of the linoleum ran under the bed; she'd have to move the bed if she was to lift the floorboards there. The corner nearest the door was securely nailed down, and so was the third corner. The fourth one, too, but the linoleum there was broken and cracked as if . . .

She put an ear to the door and listened. Not a sound. Quickly, excitement mounting in her once again, she sank to her knees beside the broken linoleum. The knife slipped in smoothly under it, and a nail came up with hardly any pressure. Her heart began to beat faster as she picked at the other ones. They, too, yielded without effort and she was able to bend over a whole strip of linoleum as easily as turning over a page.

The exposed boards were cracked and splintered. Two in particular – adjoining ones – were not complete strips running to the wall behind her but were separate pieces that had been inserted at some stage, and there was a narrow but noticeable gap where they had been fitted into the floor. Mary inserted the knife into the gap and levered. The boards were loose. She pushed the knife in further, far enough to raise them more so that she could get a hand underneath and lift. They came up without resistance.

'Jesus, Mary and Joseph!' she gasped.

Stunned, she dropped the boards, letting them fall back into place, but not before her eyes had been almost dazzled by scores of gold coins in a bed of what appeared to be hundreds of notes.

For a moment she was paralysed almost with fear of what she had discovered. Then, suddenly springing to life, she hurriedly replaced the torn linoleum and put the nails back in their holes. She wished she had something to hammer them down with, but there was no need; with no difficulty she was able to press their heads down level with the floor. She gave them a last glance. He'd never know anyone had found his hiding-place. It looked the same as it had when she first came into the room. He'd never know anyone had been at it.

Flushed now with pride and elation at having such unbelievable news to carry back to her father, she hurried out of the room. As she rushed down the corridor, the picture of all those gold coins blazed before her eyes. She'd never forget the sight.

At the head of the stairs she pulled up sharply and threw her hands up in horror. In her haste to get out of the bedroom she had forgotten to make the bed. She turned and was starting to run back when she realized there was no need to hurry. She could go back at a normal pace, make up the bed at a normal pace, take as much time as she liked at the job, for if anyone happened to interrupt her she'd be doing only what she was supposed to be doing. As for the money under the floor, she felt no temptation at all to take a second look. It was there. She had seen it. That was enough.

8

THE TROUBLE started from the moment they got into the trap. Ambrose Mercer, already in truculent mood at the thought of Elizabeth and Fahy sitting side by side while he had to concentrate on the road, suggested that Elizabeth might take the reins. She gave him no answer, her dismissal of his invitation without even an acknowledgement making it clear that in such a situation his status was that of an employee, not of someone who should have the temerity to make any sort of proposal. The insult to his pride exacerbated the feeling of jealousy growing in him at the familiarity that existed between Elizabeth and the policeman. He did not see Fahy as a rival – that would have been quite ridiculous – but the image of the two of them possibly holding hands together behind him in the trap, or indeed of what closer contacts they might indulge in given the opportunity, roused a murderous hate in his heart.

'I don't suppose *you'd* know how to hold a pair of reins,' he said to Tom Fahy, his bile turning what could have been just a casual observation into a bitter sneer.

'Oh, sure enough I do. But I'll not accept your generous offer. I need to keep my hands free – for this, you know' – and he patted his gun-holster – 'in case we meet trouble on the way.'

'I might have known you'd only want to take things easy.'

'I've got a job to do and 'tis no easy one – protecting the likes of you,' Tom Fahy answered spiritedly.

'Protecting me, too,' Elizabeth added, throwing an arm around the policeman's shoulder as if to deliver a physical taunt to Mercer as extra punishment for his bad temper.

Mercer faced to the road, his eyes smouldering, and urged the horse forward with a thunderous crack of the whip. That cursed policeman was becoming too much of a nuisance. He needed taking down a peg or two.

The fair they were going to was to be a very special event. It had been organized by some of the leading merchants of the area as a gesture of defiance against the authorities who had forbidden the holding of the long-established Listowel race meeting that year because of the general unrest. Of course these merchants were doing more than just cocking a snook – not only on their own behalf but also for the whole community – for the cancellation of the race meeting was a grave economic blow. The event always drew a huge attendance from all over Munster, and both Listowel and nearby Tralee looked forward every year to the windfall the day unfailingly provided; public houses, shops, stalls, three-card-trick men, tinkers, beggars – they'd take in almost as much as on the other three hundred and sixty-four days of the year put together. That was too vital a source of revenue to lose, so when a suggestion was made to hold an ordinary fair instead, elaborate plans were formed to turn what had looked like being a commercial disaster into a major financial triumph. A local farmer was prepared to donate a site by moving all his cattle out of his two largest fields, the streets of Listowel and Tralee were festooned with multicoloured flags and bunting, notices and posters were put up in windows throughout the county and even further afield. And when the day dawned clear and bright as if the fates were already smiling on the organizers' efforts, the locals turned out *en masse*. It almost seemed that only the bedridden, the new-born babes and perhaps their mothers were absent, while visitors from far and wide swelled the throng.

Ambose Mercer and his passengers were not long on the road when they found themselves part of the unending procession of vehicles all making for the same destination. So thick was the traffic that progress was soon reduced to little more than walking pace, and Mercer's frustration quickly had him cracking his whip and hurling imprecations at those in his way.

It was all to no avail. Every conceivable kind of horse-drawn transport was to be seen, each stuffed with twice its normal capacity of passengers. There were numerous tinkers' caravans drawn by piebald ponies that, if only they were groomed, would have looked as proud as princes' mounts. Behind the caravans trotted strings of wild-looking horses, to be vaunted to reluctant purchasers later in the day as the produce, or at least near-relations, of Derby winners. There was a company of travelling players, two families with Punch and Judy booths, and occasional flocks of sheep and herds of cattle, each prodded on and cajoled by the owners who, reckoning that because this was not an agricultural fair no other farm animals would be on sale, thought to steal a march on their neighbours. The air was full of shouting, bellowing, salutations, curses, friendly comments, not so friendly taunts, and above it all rose the neighing protests of horses being driven impatiently forward. To add to the bedlam the persistent hooting of a motor-horn swelled up from behind as one of the local gentry and his guests sought to claim right of way. For a full ten minutes Ambrose Mercer refused to draw in for them until Elizabeth, deafened by the blaring horn, told him not to be such an obstinate child. Tom Fahy could see none of his colleagues on the route but he guessed they would have set out earlier and would already be on duty at the fair, assisted by reinforcements from one or two other stations. Conspicuously absent was any evidence of soldiers, but he had no doubt they would be in the vicinity and on the alert for quick intervention if needed.

'Isn't this the life, girl?' he said to Elizabeth, his voice high with almost boyish enthusiasm. He had been at fairs before and at many 'patterns' held in honour of local saints, but he had never witnessed such a concourse as this – the people's reply to the authorities' harassment. 'Have you ever seen the like?'

Elizabeth laughed. To her it was all typically Irish, the confusion, the noise, the familiarity, the good-natured amiability of most of the travellers; it was years since she had seen anything to compare with it. And Tom Fahy's spontaneous response to the whole scene made her realize how much a part of it he was – and how wide was the social gap between them. But it was a gap she was determined to close, at least between

165

the sheets. He might not be her class – not like all the officers she had had such sport with – but then, was Ambrose Mercer her class? And having the two men to play off against each other was like old times once again. She was confident she could use the opportunity to keep Ambrose's jealousy on the boil and to make herself particularly desirable to Tom Fahy. Parties of any sort had always helped her to get a man worked up, and she couldn't remember a night following such an occasion that hadn't ended exactly the way she had wanted it to.

When Tom, taking off his heavy policeman's cap to wipe the perspiration from his brow, said, 'Wouldn't it just be my luck to be tied to that fellow there as fast as if he was handcuffed to me!' she took his cap, dumped it on her own head at a jaunty angle, and told him: 'Never mind. There's always the night – and you won't be tied to him then.'

'Begob,' Tom replied, stirred at the prospect of getting what he considered to be a just reward for all he had had to endure in the past few days, 'you're right there, Elizabeth. You're bloody right there, my girl.' And he uttered an anticipatory whoop of joy. Ambrose Mercer turned. He saw the gleam in Fahy's eyes, the teeth bared in a grin of expected conquest, the cap on Elizabeth's head that seemed already a symbol of their union, and with his body he instinctively recognized that cry for what it was. At that moment he hated Tom Fahy with all his might.

After breakfast Amelia Odron returned to her room. Once inside, she was conscious of a sense of strangeness. It was as if she had drawn into her lungs the atmosphere of some foreign place, vaguely familiar, pleasantly inviting. What was it? She did not feel ill; she had no symptoms whatever, and there had been nothing disquieting about her appearance when she looked into the bathroom mirror that morning.

Outside her window she could see that the weather, after yesterday's rain, had regained its earlier good humour – the skies were blue again, the air was still, the sun was gathering heat. Her bedroom, as she stood and looked around it, was the same room she had known since the day she had come to live in Odron House: the rich green carpet beneath her feet, the pale ceiling above her, the elegant furniture, the patterned walls.

. . . But, no, something *was* different. Her gaze was caught and held by the empty space left where her embroidered dream-mansion had been. She saw how much brighter and fresher the paper in that small rectangle was – it almost glowed with revealed life – and immediately she knew the source of the unusual sensation that had overtaken her when she entered the room. It was the stirring in her of the previous night's resolution, the decision that from now on she would look forward rather than backward, that she would live in the present rather than in the past.

She felt invigorated, delighted at having identified the cause of her strange excitement, eager to inaugurate her new-found resolution. What would she do? What *could* she do? Tell the girls? But they were out of the house. Anyway, actions spoke louder than words; it would be more effective, and less embarrassing, too, if she made them aware of the change in her by her manner and disposition rather than by any dramatic announcement. What about Charles? She could telephone him, but what would she say? He'd come rushing over, and she'd probably be sheepish and tongue-tied. There was the likelihood, too, that Charles might read too much into the situation and think she had at last decided to accept his marriage proposal. She could hardly blame him if that was his reaction. Better not disturb him. Besides, talking was still not acting. She wanted to *do* something that would establish, even if only for herself, the new Amelia.

She went to her dressing-table and took out the letters and photographs that were the mementoes of the past which had so imprisoned her. She had got rid of her piece of embroidery, why not get rid of them, too? But the embroidery had been just needlework she had fashioned even before she had ever met Alex, while the letters and photographs were all she had left of Alex himself. Could she destroy them? Having them or not having them made little difference, for there wasn't one letter that she couldn't quote by heart, word for word, or one photograph that she couldn't see again in her mind's eye. Recollection wasn't the same of course, but it would be less dangerous than keeping the letters and photographs themselves. They'd be a temptation she might not be able to resist, and so much more potent than imagination, such an aid to pretence. Pre-

167

tence! That had already been her downfall; that was the key that had locked her fast in the cell of memory.

That night, a year after Alex died, when she lay in bed in the darkness, her eyes wet with tears, her mind astray with the force of her loss, her body hungry with need. That night when her door opened and the soft footfalls approached, just as Alex had always quietly drawn near, and the voice whispered, 'Melly,' the name Alex had always used, and she did not protest: 'You are dead, you are gone.' For it was a man who had come, a man she had taken to her, whispering, 'Alex, Alex,' and he had not denied the name. She felt the grasping hand in her hair, the work-roughened fingers at her loins, the sharp teeth around her nipple, and as she used to do with Alex, she held in her hand his steel hardness until suddenly it was wrenched from her grasp and driven into her and she opened to it, drew it in hungrily, gasping: 'Oh, Alex, Alex.' Still there was no response, no denial. She clung desperately to that body, to its male limbs, its male scents, biting at its lips, raking her nails up and down its buttocks, hands pushing with each thrust, her own thighs and belly straining to climb; and, feeling inside her a tide gathering, she swam on and on into its swell, rising ever higher to its peak, until suddenly the wave broke in a thousand fountained jets that tossed and threw her in its storm. 'Alex, Alex, help me,' she screamed, until she was sobbing with a mixture of emotions she could not disentangle – ecstasy, regret, shame, self-hatred. And when her tears had dried and her tremors had ceased she found the flesh that her hands had gripped was no longer there, the weight that she had borne so effortlessly that it might have been floating on her had disappeared, and the body that had shared her bed was gone, gone from her, gone from her bed, gone even from the room. It had not been Alex – could not have been Alex – for Alex would not leave her afterwards but would close her into his embrace, stroking her to blissful sleep. That night, however, there had been no sleep, and when dawn broke the awful truth had to be faced.

For all that day and the next night she stayed in her room with the door locked, refusing all food, turning aside all enquiries, ignoring all appeals, forgetting everything – even her two young children – except the one thing she could not

168

forget. And then on the second day she gathered together all those letters and photographs – all she had left of the living Alex – and, laying them on her bed as she had also lain them this morning, she read the letters one by one and pored over the photographs image by image. It was the only way she could show contrition, the only way she could plead for forgiveness. It was the beginning of her rededication to Alex's memory, the start of her long imprisonment.

Next morning she sent for Ambrose Mercer and told him he could go.

'Go? Go where, Melly?' he asked.

'Don't call me that name,' she ordered. 'I am Mrs Odron; you are no longer my estate manager. Go wherever you please; it is no concern of mine where you go. Just leave.'

She had turned away to look out on to the rolling lawn and the little wood where she had so often walked arm-in-arm with Alex. She kept looking out, waiting to hear his footsteps leave her presence. But instead she heard his voice, coarse, brutal, threatening.

'Leave! Me leave, *Mrs* Odron! Why should *I* leave? I've been here almost as long as you have. You could say I have as much right here as you have. The colonel brought you here to be his wife and to take care of him, and he brought me here to work for him and learn to take care of his property. Well, I've learned how to do that. He taught me. I'm the only one who can take care of his property – all his property. I can take care of you, too, the way he did.'

There was silence for some time – it seemed like the longest silence she had ever endured – as the enormity of what this man was suggesting froze her in horror. Then, as soon as her senses recovered, she turned to confront him.

'How dare you! How dare you make such a suggestion! How dare you even think such a thing!'

'Oh ho, aren't we the grand lady now, *Mrs* Odron? But we weren't the grand lady a few nights ago, were we, when you were glad to have me in your bed, and to let me—'

'Stop! Stop it!' she had screamed, pressing her hands to her ears. 'No, no, it didn't happen! It couldn't have happened!'

'Couldn't it, my dear? It could and it did. Oh, you were hot with passion that night. You may have tried to fool yourself, to pretend that you were half-asleep maybe and dreaming that it was your precious husband on top of you. But you weren't dreaming. You weren't even asleep, and it wasn't your husband, was it? It was me, Ambrose Mercer. No matter that you called me Alex. That didn't fool me. I knew it was me you wanted. It was me you needed. And you'll need me again, won't you? Often. So be sensible, my dear Mrs Odron. I'm young and strong; I can serve you in any capacity for a long time to come, as long as you're likely to want a man.'

Shattered, distraught, too weak to remain standing, she had sunk into a chair. She was cold with horror, and her whole body trembled.

'Well, Melly, what do you say?'

She raised her head, squarely meeting his gaze. He looked at her, and even his stance was arrogant, suggestive.

She rose to her feet again and in a voice she could not recognize as her own said: 'Get out of here. Get out of my house. Now. This instant. I'll pay you to the end of the month. Just pack your things and leave.'

He did not move. His lips widened in a leering grin, and then he began to laugh. His laughter grew, he slapped his knee as if he had just heard the most uproarious tale ever told him. It was too much for her. She rushed at him, hammering at his chest and head with her fists. Abruptly his laughter was cut short. He caught hold of her wrists in his strong hands, propelled her backwards, and threw her back into the chair from which she had just risen. He stood over her, so close that the bulge of his crotch was almost touching her face.

'Now, listen to me, my fine lady. You may not want this any more' – and he jerked so that she had to spring back deep into the chair to avoid contact with that bulge – 'but you won't get rid of *me* so easily. In fact I don't think you really want to get rid of me at all. You don't want the whole town, the whole county to know what we did in your bed, do you? You wouldn't want people to know just how much your wonderful husband really meant to you, so much that with him no more than a year in his grave you were sleeping with his estate manager. An uncouth ignorant orphan he had taken out of the Army and given a home to. What do you think people would say to that, Mrs Odron? How would that look, eh? Do you think they'd regard that as the way to mourn your dead husband, as the way to honour his memory? I don't think they would. Do you know what I think they'd say? They'd say: "Do you mind that fine lady up in Odron House? Fine lady be damned. She's just a common whore." And you know the way people talk, especially in a small place like this. And the way they never forget. So when your two daughters grow up into young ladies I've no doubt someone will tell them. Someone will say to them that their mother is a whore.'

The words chilled her. She was unable to move. She remained seated in the chair, paralysed not only with horror at his tirade, but also with hatred of herself. She deserved this nemesis. No punishment could be too heavy for what her lust had driven her to. She sat with bowed head, speechless.

'That's better now,' he said when she did not reply. 'Much better, Mrs Odron. Let's have no more talk of me leaving. I'll be here as long as you will – maybe even longer. So don't you forget that. I'm estate manager here, and estate manager I stay. So we'll say no more about going – and as long as we say no more about that, we'll say no more about the other business either. Mum's the word all round, eh?'

He did not wait for an answer, but turned and left the room.

Time passed. Yes, she now realized, it did pass. Her daughters were grown-up ladies. *Her* daughters? They might have been distant relations for all the bond she had with them. And there was Charles – solid, helpful, dependable Charles. A suitor she rejected without ever even considering his proposal. I already have a husband, she had thought, whenever he asked her to marry him. No matter that my husband is dead, I have still to do penance for my sin to his memory as long as I live.

Amelia looked through the window, her eyes blinking in the sunlight that played on the floor of her bedroom, on the letters and photographs thrown on the bed. Today's sun, she thought, that is today's sun. The day I locked myself in for so long has no sun. It is dead and gone, kept alive only by me and by my fear of that man, Ambrose Mercer. But does he still remember? Would he still tell if . . . ? Who would believe him now, so long afterwards? Would Elizabeth? Would Victoria? Charles? They would say he was lying, that he made it all up. And, if anyone accused *me*, would *I* say he was lying? Surely the girls wouldn't

171

ask me. They wouldn't ask their own mother such a question. And Charles? Would solid, helpful, dependable Charles ask the widow of his best friend such a question? But, not asking, would he have doubts?

Amelia rose. She gathered up Alex's letters and photographs and held them all in her hands, pondering. It was time to lay them to rest, time to stop using them as solace or punishment.

She looked around the room, as if searching for a place where she could dispose of them. There was nowhere, no unused cupboard where they could gather dust, no fire in the hearth where they could be reduced to ashes. But why should she destroy them? If she was really determined to break their spell, she would put them back where they always had been – and then forget they were there.

She knelt, pulled open the drawer from which she had taken them, put them in, and closed the drawer again. Rising, she recaptured the strange feeling that had assailed her when she entered the room. This time she was able to put a name on it: it was freedom.

9

By NOON the fair was at its height. There were more people in the field than Tom Fahy had ever before seen together in one place. Movement was possible only by dint of determined pushing and shuffling, for the scores of booths, tents and stalls set up wherever their owners could find a vacant space had barely left narrow higgledy-piggledy passageways for the milling throng. The din was ear-splitting: children shrieking, babies crying, animals baying and neighing, loud music from every corner – fiddles, melodeons, mouth organs, men on the spoons and tambourine, flute-players, one with a jew's harp, and all begging the wherewithal for an extended visit to the nearest public house. Fair enough, Tom Fahy thought, what else would they do, for making music in this crowd with the noonday sun at its champion best would give a camel a thirst. He wouldn't have minded a drink himself and he wondered when Mercer might get the same idea. Damned if he'd suggest it to him. The man was obviously in a vile temper at having had to act as jarvey for the whole journey in, fuming and fretting at what the pair behind him might be getting up to. Elizabeth had taken every opportunity of stoking him up, pulling Tom's arm around her, pressing her thigh against his, throwing herself with exaggerated loss of balance into his embrace when the trap went any way fast around a bend. And whenever Mercer happened to look round it always seemed to

173

be the very moment she had her mouth close to Tom's ear and was whispering something. Tom wasn't sure whether she was pretending or not, because the surrounding noise, the creaking of the cart and the clip-clop of the horse's hoofs made hearing impossible. 'What's that?' he enquired a few times, but by then Mercer had turned away from them again and Elizabeth didn't repeat what she had said – if, indeed, she had said anything. Once he thought he caught the words 'We'll see tonight', but when he asked her what it was they'd see she only laughed and tossed her head.

Now as he forced his way through the crowds, keeping only a step behind Mercer, she pressed close beside him, holding on to his hand. It may have been only to make sure they kept together – though even if they were separated for a moment it wouldn't have been impossible to catch up again – but Tom suspected it was part of her game of making up to him. Every few moments she would give his hand a special squeeze and once she inserted her little finger into the space between their two hands and tickled his palm. All very nice, he thought, but he'd need to be careful not to get too distracted. Still, he didn't want to discourage her and spoil the night's possibilities, so when they had entered the fairground and she first put her hand in his, his momentary rejection was simply so as to release his right hand and give her his left one instead. He wasn't expecting any trouble, but there was no point in taking the chance of not being able to get to his gun quickly. He had no intention of being caught on the hop and presuming that the Sinn Fein boys wouldn't try anything on in such a crowd. You could never tell what scheme they might concoct. Not that he could see how they'd know that Mercer was going to attend the fair, but anyone who might spot him there could get word around without too much delay. Anyway, it wasn't only Mercer's presence that could be taken as an excuse for some sort of protest. The abandonment of the races at the authorities' order would be sufficient pretext if they were looking for one. Fortunately, there were no military to be seen. They'd be standing by not too far away of course, in case of emergencies, but it was as well they were keeping out of sight. Tom was quite sure that the merest glimpse of a British Army uniform would be bound to lead to violence. There were some RIC men on duty,

174

but so far Mick O'Malley was the only one he had seen from his own barracks and he hadn't been able to get near enough to him even to bid him the time of day.

'Would you like a mutton pie?' he asked Elizabeth. Mutton pies were a local speciality, and every few yards there was someone – usually a buxom red-cheeked peasant woman – with boxes of them on sale.

'I've never had one. What are they like?' she asked.

'I'm sure you've had mutton often enough. I'm getting hungry. I'll have one anyway.'

'Me, too, please.'

He tapped Mercer on the shoulder and offered to buy him a pie. Maybe if he could persude him to have one it would bring on enough of a thirst for him to want a drink, too. A man who could lower four bottles of beer with his lunch must surely have a mouth on him when the sun was high and the people pressing in on him in their hundreds. Tom suspected that Mercer's abstemiousness for the whole hot morning was deliberate; he probably guessed that Tom would be thirsty, and was cold-hearted and vindictive enough to put up with spiting himself as long as he could spite his bodyguard, too. But if Tom's plan was to kindle the man's thirst with a mutton pie, he found himself sorely frustrated.

'If I want a pie, I'll get my own,' was the surly reply. 'I don't want any favours from a policeman.'

'Please yourself,' Tom snapped angrily, annoyed as much with himself for being so foolish as to imagine that Mercer would have given him any other sort of answer, 'but I doubt that you'd get a favour anywhere else. Not your sort anyway.'

He regretted the words immediately they were out of this mouth. Apart from the fact that he didn't want to give Mercer any evidence of his frustration, he was conscious of his police-man's role – and that did not include saying something that might lead to an altercation. He wouldn't even put it past Mercer to complain him to Sergeant Driscoll, given half a chance.

All right, me bucko, Tom thought, if *you* want to be an obstinate mule, *I'm* not going hungry to suit you. Within moments he came on a convenient stall and, quickly taking some coins from his pocket, he purchased two pies.

As he and Elizabeth munched away, like children having a treat, she winked at him, broke off a piece of her pie and offered it to Mercer. With a snarl he knocked her hand down so roughly that the meat fell on the ground where a mongrel dog quickly devoured it.

'Oh, Ambrose,' she taunted, 'you *are* a naughty boy! Are you annoyed with your Elizabeth?' And, linking his arm, she pulled herself close to him. He was too surprised by her sudden attention to reject it. Tom Fahy was taken completely unawares, too, but before he had a chance to say or do anything about it she turned her head quickly and gave him a clearly conspiratorial smile. He mimed a man drinking. She nodded. Ah, yes, he assured himself, she knows what she's about, that lass – if the mountain won't come to Mahomet, Mahomet must go to the mountain.

Their slow wandering had by now brought them to a far corner of the field where a small tent stood, a cardboard sign, 'Fortunes Told', pinned to its canvas.

'Come on,' Elizabeth urged excitedly as she saw two young girls emerge, giggling with embarrassment. 'I'd love to have my fortune told.'

'That's only a lot of nonsense,' Mercer said dissuadingly.

'Oh, don't be such an old stick, Ambrose. Wouldn't you like to know your future?'

'I don't need some old tinker woman to tell me my future. I've known for a long time what my future will be.'

Tom snorted with impatience. It was typical of the man. Only a fool and a braggart could imagine he knew what was going to happen to him in the next minute, not to mind years ahead.

'Only the Lord above knows our future,' he declared. 'And, anyway, if He were to tell us what He has in store for us, we might wish He'd have kept it to Himself.'

'Well, I must say that I've never met two such stick-in-the-muds. You two needn't bother if you don't want, but I'm going in.'

'I suppose it's harmless enough anyway,' Tom allowed. 'But you'll need some money.' He reached for his pocket. 'They say you do have to cross their palm with silver before they tell you anything.'

'Come on then,' Ambrose Mercer said. 'I have money.' He felt that the policeman had already gained an advantage over him by buying Elizabeth a mutton pie and, much as he hated throwing money away, this was his chance to get even and retain the attention she had suddenly decided to give him.

Tom Fahy was in no way discomfited. He was confident of his ground with Elizabeth, and Mercer couldn't come to any harm while he was inside the tent with her. Besides, it might give him a chance of catching O'Malley's eye if he strayed into vision and have a few words with him. The sight of Mick O'Malley had made him feel suddenly lonely for the company of his colleagues from the barracks. He had been so busy himself chaperoning Mercer that he hadn't even had a chance to spend much time with Pat Howell.

'Off in with the two of you then,' he said as Elizabeth pulled Mercer with her. 'I'll be waiting here.'

Immediately the pair had gone he looked around for Constable O'Malley. It took a while for him to locate the constable, but when he did he sent a youngster over to fetch him.

'Well, well, it's yourself, Tom,' O'Malley greeted him in surprise. 'I wasn't expecting to see you here this day. I thought you and Pat were keeping watch on Mercer.'

'We are, too. At least I am – I left Pat back at Odron House.'

'Well, it's not at Odron House he is now,' O'Malley told him. 'He called into the station just before I left. And he had the young one in tow – Victoria Odron.'

'What was he doing in the station?'

'Probably collecting his letters. A few came for him. About the Police Union no doubt. You know he wrote off to some people before he was sent to Odron House.'

'Ah, that'd be it all right. He was worried about getting any replies. And so yourself is out here today keeping order? And keeping an eye out for the girls, too, I'll bet.'

O'Malley snorted. 'Small chance of any of that. I've been keeping tabs on O'Halloran since I arrived.'

'O'Halloran! Is he here?'

'He is indeed. You haven't seen him yourself?'

'Not yet. And I don't want to see him – or him to see me, for Mercer is inside the tent behind me and the further they keep from each other, the better.'

Constable O'Malley's laughter was unrestrained as he looked at the notice on the tent.

'Ambrose Mercer having his fortune told! Well, that beats all!'

'Ah, no, you gom, 'tis Elizabeth Odron is the one wanting to know her future. She's along with us. Mercer just went in to keep her company – she's making him pay for it. And good luck to her.'

'Are they long in there?'

'A few minutes only. I'd love a pint but I can't leave Mercer, especially now I know O'Halloran is in the crowd. I wonder could we spot him at all?'

Constable Fahy glanced around in all directions, but he knew that only by a rare stroke of luck would he manage to pick out O'Halloran in such a throng.

'He was over by the entrance when I left him, wandering around aimlessly,' O'Malley said. 'He had a word with a few people, but I didn't recognize any of them. Andy is watching him for me, so there's no fear we'll lose him.'

'Oh, Andy's here, too, then. Any more from the station?'

'Not yet. The rest are from other places. But Sean and Francie will be relieving us at three. I'll be glad to get out of here. The noise is giving me a fair old headache. What time are you leaving?'

'God only knows. God and Mr Ambrose Mercer. I wonder why he came at all. He hasn't spoken to anyone since we got here.'

'Yerra, who'd want to talk to him?'

'True for you, Mick. Maybe he's just come to have a look around in case there was anything going cheap that he'd want. He's certainly not here for the pleasure of mixing with his fellow-men and enjoying a day out. He's not the type, I can assure you of that.'

'And you're the one who'd know after being with him since Monday. Have you any message at all for the sergeant?'

'Divil a bit. I suppose Pat will have told him the little there is to tell. He's all right, is he? And herself?'

'Ah, sure of course you were gone before they moved her to hospital.'

'Hospital?' Tom echoed in alarm. 'Has something gone wrong again?'

'No, just that Dr Harvey didn't want to take any chances. Her time being so near, you know.'

'Ah, is that it? Won't it be great if she has her baby this time! There'll be no knowing the sergeant. Tell him to give her my best. And tell him I'll telephone at the weekend – just to let him know we're still on the job. Or earlier if anything happens.'

'I'll tell him, Tom. I'd better be finding Andy now. If you see him coming this way in the next few minutes, tell him I'm looking for him.'

Constable O'Malley pushed his way off through the crowds, leaving Constable Fahy standing outside the tent in the killing heat, lamenting that there wasn't even a bit of a wall or a pole to lean his weight against.

When Elizabeth entered the tent she found its gloom such a contrast after the brightness outside that she started back in surprise. For a moment she could see nothing and she groped behind her, feeling for Ambrose Mercer's hand. From the darkness came a scraping sound, then the sudden flare of a match and a candle was lit. She saw immediately that all the canvas panels of the tent had been screened with an assortment of dirty old rugs and mats so that no light could penetrate from outside. She supposed it was all done to produce an air of mystery, and no doubt also to persuade the customer that he or she was in the presence of a real seer and would get value for money. The more the money, the better the value, presumably. Elizabeth didn't really credit that anyone could tell the future, but then some gypsies were reckoned to have the gift of second sight, and she had always hankered after having her fortune told by a gypsy.

The light from the candle illuminated a very small area, not enough even to reveal very clearly the features of the fortune-teller. That she didn't appear to be a gypsy, or even to be dressed as one, was Elizabeth's first disappointment. She had fat healthy cheeks boasting a cherry redness rather than the burnished brown skin Elizabeth had expected. She didn't wear a tightly-drawn exotic scarf around her hair, which was thick and black and merged almost completely into the darkness behind her. And she wasn't sporting even a single brass earring.

What was more disquieting, however – and this was Elizabeth's second disappointment – was that there was no crystal ball. Elizabeth was almost ready to turn back and abandon the adventure were it not that she didn't want to expose herself to Ambrose Mercer's derision. So she quickly swallowed her disappointment, determined to make the best of things. The loss of childhood illusions was something she had long ago learned to accept as the necessary passport to adulthood.

'Come in, my dears, come in and don't be shy.'

The voice was strong and homely, almost masculine, with a decided brogue. Elizabeth took a step towards the table on which the candle had been set, and the strangeness of walking over grass in a darkened tent towards a candle-lit table was a mixture bizarre enough to stir in her a first answering thrill of excitement.

Immediately she and Ambrose stepped into the circle of light, the woman behind the table rose to her feet, surprised and impressed by the gentrified appearance of her latest clients.

'Come in, sir, come in. You're very welcome, sir, and your good lady, too. You've come to have your fortune told?'

'Not me,' Mercer answered gruffly. 'I'll tell you straight out that I don't believe in such nonsense.'

'Oh, Ambrose,' Elizabeth rebuked him, pulling at his sleeve and sitting down on one of the two hard chairs that, apart from the table, were the tent's only furniture. Reluctantly he lowered himself into the other chair.

The woman, still smiling ingratiatingly, resumed her seat and drew her heavy black shawl around her.

'Maybe the young sir will want to hear something about his own future as soon as I've told you yours, ma'am.'

It amused Elizabeth to hear Ambrose referred to as a 'young sir'; it might have been that in the gloom she hadn't seen him clearly – he was deliberately sitting back somewhat as if to deny that he had any connection with the whole proceedings – or of course she could be craftily flattering him in the hope of inducing him to take a turn after her.

'Is it to read your palm you want, ma'am, or maybe you'd prefer me to look into the crystal ball for you.'

'But you haven't got a crystal ball,' Elizabeth said.

180

'Ah, sure, God love you, ma'am, but any self-respectin' fortune-teller has to have a crystal ball. You take my advice, ma'am, never have anything to do with one if she haven't a crystal ball. They do be only takin' your money for nothing without it.' And, with an extravagant sweep of her fat arm in what she intended as a magical flourish, she lifted her crystal ball from between her feet and reverently placed it on the table.

Elizabeth smiled to herself. She recognized the cleverness of the tactic and had to admire it. To Mercer, however, the woman's trickery was transparent, and he laughed outright. Elizabeth kicked him smartly under the table. He looked sharply at her. Her face bore an expression of intense interest – a false impression, he knew, for he had never seen Elizabeth display such keenness about anything apart from getting a man into bed. It was all very well for her to pretend that she was entering into the spirit of the occasion, leading the woman on and getting her money's worth, but he was doing the paying, so it would be *his* money's worth she was getting, not her own.

'What do you charge for all this?' he put in. 'How much is it to read her palm?'

'That's a shillin', sir.'

'And the crystal ball?'

'Ah, now, that's the real thing for this fine lady, sir. There's no knowing what I'd see in there for her.'

'Yes, yes, but how much is it?'

'Five shillin's, sir, the ball is five shillin's.'

'Like hell it is. I'll give you two shillings, no more.'

'Ah, no, sir, I couldn't. I wouldn't see anything for two shillin's.'

Elizabeth couldn't suppress her laughter. It really was becoming farcical, but that was part of the enjoyment.

'Oh, come on, Ambrose, don't be so mean.'

'Half a crown then,' Ambrose snapped. 'And not a single penny more. So you can take it or leave it. I don't mind.'

The woman, recognizing that the man's offer was final – and, anyway, a half-crown was well above her usual charge for the service – quickly held out her hand before he changed his mind. Mercer took his purse from his pocket, extracted the silver coin, and passed it over. Now, he thought, we can get this nonsense over with.

'Now,' the woman said, leaning forward over the table in a businesslike manner and inviting Elizabeth to do the same. 'Give me your hands. Both of them.'

'Just a moment,' Mercer interrupted. 'It's the crystal ball I paid you for. I gave your half a crown for it and I'm not paying another penny. And I'm certainly not paying that much for you to read her palm. There's a policeman right outside this tent. He's a friend of mine, and if you're trying to fool me I'll have him in this minute to arrest you.'

Oh God, Ambrose, you *are* crafty, Elizabeth thought. You and Tom friends! The woman, however, was in no way put out by his tirade.

'Ah, sure there's no fear, sir. I always study the hands first off. They tell me a lot, you know. About the past, I mean. The future do be in the crystal ball. But sure if you have no past you have no future. Isn't that right?'

'Well, get on with it,' Mercer told her testily. Her talk was too glib by half. Probably the reason she wanted to see Elizabeth's hands was to find out whether she was wearing an engagement or wedding ring. The light in the tent outside the candle-glow was so dim that she mightn't have been able to tell before.

She had taken Elizabeth's hands in hers and was bent over them, a small moaning sound coming from her lips as if she was crooning to a baby. Elizabeth flinched at the feel of her rough hoary skin; it was like the bark of a tree.

Suddenly she looked into Elizabeth's eyes.

'Does your name begin with a V?'

'No,' Elizabeth replied immediately. 'But my young sister's does – Victoria.'

'Ah!' The fortune-teller emitted a long sigh of satisfaction.

Mercer, however, was not impressed. Obviously the woman had learned something about the prominent families of the neighbourhood but had backed the wrong horse in guessing that her customer was Victoria instead of Elizabeth.

'Yes, now,' she had resumed. 'You're older than your sister' – I've already told you that, Elizabeth thought – 'there's a fair few years between you and she do be very different from you.'

'Yes, but it's not my sister I want to hear about, it's myself. What do you see for me in your crystal ball?'

'Ah, yes, the crystal ball,' the woman echoed, but she was reluctant to release Elizabeth's hands.

'Yes,' Mercer interrupted again. Really, this charade was more than taxing his patience. 'I told you before – it's enough that I'm going to have to listen to your blarney from that piece of glass without first having to endure blarney about her hands. So let's get on with it.'

Elizabeth wished he wouldn't be so short with the woman. Having her fortune told might have started as a lark, but now that she was in the tent a part of her wanted to believe that she was not being an utter fool and that it wasn't all a game from beginning to end. There *was* a future – everybody had one – and there *were* people who could see into it.

Mercer's cajoling had persuaded the woman to do his bidding. She had pulled the crystal ball towards her and, head bent over it, was swaying and nodding. Her round face had seemed to shrink and grow white in the light of the candle, and her hands were gripping the crystal ball as if it would disintegrate should she release it from her grasp. Despite his disbelief, Mercer was entertained by the performance; but Elizabeth, eyes wide with anxiety, could not contain her impatience.

'Well,' she prompted, 'what do you see?'

'I see a house,' came the reply in a husky voice that startled by its unexpectedly eerie quality. 'I see a house,' it repeated. 'All misty and fog. It's not clear. A big house.'

Humph! Mercer thought, there's nothing smart in that. More rubbish!

'No, that wouldn't be fog; maybe it's darkness. Night, I'd say 'tis night.'

She paused a moment, then continued.

'There are people there. A lot of people. Outside. They're all looking up at the house. Moving this way and that. It's hard to see them properly. Men they seem to be, most of them. And all dressed the same.'

'What do you mean they're all dressed the same?' Mercer interrupted, leaning forward with sudden interest.

'It's gone,' was the immediate reply. 'The picture's gone.' And Elizabeth, eyes flashing and her voice edged with frustration, turned to Mercer.

'Shut up, Ambrose. Just keep quiet. You've spoilt it.'

The fortune-teller did not raise her head but she stretched out a hand to touch Elizabeth's fingers.

'It's not finished, my lady,' she whispered. 'Sometimes there do be many pictures in here, all fighting to get through. It takes a while before I can make them out. Whisht now! Whisht! There's more.'

Elizabeth grew tense. She sat hunched forward. The woman's fingers still rested on hers, and the contact seemed to establish a feeling of trust. Instinctively she moved her free hand over so that that, too, joined the others. The woman's skin no longer felt rough – Elizabeth could not feel it at all – the three hands might have been blended into a single limb. To Ambrose Mercer they appeared to be suffused with an incandescent glow, and he felt a chill travel up his spine at the sight.

'There's a picture coming now. I can see it. A person. A lady. Perhaps your grace. Tall, like your grace. And another figure. A man. Big. Very big. Bigger than any man I've ever seen.'

Mercer smiled smugly to himself, but the smile froze on his lips at what followed.

'No, not one man. Two men. They were clasped together. That's why they seemed so big. Like they might be embracing each other. But wait – 'tis not an embrace. It's a fight it is. They're struggling with each other.'

'Who is he,' Mercer hissed, 'who's the other one?' But it was as if neither Elizabeth nor the fortune-teller heard his question. They were both bent forward towards each other, the woman's head very low over her crystal ball.

'You're there, lady, 'tis yourself, to be sure,' she was saying. 'You're there still, standing watching them. They're at each other like, wrestling, slowly, as if they're tired or dragging the strength from each other.'

Elizabeth's hands were squeezing the woman's fingers so that her own knuckles were white with the force of her grip, but she seemed oblivious of her action.

'They're getting more tired now. They're falling. No, sinking down like. As if they want to sleep. They're both lying down now.'

'Am I there?' The question escaped Elizabeth almost without her knowing it.

'You're still there, but your image is fading now.'

184

She stopped.

'Go on,' Elizabeth gasped, almost unable to get the words out, 'go on. Please go on.'

'The picture is gone. We'll wait a second. Something else may come. We'll wait. Wait and see. Something . . . yes. It's the same picture again. The two men lying stretched out. And yourself standing between them, as bright as fire.'

There was silence in the tent. It was in the grip of a spell, a spell that had even made Ambrose Mercer forget, if only temporarily, his earlier scepticism. They heard the hissing of the candle as a drop of grease was caught in the flame, but they were deaf to the shouting of the crowd, the din of music, the dogs barking, the children's call of joy – all that seemed to come from somewhere far more distant than just the other side of the tent.

Suddenly Elizabeth felt a stirring in the fortune-teller's fingers. They did not appear to move, but from them a current was flowing into her own hands; she felt certain it had to presage some new revelation.

'What is it?' she asked urgently. 'What do you see now?'

The current had grown stronger. It was cold, a cold lance that travelled up each arm and then tumbled in an icy flood down into her chest to engulf her heart.

''Tis nothing,' the woman said, pulling her hand away, 'nothing at all.' Her voice no longer had a faraway unearthly tone.

'It *was* something,' Elizabeth insisted. 'I know it was. Tell me.'

'Ah, just a colour. A colour in the glass,' the fortune-teller responded reluctantly.

'A colour? What colour?'

'Dark. A sort of brown. Or red maybe.' The woman's answers were offhand, as if she attached no importance to what she had seen.

'Red?' Elizabeth said anxiously. 'Red is for danger. What danger?'

'Ah, no, love, 'tis nothing like that. I do often get that colour in the glass when the pictures do be finished.'

'Finished?' Mercer interrupted truculently, rising from his chair. 'Is that all she gets for half a crown?'

'I'm afraid there's no more, sir. Sometimes there do be a lot, sometimes there isn't.'

Elizabeth, however, was impervious both to Mercer's dissatisfaction and to the woman's matter-of-fact reply. She had forgotten, too, the original impetus that had sent her into the fortune-teller's tent, the light-hearted gaiety of a lark undertaken on the spur of the moment. The abrupt ending of the fortune-teller's account held a note of foreboding. She felt as if her soul had left her body, as if part of her – the part that bore the pulse of life – was still inside that crystal ball, imprisoned there with the two stricken men in the cloud of dust or colour or whatever it was that the woman had seen. Nor was it only the strange image itself that still held her in its grip – who were these men, where were they, was it Odron House, why had they been fighting, if indeed they had been fighting, and what was the outcome of the struggle? – but her body still tingled with the recollection of the current that had joined her and the fortune-teller together. They had become one – not just her flesh and bone, but her whole history, past and future – and what was enacted in the crystal ball was real, as if it had already happened. The shock when that scene had suddenly disappeared had left her stunned. The current had been switched off so abruptly, so savagely, that it seemed her life had been switched off, too.

She rose from the hard chair, stiff, cold, rising from a ghost of herself. Worse, as if she was somehow already a ghost, and the person who had entered the tent had been a childhood immature self, someone no longer relevant. She wished she had never so thoughtlessly decided to have her fortune told. She would never again be dismissive of fortune-tellers and their claims.

'I don't want any more,' she said, vaguely aware that Ambrose was still challenging the woman, claiming they had been cheated and threatening to have her arrested. Why is he so stupid, she thought. I don't want to hear any more. Besides. it's *my* life she was telling about, not his. Does he imagine he was one of the two men? Was he?

'Come on, Ambrose, come on,' she urged. 'I need to get some air.'

Reluctantly, still protesting, Mercer lifted the tent-flap and escorted her out. She turned for a last look at the fortune-teller. The woman was standing behind her table, her face unsmiling, her lips together, her hands still around the crystal ball. When she caught Elizabeth's almost forlorn stare, she slowly lowered her head, and Elizabeth delayed a moment, hoping she might perhaps have something more to tell that would lift the weight from her heart. But the fortune-teller remained silent.

As Elizabeth and Ambrose Mercer emerged from the tent into the blaring noise of the fair, Tom Fahy turned to greet them.

'You took long enough in there,' he said. 'She must have had a powerful lot to tell you.'

Elizabeth's face was pale, and it seemed to him that her eyes had an empty glassy look as if what she was seeing was not the scene before her but something lodged inside her head. He was about to ask if she felt all right when there was a hearty voice in his ear.

'Constable Fahy and friends! If I had my camera now, wouldn't this make a historic picture!'

He swung round to find O'Halloran, flamboyant as ever, his large florid face registering gleeful surprise.

'I can see the heading for it,' he was continuing. 'Big bold letters: "Ambrose Mercer and the fortune-teller. What did he learn about his future?"'

Mercer, still dazzled by the bright sun after the darkness of the tent, blinked when he heard his name mentioned. He screwed his eyes up, trying to identify the bulky figure facing him, but with the strong sun behind it, it was still no more than a dark shape.

'Sure there was no need for you to be wasting your money, Mr Mercer, when you had only to come to me and I'd have told you your future with pleasure. And all free, gratis, and for nothing.'

Mercer, at last recognizing his adversary, smarted at the taunt.

'Get out of my way,' he growled with a threatening lunge. 'Where I go or what I do is no business of yours, O'Halloran.'

'Oh ho, that's not a proposition I can agree with,' Tim O'Halloran answered loudly and amiably, for all the world ready to enter into a debate in which he would light-heartedly oppose the motion.

'I'm not interested in having the agreement of the likes of you. I'm not interested in your views at all. Now, get out of my way.' And, taking Elizabeth's arm, Mercer sought to push past. O'Halloran, however, was ready for him, and as their bodies made contact he turned his shoulder so that Mercer, taken off balance, almost fell back. With a snarl, he sprang at O'Halloran, and before Constable Fahy could stop them the two had come to grips.

The sudden altercation had an immediate effect on Elizabeth. Like a bucket of cold water thrown over someone lying unconscious, it shocked her into full awareness, completely wrenching her thoughts back from the future to the present. Fahy was struggling to separate the two men, grunting with the effort but making no headway against their combined determination to inflict the maximum damage on each other.

'For God Almighty sake, will ye stop behaving like children?' he appealed, anxious not to let the situation get out of hand, but his exhortation was drowned by the cries of the crowd which had instantly formed a circle around the trio. Many of them seemed to know the identity of the two adversaries, and those who didn't were quickly told. It was clear that the policeman was having no success in his efforts, and as the local favourite was holding his own nobody felt it necessary to intervene. Shouts of encouragement for O'Halloran rose from all sides, caps were taken off and waved in excitement, huge Kerry farmers brandished their sticks with gusto and spread their brawny arms wide to keep back those pressing from behind and make sure the row was given plenty of room to develop. Attracted by the cries, people rushed from adjoining stalls, adding to the throng.

'Rise him, Tim!'

'Go on, boy, get the bastard!'

'Watch out for the knee, watch out there!'

The women screamed, with enjoyment rather than with fear, shaking clenched fists at Mercer as if their symbolic blows would help to defeat him. A child was crying in fright, and two stray hounds yapped and barked madly.

Elizabeth stood at the edge of the ring, trying to prevent the jostling of the people behind from pitching her forward against the struggling men. Infected by the fever of excitement in the

188

air, something in her was stirred by the display of anger and aggression. She saw the hatred blaze in Mercer's eyes, the thick veins in O'Halloran's neck swell with strain, and although she could not hear her voice in the surrounding din, she found herself, like everyone else, urging the contestants on. Revelling in the display of brute force and energy, she didn't know which one of the two to support. She wouldn't greatly have minded if Ambrose got a bloody nose, but he *was* an Odron man and she didn't want to see someone from her own circle bested. Tom Fahy she had no fears for; he was only trying to separate the others, and she was confident he could take care of himself.

Fortunately for the policeman, the struggle between Mercer and O'Halloran was proving an equal one, and as his physical interference was preventing any really damaging blow being landed he was hoping they'd quickly come to their senses and cease hostilities.

'Take it easy now. Go easy there, can't you?' he cajoled, trying to interpose his body between them but finding that his two arms were no match for their four. When he faced Mercer, O'Halloran's flailing fists would swing around blindly from behind his back, and when he turned to subdue the latter Mercer took the chance to strike at O'Halloran over the policeman's shoulder. All three were perspiring heavily in the heat, and Tom Fahy had lost his cap, which was being kicked about and trampled into the hard dusty ground beneath his feet. Mercer's cravat was askew. O'Halloran, who was wearing an open shirt, was the least discomposed. With a mighty effort the constable managed to force both men back and almost into the shouting crowd. 'Will none of ye give me a hand with these two?' he appealed as he tried to regain balance, but the highly partisan onlookers were cheering O'Halloran and quickly backed away to let the struggle continue.

Tom Fahy could see now that both men were becoming angrier with each lunging blow thrown, and their frustration at being unable to slug it out without interference was clearly exacerbating the situation. He know he had no alternative but to call for help, and quickly he grabbed his whistle from where it was hanging at his belt and blew three sharp piercing blasts.

His action had an immediate effect on the crowd. A concerted cry broke from them – part registration of delight that

189

the policeman was admitting his inability to put an end to the fight, part expression of chagrin at the prospect of having the fight ended by the intervention of other policemen at the fair. This didn't suit them at all. Determined not to allow it to happen, they pressed firmly together in a solid ring. The other RIC men left their various posts and came at a run only to find their way barred by the mass of bodies and though they roughly pulled one or two away from its outer fringes, ranks were instantly closed again.

In the middle of the ring the two assailants had taken advantage of Tom Fahy's momentary loss of attention while he looked about him for the expected aid. They had pulled themselves away from his grip and had managed to fall to the ground, where they were now wrestling and raining blows on each other. O'Halloran, roused to an extra effort by the renewed shouts of encouragement, began to gain the upper hand, and with a giant heave he threw himself astride Mercer. From this advantageous position he clamped a hand to each side of his rival's head and was hammering it up and down off the ground with fierce regularity. Elizabeth's hand flew to her mouth with the sudden realization that the situation was out of control. 'Tom, Tom,' she screamed, 'can't you stop them? They'll kill each other!'

The constable, guessing now that his colleagues were unable to reach him, knew that he'd have to go on the offensive. He rushed up behind O'Halloran, who was still astride Mercer – on whom he was bouncing vigorously as if the man between his knees was a horse he was urging in full flight towards a fence – and putting his arm around his neck he heaved him off and threw him aside. Mercer immediately sprang to his feet, his face showing blood from a nasty cut, and mouthing oaths he made to rush at his tormentor who was now on the ground. But Tom Fahy had had enough. It was time to enforce his authority.

Pulling his gun from its holster he jumped into Mercer's path and raised his arm as if to shoot. Mercer stopped in his tracks, and O'Halloran, rising, quickly saw that it would be foolish to try to continue the battle.

'If there's any more trouble, I'll arrest you both,' the constable threatened. It was more for effect than for anything else, to

190

counteract the jeers of the crowd disappointed at the enforced conclusion of the fair's most exciting side-show. He would not have wanted to arrest either man: to take Mercer into custody would have complicated the whole Odron House assignment, while to do likewise with O'Halloran would have caused wide resentment and further local disturbances. Sergeant Driscoll would certainly not have been pleased.

'Come on now,' he appealed placatingly, anxious to lower the temperature all round. 'My advice to you is to go about your business, Mr O'Halloran.'

What matter, O'Halloran thought as he dusted himself off, I bested him anyway.

'As you wish, Constable,' he replied, a broad smile of satisfaction on his face. 'And you may inform Mr Mercer there that if the fortune-teller didn't warn him he was going to get a beating this day he should go and ask for his money back.'

The crowd cheered the sally, and Tom Fahy had to wave his gun at Mercer to restrain him from seeking to spring at his rival once more.

'You'll regret this, O'Halloran,' he screamed. 'You'll regret this, you and your rabble. And you'll regret shooting at me, too,' he added.

Tim O'Halloran raised his eyebrows in surprise.

'Are you accusing me of shooting at you, Mercer, are you? Accusing me in public – in front of all these witnesses. That's slanderous talk.'

Mercer, abashed, knew that he had gone too far.

'Well, someone shot at me,' he insisted as aggressively as he could.

'Maybe. Maybe not,' O'Halloran answered back. 'But not me. If *I* shot you, it's not standing up on two feet you'd be now, but lying down under six feet.'

He tossed his head in acknowledgement of the renewed cheers his answer drew from the crowd, and as he ambled off casually as if he had only just been passing the time of day with a few acquaintances the people parted before him, clapping him on the back and shaking his hand. Mercer stood dabbing a handkerchief to his face and trying to straighten his dishevelled clothing.

'You do look a mess,' Elizabeth said, showing him scant

191

sympathy. 'And you're lucky Tom was here or you could have got off much worse.'

'Scum,' Mercer fumed. 'They're nothing but scum. Rebels and traitors all of them.'

'Best keep your opinions to yourself,' Tom Fahy advised, 'or there'll be more than one of them here will take you on and I may not be able to save you then.'

'Save me!' Mercer spluttered furiously. 'A lot of good you were. I wouldn't be surprised if you were in league with him. You're all the same, you Irish.'

'That's enough now,' Fahy told him. 'You want to get those cuts seen to and get yourself cleaned up.'

'I'm dry after all the excitement,' Elizabeth announced, her cheeks flushed. She had never before witnessed anything like it. What a tale she'd have to tell when they got home. 'I'm quite hoarse, too. Couldn't we get a drink somewhere?'

'Good idea,' Tom declared enthusiastically. 'And it'll be a chance to get Mr Mercer's cuts washed. We could all do with a drink to cool us off. Come on.'

Elizabeth put her arm through Ambrose's, jollying him into agreement as Tom shepherded them through the crowd and out of the field. He really needed a drink. He felt he really deserved a drink; it was no more than his just deserts that he was going to get one after all.

10

'THIS IS SO PLEASANT. Quite heavenly really,' Victoria said. 'I haven't been on a picnic since Elizabeth and I were children. I'd forgotten how exciting it could be.'

She and Pat Howell were sitting in a field, their backs to the ditch between themselves and the road, their bicycles lying together beside them. They had restored Saucy to her perch on the barracks window-sill where, having turned in a few tight sniffy circles to confirm her surroundings, she had immediately resumed her interrupted siesta.

'I'll bet those picnics of yours were more high-class than this,' Pat joked as he shared out their small stock of apples, chocolate bars and lemonade. 'What did you have? Tea and cakes?'

'Yes. And cucumber sandwiches, and biscuits, and ice cream, and sweets.'

'Well, you haven't anything like that today, I'm afraid.'

'Oh, there's nothing wrong with this. I was only a child then, and when you're a child the food is the attraction. When you're grown-up, the food isn't the most important thing, is it?'

'What is, then?' Pat asked, not altogether innocently. He, too, remembered the ecstasies of anticipation the food had aroused in his own childhood picnics, but the thrill of excitement he felt as he pushed his bicycle through the gate a

193

few minutes before had not, he knew, anything to do with food.

'The company, of course,' Victoria replied. 'It's the company that's important now. Don't you think so, Pat?'

She was biting into an apple, her soft brown eyes turned on him and the white of her teeth sparkling against the red of the apple skin. He wanted to agree with her, to tell her that the company – her company – was the attraction of this picnic for him, but having invited the opportunity, he was too shy to take it. Pretending to be absorbed in selecting between two varieties of chocolate, he put a clownish garb on his answer.

'Oh, of course it's the company all right. I mean, we can have an apple and an oul' bar of chocolate any day. Sure the dullest of company would be better than that.'

Victoria sighed, but more in understanding than in exasperation. Trying to penetrate Pat's reserve had been unrewarding so far, but each time he rejected her advances had she not sensed some uncertainty and hesitation?

'Why don't you read your letters?' she asked. 'I never get any letters, but if I did I wouldn't be able to wait as long as you have to read them. They'd burn a hole in my pocket.'

Pat shrugged. 'Ah, they're not important.'

'How do you know until you open them? You told me you were worried about replies to the letters you wrote on Sunday about a Police Union. Now that you have replies, I don't know why you won't find out what they say. Or is it that you're being too well mannered to read them in front of me? I won't mind. Honestly. I won't think it rude.'

A light breeze rustled her hair, blowing a strand in front of her face. She puffed it away, and her eyes caught his. They seemed to have a mischievous glint that made him notice her mock-serious expression.

'You're very like your sister, aren't you? I mean the way both of you like to tease. Tom says that Elizabeth is always behaving like that.'

Victoria laughed, then fell silent for a moment.

'The trouble is', she answered eventually, 'that Elizabeth teases all men – all young men anyway. She just can't seem to help it.'

'But why? Why does she do it?'

'To make men jealous. Or excited. Something like that. I

194

only do it with you because I like you. And because you take it so seriously.'

'It's a funny way to treat someone you like – to tease them,' Pat said quietly.

'Oh, nonsense,' Victoria declared. 'People do it all the time. Haven't you ever seen parents talk to their children? Didn't your parents ever tease you? It's a way of showing affection.' She paused, then added with assumed casualness: 'Sometimes even love.'

Pat, munching a piece of chocolate, stopped suddenly. He stared down at the ground between his feet and idly plucked a blade of grass. Then he turned to look up at Victoria, who was kneeling beside him.

'Supposing,' she said, her voice casual, speculative, 'supposing *you* loved someone and supposing you wanted them to know but you weren't able to say it. How would you show it?'

She tried to give her question no weight, but Pat guessed it wasn't meant just as a piece of light conversation. After almost four days in Victoria's company he had learned a lot about her, and her hints had left him in no doubt of her feelings. He was bewildered by what was happening, bewildered by the knowledge of what his answer to her question should be. He knew what it would be if Tom Fahy was in his place. Tom wouldn't hesitate or waste time about it. He'd have the girl in his arms before you could say 'Jack Robinson'. Yes, but next day it would be a different girl, if the chance arose. Pat didn't see how he could take a girl in his arms unless he meant it to mean something . . . something permanent. And how could there be anything permanent between him and Victoria Odron? It was ridiculous.

Savagely he tore up a whole tuft of grass and then dashed it back into the ground. He knew, without turning his head to look at Victoria, that she was waiting for an answer, but he could not give her the answer she wanted, much as he might have wanted to himself.

'Oh, well, if you've suddenly been struck dumb, there's no use in my talking to you,' she said at last, moving away from him and turning her attention to the food. 'I could starve while I'd be waiting for you to say something. You go on and read your blessed letters. Perhaps they'll cheer you up a bit.'

195

For a minute Pat did not move. He felt disgusted with himself, sick with shame at his awkwardness, fearful that Victoria would decide he was only a tongue-tied yokel and give him up as a bad job. Yes, he might as well read his letters now, but the prospect of what might be in them failed to excite or even interest him. The Police Union . . . it was dead anyway, wasn't it? He was surely only hitting his head off a stone wall trying to revive it. Despairingly he took the two envelopes from his pocket and tore them open.

He glanced through them quickly, then read them both again. They were brief. Brief and blunt. One from Galway told him that there was virtually no support in that area for a Dublin meeting. That didn't surprise him. Out in the west they were so isolated from everything – from Sinn Fein attacks as well as from the close attention of the authorities – that it was hard to envisage them disturbing their easygoing routines to rally to a cause they knew could land them in trouble. The second letter was the really bitter one. It came from one of the Dublin wards, a station which had been among the first advocates of the idea and aims of the Union, but now it was all regrets and apologies. Interest had waned, support on any significant scale couldn't be guaranteed – indeed, would be hard to drum up. If prospects improved, they'd be in touch again.

Pat stuffed the letters back in his pocket. He looked at what was left of the picnic, but it didn't entice him any more. He had lost all appetite. Along with everything else. The Police Union dream . . . it seemed that was all it really amounted to: an empty dream. And Victoria? It was stupid to let her excite him. His job was to protect her and everyone else in Odron House from attack. That was all. If he imagined there was anything else in it, he was mad. It was just the kind of silly fancy an innocent schoolboy would get – imagining he was falling in love with the first girl he had ever spent any time with. And to fool himself into thinking that she might be falling for him, too. . . . God, had he taken leave of his senses at all? What a laugh Tom would have if he knew.

'That didn't do you much good – reading those letters, I mean,' Victoria interrupted his thoughts. 'Here, have a bit. It's the last bar.'

She broke off part of the chocolate she was holding and offered it to him. He stared at it as if he had never seen chocolate before but made no move to take it.

'Come on,' she said. 'Open up' – pushing it against his closed lips.

He turned his head away, annoyed at her treatment, trying to feed him as if he was just a sulking child. Women! They had no sense of proportion.

'Please yourself,' she said, eating the piece herself. 'I'll keep a half aside in case you change your mind.'

'I'm not hungry. Eat it all yourself.'

'Those letters,' she said. 'They *were* about the Police Union, weren't they?'

'Yes.'

'And they weren't very encouraging, that's plain to see.'

He didn't reply apart from a reluctant grunt to indicate that he didn't want to discuss the subject.

She tapped him on the shoulder, and when he turned to look at her she took his face in her hands and gazed into his eyes. Embarrassment and nervousness made him raise his own hands in an effort to remove hers.

'Uh-huh,' she said threateningly.

He stopped halfway.

She held his face as tightly as she could and slowly lowered hers until their lips were touching. Pat did not move. After a few seconds she released him and sat back on the grass.

His heart was beating like a drunkard on a drum, so hard that he was sure she would hear it and know how excited her kiss had made him. Even if she didn't hear it she could plainly see his blush. His cheeks must have turned beetroot red, so fiercely did they burn. She'd guess he had never been kissed before.

He licked his lips. They tasted of chocolate.

'I'll have a bit of that chocolate now,' he said.

'Oh, that brought your appetite back, did it? Not very complimentary, I must say,' she commented as she broke off some of the bar and handed it to him.

'Why not?'

'A woman's kiss is supposed to make a man forget food, not the opposite.'

197

He was about to deny her implication when he suddenly realized what she was up to.

'Ah, you're teasing me again, aren't you?'

'I have to.'

'Why?'

'Because I can't seem to make you take me seriously. Don't you like me?'

After a lengthy pause he hung his head in confusion and replied: 'Oh, I like you all right.'

Victoria clapped her hands in mock elation and bounced up and down on the grass.

'Hurrah! Hurrah! Constable Howell makes a damning admission. He likes the lady "all right".'

'What do you expect me to say?' he protested angrily.

'Oh, just that and no more. If, that is, there's no more to say. It's just that I had the feeling you liked me more than that. But, then, you're the first man I've really liked, so maybe it was all wishful thinking on my part.'

'Well, you're the first—' He broke off, then turned to face her. 'Look, I've been sent to Odron House on official business, to guard you and your family and Mercer. I wasn't sent to . . . to. . . . You know what I mean.'

'I think I do, but getting it out of you is like getting blood from a stone. Now, you listen to me. When a boy and a girl like each other, it's not really important how they happen to meet, is it?'

'That's not what I mean,' Pat said. 'There's a lot more than that to it.'

'Do you mean all the differences between us?'

Pat suddenly lost his patience. 'For goodness' sake, what are we talking about? That is all a lot of nonsense. And I've enough to worry about without . . . without. . . .'

'Your Police Union?' Victoria asked.

'Yes.'

'Pat, do you really imagine you'll ever get it going? Do you really think there's the slightest chance it will ever be allowed by the powers that be?'

Pat stood up, uncomfortable under her questioning and stung by her practical realism.

'I can't give up. I have no alternative but to keep trying.'

198

Victoria rose, too, and faced him.

'That's pure obstinacy. What's the point of continuing if you don't really believe you can get what you want? And you don't believe you can, do you?'

'You don't understand. It's too late to turn back. I'm already in the authorities' bad books, and when they find out about these letters I wrote there'll be no hope for me. They'll either send me to some hole-in-the-wall where I'll never be heard of again, or more likely they'll get rid of me altogether. So my only hope is to get the Union going. If I can do that, it might be some protection.'

Victoria despairingly looked up to the skies.

'Men! They can't see further than the nose on their face.'

'What do you mean?'

'I mean that the sensible thing for you is to forget about the Police Union – just drop it, it has no chance anyway – and think about your future.'

'But, for goodness' sake, girl, haven't I just explained! Without the Union I *have* no future.'

'Not in the RIC maybe. But there are other things you could do.'

'I'm not going back home. There's nothing for me there.'

Victoria did not answer for a moment. Then, putting her hands on his shoulders, she said: 'We could go away . . . together.'

Pat stared at her in amazement. He was so astounded by her suggestion that for once he did not blush. He took hold of her arms and lowered them to her sides, but resolutely she held on to his hands and refused to release them. He did not try to break her grip. He felt calm and collected, in control of himself at last.

'That's a great joke—'

'It wasn't meant to be a joke,' she interrupted.

'I don't think your mother would regard it as a joke, either. If she'd be shocked by the idea of your sister marrying Ambrose Mercer, how do you think she'd feel about us – you and me, I mean. For goodness' sake, where's your sense? We're not even the same religion.'

Victoria regarded him silently, then her face softened into a smile.

'What's so funny now?' Pat demanded. 'You certainly seem to have a queer sense of humour.'

'I'm not smiling because I see anything funny,' she said quietly. 'If you must know, my smile is a smile of satisfaction.'

He looked at her, totally uncomprehending.

'Of all the reasons why you couldn't come away with me,' she said, 'you picked the least important ones – that my mother would object and that we're not the same religion – and you didn't even mention the most important one.'

'What's that?'

'That you don't want to come away with me. Why didn't you say that?'

Pat looked surprised. Why hadn't he said that?

'I don't know,' he answered slowly.

'Are you sure?'

'I don't know,' was all he could repeat. The whole thing was madness. He'd be back in barracks in a few weeks and they'd soon forget each other. Best thing, too.

He moved away from her and picked up his bicycle.

'Come on,' he said. 'We'd best be getting back.'

Victoria followed without protest, but the smile had not left her face.

Dinner at Odron House that evening started on a strained note. Ambrose Mercer refused to wait in for it, insisting on going down to the village for 'a few drinks, or maybe more than a few'. Tom Fahy had tried his best to dissuade him, but short of putting him under arrest there was nothing he could do about it. It was sheer bravado on Mercer's part of course, his way of showing the locals that the morning's set-to with O'Halloran wasn't going to make any difference to his attitude. 'No bloody Shinners are going to frighten me, Fahy,' he declared. 'A lucky blow that grounded me, that's all, and then when that oaf got on top of me he was too heavy to shift.'

'Maybe,' Tom said, 'but this is no night for you to go out among them. Most of them will be drunk, and it'll only be by the grace of God that you won't get into another fight.'

'Don't be so lily-livered. I'm not afraid of them, even if you are. And you'll be carrying a gun, so what have you to worry about?'

'Don't be a stupid bastard,' Tom Fahy said angrily. 'If I fire a single shot in that crowd, I'd have so many on top of us that they'd have the life beaten out of us in two twos. That's if we're lucky enough not to get shot to pieces ourselves first – I'd say there'd be a couple of those boyos might be armed themselves.'

'Well, no one is asking you to come along. I don't want a nursemaid. I never wanted you on my coat-tails. It's the women you should be protecting, so stay with them. You'll be safest doing that. You can't stop me, and I warn you not to try.'

The two men glared at each other until Mercer strode away and out of the house.

'Blast!' Tom muttered as he went after him. 'Damn and blast!' He had missed his lunch and now he was going to miss dinner as well.

Amelia, who had not seen her daughters since their return from their morning's outings, was not surprised at the absence from the dinner-table of Ambrose Mercer and Constable Fahy. She was almost beginning to regret her action in asking Sergeant Driscoll for protection at all. It had seemed the right thing to do at the time but, really, Mercer had behaved so badly since the policemen arrived that he didn't deserve their protection. They were being given such a hard time by him; at least Constable Fahy was, the other one had by far the easier job in looking after Victoria. One might have thought they had been friends for years, so much were they together. Amelia was not disturbed by their closeness. Victoria seemed to live so much a solitary life that company was good for her. It would bring her out of herself. Of course Elizabeth needed company, too. But a different sort of company – the company of responsive men. Looking at Elizabeth's vivacity on such occasions, listening to that subtle modulation in her voice that was often akin to a verbal caress, seeing the suggestive way she moved to a man or walked beside him – these were all signs that a woman could recognize. Elizabeth would have no trouble making a man happy when the time came. But when would that be? She was twenty-six; she should be married by now. Amelia was twenty-six when she met and married Alex. But that had been in England. Here in Ireland, Elizabeth was marooned in a country virtually at war, with no immediate prospect of meeting a suitable man. As Amelia looked at her

201

two girls, chattering away brightly over the soup, she had an almost uncontrollable urge to clasp them to her as if they had been years and years away on some remote island without any contact at all. But it wasn't they who had returned, it was she – not, she hoped, too late.

Elizabeth was telling Victoria some story about a fight at the fair that morning between Ambrose and Tim O'Halloran. Amelia listened with growing concern. Anything that increased the hostility between those two men was disturbing, even frightening. But Elizabeth's account didn't seem to suggest that the confrontation had been too serious: Mercer appeared to have got the worst of the bargain, and the people at the fair evidently were all against him – which was only to be expected. So that's what had put Mercer into a sulk and made him miss dinner. Well, more fool he! But he never did like being bested.

Pat Howell, however, did not join in the laughter at Elizabeth's description of Ambrose Mercer pinned to the ground by O'Halloran and flailing unsuccessfully at him like a crippled windmill. Tom Fahy had given Pat a more accurate report of the fight in his room that afternoon, while Mercer was bathing his cuts, and Pat, like Tom, feared that the encounter could only have sharpened the animosity between the two men. Why, he wondered, was Elizabeth making out it had all been such a lot of fun?

Victoria, also, was puzzled by her sister's high spirits. She was used to Elizabeth's ways, used to recognizing the spontaneity and naturalness of her gaiety, and she was certain that on this occasion there was something about it that did not ring true. A fight between Ambrose Mercer and Tim O'Halloran in which they actually came to blows in full view of the public was not a joke; it couldn't seriously or sensibly be treated as a matter of fun. And that it *had* been serious, and quite bruising, too, was clear, for Victoria had seen Ambrose Mercer on his way to his room when he returned to Odron House and he had looked very much the worse for wear; she wasn't at all surprised that he hadn't turned up for dinner. She recalled suddenly what Pat had told her that morning, that Mercer had been boasting he was going to marry Elizabeth. It had seemed an outlandish story – but supposing Mercer had some basis for it. . . . Supposing there was an understanding between him and Elizabeth, that would be something she'd not want her mother to know about until she was ready to tell her. They might be planning to elope. Nonsense! Yet, if some sort of scheme had been hatched, Elizabeth would be at pains to hide any feeling she had for Mercer and so might well be artful enough to pretend she had enjoyed his discomfiture at the fair. It was all very worrying. The time, she decided, had come to have a serious talk with her sister without delay.

'Really,' Elizabeth was saying, evidently still insisting that the whole spectacle had been a rare old treat, 'you should have seen Ambrose, he was like a pricked balloon. And full of excuses afterwards. But it won't do him any harm at all to have met his match.'

'Perhaps,' Amelia said, 'but on the other hand, it might make Mr O'Halloran and his awful Shinners even more aggressive. Have you thought of that?'

'Oh, no, Mother,' Elizabeth rejoined, 'quite the opposite, I'd say. If he had beaten O'Halloran, then no doubt the Shinners would want revenge, but I'm sure they must be very happy with their man's victory.'

'What do you think, Constable?' Amelia addressed Pat. 'Do you think the fact that they won what appears to have been only a minor rumpus will satisfy them?'

Pat didn't for one moment think it would. He knew that what had happened would have no bearing on the issue between the Sinn Fein demands and Mercer's position. If anything, even though O'Halloran, according to Tom's description, had administered a really powerful drubbing to his adversary, the fact that Mercer had been humbled once could spur on O'Halloran and his followers to strike when the iron was hot and somehow or other put paid to Mercer altogether. A physical drubbing was a nice taster for them, but that's all it was. It still left Mercer boss of the Odron House lands. But Pat was careful not to voice his real thoughts. He was there to reassure his charges, not to frighten them with his fears of what might follow.

Elizabeth, however, was paying no heed to his answer. Even while she had been giving her version of the morning's fight, the scene in her mind had not been that of the two men struggling with each other, of the ring of red excited faces surrounding them, of the throaty hostile shouts, of Tom Fahy desperately trying to come between the combatants and subdue them; all that was just the dust of words she was throwing out in the vain hope of dowsing the awful image in the fortune-teller's crystal ball. All the way home from the fair the picture had haunted her – the two fallen men, the ominous red cloud, and herself. In some way she could not identify, the fairground mêlée seemed to be connected with the scene in the crystal ball. But in the fairground there had been three men involved – Ambrose, O'Halloran and Tom; in the crystal ball only two, and these too vaguely defined to be recognizable. And what about all that red the fortune-teller had seen? Of course Ambrose's face had been cut in the fight and was bleeding, but that could hardly be described as a cloud of red. No, she was only imagining things. It was childish of her to let herself become obsessed by a silly old peasant woman's predictions. It had all been just a carefree escapade, a bit of fun. And that was how to regard the fight, too. Of course it was angry and bad-tempered while it was taking place, and it might easily have ended tragically, but it hadn't; so, looking back on it, it was the ludicrous sight of Ambrose like a beached whale on the ground trying ineffectually to dislodge O'Halloran that Elizabeth clung to, and her mother's amusement at her version of the whole affair was some much-needed reassurance.

'And, I suppose, after all that excitement,' she heard Amelia saying, 'you forgot to get the thread I asked you to buy. You haven't mentioned it, so I presume you must have forgotten it.'

'Oh, Mother, I'm so sorry,' Elizabeth apologized. 'I'm afraid you're right. The high jinks did put it clean out of my mind. Can you wait until next week? I'll go in again then.'

Amelia, however, was showing neither disappointment nor annoyance.

'It doesn't matter. I have some thread to be going on with.'

'You have? Where did you get it?' Victoria asked. 'Don't tell me you had it put away for years.'

'No, not at all. I simply unpicked the thread from that piece of embroidery in my bedroom.'

'The one on the wall?' Elizabeth said in surprise. 'Whatever made you do that?'

Amelia smiled, but her answer was noncommittal. 'Let's say I felt like a change. It had been there far too long. Waking up to it day after day – it was beginning to make me feel old. And, even if one *is* old, there's no need to surround oneself with ornaments that make one *feel* old. But, then, that's not something that would concern you girls at your age. Or you, Constable Howell, either.'

'No, ma'am,' Pat agreed, but Elizabeth and Victoria exchanged glances. They knew that that piece of embroidery had represented something of significance to their mother. When, as children, they had asked her about it, she had told them it was something she had made before they were born, before even she had been married. They had often asked her if it had been based on a real house, and she had replied, 'In a way, I suppose it was'; and when, as children do, they had persisted and wanted to know where the house was, she had seemed to grow sad and would say no more.

Elizabeth was able to recall how affected Amelia had been by such questions, and yet now she appeared quite unmoved by the fact that with her own hand she had destroyed something that had meant so much to her. Perhaps it had not been a particularly happy memory after all, and getting rid of it at last had led to the change in her that evening. It wasn't a change of appearance or demeanour – more one of mood. No, that wasn't quite it, either. What, then? Essence? Yes, in essence she was different, and observing her closely it seemed to Elizabeth that her mother now had what, for them, she had never had before: presence. She diffused an aura which, curiously, was part of her own self-awareness and in which she seemed to take comfort and pleasure.

That Elizabeth's apprehension of such a change was not a trick of her imagination was confirmed for her later by Victoria, when her sister knocked on her bedroom door and entered her room.

Elizabeth greeted her with a cheeky smile and the question, 'Why did you knock, sister dear?'

'I always knock,' Victoria replied. 'You know that.'

'Oh, yes, you're always very discreet, just in case I'm not alone. But I could hardly have had someone in my room now, could I, with both Ambrose and my policeman out of the house? Unless, of course, I had nabbed *your* policeman.'

'Oh, Elizabeth, don't be so silly.'

'But he *is* your policeman, isn't he?' Elizabeth teased. 'I'm not blind, you know. It was plain to see at the table that you've – what do they say? – given him your heart. Why, you could hardly take your eyes off him.'

'Oh, gosh, no! It wasn't that obvious, was it? Do you think Mother noticed?'

Elizabeth patted her sister's hand. 'You don't need to worry about Mother, she usually never notices anything.' She paused, then added: 'Though I thought she seemed different this evening. Did it strike you by any chance?'

'Yes,' Victoria agreed. 'It hadn't occurred to me but, now that you mention it, she *was* different. More alert, more ready to join in. Happier, too, I suppose.'

'Yes, that's it. I wonder why. And there was that business about the thread. All of a sudden she seems to have come to life. I'm glad it wasn't just my imagination. If you noticed it, too, despite all the sheep's eyes you were making at Constable Howell, then it must have been pretty obvious. You *have* fallen for him, haven't you, Vicky? You *have* given him your heart?'

Victoria made a wry smile. 'How can you give someone something they don't want?' she asked, flopping down on to her sister's bed.

Elizabeth was immediately all sympathy. 'Oh dear, has he not fallen for you, then? It seemed to me that he had, and I can usually tell.'

'I'm not sure. I *think* he has, but he's so shy. Shy and afraid.'

'Afraid of what?'

'Of us, I suppose. Ourselves, I mean, and all the barriers and differences between us.'

Elizabeth laughed. 'For goodness' sake, Vicky, why should either of you worry about these things at this stage? I mean, you're not taking this that seriously, are you? Surely you don't imagine this is going to be the big love of your life?'

Victoria stood up and then suddenly fell back again on to the bed as if a great weight had pushed her down.

'I don't know. How *does* one know these things?'

'Are you asking *me*?' Elizabeth said in amusement.

206

'Well, I've no one else to ask, have I? Besides, you . . . well, you know about men.'

Elizabeth laughed wryly. '"Out of the mouths of babes and sucklings . . ."' she murmured.

'Whatever do you mean?'

'You said I know about *men*. You didn't say *love*.' There was a harsh note in her voice, a note more of self-anger than of self-pity, a note which Victoria couldn't fail to catch.

'But what about Ambrose?' she asked. 'Aren't you in love with him?'

'Ambrose? In love with Ambrose! Just because I've slept with him? I don't have to be in love with a man to sleep with him. I'm sure you've noticed that.'

'Then, you're not going to marry Ambrose?'

Elizabeth turned to her sister, a stern look on her face. 'Now, why in the world should you get that idea?'

'Well,' Victoria started to explain, 'you go to bed with him a lot. Oh, I know what you just said – that you don't have to be in love with him to do that – but you've been sleeping together for so long that I thought by now you would have been fed up with him if you didn't love him. And then. . . .'

'And then what?'

'Well, I know of course you've slept with other men – perhaps even with Constable Fahy, too – but I presumed that was all done to make Ambrose jealous.'

She paused, but did not yet seem to have exhausted her arguments. Elizabeth faced her, waiting.

'And also', Victoria resumed, 'Ambrose has been boasting in the public houses that the two of you are going to get married.'

It was Elizabeth's turn to collapse on to the bed.

'Ambrose has been . . .,' she echoed in stunned amazement. 'Wherever did you hear that?'

'Pat told me. It's all the gossip down in the village.'

Elizabeth was silent for some time.

'Is it not true, then?' Victoria asked. 'You haven't been planning anything? To elope, perhaps. I mean, I saw Ambrose after he returned from the fair today and it looked to me as if he'd had quite a beating, much worse than you made it sound. I thought perhaps that you made a joke of it at dinner tonight so as to fool Mother, to hide your true feelings for him from her. Was I wrong, then?'

'As far as present intentions go,' Elizabeth said jauntily, 'you were wrong. And Mr Ambrose Mercer is wrong, too. He's always pressing me to marry him, but I've always put him off.'

'Is he in love with you then?'

'I don't think Ambrose is in love with anyone but himself. I don't think he's even capable of love.'

'Then why does he want to marry you?'

'Oh, my little sister, you're so naïve. Ambrose Mercer is a nobody, we're somebodies. We have a name, a reputation, land, roots. They may not mean a great deal to me – they don't, in fact – but they would to him.'

'But that mightn't last much longer. Things are changing in Ireland.'

'Oh, nonsense. All this Sinn Fein business is only a storm in a teacup. It'll soon blow over, and the country will return to normal. Our people will always be on top here. And Mr Mercer would very much like to be really one of our people – on top *with* us rather than be just one of our employees. That's why he wants to marry me.'

'And you're certain you don't want to marry him?'

'I'm certain I don't want to marry anyone at the moment. As to how I'll feel in the future – well, I hate predictions. . . .'

Her voice trailed off as she suddenly recalled the fortune-teller's predictions, and a shiver ran through her. Victoria, lying on the bed, noticed nothing but was quick to catch her sister out.

'You made a prediction a moment ago – that everything would get back to normal in Ireland soon. What about that?'

'Oh, that,' Elizabeth laughed, shaking off the memory of what the fortune-teller had seen, 'that's only a general prediction, the sort everyone makes. An opinion more than a prediction. Really I'm much more interested in the present. That's what counts with me – what's to happen tonight or tomorrow is as far as I want to plan.'

'And what *is* going to happen tonight, if it's not too indelicate to ask?' Victoria said lightly, rising from the bed. 'Ambrose Mercer or Constable Fahy?'

'It *is* indelicate to ask,' Elizabeth replied, and added with a laugh, 'and none of your business either, missy. You have a man of your own to worry about.'

Victoria strolled pensively to the door. 'I have a man to worry about certainly, but I doubt that he'll ever be mine. Wouldn't it just make you mad! The first time I find a man I really like and he has to be an Irish Catholic policeman. Ye gods!'

'Well, my girl, gather ye rosebuds while ye may. That's my advice. That's what I'd do in your shoes.'

'I'm not you,' Victoria declared firmly as she opened the door and stepped into the corridor.

'There's no need to sound so pleased about it,' Elizabeth called after her, though in fact she was very glad indeed that there was such a great difference between them.

With Victoria gone, Elizabeth settled down to wait. It certainly would be some hours before the two men returned. They would be full of drink – at least Ambrose would be, but Tom, being in a sense on duty, would probably have been careful to remain fully sober. That pleased Elizabeth; men who were half-drunk, or even only merry, were never much fun, always impatient with love-play, anxious to have her and then go to sleep. That wouldn't suit her at all. Of course Tom would be tired; he already had had a trying day, and keeping Ambrose out of trouble in the pubs with the atmosphere likely to be tense and Ambrose quite possibly making belligerent noises wouldn't allow him a moment's relaxation. But tiredness in a man, as long as it wasn't sheer exhaustion and provided at least the spirit was willing, had never been a problem. What about food? She had nearly forgotten that. He was bound to be hungry. He had missed dinner, hadn't really had a proper meal all day. The poor man would be starving, but that was something she could turn to her advantage. She went to the kitchen, prepared a plate of sandwiches, placed them with a glass of milk on a tray, and put them by his bedside. She smiled to herself: that would satisfy one appetite, and his gratitude would help whet another.

As she passed Ambrose Mercer's door it occurred to her that he would have had no more food than Tom during the day and so was likely to be just as hungry. But he'd be so full of drink that he'd hardly be looking for food, so there was no need to

209

worry about him. Besides, she was still smarting at his cheek in telling people that he was going to marry her. He wasn't in love with her; she believed what she had said to Victoria, that the only person he could love was himself. But what about her? She had never loved a man – only men; loved teasing them, exciting them, wanting them, and then having them. If what she loved was loving, did that not mean that she herself was the only person she really loved – her desires, her urges, her body's hunger? So how much better was she than Ambrose – if she was any better at all? At least he had always been faithful to her, even if it was only lack of imagination that prevented him from being otherwise. Maybe that meant that in his own way he *did* love her. Maybe it also meant that they were well matched.

Elizabeth lay down on her bed, surprised by the thought. The possibility that she and Ambrose suited each other had never previously entered her mind. Now that she considered it, she had to admit that it wasn't really very wide of the mark. Oh, he could be a surly brute and they had their rows occasionally, but usually it was she who provoked the rows with her teasing and her nights with other men. If they were married, that would all have to end. But would it? As long as she was legally bound to him and as long as she continued to satisfy him in bed, would he really care who else she had? Perhaps it wasn't such an out-landish idea after all. She could continue just as she had always done and have Ambrose as her secure future. Maybe even Odron House also, in time. Ambrose was the only one who could run the estate, so obviously they'd live there, and Victoria could live with them until she got married herself. And their mother, too, of course. Amelia wouldn't at all like the idea of having Ambrose as a son-in-law but she'd get used to it in time.

Elizabeth found that thinking about marrying Ambrose was diverting enough to while away the time waiting for Tom Fahy to return. But as the hours passed she grew more and more bored, and once again the scene in the fortune-teller's crystal ball returned to haunt her. What did it mean? Who were the two men? Ambrose, she supposed, could be one, but who was the other? And that red cloud that seemed to engulf the three figures in the end, what could that possibly be?

She was half-asleep when eventually the noise of the men's return made her sit up with a start. She looked at her watch.

Only eleven o'clock. Not too late at all. She'd give Tom plenty of time to have his little snack before the real midnight feast.

She undressed to her slip, sat down at her dressing-table and readied herself, her blood warming with anticipation. Then, when she judged the time had come, she took off her slip, admired her naked body in the mirror, put on her dressing-gown and left the room.

She did not knock on the policeman's door but quietly opened it and looked in. He was standing by his bed with his back to her and, although she had made no sound, he swung around sharply and drew his gun from its holster in the one action. Elizabeth stood stock still without flinching.

'I must say, you're still alert for one who's been on the go all day,' she said, going into the room and ignoring the raised gun.

He reproved her sternly. 'Don't ever come into my room like that if you value your skin.'

She smiled archly. 'It would rather spoil the night if you had shot me. For both of us – in more ways than one.'

'A pity these old houses don't have keys in their bedroom doors. That would help a lot.'

'Don't worry. No one else will come in. You needn't fear we'll be disturbed.'

'Just as well, isn't it?' he said, dropping on to the bed.

She saw the tray she had left on his table, the sandwiches no longer there but the milk hardly touched.

'You haven't finished your milk,' she said.

He laughed.

'Whoever left that doesn't know much about policemen. It was very welcome, apart from the milk. I don't like milk, except in a cup of tea.'

'As a matter of fact it was *I* left the food. I thought you might be hungry. I'm sorry I hadn't anything stronger for you to drink.'

'Apology accepted, and it was very good of you to think of my well-being. It was very tasty.'

'Good,' Elizabeth replied. 'I'm glad. But I also thought you'd be in bed by now.'

'Ah, sure there was no rush. Did you come to tuck me in, then?'

'Yes, but now I can do better than that. I can actually put you to bed.'

'That will be a new experience for me.'

'Have you never had a woman put you to bed before?' she asked.

'Not since I was a nipper,' he replied. 'And the woman was my mother. I see you're about ready for bed yourself.'

Elizabeth looked into his eyes. He was still sitting on the bed, looking up at her as she stood in front of him.

'As you say,' she replied. 'About ready for bed.'

Smiling at him, her eyes half-closed, she slowly opened the cord of her dressing-gown and gradually eased the gown off her shoulders, allowing it to slide down to the floor. Tom Fahy drew in his breath sharply.

'Jesus!' he whispered and swiftly crossed himself.

'Oh, no,' Elizabeth protested. 'Surely you're not outraged.'

'Outraged?' Tom echoed in a puzzled voice.

'You made the sign of the Cross, didn't you? Was that to drive away the Devil?'

Tom burst into laughter.

'Ah, sure that was because I took the Lord's name in vain. I wasn't thinking of driving you away, devil though you are.'

'Well, that's a relief. Come along, then.'

She unbuckled his holster, letting it fall behind him on to the bed, and she bent towards him to unbutton his coat. Her breasts, like two cherry-tipped exotic fruits, offered themselves to him, their intoxicating scent an irresistible message. Tentatively he leaned forward to put his face between them. He felt Elizabeth's hand at the back of his head, pressing him into her. He turned just enough to urge one of her nipples into his mouth. It hardened instantly as his tongue caressed it, and he was aware of her free hand struggling to open his trouser buttons.

'Come on,' she whispered. 'Let's get you undressed.'

Speaking no words, together they made him naked and then sank back on to the counterpane, their bodies entwined each to each.

Almost an hour later, Ambrose Mercer, still fully dressed, suddenly rose off his own bed where he had been lying brooding on the events of the day. Gingerly he fingered the cuts

212

on his face, still tender and sore. But the fight with O'Halloran was not uppermost in his mind. If that damned policeman hadn't hampered him, O'Halloran would never have put him down and there'd have been a far different outcome to the struggle. Curse Fahy – he was the real enemy now; he was the danger with the way he was making up to Elizabeth, whispering with her, pressing close into her. And she was fool enough and man-mad enough to welcome all that attention. It was one thing to flirt with house guests and British officers – at least they were British, her own kind, and Mercer knew she'd be back with him when they left the scene. But a bloody Catholic, an Irish policeman – that was another kettle of fish altogether. Didn't she realize that if she let him have his way with her he'd not only tell all his colleagues and spread the story throughout Gortnahinch, but he'd have to tell it in Confession, too? It was galling – a common Irish bogman to be canoodling with her! He'd not stand for it. He had been patient long enough. It was time to make her knuckle down before she gave Fahy any further encouragement, time to tell her what was what, to make her realize that he wasn't going to give her up. And, by God, while he was at it she'd make up to him, too, for the frustrations and annoyances she had made him suffer since Fahy had come to Odron House.

Determinedly Mercer strode into the corridor and without thought or hesitation threw open Elizabeth's door. If she was asleep, no matter. She could bloody well wake up, listen and submit.

The room was empty, the bed undisturbed. Ambrose Mercer stared at it. Shock, anger, humiliation coursed through him. Was he too late? Was the bitch nuzzling with that Irish dog already? He whirled around and rushed to Constable Fahy's room, putting an ear to the door to listen. What he heard confirmed his suspicions. Slowly he returned to his own room, struggling to suppress his rage. All right, Constable, all right, then, enjoy your night, because you'll not have another one like it. I'll see to that. One way or another, Constable bloody Thomas Fahy, I'll do for you. One way or another, I'll get you.

If frustration and anger kept Ambrose Mercer awake most of the night, it was elation and a feeling of deep satisfaction that banished sleep from Charles Renfrew. Around midnight he had been sitting up in bed reading, when he thought he heard footsteps approaching his front door. He waited, but there was no further sound. Unconvinced, he donned a dressing-gown, took a gun and a torch from a drawer and quietly crept downstairs. At the bottom of the stairs he was able to see a piece of paper that had evidently been pushed through his letter-box. He took up the note, shone the torch on it, and read. Three words were written there – 'You were right' – followed by the bare initials 'T.O'H.'

11

ON FRIDAY MORNING Ambrose Mercer had his usual early breakfast, but to Tom Fahy's surprise and relief he took himself back to his own room instead of making his morning round of the estate. He refused to have any conversation with the constable, giving him no reply even when he was bade 'Good morning'. Tom supposed he was still smarting over the previous day's ignominious defeat by Tim O'Halloran; the cuts on his face looked raw, like his pride, not having begun to heal. Tom wasn't upset by the change of routine. He'd be very glad of a rest after last night, and particularly as Elizabeth had warned him to be ready for her again that night. So he'd be more than happy to stay in the house all day if that was what Mercer wanted.

Ambrose Mercer, however, had no intention of staying in his room all day. As soon as he judged that breakfast would be over for everyone and Amelia would be busying herself in the sitting-room, he made his way there.

She looked up in surprise when he entered. For a moment she was confused – his usual morning visit to her to report on the estate took place on a Saturday, and at the end of the month. Was today Saturday? Surely it was Friday. Surely she hadn't skipped a day. And it wasn't the end of the month, either.

'Are you looking for me?' she asked.

'Yes.' His tone was curt, almost threatening. 'I have something to say to you and you'd better listen.'

Amelia stiffened in her chair. That tone sent a chill through her. Eighteen long years before, when, after her terrible night of shame, she had spurned his further advances, he had used the same tone, almost the same words. 'Listen,' he had said then, 'you'd better listen.' And now it was echoing in her ears again, after all that time: 'I have something to say to you and you'd better listen.'

'What?' she asked, her voice steady but her body quivering like a leaf.

'I'm going to marry Elizabeth. We're going to be married.'

She made no reply. Thought froze, as if her mind had been bundled into a box and a lid closed on it. Her lips refused to open. Her eyes were locked, staring straight ahead at the scene of warm swaying nature outside the window. Only her heart continued to beat, its persistent pulse telling her that she was still alive and would have to live through the awful future Ambrose Mercer was threatening.

'Do you hear me?' he repeated. 'Elizabeth and I. I'm going to marry your daughter.'

'Never,' she breathed. She did not turn to face him. So quietly had she spoken that her reply sounded not so much for him as for herself. Then suddenly she swung around and thundered at him: 'Never!'

The very force of determination in her voice made him recoil. He had not expected such ferocity. But he was glad of it – it satisfied his thirst for revenge for the humiliation Elizabeth had made him suffer. The more he could hurt, the more pleasure it gave him. All the long years he had spent at Odron House – what was he but a tolerated underling? Trained to serve the colonel, respond to all his instructions, do his bidding as if he was still in the Army and under his command. And, when the colonel died, used at first by his widow to manage the estate and keep her in luxury until the time her need made him for one night truly her master, made him believe that that mastery was at last to be his permanently and as of right – only to have his belief shattered when her lust had been satisfied. Then to be treated as a plaything by her daughter, taken up when there was no one else to satisfy *her* hunger, and tossed

216

aside at her slightest whim for any and every casual half-capable male who might arrive on the scene, be he soldier, sailor, civilian, or even the dregs of the common native horde. These Odrons! They considered themselves gentry! They were looked up to as 'the quality'! He knew well what sort of quality they were. Well, they'd suffer for all their slights. If he couldn't strike at Elizabeth, not just now anyway, he could strike at her mother. And what better way than to tell her what he knew would cause her most suffering, true or false? It would be true anyway, eventually. By God it would!

'Oh, yes,' he replied calmly, 'marry her I shall.'

'She'd never have you,' Amelia told him in as dismissive a tone as she could manage. 'Not you.' But she was remembering that birthday present he had given Elizabeth – a ring which he had said she could regard as an engagement present if she wished; and, although she had appeared to treat the idea with amusement, she hadn't been insulted or outraged by it.

'Oh, she'd have me all right. I've asked her, you know, plenty of times. She hasn't said yes yet, but she will, because you're going to tell her to, Mrs Odron.'

'*I* tell her! Certainly not.' But Amelia's voice was unsteady. She well knew the threat Ambrose Mercer could make to persuade her to do his bidding.

'Brave words, Amelia Odron. But did you think I had forgotten about our night together? It might have been many years ago, but it's not something I'll ever forget. Or you'll ever forget, either, eh? I've told nobody since then. I've kept silent, not breathed a word. But I'll tell now. I'll tell the whole townland, if you persist in your stubbornness.'

Amelia had lowered her face in anguish into her hands. Her flesh burned with shame and self-recrimination. Only yesterday she had determined to bury the past. What a fool she had been even to think she could bury that part of it! What a fool she had been to imagine that she wouldn't have to pay for it eventually, that one day it wouldn't come back to destroy her.

'You don't dare tell,' she warned spiritedly. 'If you did, Elizabeth would be bound to hear it, and do you think she would marry you then? It would turn her against you.'

Mercer laughed.

'Oh, she'd hear it all right. But I don't think I need worry about her believing it. I'd just deny it, that's all. I'd say it was just a bit of slander put around by the people in the district who don't like me. There are plenty of them, I know that. So I don't think I'd have much trouble convincing her that the story was a lie. And it'd be just as easy for me to convince everyone else that it was true – make no mistake about that. The people here may not like me very much but, by God, if I tell them something, they know they can believe it. So, you see, you have no way round it. Much better for you to have a quiet word with Elizabeth and tell her it's time to settle down and become my wife.'

Amelia felt as if she had been struck dumb. She had never guessed that, crafty and base though he was, he could be capable of such fiendish duplicity. He had it so cleverly worked out. And she knew that, if he set himself about it, he could indeed make Elizabeth believe that black was white while making others believe that white was black. But how could she stop him? What alternative did she have?

'Of course you could tell Elizabeth yourself if you like. If you're so certain it would turn her against me, you could do that.'

He was looking at her, enjoying to the full her agony and humiliation. She could stand him no longer. She had to be rid of him.

'Go away! Get out of my sight!'

'You'll do as I say, then?'

'I'll talk to Elizabeth,' she agreed shortly. 'I'll talk to her. Now, get out.'

Charles Renfrew spent Friday morning at home, feeling happier than he had for many a day. After breakfast he sat in his deep armchair with the previous day's *Irish Times* which had just been delivered. He recalled with a sense of amusement how people who ever visited him from Britain were often surprised – indeed, almost shocked – that the national newspapers were always a whole day late. The fact that they might be had on the day of publication only in Dublin and its surrounding areas seemed to them to confirm their conviction that Ireland was still a primitive country. It justified the prevailing impression they had brought with them from their own bustling cities, busily matching up to what they believed the twentieth century, young though it still was, required of their society, that this island at their back door was really too lazy, too feckless and too unruly also to be allowed to govern itself. When Charles pointed out to them that as the Irish were not, in fact, ruling themselves they could hardly be blamed for the shortcomings of the imperial administration that was running their affairs, they would look at him askance and mutter to each other behind his back that he was letting the side down, that making excuses was just the sort of thing the natives did.

Charles, however, had always felt that there were welcome advantages in getting one's newspaper a day late if one lived in Ireland, and especially if, like him, one was retired. It fitted in with the tempo of life and helped to give the feeling of being away on holiday, for the news in the paper was always stale. These days it was always bad, too, but one always lived in hope, and bad news that was actually stale helped him to sustain hope.

His sense of well-being on Friday morning could not be dispersed by anything he read in the *Irish Times*, for what was more important to him was that his own prospects had suddenly taken on a rosy hue. He felt entitled to congratulate himself on his cleverness, his wisdom, and his boldness of decision. It was almost like planning an inspired but risky battle-manoeuvre that had come up trumps and scattered the enemy. He took the precious note out of his pocket and read it again with a feeling of lightness and anticipation. 'You were right. T.O'H.' His news would surely make Amelia happy as well, presumably resulting in a substantial improvement in her fortunes as soon as all the stolen money was recovered. That might take a little time of course, depending on where it was. Probably in a bank account somewhere in the country. In which case there could be a lengthy legal action to prove Amelia's ownership – unless, of course, a deal could be struck with Mercer not to tell the police as long as he restored his stolen gains and left Ireland. By Jove, that was a good idea! Charles glowed with pleasure at how well he was handling the whole business and how sharply he was dealing with every development. It made him feel young again. And it couldn't but create a powerful impression on Amelia. Bound to do his chances of winning her no end of good. Could hardly fail, in fact.

The first requirement was to find out where the money was. Presumably O'Halloran would call on him during the day to tell him. But when, by lunch-time, there had been no word from him Charles could wait no longer. Action: that was the keynote. He set out for O'Halloran's workshop.

To his disappointment, however, he found that only Myles Barratt was there, and he proved to be very unforthcoming.

'No, I don't know where he is,' he replied to Charles's enquiry.

'He sent me a note last night,' Charles offered, taking the piece of paper from his pocket, to show his credentials as it were. Myles Barratt, however, hardly cast a glance at Charles, keeping his bald head down over his work as he said dourly: 'I don't know anything about that, Mr Renfrew.'

His studied reluctance to encourage the conversation made Charles Renfrew refrain from asking him about the hidden money in case O'Halloran hadn't told him. That seemed to Charles most unlikely, but he concluded it was foolish to assume anything where these Sinn Fein boys were concerned. They were, after all, an illegal and secret organization; one simply had no idea what their chain of command might be or how much any one of them might know about another's activities, even if they were both lifelong friends and working under the same roof.

'Any idea when Mr O'Halloran will be back?'

'He didn't say.'

'I suppose he could be gone to find me. I might have misssed him. Perhaps I should wait.'

Myles Barratt looked up. 'Well, as to that, since he didn't say where he was going, I don't know where he might be. And, since he didn't say when he'd be back, you might have a long wait.' He paused as if to let his discouraging advice sink in, and then, in case he might seem to be too unaccommodating, added: 'But you may please yourself about that.'

Charles grunted. It was obvious that he would get nothing out of the man.

'Well, when he comes back, please tell him I was here. Tell him I expect to hear from him.'

'I'll do that,' Myles Barratt answered, his tone more friendly now that his visitor was about to leave.

But Charles did not leave immediately. Instead he sat in his trap for ten minutes, hoping that Tim O'Halloran might show up. When he didn't, he reluctantly returned home, keeping a sharp look-out all along the way. But there was still no sign of O'Halloran; nor had he called while Charles was out; nor had he sent any message.

Charles settled down for the afternoon, certain that word from O'Halloran would not be long delayed. He was impatient to go over to Odron House and tell Amelia the good news but unwilling to do so when he had only half the story. After all, all he could show was a cryptic note from O'Halloran. If Mercer had been stealing from her, she would surely ask 'Where is the money?' And Charles didn't know.

The afternoon passed, he still didn't know, and now he was beginning to feel worried. O'Halloran had confirmed his suspicions about Mercer, but now Charles was beginning to have suspicions about O'Halloran. The terseness of his note began to take on an ominous significance that Charles had not given any thought to before. Why hadn't it said where the money was? It would have been natural for it to have conveyed that information. There could be only one reason: O'Halloran had no intention of letting Charles know where to find the money. He was going to take it for the Sinn Fein cause. That was surely it. He would almost certainly regard it as money squeezed out of land that rightly belonged to his countrymen and so the money, too, belonged to them. As soon as the explanation occurred to Charles he had an unassailable intuition that once again his reasoning was correct. But this time his logic gave him no pleasure at all.

When Ambrose Mercer left Amelia sitting in her armchair after his ultimatum, she stayed there so silently, so motionless, that she might have taken root there. Even her eyes, which were fixed on the scene outside the window – the perfect lawns, the friendly trees, the warming blue sky – remained still. No swooping bird drew them to its course, no buzzing wasp awakened them from their locked gaze. Only her mind was active.

Her initial inclination, once she was alone, was to retreat, to flee to her bedroom where she had spent so many years cocooned between its protecting walls and anaesthetized from Time's advance by the memories it enshrined. Had she been able to recover the immediate power of her limbs, she would have left her chair and rushed there. But even while she was waiting to gather her strength her mind began to work its own salvation. What was uppermost in her thoughts was the irony of the situation. How bitter life could be! Just when she had at last, after so long, resolved to turn aside from the past, it had returned to crush her. What was it about life that could make it so cruel? Was it that, once deserted, it exacts its revenge on anyone who seeks a way back? 'When you had me, you didn't want me, so now you can stay with your past.' That's what it was saying, and back again she was being thrown into the lonely cell of the years that were gone.

After many minutes Amelia rose to her feet and forced herself to take stock. Her head turned towards the door: that way lay the quiet hall, the beckoning stairway, the bedroom that would welcome her back and shield her as it had always done with its treasury of symbols and memories. But how could it protect her now? Its memories were impotent against this new threat, its symbols but ciphers, even the dream house that had hung on its wall was no more.

She turned away from the door and once again looked out the sitting-room window. She saw a world out there, nature on parade, proud and resplendent. Rooms and walls were but bricks and mortar, without life, devoid of sap. Almost unaware of her progress, so automatically did her movements respond to long-forgotten surroundings, she found herself in the Odron gardens. Instantly, she was dazzled by their colour, bewildered by their variety. She knew that winter would see them numb and denuded, sunk in a frozen torpor that would spread its ugly skin over them; and then, next summer, they would be gloriously triumphant once again. Just as they were now after last winter. Just as they had been every summer despite the deadly clutch of each preceding winter.

She wandered among the trees, leaned against the strong fortress of their trunks that repelled the anger of the winter's worst storms, ran her hand over the rough grooved bark that

222

protected the life inside them. They were sturdy, they held firm. She rested awhile beside the stream, refreshed by its liquid-vowelled chatter; she strayed to the edge of the pasture and studied the animals – cows tearing at the grass and then lifting their heads to stare about them as they chewed, horses wheeling and cavorting, one putting its nose against another's head as if discussing their next game. In the distance she saw Victoria and Constable Howell sitting together and she stood watching them until the policeman suddenly arose and gave his hand to Victoria to help her up. Amelia was not surprised by what happened next. A flash of intuition prepared her for what seemed to be a long-held tableau of the two of them standing facing each other, hands linked, then the slow, almost reluctant coming together of their bodies, as if despite themselves they were having to submit to a force they could not resist, and then the embrace, the quick fearful kiss that would not be refused, and the further long embrace full of joy, hope and unutterable poignancy.

As all this was happening Amelia stood and watched, surprised by none of it, shocked not at all. In her mind was a picture of another couple – a girl and a tall cheeky soldier meeting under such a hot summer sun many years ago. True, Constable Howell was a policeman, not a soldier; but then she herself had been an ordinary shopkeeper's daughter while Alex was well born with – how many was it? – five Christian names. If Amelia had to choose between the two couples, Victoria and Constable Howell as against Elizabeth and Ambrose Mercer. . . . Oh God, if only she were given such a choice! She saw them move slowly off, still hand in hand, towards the house. They would go in to lunch, and if she joined them – if anyone joined them – they would endeavour not to catch each other's glance, behaving with restraint and propriety, as if there was nothing between them, as if their hearts and bodies were not bursting with the force of their desire for each other and their longing to be alone. Well, let them enjoy their discovery and excitement to the full. Amelia hoped they might be lucky enough not to have to share the lunch-table with anyone else. She, at least, would not disturb them. Besides, she wasn't hungry. Food was the furthest thing from her mind.

223

Sergeant Driscoll stood by his wife's bedside gazing down at her sleeping figure. Her black hair was arranged neatly around her face like a dark frame etched against the snowy whiteness of the pillow. Her face itself looked calm and unworried, and her arms were outside the counterpane, lying motionless at her sides. Many times in the last few days the sergeant had thought the worst thing that could happen was not that Lucy should have another still-birth, but that in trying yet again to give both of them a child she would be overcome by the effort and die. In such black moments he saw her as he was seeing her now, as he had in his time seen many a corpse – stretched out on its back on a neat bed, eyes closed, hair groomed, lifeless and still. But, God be thanked, this was not the way with Lucy; nor, according to Dr Harvey, was there any fear of such a tragedy. For Lucy was herself alive, and their child inside her was alive, too. But keep your fingers crossed, Dr Harvey had advised. Nothing should go wrong at this stage, he had said, but on the other hand nothing could be taken for granted. The sergeant would realize that. A man in his position and with his experience of life and its pitfalls. Sergeant Driscoll had nodded and said nothing. There was nothing to say unless a prayer.

He looked down at his wife and, though his lips did not move, he was praying. Then he turned, made silent nods of farewell to the other patients, and slowly picked his steps out of the ward, careful not to let his boots creak until he was back in the corridor.

The knock on the door surprised Elizabeth. It could only be Tom Fahy, for she couldn't imagine that anyone else would be looking for her an hour before dinner – except, possibly, Victoria.

'Come in,' she called.

She was sitting at her dressing-table and she swung round in amazement at what she saw reflected in the mirror. But there was no mistake, no distortion; her mother stood on the threshold.

'What is it? Is there something wrong?'

'May I come in?' Amelia said, the false brightness in her voice failing to disguise her embarrassment.

'Of course.'

224

Amelia closed the door behind her and smiled at her daughter. Then she stood and looked around the room as if, it occurred to Elizabeth, she was seeing it for the first time. But she is, Elizabeth thought wryly, at least for the first time in many years.

'To what do I owe the pleasure . . .?' she asked lightly, unable, even in the face of this mysterious visit, to suppress her teasing disposition.

Amelia leaned back against the door and sighed.

'Is it a pleasure?' Now that she had taken the first step, she did not know how to go on. It wasn't going to be a pleasure for her, nor for her daughter, either.

Elizabeth laughed and turned on her seat.

'Well, pleasure or not, don't hang about at the door. Come in. Though I can't pretend that it isn't a shock to see you.'

Amelia went and sat on the end of the bed. She could feel her legs and arms quivering with nervousness.

'That's what I like about you, Elizabeth,' she said. 'You don't pretend. You say what you think, straight out. Your father was like that, too. It's the sign of a passionate person. Are you passionate?'

Elizabeth blinked, quite taken aback.

'What a strange question!'

'Yes, I suppose it is. Especially for a mother to have to ask her grown-up adult daughter.'

'Why do you want to know?' Elizabeth asked, wondering if somehow Amelia had learned about her paramours and had come to rail at her. Her mother didn't appear to be nursing any anger, however; but, then, Elizabeth was conscious that she knew as little about Amelia as Amelia knew about her.

Her question received no answer. Instead her mother went on: 'I like passionate people, the sort who speak their mind, who don't keep you in the dark. I suppose that's because I'm the sort of passionate person who keeps things all bottled up so long that they become bitter. And quite poisonous, too.'

Elizabeth remained silent. Her mother passionate? What on earth was she getting at?

'Victoria, is she passionate, too? I think she may be. Not the way you are, of course. She's not quite as outspoken, is she? And not the way I am, either, although she does tend to live in her mind.' Amelia paused, then resumed. 'I saw her in the garden this morning. I was taking a walk. The weather has been so wonderful, hasn't it? I thought I really shouldn't waste it. She was with one of the policemen, the younger one, Constable Howell.'

So that was it! She had come to talk about Victoria. God knows what she had seen her sister and the policeman up to! But surely not, not Victoria, no matter how much she had fallen for him. And, anyway, that young man was clearly too innocent to make improper advances.

'They appeared to be in love,' Amelia said suddenly. She looked up at her daughter. 'I suppose it's not altogether surprising. Two young people thrown so much together the way they have been – Victoria has known hardly any men. I do hope she'll be sensible about it. I do hope she'll not get hurt.'

So that was it, Elizabeth thought. That was the purpose of her mother's visit – to suggest Elizabeth have a quiet word with her sister. Perhaps she felt that gentle discouragement, mixed with sympathy, no blatant disapproval, and coming from Elizabeth rather than from herself, would be the best sort of dissuasion. Clever: Amelia was not, when it came to it, as out of touch as Elizabeth had thought.

It was not Victoria, however, who was the subject of her next enquiry.

'Have you ever been in love, Elizabeth?' she suddenly asked.

All Amelia's conversation in the few minutes she had been in the room was so baffling, so unpredictable, that the question did not surprise Elizabeth as much as it might have. Nevertheless her experience of love was not a topic she felt quite ready to discuss with her mother.

'I don't know,' she answered, adding unthinkingly: 'How does one recognize love?'

'If you can ask that, then you haven't been,' Amelia declared firmly. 'I know. I was in love once. With your father of course.'

Elizabeth was bewildered. That was the second time her father had been referred to, twice more than her mother had spoken of him in goodness knows how many years. What on earth had come over her? Did she at last want to break her silence about him? Perhaps if Elizabeth gave her some encouragement. . . .

'I'm sure you were. After all, you did marry him,' she said.

'Yes. But that doesn't always prove anything. I mean, so many people marry for reasons quite other than love.'

Elizabeth made no comment. That piece of wisdom certainly struck a chord. But Amelia had got up and seemed not to know what to say or do next. She moved over to the dressing-table and stood beside her daughter. Looking down, she saw Elizabeth's sapphire ring lying there. She took it in her hand.

'Do you love Ambrose Mercer?' she asked sharply, almost accusingly.

Elizabeth burst out laughing.

'What makes you think I might?' she countered. She supposed Amelia's question was the kind a mother was entitled to ask; but, then, hadn't Amelia long ago forfeited her right to such information?

'Well,' Amelia answered, 'this ring. I know it was a birthday present, but didn't he say you could regard it as an engagement present also if you wished?'

'He did. But I don't see why I should let Ambrose get away with being such a miser.'

'Does that mean that you'd expect another ring for your engagement? Does it mean that you intend to marry Ambrose Mercer, Elizabeth?'

Elizabeth immediately sensed the marked change of tone. Amelia's voice was strained, almost at breaking-point. This, then, must be the real purpose of her visit.

Elizabeth remained silent. She saw, in the mirror, the expression on her mother's face, the anxiety in her eyes. Of course as a mother she was entitled to know if her daughter had any thoughts of marriage. But why did she want to know *now*?

The silence and the waiting proved too much for Amelia.

'Well, Elizabeth, tell me,' she insisted. 'Are you going to marry Ambrose Mercer? I have to know.'

'I don't know. I might,' Elizabeth answered, her tone clearly conveying that the question held no urgency for her. But her answer caused Amelia even greater agitation. She put a hand on her daughter's shoulder, squeezing it painfully.

'No, Elizabeth. That won't do. You *must* tell me, yes or no. Surely you know by now whether you intend to marry him or not.'

227

Elizabeth felt her mother's nails biting into her skin, and her body flinched. Amelia, realizing that she was hurting her daughter, took her hand away.

'I suppose I *might* marry Ambrose. It's not impossible. It isn't as if there's anyone else on the horizon, is there?'

Amelia turned and stood with her back to her daughter. There was a long silence. Elizabeth remained sitting. She was certain the conversation was not over. She was certain her mother had more to say.

Eventually Amelia turned back to her and, as if having to force out the words, she said: 'You must not marry Ambrose Mercer, Elizabeth.'

'And you must not be such a snob, Mother,' Elizabeth retorted sharply. Ambrose, of course, wasn't born in their class, and he was their estate manager – an employee – but, for goodness' sake, he had been at Odron House almost as long as Elizabeth, even almost as long as Amelia herself. He was hardly on a par with their plumber or groom or one of the labourers. And Elizabeth wasn't going to be told by anyone whom she might or might not marry. Whoever it would be, it was she, not her mother, who'd have to live with him.

'I may be a snob, Elizabeth,' Amelia answered quietly, 'but that's not why I don't want you to marry Ambrose. I give you my word on that.'

Elizabeth was surprised, but when she turned from the mirror to face her mother it was instantly clear to her from Amelia's expression that she was telling the truth.

'I believe you,' she said. 'But obviously you have *some* reason, and I'm entitled to know what it is. That's not an unreasonable request, is it?'

Amelia passed a hand over her eyes. It was an uncharacteristic gesture and plainly revealed to Elizabeth the stress under which her mother was labouring.

'No, that's not an unreasonable request. Not at all unreasonable,' she replied, as if she was trying to think ahead, to work out what she'd say next. 'And it isn't that I want to avoid it,' she went on. 'Really it isn't – but when I've told you, you may wish you had never asked.'

Amelia sat on the bed, her hands clenching the coverlet on either side of her. She lowered her eyes, refusing to meet her daughter's puzzled look.

Elizabeth waited. The warning made her experience a sudden chill. She remembered a similar sensation in the fortune-teller's tent.

After a long pause Amelia lifted her head again.

'Please don't look at me while I'm telling you,' she begged. 'Please look away until I've finished.'

The force of her plea touched a chord in Elizabeth. It almost made her spring to Amelia's side and promise that she wouldn't marry Ambrose Mercer just so as to save her even more agony and anguish. But something restrained her, some intuition that what she was to hear would not only explain the mystery of her mother's long isolation but would also establish between them the bond they had never had.

'All right, Mother,' she whispered, turning fully round on her seat so that her back was to both Amelia and the mirror which still reflected every detail of her distress.

'You never knew your father,' Amelia commenced quietly. 'I don't suppose you even remember him, you were so young when he died.'

Elizabeth was about to interrupt, to say that she did indeed have some recollection, some picture in her mind of what her father was like. But how could she be sure that the recollection was real, that it wasn't a figment of her imagination based on the photographs downstairs of the tall fair-haired military figure? She said nothing.

'I never forgot him. You see, I loved him.'

Amelia gave a tiny wry laugh.

'That must seem a peculiar thing to say,' she continued. 'I mean, you'd expect me to love him, wouldn't you? But I didn't just love him – and he didn't just love me, too. We lived for each other. We were young, we had energy, we were full of passion. It's so important, Elizabeth, in a marriage – passion, I mean. Oh, I'm not making myself clear. This is so difficult.'

Elizabeth was about to turn to her mother, but Amelia checked her sharply.

'No, no, don't turn round. Don't look. I must tell you.'

There was another pause before the story was resumed.

'If I say we made love, I don't know how much you'd understand from that. I mean about how it was between your father and me. I know I've never spoken to you about . . . about sex. Mothers are supposed to tell daughters about that sort of thing but, then, I wasn't much of a mother. But you're a young woman already, Elizabeth, and these days . . . the war . . . things like that . . . all the people we used to have in the house . . . soldiers . . . others. I never bothered – I suppose I just decided that one way or another you'd learn by experience. Maybe you did. I don't know.'

Amelia paused, and Elizabeth thought how blind her mother must have been not to have seen that the person who could really teach her about sex was there, under her own roof, long before any soldier or other visitor entered her life.

'I don't know,' her mother repeated. 'I don't want to know. I mean whether you did learn. I know mothers prefer their daughters not to have . . . to be virgins until they marry.'

Amelia broke off. Elizabeth could tell that she was embarrassed and confused. Her next words confirmed it.

'Oh God, what am I saying?'

She got up from the bed and went to face her daughter, sinking down on her knees and taking Elizabeth's hands in hers.

'Perhaps I should just come straight out with it. I've been a coward long enough. And trying to talk to your back is a coward's way – not that it makes it any easier, either.

'Elizabeth, when your father died I was desolate, completely distraught. For that first year it was hell for me, not only because I had no husband and was left with two very young children, but also because. . . .'

She held Elizabeth's hands tightly.

'Because I had no one in my bed. No one to make love with. Do you understand me? No, don't say anything. You see, my dear, I was so used to making love with your father – night or day, it didn't matter. He was perfect . . . well, perfect that way. Without him I was bereft, starved. It nearly drove me mad, just the longing. And then, about a year after he died, one night. . . .'

She looked into Elizabeth's eyes, her own face twisted with remorse, her eyes brimming with tears. Elizabeth stared at her, a growing premonition gripping her thoughts.

'One night, he came to my room. . . .'

Elizabeth opened her mouth to ask 'Who?' but before she could Amelia had told her.

'The man who wants to marry you. Ambrose Mercer. He came to my room. Oh, I could say that before then he had tried to help me, to offer me sympathy and comfort. I think he did . . . I don't remember. But it wasn't for his sympathy that I took him to my bed. It was for . . . for his body. Yes, for that. I made excuses to myself of course. In the darkness I pretended that it was Alex – your father – beside me. Yes, I was that mad. But when it was over I couldn't pretend, could I? I hated myself. I've hated myself ever since that night for what I did.'

Elizabeth was about to speak, but Amelia wouldn't let her.

'No, that's not all. There's more. Oh, I didn't sleep with Ambrose Mercer again. He tried to make me of course. He said he wanted to marry me. Yes, Elizabeth, he wanted to marry me. Do you know why? Not because he loved me. Oh, no, love means nothing to him. Greed is his god. He wanted to take Alex's place not because he wanted *me* but because he wanted Odron House. His ambition, once Alex was dead, was to become master here. So he took advantage of my grief and loneliness. He knew how to run the estate and how much I relied on him for that, so he thought that by compromising me I'd have to marry him and he'd be made for life. He was wicked, Elizabeth. Wicked, crafty – and foolish, too, because if he had acted honourably, and taken his time, who knows . . .? But I hated him for what he had done to me. I tried to dismiss him. I told him to go, but he threatened that if I insisted he'd tell everyone about the night he had spent with me. I couldn't face that. I couldn't bear the idea of all the people here, who admired Alex, knowing what a slut his wife was. I couldn't bear what it would do to his reputation and to his memory. So I said no more. I allowed Mercer to stay on as estate manager but I was never familiar with him again.

'Now you know why he wants to marry you. He believes that's the only way he could become master here eventually. Without you as his wife he'd have no chance. And that's why he came to me today and threatened once again to tell people what happened if I didn't try to persuade you. Now you know why you mustn't marry Ambrose Mercer, ever.'

The two women looked into each other's eyes, Elizabeth gripping her mother's hands hard, Amelia still on her knees like a supplicant.

With a sob Elizabeth leaned forward and put her arms around her mother, hugging her fiercely. Wordlessly the two of them held each other in shared understanding and compassion, until Elizabeth suddenly disengaged from the embrace, an expression of consternation on her face.

'But if I reject him', she said, 'won't he tell his story anyway?'

'Let him,' Amelia answered, rising. 'I'll just have to face it. As long as you never become that man's wife, that's all that matters to me.'

Yes, but I've been that man's mistress for years, Elizabeth thought. And I can't possibly tell you that. But what if *he* tells you? He certainly would if I turned him down.

'Look, Mother,' she said, 'he's been asking me to marry him for years, and I've always put off giving him an answer. I can do so for a while longer until we've had a chance to think about how to keep him quiet permanently. I can tell him you've spoken to me and I'm seriously thinking about it. That will stop him annoying or threatening you. Don't worry, Mother, we'll think of something. We'll take care of Mr Ambrose Mercer between us.'

Amelia rose but she could not speak. She just nodded, and as she did so her tears ran down her cheeks and fell on Elizabeth's hands.

Ambrose Mercer was not yet completely satisfied with the day's business. Certainly he had taken a step forward in confronting Amelia, but there was still Constable Fahy to attend to. What was really galling was that but for himself the damned policeman wouldn't be in Odron House at all. If he hadn't concocted that story about being shot at, Amelia wouldn't have demanded that Sergeant Driscoll send out somebody to protect them. It seemed the best way at the time of keeping Amelia from running off to Charles Renfrew. And it was a good plan, too; it would have worked like a charm but for Elizabeth's behaviour. Well, it wouldn't be long before he had her tamed and trussed up. With Amelia's help – and what alternative had she but to do his bidding? – Elizabeth would soon be brought to book. But he'd have to get rid of that policeman first. As long as Fahy was on the premises to provide amusement for her, the harder it would be to put an end to her gallop and make her agree to become engaged to him. Well, there was nothing like striking while the iron was hot. He had dealt with Amelia; it was time to deal with Constable Fahy.

He knew the policeman would be hanging around somewhere in Odron House, ready to keep on his tail like a stupid little puppy if he as much as stepped out to the front door. He left his room and went down to the hall. He could hear voices in the sitting-room and he opened the door to look in. Victoria was in there, sitting with the other policeman, Howell.

'Where's Fahy?' he asked roughly.

'I left him in his room a while back,' Pat Howell said, turning. 'Have you tried there?'

Without a word Mercer retraced his steps back up the stairs. Face set, he strode determinedly towards Constable Fahy's room. At the door he paused to listen. He heard nothing. Fahy might be in there alone, or Elizabeth could be there with him. If they were in bed together, they wouldn't be making much noise. There was no point in giving them any warning. Without knocking, Mercer threw open the door and went in.

Tom Fahy looked up in surprise. He was lying on his bed, smoking a cigarette. His tunic coat was thrown over a chair, and Mercer noted that his gun and holster were lying on top of it.

The policeman took the cigarette out of his mouth but did not get up from the bed.

'Come in, Ambrose,' he said. 'Were you wanting me?'

'I don't want *you*,' Ambrose Mercer replied tartly. 'I just want a word with you.'

Tom Fahy smiled. 'Begob, Ambrose, you have a bit of wit in you after all. Well, I'm at your service. What is it you've got to say? Shut the door and speak your spoke.'

Mercer, however, took no notice of the request but remained standing in the open door.

'I'm going to telephone your sergeant and tell him that there's no need for you and your friend to be here any more.'

Tom Fahy said nothing. He stubbed out his cigarette, got up off the bed and walked towards his visitor. Mercer immediately tensed, flexing his muscles and raising a fist quickly as the policeman's hand shot forward.

233

'You're a bit nervous, Ambrose, aren't you?' Fahy said with a sly grin. 'I was only going to shut the door since you didn't yourself. There's no need for the world and his wife to be hearing our conversation, is there?'

'We won't be having any conversation,' Mercer retorted. 'I've told you what I've decided.'

The constable returned to his bed and sat on its edge.

'You'd be wasting your time. You don't think Sergeant Driscoll would be taking orders from you, do you?'

'I'm sure he'll be glad to have you back with him,' Mercer replied confidently. 'Times like these no doubt he could do with all the men he can get.'

'Oh, you're right there. Even so, he'd not pay any attention to you. Remember, it wasn't you who asked for protection, it was Mrs Odron. Though of course we were more worried about *your* safety, you being the one was shot at.'

Ambrose Mercer snorted in derision. 'Well, that's easily taken care of. I'll just go to Mrs Odron and tell her to telephone the sergeant. She'll listen to me.'

Fahy refused to be rattled.

'I wouldn't know anything about that,' he said noncommittally. 'But you don't know our sergeant very well. He makes up his own mind. He's got many years experience behind him, has Sergeant Driscoll, and it would be my guess that he'd prefer to keep myself and Constable Howell here yet. Seeing the times that are in it like. Do you follow me?'

Mercer remained silent. His eyes burned with anger and resentment.

'Anyway,' Tom Fahy continued, his tone light and easy as if the topic was of no more weight than a casual enquiry about the time of day or whether the weather would hold up, 'the sergeant would want to have a word with me first, as the man on the spot so to speak, before coming to any decision. And I can tell you that my recommendation would be that we stay here until further notice.' The constable paused to let the message sink in. 'Besides,' he went on, 'you could never tell what O'Halloran's boys might get up to if Constable Howell and I left. They might decide that the little altercation you had with O'Halloran yesterday should be followed up. That little affair couldn't have increased your popularity with them, could it? And, sure, even before that they liked you so much that one of them even thought you deserved to join your Maker – with a bullet in the back of your skull. So, all in all, Ambrose, it looks as if you'd be wasting your time telephoning Sergeant Driscoll. And wasting his time, too.'

The sarcasm and increased sharpness of the policeman's final words stung Ambrose Mercer. He stood at the door, undecided, angry at the idea of being bested by Constable Fahy.

'He'd change his mind if he knew that there was no need for you here,' he said aggressively. 'He'd change his mind if he knew that no one shot at me at all. That was only a story I made up.'

Tom Fahy shrugged and stretched himself out once more on the bed. He kept Mercer waiting before he made any reply, extracting another cigarette from the box on the table, searching for the matches, slowly striking one and then taking a few leisurely puffs.

'You don't think that's news, Ambrose?' he said at last. 'Sure I've known that almost since the moment I arrived here.'

Mercer was dumbfounded.

'You couldn't have known it,' he blustered. 'How could you? You're lying.'

Tom gazed up at the ceiling and blew a few ragged smoke-rings. He knew he had Mercer on the run and he wasn't going to surrender his advantage.

'Ah, no, boy,' he laughed. 'You've got it all mixed up. It's you who was lying, not me. Didn't you just say so yourself? Mind you, I don't know why you made up such a cock-and-bull story and I can't prove it was all a yarn, but I don't need to, do I, now that you've admitted it? Still, yarn or not, it'd make no difference to Sergeant Driscoll or to what would be my advice to him. Here I am and, if I have any say in the matter, here I stay.'

'You might not be so sure of yourself if I tell your precious sergeant just why you're so keen to stay here,' Mercer threatened. His voice was low with the barely controlled ferocity of his mood.

There was a long silence while Tom Fahy continued to smoke, as if he hadn't heard what Ambrose Mercer had said.

Then he took two quick drags on his cigarette before topping it, only half-finished, between finger and thumb and depositing it in the ashtray. He swung his legs over the side of the bed and faced his man. Mercer, however, seemed not to take in the storm signals or, if he did, seemed to be determined to ignore them.

'Ah, I thought that might make you change your tune. Don't think I don't know what you were up to.'

'And what is it, friend, that you think I'm up to?'

The question was calm and controlled, but the casual note had gone from Constable Fahy's voice.

'You can't fool me,' Mercer rasped. 'I know damned well you had Elizabeth in that bed with you last night. I may not be able to prove it, just as you can't prove that I wasn't shot at, but I know it's true and if I tell Sergeant Driscoll you'd be out of here pronto. Now, put that in your pipe and smoke it.'

Tom considered Mercer's accusation for a few moments. There was a touch of braggadocio in his voice that suggested he may have regretted the words almost as they were issuing from his mouth.

'I'm not concerned with what you might tell Sergeant Driscoll about me – be it true or false. The sergeant is unlikely, anyway, to believe daylight out of the likes of you. But I'm surprised to hear you saying that sort of thing about the woman you've boasted you were going to marry.'

'And marry her I will,' Mercer asserted. 'Rest assured on that. And when I do there'll be no more playing around by her with any man she can entice into getting on top of her, and certainly not with a common Irish pig who's no better than the rabble that follows O'Halloran. Of course Elizabeth was always fooled by a uniform. I shouldn't wonder that she got a shock when you took yours off for her. The smell of the pigsty and the bog must have fairly knocked her out.'

In one swift action Tom Fahy sprang from the bed, rushed at Mercer and grabbed him by the lapels of his coat. The force of his weight threw Mercer back against the door with a thud.

'I'll take no insults from a guttersnipe Englishman. By God, Mercer, put a snaffle on that tongue of yours or you'll find yourself in right trouble.'

Ambrose Mercer, however, feeling the constable's knuckles

236

digging into his chest, was glad that the argument had come down to force rather than to words. That was the level at which he felt a match and more for Fahy, and with a savage jerk he brought up his knee into his adversary's groin.

The blood drained from Tom Fahy's face, and with a grunt he bent almost double. But he retained his grip on Mercer's coat and, while pretending that he was still in too much distress to take any effective action, he pulled Mercer around with a desperate wrench, pinning him to the floor and returning the compliment by digging his own knee into the latter's groin. Mercer's eyeballs bulged with pain and shock. He struggled furiously to free himself, but Tom held on grimly. Their breath came in pants, and each was grunting with exertion. With a mighty heave Mercer managed to lurch sideways, enough to throw the policeman off balance, and both men wrestled on the floor, trying to regain the advantage over each other.

Suddenly the door burst open and Constable Howell rushed in. Grabbing at Mercer's threshing legs, he locked them together so that Tom was able to get Mercer's shoulders on the ground again, with a knee imprisoning one arm, his right hand holding down the other and his free arm pressing on Mercer's neck under his chin.

'All right, Pat, I have him now,' he said, gasping.

'A good job I came,' Pat replied. 'I knew he was looking for you and I guessed he might start some trouble, so I followed him.'

'Are you going to be a good boy now and go back to your room?' Tom said to his prisoner.

'Damn you,' Mercer answered, his words almost choked with the weight of the arm on his throat. 'You're brave enough with someone to help you.'

'Now, listen, boyo,' Tom Fahy told him, his voice hard and uncompromising, 'any more lip out of you and I'll have to take you into custody and charge you with obstructing a police officer in the execution of his duty. Is that what you want? Because if it is, just say the word.'

Mercer glared at him, but said no word.

'All right then. I'm going to let you up now and I don't want to have any more trouble from you. Understand?'

'Let me up,' Mercer growled truculently, but Tom Fahy

judged that the threat of arrest had brought him to his senses.

'Let go his legs there, Pat,' he ordered, rising himself from the prostrate figure.

Mercer got himself up from the floor.

'You'll hear more about this,' he warned. 'I'm not finished with you yet, Fahy.'

'You are for tonight anyway,' Tom told him.

With a muttered oath Ambrose Mercer left the room, promising himself that one way or another he'd get his revenge.

12

For Sergeant Driscoll the blow fell on Saturday morning.

He had woken and got up in the best of moods. Not that he had slept a great deal during the night, but the cause of his sleeplessness had been neither stress nor worry, but excitement. Try as he might, he had found it impossible to suppress his hopes about Lucy. He had phoned the hospital last thing on Friday night and learned that there was no change in her condition – 'in her very satisfactory condition' was exactly what Matron had said – and in bed afterwards the prospect at last of having a child kept his thoughts buzzing.

After breakfast he filled a fresh saucer of milk for the cat and went to the back door. 'Pish, pish,' he called, 'come on, pussy, breakfast.' But Saucy failed to appear. She'd come in in her own time, he thought, as like as not with a fieldmouse dangling from her mouth to prove she had been up before everyone else. Then the sergeant drank his second cup of tea, wiped his lips, and in leisurely, almost lazy fashion lit up his pipe. It tasted sweet, and the first puff of smoke he exhaled wafted its way up a lightly dusted sunbeam towards the open window.

As he went downstairs to his office he almost felt as if he was wafting along, too, so buoyant was his step. He shut the office door behind him, sat behind his desk, and leaned back in his chair, taking the pipe out of his mouth only to deliver himself of a cavernous yawn that banished the very last of the night's cobwebs from his brain.

Then the blow fell.

He spotted immediately in the sparse Saturday post the single official envelope. There were envelopes such as this every morning, frequently more than one at a time, and more often than not they were of no particular interest or importance. Even when they did contain an official Order, it might not be relevant to his barracks; even if it *was* relevant, it still seldom made much difference to regulations or routines. Yet something told him that was not the case this time. The premonition was so strong that he was quite certain he wasn't making a mistake. Life was at it again, indulging in its little game of coming up with one of its cruel ironies just when he thought things were going really well for him. Probably *because* things were going really well for him.

He opened the other correspondence first – apart from one letter addressed to Constable Howell, no doubt about his Police Union – glanced quickly at it and put it aside. He took up the official envelope and held it in his hands, staring at it for some time. It was no use cursing it up hill and down dale; that wasn't going to change its contents.

With a grunt that was a mixture of resignation and rebellion he tore open the envelope and took out the two sheets of white paper it contained. The top sheet read:

Divisional Commissioner Smyth's Office in Cork
Order No. 5
By Lieutenant-Colonel G. F. Smyth, DC

You are hereby notified of the transfer of constables from Gortnahinch RIC as per attached list effective immediately. All men named in that list are to vacate Gortnahinch RIC barracks by twelve noon on Monday, 16 June 1920, at which time the British military under the command of Captain Chadwick will take possession of said barracks.

[Signed] G. F. Smyth, Lieutenant-Colonel,
Divisional Commander, RIC

Sergeant Driscoll looked at the second sheet of paper, the list of men being transferred. They included every constable serving in Gortnahinch RIC station except two, himself and Tom Fahy.

He sat like a statue for some minutes, unable to move, unable even to contemplate the enormity of what had happened. His worst fear had been realized. All the splendour and promise that he had thought the fine morning presaged had been swept away. And there was nothing – absolutely nothing – he could do about it.

There was a rumble in his stomach, and the acid floated up into his throat. That cursed indigestion again. He might have known it would be lying low, biding its time until it could get him when it would be least welcome.

He laid the Order aside and waited for the spasm to pass. When it had run its course, he tried to concentrate on the dilemma facing him. Should he stay or should he resign? It was a decision on which he knew he should consult Lucy, but how could he at such a time? It would be cruel. It would be mad, too, for the worry could easily cause yet another still-birth. Right or wrong, this was a problem he'd have to decide for himself and by himself – and pray God that he'd make the right decision. At least he had two full days to think about it. Even two full days to act if he decided immediately that there was no place for him in the kind of RIC the Force would become under military command, doing the sort of thing that would mean total loss of authority, pride, self-respect, and perhaps eventually life itself. If that was to be the sum of his conclusions, then it would be wise to tot up that sum and draw the line sharpish so as he could set about finding somewhere to live, somewhere to bring Lucy when she'd come out of hospital, somewhere perhaps – oh God, why now and not earlier? – to bring their gift of a new life also.

As soon as he felt able, Sergeant Driscoll stirred himself and automatically commenced to fulfil his invariable morning routine. He made an entry in the diary recording that the barracks orderly had paraded at 8 a.m., and that a general parade had been held at 9 a.m. Then he realized that these entries were pointless if he intended to resign. He flicked back the pages for the part of the year that had gone – every morning the same, every morning identical entries. Of course in their way they had been meaningless, too. They were all camouflage, all pretence. He never asked what time whoever was barracks orderly for the day had paraded – and what a stupid idea that was, as if one man could or would parade alone, and he certainly hadn't for many years held a general parade – not, at least, the way they had been taught in training school. The men got up around eight, like himself, shaved, had breakfast, and then were ready for the day's duty. The day's duty – ah, the duty roster; they'd be waiting for it in the dayroom, even though it was usually no more than a concoction of routine regulation duties and tasks, most of which were never carried out or needed to be carried out, and were pinned up on the wall only in case an Inspector dropped in unannounced. Well, there wasn't much point in even a bogus duty-roster today seeing that the men were only technically still attached to Gortnahinch barracks. And bugger an unexpected visit from an Inspector – the sergeant felt very much in the mood to take a chance on that.

With a sigh he rose from his desk to take the Order and present it to the men waiting for him in the dayroom. Before doing so he looked more closely at the list of transfers to see where they were being moved. As he expected, they were all being sent to different places, far-off outposts where their real or alleged disloyalty to the Crown would find little on which to focus its opposition and where it might well wither away through sheer boredom. Andy Doyle was destined for County Sligo; perhaps, Sergeant Driscoll thought, they'd consider his Sunday cooking too metropolitan for their taste. Francie O'Leary was being marooned up in County Donegal; that would take the edge off his humour. Kesh caught the sergeant's eye; Aengus Rafferty was aimed there. Kesh, County Roscommon, the little roadside station that had been the sergeant's own first billet. God, he wouldn't mind now being back there himself, with Lucy beside him, with or without a child. But what about Pat Howell, where had they found for him? The sergeant shook his head as he came on Pat's name and destination. The furthest point they could find in the wildest part of the most remote district of the west of Ireland. Another step and he'd be in the Atlantic Ocean. Ah, the cute hoors, they were burying poor Pat and his Police Union for good and all.

Well, what could he expect? Sergeant Driscoll slowly made the few steps across to the dayroom and went in.

The usual good-morning calls greeted him, the usual comments that he had heard, day in, day out, for so long, the usual praise or blame for the weather. Sean Hogan asked if there was any more news of Lucy's welfare.

'Not since last night, Sean,' Sergeant Driscoll answered. He'd telephone the hospital to find out as soon as the unpleasant task in hand was over.

Constable O'Leary noticed that the sergeant held two sheets of paper in his hand instead of the usual one for the duty-roster.

'Looks like you have a busy day for us, Sarge,' he said with a laugh.

'On the contrary, Francie. It looks as if you'll have nothing to do at all.'

He took down the previous day's roster, pinned the two sheets to the wall, and then turned to face his men.

'Sorry, lads,' he said. 'I'm very sorry.' And quietly he returned to his office.

The first thing was to telephone the hospital. He lifted the receiver and waited for Mrs Kelly in the Post Office to get to her switchboard from wherever she might be and ask what number he wanted. He knew there should be no reason to feel tense and nervous; if there had been anything wrong during the night, the hospital would surely have got in touch with him. Nevertheless, it was only when he was at last speaking to Matron to learn that Lucy was doing fine that the thumping of his heart died down.

'She slept well, Sergeant Driscoll,' the sing-song voice told him, 'and she ate her breakfast and she's dozing off again. There's no sign of anything at all happening, but sure you know that's quite usual. With God's help she'll have no trouble at all, and I'll be sure to let you know the very moment you're needed.'

'That's great, Matron. Look now, would you do something for me? When she wakes, would you tell her I'm not certain of being able to get in to see her today. Tell her not to worry if I don't. We may have an Inspector in some time. I'm not sure. I'll have to wait until he comes. If he does come, that is. I might be stuck in the barracks. Lucy will understand. Will you tell her that, please, Matron?'

The sergeant wasn't at all certain he was making sense. It was only on the spur of the moment it had occurred to him that, if he were to visit her today in his depressed state, she would be bound to notice and want to know what was ailing him. He wouldn't be able to keep his worry to himself, and lying to her would be useless; he'd never lied to her, he wouldn't know how, and she'd be sure to catch him out. So better keep away from the hospital until next day, hard though it would be on him. He could telephone again during the day, and later in the evening, too, if he wished. That would have to satisfy him – poor Lucy also.

Immediately he put the receiver down and rang off there was a knock at the door. 'Come in,' he called.

It was Sean Hogan, who, he guessed, had been sent in by the men to discuss the shattering news they had had.

'Sit down, Sean, sit down,' he said.

Hogan lowered himself into a chair. His lined face hadn't lost its usual unflustered expression, but his eyes were restless and troubled.

'Before you say anything, Sean,' Sergeant Driscoll told him, 'I know no more about this than is in that damned paper on the wall. I knew there was a possibility it might happen. It's happened elsewhere. But I didn't want to say anything before. There was no point in upsetting anyone without reason, and sure I hoped the axe would never fall on us. Wishful thinking, I suppose. I can see that now. How are the men taking it?'

Sean Hogan coughed and sighed.

'I don't think it's sunk in yet, John. They asked me to talk to you about it. Sure I know you can't change anything. But it will give them a few minutes to absorb the shock, you know, and when they think on it I daresay one or two of them might be happy enough to remove themselves from the troubles here, once they get over the blow to their pride at being moved at all.'

'I dare say, Sean, I dare say. But, if I know my men, they'd prefer to be allowed to stick it out here. This is their barracks, they're a fine force, and they're proud of their record. They won't want to be torn apart and scattered to the four corners of Ireland. This place has become their home. How will you like it up in Donegal?'

Constable Hogan tossed his head. 'Ah, at my age I'm not

244

ever going to make sergeant, so I won't mind too much. At least you're not being transferred yourself. That must be a relief to you.'

Sergeant Driscoll stared hard for some time at his old friend. Then he pulled open a drawer in his desk, rummaged among the papers in it, and drew out the copy of Order number 5 he had received a few days before. Without a word he passed it across the desk, then took up his pipe and put a match to the tobacco. In between puffs to get the pipe going he looked up at the constable.

'Point Three, Sean, point Three,' he directed. 'That's the killer.'

When Sean Hogan handed back the Order, the sergeant commented; 'You know what that means, don't you?'

Constable Hogan nodded.

'What'll you do?' he asked.

'What *can* I do? I can resign and move out. But where would I go? Where would Lucy and me live? And if we have a child, eh? What about that, Sean?'

The sergeant fell silent. Sean Hogan made no response. He could find nothing to say. His heart bled for the man under whom he had served so long and so happily, the man he respected and, yes, loved.

'I'd best get back to the men. At least Tom Fahy is being left with you. Will you bring him back now from Odron House?'

'I don't think so, Sean. He's needed there, more so now that I'll have to recall young Howell. I'm sorry for that young fellow. I suppose he's too idealistic for his own good. He'd really be better off getting out and trying his luck in America. Still, he's young and strong and ambitious. He'll not let this get him under.'

The sergeant took up the telephone again.

'I suppose I'd better let Fahy know the news and tell him to send Howell back. I'll be in to talk to the men later on.'

Sean Hogan nodded and got up. His eyes met the sergeant's. The look that passed between the two old colleagues said everything they could find no words for.

Amelia was finding it almost impossible to credit what Charles had just told her. Immediately she learned he was paying her a visit she guessed he must have had some pressing reason – he never called on a Saturday. But not in her wildest dreams could she have imagined such news. If it were true, it could mean the end of the awful burden she had been carrying for so long, the end of Mr Ambrose Mercer in her life. That he was an unscrupulous rough-tongued bully she knew to her cost. But a thief? That had never occurred to her. To have been harbouring under her roof all these years someone who was month after month systematically robbing her! What a fool she had been! But she deserved it. If she hadn't been so sunk in self-pity, if she had taken more interest in her affairs and in her family, all this might have been avoided. Why, she could well have learned how to manage the Odron estate herself. It would have taken time, but Charles would have helped her. Sterling Charles! He certainly had proved himself. Armed with his discovery, she could surely now safely get rid of Mercer and let everyone know the reason into the bargain. If he tried to spread his vile story about her among the townspeople, she could treat it with contempt, and no doubt the general opinion would be that he was just making it up to gain his revenge for being unmasked.

'How wonderful of you!' she said, turning to Charles Renfrew. 'I just can't believe it.'

'Well, *I* couldn't believe that the estate here should be doing so badly. It just didn't make sense to me. So I put two and two together, and O'Halloran did the rest.'

'But how much money did he find? Can we be sure it was stolen from me? Perhaps it was just Ambrose's savings – he's been here a long time after all.'

'I don't know how much O'Halloran found; he didn't say. But, if it was only savings, why should Mercer hide it? A crafty beggar like him – he would have put it in the bank, earning interest. No, no, I'm sure it wasn't money he saved.'

'Where did he hide it?' Amelia asked.

'I'm afraid O'Halloran didn't tell me that, either. I've been trying to see him to get more details, but he's a hard one to pin down.'

Amelia was silent for a moment. Then, almost fearfully, she said: 'Charles, you don't think . . .?'

'Think what, Amelia?'

'O'Halloran. . . . I mean. . . . If he got his hands on the

246

money, it might never be seen again. He might keep it all for his cause.'

'Yes,' Charles answered, 'I know what you mean. And I fear our fine friend may be deliberately avoiding me. But I'll keep after him. I'm not going to let him get away with anything.'

'Should we tell the police?' Amelia asked. 'If we don't get the money, I can't possibly make any accusation against Ambrose Mercer, much less dismiss him.'

'I know, I know. But wait until I get hold of O'Halloran and find what he has to say. I'll go out to his place again now. I just called in here to let you know what's happened. I couldn't keep the news to myself any longer.'

Amelia took his hand and touched his cheek with hers. He blushed furiously, and his heart gave a jump of joy.

'You're so good, Charles,' she said. 'Such a good friend.'

'More than just a friend, may I hope?' he suggested almost coyly.

'Of course, Charles. You're much more special than just a friend.'

She went to the front door with him and waved as he drove away in his trap.

'I'll be back as soon as I can,' he called.

Amelia returned to the sitting-room, hope rising in her as it hadn't done for as long as she could remember. Above her head, under the floorboards in Ambrose Mercer's room, the money he had stolen from her continued to gather dust.

13

WHEN TOM FAHY put down the receiver he wished he didn't have to tell Pat Howell the bad news immediately, but as he didn't know how far afield Mercer would drag him that day or how late he'd be getting back he had no alternative. God, the west of Ireland! A man could rot out there and never be heard of again. Pat was a tough and resolute youngster, but that was a pill that would take some swallowing. Tom wished he wasn't the one to have to administer it.

The sergeant had said that Pat could stay on at Odron House over Saturday night. He could hold the fort there on Sunday morning while Tom was getting early Mass and then he could report back to barracks and get a later Mass himself in Gortnahinch. There wasn't any point, Sergeant Driscoll suggested, in dragging him back in a rush; he wasn't due to be transferred until Monday, and a full day would be sufficient time for him to prepare himself for the long journey to the west. Besides, why weaken the Odron House protection a moment earlier than was necessary? Sergeant Driscoll was too long in the tooth – and too long in the district also – not to have learned how quickly even confidential information got around, and he wouldn't put it past O'Halloran to find out about the changeover at the barracks almost as soon as he himself learned of it. If he did, he'd have no difficulty mounting a quick attack on Odron House while Tom Fahy was the only defender left. At least if Pat Howell was still there on Saturday night, O'Halloran would have only Sunday night to take advantage of the changed situation before the military commander made arrangements about reinforcements for Fahy on Monday. That was how the sergeant saw it, and Tom agreed with him.

He got his unpleasant task over with the minimum of fuss and without beating about the bush. To his relief Pat took it well.

'Where are they sending *you*, Tom?' he asked.

'Nowhere. It seems the sergeant and I are to stay in Gortna-hinch, but under the command of the military. Aren't you glad now that at least you won't have to suffer that insult?' Tom made the comment lightly, trying to show his young colleague how to put the best face on his own fate.

Pat, however, didn't need any such hint.

'I'd not stay, Tom,' he said, 'not under these conditions. It's bad enough that we're half-soldiers already, what with having to carry arms and having arms in the barracks, but to put soldiers in command of us on top of that – they might as well put soldiers' uniforms on us altogether and make us take the King's shilling.'

'So you think I should resign, then, is that it?' Fahy asked.

'Oh God, no, Tom. I didn't mean to be telling you what you should do. All I'm saying is that, if it was me, I'd get out.'

Tom Fahy was aware that over the next few days he would have to work out what attitude to take. There was nothing to gain in putting off consideration of the dilemma, and he was happy to discuss his position with Pat. He respected Pat's intelligence; for a young 'un he had a lot of sense.

'Yes, but what would I do if I resigned? And how long can all this fighting continue? If I stay in, I wouldn't be surprised to see things settle down very soon, and then wouldn't I be sitting pretty with a career for life?'

Pat made no reply, but Fahy knew what was in his mind.

'Oh, yes,' he continued, 'you're looking at it from another angle altogether, aren't you? You're thinking of the principle of the thing. Well, I don't have to tell you, Pat, that I don't see it quite the same way as you do. And it isn't that I'm just playing safe. After all, I was willing to join the Police Union if you got it going again.'

249

'Fat chance there is of that now,' Pat interjected.

'I suppose you're right. But at least I was on your side – and for all I know that might still tell against me with the powers that be. But, as I see it, for me resignation-point hasn't been reached yet. I'll wait and see. Remember, once I resign, I can hardly get back in again, can I? If I'm out, I'm out for good.'

'True for you,' Pat agreed. 'And at least, if you've backed the right horse by staying in, you're certain sure to be on a winner. But where will *I* be? Right at the tail end of the field, that's where I'll be. The miserable whipper-in! Oh, they've made sure to put an end to my gallop all right. The west of Ireland, County Mayo. It's like being exiled to Siberia, to be sent out there. It might be fair enough for a short spell, a bit of experience like. But I'll never get out of there, you can be certain of that.'

The despair in his voice troubled Tom Fahy. It was cruel that a young lad like Pat Howell, with all his fine qualities – all his enthusiasm, idealism, loyalty, and his sense of pride in his job – it was cruel that blundering brass-hatted idiots, intent on crushing all individuality, could break him for life.

'Well, what will you do?' he asked. 'Would you resign and go back home?'

'No, never go back home. Resign? I might. But, if I do, I won't go backwards. 'Tis forward I'd be thinking of going.'

'Meaning?' Tom queried.

'Well, if they're going to send me out to the west, I might go further west than they bargained for. Much further west.'

'You could do worse,' Tom said consolingly. 'At least you'd find plenty of Irish there before you.'

'I'll wait and see anyway. And talk to Sergeant Driscoll first and see what he says. I'd better go find Victoria and tell her.'

'Oh ho, oh ho, is that so urgent, then? Has she got her hooks into you already that you have to run to share the news with her?'

When Pat hesitated about answering, Tom Fahy's expression changed from one of teasing levity to surprised gravity.

'Begob, Pat, I'm sorry. I only meant it as a joke, but judging from your face it's more serious than that. You haven't fallen for her, have you?'

Pat endeavoured to throw off any need for concern. As if to put himself in his place, he said disclaimingly: 'Now, wouldn't I be the real gom to think I may have fallen for her! She's a fine girl, I'll grant you, and I won't deny we hit it off from the start, but I wouldn't make any more than that of it.'

Tom Fahy said nothing. Pat Howell's wisdom, he knew, did not extend to affairs of the heart or dealings with the fair sex, but his own did, and he'd have put money on it that Pat's face showed all the signs of a man who had lost his heart.

When Pat went looking for Victoria he found her in her favourite spot, stretched out on her back beside the little stream that bordered the front lawn. By that time the expression on his face had changed from that of a man who had lost his heart to one of a man who had lost everything else as well.

Victoria did not move when she heard his footsteps approach over the grass, but immediately he arrived at her side and stood looking down at her she knew he was troubled.

'What's wrong?' she asked, sitting up quickly.

Pat flopped down beside her, plucked a stem of grass to put in his mouth but then flung it away in frustration.

'Everything. I have to go back tomorrow.'

Victoria felt a shock of disappointment, but the shock also carried a small current of joy that his unexpectedly early departure was the cause of Pat's glum countenance. It was proof of what she meant to him.

'But we'd still be able to meet again, wouldn't we? We'd be able to see each other often.'

Pat gave a derisive grunt.

'Have you ever been to Dunnabaun?' he asked.

'No. Where's that?'

'No. I didn't suppose you had. Well, that's where you'd have to go if you want us to meet again.'

He paused.

'You're not—?' Victoria started before her voice was stilled.

'Being transferred?' Pat cut her short roughly. 'That's what it's called. But banished would be nearer the mark. You see, Dunnabaun is in County Mayo, a wild savage place where no one ever goes and nothing ever happens and divil a soul lives there. Or almost. It's about the furthest point west in the whole country that you'd find a police station.'

251

His litany of gloom awoke a surge of sympathy in Victoria, and she put a hand in his.

'But why?' she asked. 'Why this out of the blue?'

Pat told her about the impending takeover of their barracks by the military and of the mass transfer that was to follow. His new posting, he had no doubt in the world, was chosen as a punishment for his Police Union activities. It was meant to put an end to that for good and all, and to him, too.

'Can't you do anything about it?' Victoria pleaded. She knew the question was pointless; it was really an expression of her stunned despondency at the thought of never seeing him again.

'What *can* I do?' Pat said in despair. 'It's like the Army. You do what you're told.'

'But you can't resign from the Army, you can from the RIC. Plenty have. They're resigning every day, aren't they? The newspaper reports have published the figures. I'm sure I've read them.'

'Oh, yes. Plenty of the lads are unhappy with the way the Force is run. And unhappy about what may become of the RIC in the future, too, if the present troubles continue,' Pat agreed. But he did not go on to discuss Victoria's implication that he might consider resigning, and she did not pursue the point. She knew how much his career meant to him and that, if the question of resignation was at all an option he'd consider, he would need time to think about it. She was tempted to suggest once more that they should go away together, but remembering the derision he had poured on that idea when she had first mentioned it on the picnic, she guessed the time was not yet ripe to bring it up again.

'Couldn't I visit you in Dunnabaun?' she said.

He turned on her in amazement.

'Are you insane, Victoria?'

'No,' she whispered, 'I'm not mad. Unless you think it's mad to fall in love with you.'

Pat stared into her eyes. His thoughts were in confusion, pushing and pulling him, now one way, now the other. He felt that something had ended in his life . . . or had it? That something else was starting . . . or was it? He realized that the turn of events had suddenly given him the challenge of deciding his own future, but with Victoria's warmth and closeness making his heart thump he had no idea how or when he could make such important decisions, much less what they should be. Involuntarily he leaned nearer her, and their shoulders touched. He felt the softness of her flesh against his. The touch seemed to weld them together. Unable to stop himself – unable even to want to stop himself – he threw his arms around her, pulled her down on to his lap and awkwardly, like a frightened schoolboy still learning how to kiss, clenched his lips against hers. Victoria held him, her heart racing for joy. Then slowly she moved her hands up and down his back, drawing out his tension, easing his bewildered nerves, until the pressure of his mouth on hers became lighter and gently their lips began ever so slightly to move in unison with their caressing arms and the kiss became at last a blissful confident celebration of their love.

14

PAT'S RETURN to barracks drew only the most subdued greet-ings from his colleagues. They were sitting around in various poses, a few of them polishing their belts and buckles with a slowness of movement that clearly showed how little else they had to do, others engaged in silent time-wasting tasks or activities that could hardly have distracted them from forlorn contemplation of the morrow.

'I declare,' Pat commented, looking around him, 'but it's like coming into a wake.'

'Sure what else is it but a wake?' Mick O'Malley gave back.

'Where are *you* being buried, then?' Pat asked with a touch of aggression, feeling that wherever O'Malley was being sent he'd really have something to grouse about if he were in Pat's shoes.

'Never mind him,' Francie O'Leary joked, ready, no matter how daunting the future looked, to knock a laugh out of it. 'He's being sent to King's County and he thinks it's an insult to the Irish that a whole county should bear the indignity of a name making it the private property of the British monarch.'

'You might take a look at the list on the wall there, Pat,' Sean Hogan chipped in. 'That'll give you all our whereabouts.'

'And write it all down,' Francie added. 'I don't want my Christmas card from you going astray.'

'How's the bould Tom?' Sean Hogan asked as Pat was

perusing the fateful order. 'He's still in one piece, I gather.'

'Just about,' Pat answered, turning with a shrug. 'I've been seeing precious little of him, he's been so busy keeping step with Mercer.'

'He's more than kept step with him,' Andy Doyle commented. 'Didn't they have a right set-to at the fair the other day?'

'I wasn't there,' Pat replied, 'but Tom told me about it. It wasn't his fight. He was only trying to keep Mercer and O'Halloran apart.'

'Aye, that's what I heard, too,' Sean Hogan agreed. 'Are you going in to see the sergeant? He'll no doubt want a word with you about your time at Odron House.'

'Yes, I'll go in now so. How's Mrs Driscoll?'

'That's the only good news we've had in the past few days,' Francie O'Leary told him enthusiastically. 'She's doin' fine. Isn't that right, Sean?'

'Aye, so the sergeant says. With God's help we'll have another recruit any time now – providing it's a boy.'

'What if it is?' O'Malley declared, still in mourning over his fate. 'He won't have a barracks to join here, will he?'

Sean Hogan smiled and nodded his head at Pat, motioning him towards Sergeant Driscoll's office. 'Have a word with himself, then,' he said, 'and when you've finished we'll arrange to have a meeting – all of us together now you're here. We'll discuss the whole matter of this takeover by the soldiery.'

'What the hell is there to discuss?' Andy Doyle grunted. 'We have our orders.'

'We have, lad, we have,' Sean Hogan replied placatingly. 'Isn't that what we have to discuss?'

Like Constable Doyle, Pat didn't see what they could do about the situation; they could hardly get the order withdrawn. But, unlike Doyle, he was glad they were all to discuss it. At least they weren't going to go like complete lambs to the slaughter, without even a bleat between them.

As soon as tea was over and cleared away, the meeting commenced almost by a process of spontaneous combustion. Everyone had been looking forward to it all day, more out of curiosity than out of hope. Nobody saw any prospect that a discussion of the takeover would change anything, but feelings about it were so deeply aggrieved that a desire to give voice to

255

their anger kept tempers high. It would, at least, afford a chance to let off steam, reiterate principles, rail against the bloody-mindedness of authority, pledge mutual support, refer to local pride – to say anything and everything that would record loudly their sense of frustration.

The whole complement of Gortnahinch RIC station, apart from Tom Fahy and Sergeant Driscoll, was present in the dayroom when, tacit agreement backing seniority of service, Sean Hogan took the chair.

'No,' Sergeant Driscoll had earlier told Pat Howell, 'I won't be at your meeting. If I were there, some of the men might feel reluctant to speak their mind. They might be, you know, a bit awkward about giving out. In a way, you see, I represent the authority they'd be protesting against. And, anyway, it's they who are being broken up and transferred, not me, so no doubt they reckon that they have far more to cry about than I have.'

'So what'll you do, Sergeant, while we're having the meeting?' Pat had asked.

'Better if I'm off the premises altogether. I'll go in and see the missus. It won't be visiting hours, but sure I don't suppose they'll lock the door on me. I can say I'm on official business, investigating the mysterious disappearance of a bar of soap.'

Pat was used to the sergeant's occasional quiet humour, but this time the usual accompanying twinkle in the eye was absent. His face was heavy, his expression wan, and he was drawing on his pipe so much that it glowed on and off like a distress signal. Poor Sergeant Driscoll! He had enough on his mind worrying about Lucy, Pat thought, without having to cope at the same time with the worst crisis he must ever have had to face in his career.

'Give her my love, will you, Sergeant? I'd have gone to see her more than the once if I hadn't been out at Odron House all week.'

'Ah, she knows that, lad, she knows that.'

'I won't see her again now, I suppose,' Pat lamented. 'Not if I'm to be off to the wilds of Mayo tomorrow.'

'Ah, sure,' Sergeant Driscoll rejoined wistfully, 'if all goes well with her and we have a third Driscoll in the house, you might come back some time and make his – or her – acquaintance.' The sergeant didn't add: 'If I'm here myself, that is.' There was no point in drawing young Howell into his own problems.

But Pat was in no mood for wistful speculation. 'If I go out to that place, Sergeant,' he declared, 'then your son, if it is a son, will have his stripe before I'll come back here, and that's the truth.'

Pat felt the same way when Sean Hogan called the meeting to order, and his truculent emotions were matched by those of the men. Individually no one could see what could be done about their situation, but when Constable Hogan cleared his throat and said, 'Come on, now, lads. We have serious matters to discuss,' there was a change in their demeanour. Those who had been lounging in their chairs sat up straight, while the few dawdling around or leaning against the wall in private conversation came to join them, and the consequent feeling of solidarity and strength in numbers made everyone lean forward, eager to show that at Gortnahinch they were a proud force, a forced to be reckoned with.

'Now,' Sean Hogan commenced, 'we all know the position. We all have our orders. Either we accept them, as we are bound by our oath to do, or we don't. If we don't accept, what do we do? And I'd like to say that, while it might make more of an impression if we could be unanimous about our decision, let no one be unduly influenced by that consideration. Each man has a life of his own to plan and he's entitled to make up his own mind. So don't be afraid of what the fellow next to you might be saying, even if he shouts louder. Speak your own mind and let no one begrudge you that right. Now, lads, I'll hear views.'

He looked around, waiting for someone to be first into the breach. While waiting he lit up his pipe; some followed suit, cigarettes were passed around. It was as if each man wanted it to be seen that he was momentarily occupied and so couldn't be the first to speak.

'Come on now,' Constable Hogan encouraged. 'You all had plenty of guff out of you all day. What's holding you back now?'

Constable O'Malley, still smarting about being sent to King's County, made the first contribution: the basic suggestion that they should appeal to the authorities to reconsider their decision. This was enough to open the flood-gates, his

257

idea being ridiculed on all sides on the grounds that there was clearly no time for such a course.

'Well, if you're all so smart,' O'Malley shouted, glaring around, 'why don't one of you come up with something?'

'Easy now, easy,' Sean Hogan called. 'There's no need to get excited. If we're all going to start off on such a high note, we'll never get anywhere. Let's just keep calm and don't all speak at once.'

Constable Aloysius Power, who was the quietest and most studious of the group, helped to get the meeting back on the rails with a succinct analysis of the authorities' tactics. He wasn't telling his colleagues anything they didn't already know, but his ponderous delivery allowed time for the initial temper-flushes to cool down. Speed and surprise, he pointed out, were time-honoured well-proven tactics; that was why the authorities had employed them. He had reluctantly to accept that in this particular case they rendered any formal protest or request for reconsideration pointless. He called it a *fait accompli*; the strange phrase effectively persuaded the men that, if they contemplated any action at all, it would have to be more radical than Constable O'Malley's suggestion.

This met with a great deal of nodding of heads and muttered agreement. There was a spontaneous feeling that Constable Power's words pointed to the only way forward if what was in their minds was to put up a real fight, but each was waiting for someone else to make the fateful proposal.

Sean Hogan decided to push the matter along with a little prompting.

'Thanks, Aloysius, that cleared the air, I think. It's great to have someone with a logical mind.'

There was a moment of lightness as Constable Power was ribbed by his colleagues. Then Sean Hogan resumed.

'All right, then, we know what we won't be doing. We won't be asking for any favours. We'll either be going our way where we've been sent, or—'

He left the rest unspoken, inviting their reaction. To everyone's surprise it was the youngest of the party, Denis O'Sullivan, who came out with it.

'Couldn't we all just resign rather than go on the transfer?'

The lilt in his voice seemed to suggest that he might be only making a joke, that he didn't for a moment imagine such an unprecedented action was even feasible. It was greeted with a subdued cheer from the majority of those present, as if they, too, couldn't quite take it seriously; the principle behind it reflected their feelings, but it wasn't really practical, was it?

'Well,' Sean Hogan temporized, 'it certainly is an option we have, so I suppose we should talk about it. But what reason could we give? We couldn't just say we didn't like our transfers. All members of the RIC are liable to transfer at a moment's notice. We're told that when we join. And, anyway, haven't most of us come here on transfer from other stations? So it's a bit late in the day to be raising any objection to that rule.'

Aloysius Power weighed in again.

'Well, Chairman, there's the question of *esprit de corps*. Could we say we object to the transfers because they amount to discrimination? I mean, the sergeant and Tom Fahy aren't being transferred. It's not that I'm saying they should be, too. I'm just wondering if it gives us any grounds for complaint.'

'Rubbish!' someone commented derisively, and Francie O'Leary laughed, saying: 'If Tom Fahy was here, I know what he'd think of that idea. Where would he be if they listened to us and moved him out as well?'

A chorus of agreement rose on all sides, but Pat Howell did not join in.

'Wait, lads, wait,' he called, and when Sean Hogan had restored order he went on: 'Aloysius has a good idea – if we turn it upside down.'

There were raised eyebrows and grunts of puzzlement.

'Look,' he explained, 'we could refuse to go on transfer, not because two of us are not being moved also, but because out of loyalty to them we prefer to stay in Gortnahinch with them. We can say it's not fair that they should be left alone with the military.'

'Arrah, that's not very convincing,' Constable O'Malley objected, and the inclination was to agree with him until Sean Hogan spoke.

'Well, now, it mightn't convince the authorities, but there's a lot in it that convinces *me*. You've all read the order, men, but there's something else you haven't seen. Just hould your whisht a moment.'

He left the dayroom and went into Sergeant Driscoll's office, emerging a minute later with a sheet of paper in his hand.

'This is another Order, an earlier one that the sergeant didn't show you because he didn't want you to be too worried. He only showed it to me yesterday. Read it for yourselves. Here, I'll pass it around. And have a good look at Clause Three.'

He handed the order to Pat Howell, as the one whose intervention had prompted him to put all the facts before the meeting. The others, too impatient to wait their turn, crowded around Pat, and gasps of amazement and anger were voiced as they read the document. 'The bastards!' someone breathed. 'Yerra, what else could you expect from them?' another grunted. When everyone had digested the information and resumed his seat, Constable Hogan continued.

'As you can see, there are two reasons why the sergeant and Constable Fahy have been left here. The first is to comply with that Order that not everyone can be transferred from a station. The second reason is what's behind Clause Three. The military will need someone who knows the area and the people well, and who can be a spy for them, giving them all the information and direction they need to catch the Sinn Fein. Now, I'm not holding any brief for that organization, but I don't have to tell you the position Sergeant Driscoll and Tom Fahy would be in if the rest of us go and they have to stay.'

There was silence for some moments before the men turned to each other, debating among themselves the pros and cons of the situation.

'I'll put this back in Sergeant Driscoll's drawer while you're thinking about it,' Constable Hogan said, taking the Order sheet and returning to the sergeant's office. When he came back, he addressed Pat Howell.

'Well, Pat, how do you feel now about your suggestion?'

'It certainly doesn't make me feel any less in favour of it, Sean,' Pat Howell replied. 'But I've been thinking: it seems to me there's a lot more at stake than wanting to stay on here just out of loyalty to the sergeant and Tom.'

'We're listening, Pat,' Sean Hogan encouraged, and Andy Doyle added: 'We're all ears, as long as you're not going to bring up your Police Union argument again.'

'No, I'm not,' Pat said, 'it's a wider question even than a

Police Union. It's obvious that all the mass transfers and the military taking over mean that something big is afoot. If you ask me, it's all a preparation for an all-out war on Sinn Fein. And, if I'm right, men, we'll be the ones in the middle.'

'How so?' a voice asked.

'Well, we'd have to make a decision, wouldn't we? Supposing we stood by the British Army and together we beat Sinn Fein, what would happen to us when the troops would be eventually withdrawn? I don't think we'd find our position very pleasant in that event. Supposing, on the other hand, Sinn Fein happened to beat *us*. That might seem unlikely, but if it did happen we might be even worse off. So it seems to me that either way we can't win.'

'Wait a while now,' Aloysius Power said, 'there's a flaw in your argument. If we accept the transfers, we won't be put in the position of having to help the military against Sinn Fein, will we?'

'Ah, but how can you be sure,' Pat asked, 'that you wouldn't soon be faced with the same problem wherever you're sent?'

There were noises of assent from most of the men, and Sean Hogan's voice rose above them.

'All right, Pat, what you've said makes sense. A very valuable point, I'm bound to say. But where do you go from there? Where does it lead us?'

'It leads us', Pat Howell declared, 'to making our minds up not to get involved at all.'

He sat down and allowed his words to sink in. After a moment there was a frustrated, almost angry yelp from Constable O'Malley.

'In the name of God, how can we not be involved? Aren't we Irishmen, and policemen?'

'What Pat means, Michael,' Sean Hogan interjected, 'is that we should try not to get involved in an all-out war between the British army and Sinn Fein.'

O'Malley looked over at Pat Howell, and when the latter nodded his agreement he barked truculently: 'How?'

Aloysius Power's quiet voice supplied the answer.

'Refuse to go on transfer *and* refuse to hand over to the military.'

A chorus of whistles and gasps arose; and, to everyone's

261

surprise, young Denis O'Sullivan struck a fist into his palm and declared: 'Begob, I'm ready.' Sean Hogan made no comment. The issue had been put fairly and squarely to the men. It was almost certainly the most difficult decision they had ever in their lives been asked to make, and he wouldn't rush them into voting on it. He was content to let them debate it among themselves before calling them to order again, but above the hubbub of their voices there was suddenly a thunderous rumbling from the yard at the back of the barracks. Immediately the men, led by Sean, jumped to their feet and made for the corridor, those who weren't armed buckling on their holsters as they went. Was it their turn to have a Sinn Fein raid? In daylight?

At the back door they came to an amazed halt, the ones in the rear pressing forward to see until all of them had spilled out into the yard. There, in front of their eyes, a military lorry had pulled in and dumped its full load of coal onto the ground, scattering lumps haphazardly. Already the soldier driving the lorry and his helper were back in the cabin, and with neither sign nor word to the policemen they drove off.

'The bastards,' Constable Doyle moaned. 'Will you look what they've done to my flowers?'

'Flowers be damned,' Michael O'Malley said quietly, 'but that's bloody provocation.'

'It is that,' Sean Hogan agreed. 'The message is as clear as if a note was tied to every lump of coal there. The military are going to take over and they're preparing to settle in for a long stay.'

There was an angry edge in his voice, and his resentment at what seemed to him an overbearing action was reflected in his colleagues' demeanour. Recriminations and threats were freely uttered as tempers rose.

'Come on back, men,' Constable Hogan directed, 'we have business to attend to.'

'We have that,' they agreed with each other. Their spirits were roused, their mood threatening.

When they were all assembled again in the dayroom Sean Hogan readdressed them.

'We can discuss it if you want, or we can vote on it straight off. Do we refuse to hand over our station? That's the long and the short of it.'

'Vote! Vote!' came from all sides.

'All right, all right, then,' Constable Hogan quietened them. 'All in favour of refusing to budge, hands up.'

Like a shot everyone present raised a hand. Francie O'Leary raised both and then waved them in the air when he saw that the response was unanimous. A great cheer was heard, and the men clapped each other on the back, their eyes shining, their faces proud.

'Hold on now, hold on,' Sean Hogan shouted. 'That's fine. We've made our decision, and I'm pleased we're standing together on this. But we're not finished yet. Someone has to do the talking. Someone has to get in touch with the County Inspector in Tralee and inform him.'

'Yourself, Sean, yourself,' Pat Howell suggested, but someone else said: 'No. It's Pat should do all that. He's the organizer among us. He's the one who's been writing letters all over the place about the Police Union.'

The call was taken up enthusiastically and backed by Constable Hogan.

Pat blushed at the degree of acclamation he was getting. He felt elated with the way the meeting had gone and proud to count himself one of such a band.

'Go on, Pat, telephone the County Inspector now,' a voice urged.

'Yes,' Constable Rafferty added, 'before we change our minds.'

Pat Howell, however, was certain there was no fear of that. Although all the men present had been serving in Gortnahinch for far longer than he had, he knew they were a sterling group who would never let each other down.

Sean Hogan nodded to him and, followed by everyone, he went to the sergeant's office where the telephone was. They crowded in after him as he sat behind Sergeant Driscoll's desk and lifted the receiver.

He gave the operator the Tralee number and waited, looking round at his colleagues. They stood tense and silent, all eyes boring into him.

He was put through to his number and he asked to speak to the County Inspector. The answer he received made him look up in consternation.

263

'He says it's late. He doesn't know if the Inspector is still there. He's gone to see.'

There was a lengthy wait. No one spoke. Pat put the receiver down for a moment while he wiped the perspiration from his palm. When he took it up again, a voice at the other end said: 'Yes?'

'Is that the County Inspector?' Pat asked.

'Speaking.'

'This is Constable Patrick Howell, Gortnahinch RIC, sir,' Pat said. 'I'm telephoning you about the order we received from Divisional Headquarters in Cork notifying us that the military will be taking over our station tomorrow at noon.'

'What about it?' the Inspector barked.

'Well, the men here have just had a meeting. All of us except Sergeant Driscoll who is out at the moment and Constable Fahy who's on—'

'Never mind all that, Constable,' the voice cut in. 'Get on with it. What do you want to say?'

'I want to say, Inspector – I've been authorized to tell you that by unanimous vote we are all refusing to go on transfer and refusing to hand over Gortnahinch RIC station to the military.'

A heavy silence followed. Pat clenched the receiver and stared down at the desk-top. The men held their breath. Suddenly Pat put the telephone down.

'What happened?' voices demanded.

'He just rang off,' Pat answered, completely taken aback.

'But what did he say when you told him?'

'He just said "Thank you, Constable" and then rang off.'

'Ah, sure,' Sean Hogan explained, 'no doubt he'll report up the line. I'd say we haven't heard the last of it yet. We'd best get out of the sergeant's office now. He might be back any minute.'

'What will you tell him, Sean?' Pat asked.

'I'll tell him what we decided of course. What else would I tell him?'

'Will he be mad angry?'

'Angry?' Sean Hogan lit up his pipe. 'If I know John Driscoll, it's proud he'll be, not angry.'

And proud he was. He showed no surprise while Constable Hogan was retelling his account of the evening's proceedings, but when he finished the sergeant went to look out the window of his office. From that vantage-point he had his back to his colleague and so was able to hide the tears in his eyes. He was still standing there, trying to swallow the lump in his throat and telling himself how lucky he was to have such men serving under him, when the telephone rang.

He went to his desk and took the instrument up.

'Sergeant Driscoll speaking. Gortnahinch RIC station.'

He listened while the voice at the other end spoke, his face betraying no expression. After a few seconds and without saying a further word, he put the telephone back.

'That, Sean, was the County Inspector.'

'I thought he might be back again,' Sean Hogan said. 'He was brief anyway.'

'Brief and to the point. He told me that all the men in the station are to be on parade at ten o'clock tomorrow morning, complete with side-arms.'

'March orders, eh?' Constable Hogan said. 'So they still mean business.'

'Of course they do,' the sergeant replied.

'Begob, then, so do the boys. They'll not weaken. You'll see.'

'No need to tell me that,' Sergeant Driscoll smiled. 'I know I can depend on them. That's my least worry.'

'Sure of course, of course,' Constable Hogan said apologetically, 'with all the excitement I was forgetting Lucy. How did you find her?'

'In great form, thank God, in great form. And all the signs are still favourable. Any day now, they say. Any moment even.'

'It looks as if we have an exciting day ahead of us, doesn't it?'

'That's about the size of it, Sean. Exciting,' the sergeant agreed.

Had he and Constable Hogan known of a second meeting that had taken place that evening in Gortnahinch, they might have also agreed that a stronger word than 'exciting' was likely to be needed to describe the day in prospect. Tim O'Halloran had soon learned of the proposed military takeover and he knew this was the opportunity he was waiting for. Quickly he summoned his command council and set out his plan. He was well satisfied with the response. If he had been asked, he wouldn't have said that the next day was going to be merely exciting. As far as he was concerned, it was going to be memorable.

15

FEW OF THE MEN in Gortnahinch barracks got a proper night's sleep after Sunday's unprecedented events, and next morning many breakfasts were only picked at. It was difficult to remain unaffected by the knowledge that before the day was out they might all be unemployed or even under arrest. The sun had risen bright and full, as confident of its reign as it had been for weeks past, and the barracks seemed to float in light. But that morning its writ did not run within the barracks walls, and from the moment the men began to assemble in the dayroom the mood was sombre and strained.

Anxiety had got them up even earlier than usual, and so they were all ready, spick and span, well before the appointed hour of ten, with nothing to do but polish and repolish buttons, buckles and side-arms. They were determined to put their best side out, to make pride in their appearance reflect the pride they felt in their job. Ill-at-ease for the most part, from time to time they would rise from their seats to wander here and there in the dayroom and gaze out the window at the area in front of the barracks, now silent and still. Each in his mind imagined how the military would arrive; some saw a platoon of soldiers marching down the street, their drilled steps echoing, and snapping to attention in front of the barracks, almost threatening to engulf it by force of numbers; others saw Army lorries whizzing down on them, screeching to a halt and disgorging hordes of khaki-clad soldiers who would rush in as if they were attacking an enemy encampment.

The tension was broken a little before ten by Sergeant Driscoll, coming to join his men. He was in full dress, and when he entered everyone present stood up and saluted although he had issued no command.

'At ease, lads, at ease,' he said. 'I have a few words to say to you before our visitors arrive.'

The sergeant half-sat, half-leaned on a corner of the table, one leg swinging loosely, and his casual pose encouraged the men to relax and take up seats themselves.

'This is a big day, lads, a big day,' he commenced uneasily. 'I suppose it's the most important day you've had yet in the RIC. It's important to me, too, though my own position isn't threatened. Not at the moment anyway, since I haven't been put on transfer like you. But—' He paused and swallowed, seeming to be suddenly lost for words.

Embarrassment at the silence made some of the men shuffle their feet or clear their throats. The noises stirred Sergeant Driscoll to continue.

'Constable Hogan gave me a full report of the meeting you had last night and of the decision you made. It was a brave decision, and I respect it; I know how much courage it took. I know your reasons, too, and I admire them. Sean told me that you were unanimous—' Here the sergeant once again appeared to be struggling with his emotions. 'That was great to hear. To know that you're all standing together in this. That's as important as what you're doing. You know it yourselves – you'd have no chance if you didn't show that you're determined to be loyal to each other. So stick together, lads, no matter what happens.'

He stood up and made towards his office. There was total silence as he turned at the door.

'Good luck,' he said. Then again, 'Good luck to all of ye,' and he left the dayroom.

Conversation and debate broke out anew and, even though every conceivable aspect of the situation had already been discussed the night before into the small hours, speculations, theories, possibilities were voiced again as the minutes ticked by towards ten o'clock. How many military would there be?

How would they arrive? What RIC officials would accompany them? Would there be other RIC as well? They'd be needed if it was a question of arresting everyone at Gortnahinch apart from the sergeant, for the military wouldn't have the authority to take them into custody.

'Isn't that right, Pat?' Constable Doyle asked, evidently to support his argument with Francie O'Leary. 'It's from RIC Divisional Headquarters that the Order has come, so it's with them we'd be dealing, not with the soldiers?'

'That would make sense,' Pat replied. He himself wondered what high-ranking officers would show up. Would the new Divisional Commander, Lieutenant-Colonel Smyth, be one of them? It was he who had issued the fateful Order for the takeover, so he might well come along in person. Pat felt a cold wave of apprehension pass over him at the thought of having to confront Smyth and especially at having to refuse to obey him. It was less than a few months since his appointment as Divisional Commander of Munster, but his reputation had travelled before him. Indeed, his appointment was widely regarded as incontrovertible evidence that the British government's policy was one of complete suppression. Why would they draft a high-ranking Army commander into the RIC unless they intended to crush all opposition ruthlessly? Smyth, Pat learned, had been born in India, had fought in France during the Great War – indeed, had lost an arm in battle, gaining bravery awards for his exploits. Obviously he'd be a formidable person to oppose. And he had the authority of the British government behind him. What authority have I, Pat asked himself. Only the agreement and support of all my colleagues – provided none goes back on his word.

Pat knew there must be a danger that one of them would break under the stress – and, if one did break, would others follow? Not that they could be blamed if they lost their nerve. It was one thing to feel brave and confident in the heat of the moment at a meeting among themselves; it would be another thing to stick to their guns when the time came to say No to authority and face the possibility of dismissal or even court-martial. After all, what they were about was a mutiny. There was no point in mincing words – it was blatant mutiny. Even the thought of the word set Pat shivering. God knows, he was frightened out of his wits himself at the course they were taking; he wasn't regretting it but he wasn't relishing it. And, being their spokesman, it was up to him to stand firm. They would be relying on him – the sergeant would be, too. He was determined not to let them down. What's more, if he did stand firm, that would help them all to keep their nerve when the test came.

There were now only a few minutes to go to ten o'clock, and conversation gradually petered out. At a minute to ten Constable Hogan stood up and motioned the men to do likewise. They lined up, the dayroom table behind them, the closed door facing them.

'Attention, men,' Sean Hogan muttered, and each one stiffened, stood tall and straight, Pat Howell near the middle of the line. So complete was the silence that they could clearly hear the ticking of the big clock on the mantelpiece behind them. Eyes front was held thus, each listening to the steady rhythmic tick-tock and their own heavy breathing. Then they heard the tinkling melody of the chiming clock across the corridor in Sergeant Driscoll's office. Note by note it held them. They had heard it thousands of times before, but now for the first time in their lives they were really listening to it, urging it on, wanting it finished so that they would be that much nearer the end of their waiting. Then, when the last phrase had sounded, it was all they could do not to count aloud, in unison with each other and with each ticking stroke – one, two, three, four, five, six – only seconds left – seven, eight, nine, ten!

Silence in the dayroom.

Silence from outside.

They stood to attention for some minutes. Nothing happened. Muscles no longer able to bear the strain softened and relaxed for a moment until stiffened again by the growing tension. They wanted to dry their hands and wipe the perspiration from under the rim of their caps, but they dared not move until Constable Hogan himself pulled out a large white handkerchief and blew his nose. He didn't need to, but he knew the men would take it as his signal for a moment's respite.

'Now, lads,' he said quietly when he judged they should be ready to screw up their courage once more. They responded to the brief muttered hint and came to attention again. 'They should be along any minute now,' he added.

Almost ten minutes passed. Then in the distance they heard a low humming sound. As it grew in volume, there wasn't one among them who didn't recognize with awesome certainty the familiar tone of a Crossley tender. All eyes turned to the window, and within seconds the vehicle swung into view and came to a halt inside the main gate. To the constables' surprise it was packed not with soldiers, but with fully armed and helmeted policemen. Barely had this ominous detail registered on them when down from the tender's cabin stepped two police officers in the full dress of their high rank. Their attention was immediately captured by the resplendent, almost bizarre appearance of the first of the officers. Sprouting from his helmet was a large snow-white ostrich feather, and across his breast, like a line of party bunting, stretched a row of medals. It was Sean Hogan who recognized him.

'Tudor,' he murmured quietly.

Pat had heard of Tudor but had never seen him before. A veteran of the Boer War and the Great War, Major-General Sir Henry Tudor had only months earlier been appointed police adviser to the Viceroy of Ireland, but it was strongly rumoured that his real task was to rebuild the RIC's detective force which had been seriously weakened by Sinn Fein successes.

As the two officers approached the barracks Pat wondered at the apparent change of tactics. Policemen instead of soldiers – that presumably was to counteract any objection that the military didn't have the right to take over an RIC barracks and arrest its occupants. Or maybe it was more subtle than that. Maybe it was meant to soften the blow to their wounded pride. Divisional Commissioner Smyth might have reasoned that they'd be more amenable if it was colleagues of their own who were replacing them – even if only to relinquish the post to soldiers later on – instead of soldiers themselves. At any rate, it appeared that it was to Tudor, not to Smyth, that Pat would have to make his declaration. He took a deep breath and rubbed his perspiring palms against his trousers.

To the men's suprise, however, Tudor and his companion did not enter the barracks, but stood outside, chatting. In a moment they were joined by Sergeant Driscoll, who greeted them, saluting and shaking hands with each, and then engaged

271

them in conversation. What were they talking about? Why were they delaying?

Before Pat and his colleagues had time to speculate further, a second Crossley tender appeared, crammed with British soldiers, rifles cocked, and led by two officers.

This is it, then, was the thought that immediately flashed through Pat's mind. The first group of policemen was only for show, a sort of decoy, perhaps to lull the suspicions of the Gortnahinch men, or even to undermine their confidence. It seemed to Pat to be a pointless tactic, but then it occurred to him that its apparent pointlessness might have been intended, to confuse him and his colleagues. Whether or which, the confrontation was surely now imminent.

Yet still no one made any move to enter the barracks, and within a minute the situation became even more threatening when a third Crossley tender swung in behind the other two, this one disgorging further armed and helmeted police and two more officers. The latter joined the other officers outside the window, where they casually lit up cigarettes, each one making a great show of taking out a gleaming cigarette-case and trying to persuade his companions to put their own cases back in their pockets. The men in the dayroom looked on in fascination at the unreal scene. It was like a group of actors assembling in the wings and chatting among themselves, until the arrival of the star would allow them to take their places on the stage and the real drama would commence.

That's why they're not coming in yet, Pat realized. He was certain he was right. The men outside were only extras, gathered together in force to underline the seriousness of the occasion, to give the utmost weight to the Government's intention not to brook the slightest opposition. Gortnahinch, even though it was of limited importance – Tralee, so near to it, was the major barracks in the area – was nevertheless to feel the whole might of British authority. It was to be made an example of, a warning to every other barracks of what would happen if any dared challenge the Government's rule.

As the atmosphere outside the dayroom appeared to grow lighter and the conversation more cordial, with much laughter and geniality, inside the tension was at breaking-point. Pat was sure now that his earlier fear of being confronted by Divisional

272

Commissioner Smyth would be realized. But he said nothing; there was no point in making his colleagues even more nervous than they already were.

'Jesus, I wish something would happen,' Constable Doyle said, the crack in his voice making evident the effect the strain was having on him. Pat turned to reassure him, but Francie O'Leary, equally solicitous, spoke first.

'Pray for rain,' he said.

Doyle and the others looked at him in puzzlement.

'All we want is for the heavens to open and that crowd wouldn't be long coming in like a shot off a shovel. We'd soon get things started then.'

There was laughter at Constable O'Leary's joke. Good man, Francie, Pat said to himself, that'll help. It gave the men a moment's respite before at last what Pat had been waiting for came about.

It was a fourth Crossley tender, with yet further British troops, that brought Lietenant-Colonel Smyth on the scene. It swung in the barracks gate between the other vehicles, coming to a stop broadside on as if to emphasize the higher rank of its main passenger. Two officers jumped to the ground, came to attention alongside the driver's seat, and saluted smartly as the Divisonal Commissioner stepped down. He was wearing full dress, his heavily braided tunic carrying a row of medals across his breast. Tall and straight, his left sleeve hung emptily at his side as he almost languidly acknowledged the salutes from the other waiting officers. As he joined them outside the barracks, the eyes of all the men in the dayroom were pinned on him.

'That'll be Smyth,' Pat curtly informed them. 'He's the one who signed the Order.'

The policemen looked at each other in consternation. They had never expected such a show of force. That the Divisional Commissioner himself was there to face them, backed up by so many troops and other policemen, made it clear that they were really up against it. If they were to persist in their rebellion, they might well be facing a court-martial. It could even end in some of them being shot. They turned from the window to look at Pat. Their eyes betrayed their conflicting emotions – fear, bewilderment, appalled realization of what they had talked

273

themselves into. On their tongues was the unspoken question: have we gone too far?

Pat caught Sean Hogan's eye. Constable Hogan nodded encouragement to him and then called the men to attention again.

'Remember, lads,' Pat Howell urged, as if to show them that if *he* wasn't wilting they needn't be, 'this is our barracks. Don't forget that. And Sergeant Driscoll is on our side, too. At least that's one who isn't against us.'

'Remember, too,' Sean Hogan hastened to add as he saw the group approach the barracks door, 'Pat speaks for us all. Leave it to him, let ye.'

There was no time for any further comment or instruction before all the officers, led by Lieutenant-Colonel Smyth, entered the dayroom, Sergeant Driscoll bringing up the rear. The sound of their boots on the floor rang in the silence as, amid a barrage of perfunctory coughing and clearing of throats, they ranged themselves in front of the empty fireplace, the Divisional Commissioner in the middle, the dayroom table between them and the men. As soon as they had settled them-selves to their own satisfaction, the Commissioner threw a glance to each side of him to check that they were all ready, and then turned his gaze on the men of Gortnahinch RIC barracks.

For half a minute he did not speak, appearing to examine the constables one by one, as if either to gauge each man's strength and temperament from his expression or perhaps to imprint each face on his memory. His eyes were small and dark, two hard pebbles that were flicked from man to man as he con-tinued his examination. His face was small, too, the satiny skin and puffed cheeks giving a schoolboyish impression that his thin black moustache did little to counteract. As his eyes roved steadily on, each constable met them without flinching, determined to let him see that they were not going to be overawed or browbeaten, determined to show their mettle.

His appraisal completed, he abruptly placed his right foot on the form at his side of the table, leaned forward with his elbow on his knee and, stretching his arm across his body, took his empty sleeve in his hand.

'I am Colonel Smyth, Divisional Commissioner over all police and military in Munster,' he rapped out in a series of

274

short barks. 'I was appointed by the Prime Minister of Great Britain. He is my sole superior officer.'

He gave a crisp cough as if to indicate that that was all there was going to be in the way of formal introduction, but before he could address the men further Pat Howell interrupted him.

'Excuse me, Colonel Smyth,' he said, 'but it was our understanding that this meeting was to involve RIC personnel only, and we question the right of military officers to be present.'

This was met with much raising of eyebrows and some embarrassed coughs from the high-ranking soldiers. Colonel Smyth made no comment in their defence. Evidently taking this as a vote against them, they passed each other a look and, mustering as much dignity as possible, shuffled noisily out of the dayroom. Outside the window, the men could see the other police and military milling around, while at the barracks gate a knot of passers-by had gathered, their curiosity aroused as they wondered among themselves about the reason for the unusual activity.

Colonel Smyth gave two short raps on the bench with the toe of his boot and readdressed the policemen.

'Well, men, I have something to tell you. I am going to lay all my cards on the table, but I must reserve one card for myself. Now, men, Sinn Fein has had all the sport up to this; we are going to have the sport now. The police have done splendid work, considering the odds against them. They are not sufficiently strong to do anything but hold their barracks. This is not enough, for as long as we remain on the defensive so long will Sinn Fein have the whip-hand. We must take the offensive and beat Sinn Fein with their own tactics. I am promised as many troops as I require from England. Thousands are coming daily. I am getting seven thousand police from England.'

Pat Howell could sense the physical shock of alarm that passed through his colleagues at the Commissioner's words. He wanted to tell them to be strong, to remind them that threats were cheap and easy, but he judged that this was not the point at which to make a second interruption.

Colonel Smyth had paused and was running his eyes along the policemen's faces, allowing what he had said to sink in, perhaps sensing himself that they weren't now quite as sure of themselves as they had been. Pat stole a glance at Sergeant

Driscoll, standing at the end of the table, a gap between him and the officers as if to emphasize that he was not necessarily on their side.

After a moment, the colonel's address was continued.

'Now, men, what I wish to explain to you is that you are to strengthen your comrades in the out-stations. The military are to take possession of the large centres where they will have control of the railways and lines of communication, and be able to move rapidly from place to place. Unlike police who can act as individuals and on their own initiative, military must act in large numbers and under a good officer – he must be a good officer or I shall have him removed. If a police barracks is burned, or if the barracks, already occupied, is not suitable, then the best house in the locality is to be commandeered and the occupants thrown out into the gutter. Let them die there, the more the merrier.'

At this there was an audible rumble of protest, but Colonel Smyth ignored it.

'The military and police will patrol the country roads at least five nights a week,' he went on, emphasizing the last four words with four tugs of his empty sleeve. 'They are not to confine themselves to the main roads but to go across the country, lie in ambush, take cover behind fences, near the roads, and when civilians are seen approaching shout: "Hands up." Should the order be not obeyed immediately, shoot, and shoot with effect. If the persons approaching carry their hands in their pockets or are in any way suspicious-looking, shoot them down. You may make mistakes occasionally, and innocent persons may be shot, but this cannot be helped and you are bound to get the right persons sometimes. The more you shoot, the better I will like you, and I assure you that no policeman will get into trouble for shooting any man. In the past policemen have got into trouble for giving evidence at coroners' inquests. As a matter of fact, coroners' inquests are to be made illegal so that in future no policeman will be asked to give evidence at inquests.'

One or two of the men, appalled at what they were hearing, looked at Pat Howell as if he must surely speak up now. Pat glanced towards Sergeant Driscoll. The sergeant's head moved almost imperceptibly, and to Pat it was a clear signal to hold

276

his fire. He was glad of the silent advice, for his own feeling had been that the Commissioner should be allowed free rein. The more obscene and outrageous his speech, the more resolute the angry policemen would become, the more justified their refusal to co-operate appear. Pat's plan seemed to be working, for Colonel Smyth, his eyes now blazing with zeal, his hand white with the strength of the grip he was exerting on his empty sleeve, was becoming even more fanatical.

'Hunger strikers will be allowed to die in gaol; the more the merrier. Some of them have died already, and a damn bad job they were not all allowed to die. As a matter of fact, some of them have been dealt with in a matter that their friends will never hear about. A ship will be leaving an Irish port in the near future with lots of Sinn Feiners on board. I assure you, men, it will never land.'

'That now is all I have to say to you. We want your assistance in carrying out this scheme in wiping out Sinn Fein. Any man who is not prepared to co-operate is a hindrance rather than a help.'

The ominous note of veiled threat marked the end of Colonel Smyth's address. He took his right foot down off the form and planted it on the ground with a firm crack. Then, while the policemen were still feeling stunned both by the ruthlessness he was ready to employ and by the obvious relish he took in it, he released his empty sleeve, pointed at the first man in the line facing him, and rasped belligerently: 'Are you prepared to assist me wipe out Sinn Fein?'

It was Denis O'Sullivan he addressed, the most recent recruit. Pat Howell mentally upbraided himself for exposing their most inexperienced member to the ordeal of being the first to come under fire. He should have been more alert to such a danger; he should have anticipated the possibility and tucked young Denis away in the middle.

Constable O'Sullivan hesitated for only a moment, and then, closing his eyes tight, he sang out: 'Constable Howell is our spokesman, sir.' It was like something he had learned by rote, a spell he had been taught to repeat when any danger threatened. Pat Howell's heart surged with joy.

The Commissioner proceeded from man to man, asking each the same question, getting from each the identical answer, until he reached Constable Howell near the end of the line.

As he moved his pointing finger and repeated his question, Pat Howell took one firm step forward and coolly replied: 'You're an Englishman. You forget that you're addressing Irishmen.'

'Just a moment, Constable,' the Colonel interjected sharply. 'I may not have been born in Ireland, but my people were. They came from County Down – Banbridge, County Down.'

Pat, however, was not to be put off. 'I am an Irishman,' he announced almost aggressively, 'and I'm proud of it.' Then, sweeping off his cap, he half-pushed, half-threw it onto the table in front of Commissioner Smyth.'

'This is English,' he declared in an unmistakably derogatory tone. 'I don't want it. You can have it as a present from me.'

His action seemed, by its very momentum of anger, to push him into even further challenge. Unbuckling his belt and bayonet with fingers that trembled with fury rather than with nervousness, he banged them down onto the table on top of his cap.

'You can have these, too. They're English also. And to hell with you, you murderer.'

Colonel Smyth coloured visibly but held his temper. He turned to Sergeant Driscoll.

'Arrest that man,' he ordered. His voice was low and quiet.

The sergeant looked at him for a moment, then motioned to Mick O'Malley who was next to Pat Howell. Constable O'Malley hesitated, but Pat resolved his indecision by turning to him and saying: 'Go ahead.'

O'Malley took hold of Pat's arm and led him out of the dayroom, turning towards the kitchen at the end of the corridor.

In the dayroom there was an awkward silence, while Colonel Smyth quietly conferred with his officers. The Gortnahinch policemen, their members now badly depleted, were for the moment uncertain as to what to do. Then suddenly Sean Hogan took over.

'Are we to understand that you've placed our spokesman under arrest?' he quietly asked the Divisional Commissioner.

'Yes. That is correct,' Smyth replied.

The policemen's murmuring quickly rose to a crescendo of

278

protest. Colonel Smyth's action was too authoritarian for them to stomach. Without Pat they had been deprived of the one man they were relying on to express all their objections and frustrations in a fashion none of them was equal to. Ordering his arrest was dirty play, and they were outraged.

'By God,' Aloysius Power cried, 'we're not going to let him arrest Pat. He's our spokesman. Come on, lads.'

Fired by his outburst, the men broke in a body from the dayroom and stampeded down the corridor to the kitchen.

'Come out of there, Pat,' they shouted.

'No bastard Englishman is going to arrest you!'

'Let him go, Mick.'

'Arrah, I don't want to hold him,' Mick O'Malley replied.

Pat, grinning in triumph, his back almost broken with the thumps of encouragement he was getting, was pushed and pulled forward, jostled down the corridor and back into the dayroom. It was empty and silent apart from the ticking clock.

Pat quickly looked out the window, but the officials were not outside. Indeed, most of the supporting soldiers and police had disappeared, too, and he guessed they were all in the nearest public house. That meant that Colonel Smyth and his companions were in Sergeant Driscoll's office, along with the sergeant himself.

In the dayroom Pat's colleagues were raising a loud hubbub, elated at having defied Smyth's arrest order and convinced that they had forced him to retreat and consider his position.

'If anyone lays a hand on you again, Pat,' Andy Doyle said loudly, 'I'm telling you, they'll pay for it. This place will run red with blood!'

Cheers greeted his outburst, and the atmosphere was electric. The men were full of fight. Too full of it, Pat thought; in their present mood they could easily overreach themselves and go much further than would be wise or advantageous. There was no knowing what Colonel Smyth might do next. He'd be bound to make some comeback. He certainly wasn't the sort of man to take what happened lying down.

'Go easy, men,' Pat urged in an effort to restore calm. 'We'd better have a quick talk while we have the chance. Smyth is probably telephoning Tralee for more soldiers, so we'd better have some plan ready.'

Constable Power laughed. 'He can telephone as much as he likes but he won't get anywhere.'

'Why not?' Pat asked.

'Because I disconnected the telephone,' Power revealed, looking around gleefully at his colleagues.

'Good man yourself, Aloysius,' they roared. 'That'll give him something to think about.'

In fact Colonel Smyth *had* tried to telephone Tralee, and his failure to get a sound out of the instrument was indeed giving him something to think about. It did not worry him that, with communication with the outside world cut off, he was in a way as much a prisoner in Gortnahinch RIC barracks as its policemen were, but what did worry him was that if he tried to use force to overcome them they would certainly resist, and injuries, even deaths, could follow. Sitting at Sergeant Driscoll's desk, he discussed the situation with his officers, seeking some way of establishing his authority.

In the dayroom there was also a discussion proceeding, but it was made up mostly of reiterated declarations not to surrender rather than of what to do if the Commissioner returned or ordered the troops to use force. Pat feared that, if Colonel Smyth did resort to force, it would not be the British soldiers he would use but the RIC reinforcements. If Pat and his colleagues resisted, blood could well flow, and while Pat would not hesitate to defend himself against an attack by a British soldier it was against his principles to fight his fellow-Irishmen in the RIC.

Nothing happened for almost an hour, and it seemed as if the tactics Smyth was adopting was to play on the men's nerves. Then suddenly the door opened and Sergeant Driscoll entered. His face was pale, his expression drawn; the men appreciated how difficult a situation it was for him.

'Lads,' he said, 'General Tudor would like to say a few words to you.' His request was met with silence, and he hastily added: 'As a friend.'

The men turned to Pat for direction.

'No, Sergeant,' he said respectfully, 'we have nothing to say to General Tudor and he has nothing to say to us.'

Sergeant Driscoll looked at Constable Howell for a moment, but his expression gave no clue to his thoughts. As he turned to go back to his office, Pat added: 'And, Sergeant, it'd be as well to tell the Commissioner that he'd better get himself and his officers out of the building. The way we're feeling here, if he tries anything, we won't answer for the consequences.'

'That's telling him, Pat,' Mick O'Malley supported with a confirmatory nod.

Sergeant Driscoll returned to his office but was back in the dayroom within a minute.

'Look, lads,' he appealed, 'I told them what you said, but General Tudor still wants to speak to you. If you take my advice, it might be a good idea to listen to him. I don't know what he wants to say, and I'm not saying you should do anything he might suggest, but it would make you look very unreasonable if you refuse even to give him a hearing. He may be a soldier really, but remember his present post is police adviser to the Viceroy, so he has every right to talk to you.'

Pat Howell looked around at his comrades. They said nothing one way or the other. Pat knew they were in no mood to listen to General Tudor, police adviser to the Viceroy or not, but he guessed they wouldn't want to make the sergeant's position any more difficult by sending him back once again with a flea in his ear.

'All right so, Sergeant,' Pat agreed. 'Tell him he can talk to us.'

The sergeant, plainly relieved at not having to go back empty-handed, went out once more, and in a moment General Tudor entered the dayroom. To the men's amazement he was no longer dressed in his bemedalled uniform and ostrich-feathered helmet but in a sober brown tweed suit. He strode to the table, turned, and stood for a few seconds, fingering his moustache as if uncertain how to begin. He was faced with a line of stolid unhelpful expressions and, obviously discom-fited, he made a few nervous sounds in his throat before eventually finding his voice.

'Well, men,' he started, 'I would just like to say a few words to you as a friend. Just to show that I *am* a friend, I will shake hands with each of you.'

To the policemen's bewilderment he started off down the line, offering his hand to each. Awkwardly, with various degrees of embarrassment, each man took it and submitted to a perfunctory shake. It appeared to them a pointless exercise, but at least it wasn't hostile, and an innate sense of politeness told them it would be rude to reject his handshake.

Courtesies completed, he returned to his place at the table, and now he seemed to find no difficulty in knowing how to proceed.

'I am an Englishman,' he said, 'but my ancestors came from Ireland and I like the Irish.'

He paused to see what effect his announcement was having, but Pat knew that if he thought such patronizing sentiments would impress them he was making a big mistake.

'I want to tell you that there are a lot of changes on the way, and some of them are of the greatest importance to you men. Dominion Home Rule, for instance, will soon be extended to the whole of Ireland and that will greatly improve the standing and conditions of the RIC. For one thing, each man will have twelve years added to his service for pension purposes. You can work out for yourselves what this will mean. It's no small thing.'

The men were silent, and Pat could see that the general was beginning to catch their interest. If he were allowed to proceed, goodness knows what he might come up with to lull them into a more conciliatory mood. Quick action was called for.

'We've had promises like that in the past and they came to nothing,' he intervened. 'If you were really serious about bettering the conditions of the RIC, why did you reject all our efforts to start a Police Union? And why have you allowed Colonel Smyth to send soldiers to take us over? We've had enough of your kind of talk.' Before the general could dissuade him, Pat gave the command, 'Men, dismiss,' and immediately the line of men broke. 'Come on,' Pat called, 'follow me.' Someone began to sing 'A Nation Once Again' and the others quickly took it up. Leaving General Tudor in open-mouthed dismay, Constable Howell led his comrades out to the back yard where they finished their song and then roared lustily on into 'Wrap the Green Flag Round Me, Boys', before Pat called them to order and commenced another impromptu meeting.

After half an hour they returned to the dayroom, only to find it empty. Pat crossed over to the sergeant's office. He knocked on the door and opened it. To his surprise only the sergeant was there, sitting behind his desk, his unlit pipe in his hand.

'Where are they?' Pat asked.

'Oh, they've gone.'

'All of them?'

'All of them.'

'Where to?'

'To Tralee, I believe.'

'Are they coming back?'

'I doubt it.'

'What about the police and the soldiers outside?'

Sergeant Driscoll turned his head to look at Pat Howell, who was still standing at the door.

'Well, as long as they stay out there, we'll have to stay in here.'

The sergeant sounded tired, and Pat realized what a strain he had been under.

'Sergeant,' he said quietly, 'we – I mean the men and me – we know you're on our side and we're all grateful. But we don't expect you to back us openly. We appreciate that if you did, you'd be finished. Not only here but in the RIC altogether. None of us wants that to happen to you.'

Sergeant Driscoll rose from behind his desk. He had tears in his eyes as he walked past the constable and stood at his open door, looking across the corridor into the dayroom.

'Pat,' he said, his voice low, 'when I think of the men in there, those fine lads who have shown such courage and bravery, I feel that I am the happiest man in Ireland. It has been my great privilege and honour to have been placed in charge of such men, and as an Irishman I would be unfit to live were I to desert them.'

He turned, went back to his desk, sat down and looked up at Pat.

'That I shall never do. And may God bless you all.'

Pat could say nothing. He walked towards the dayroom to rejoin his comrades, but at the door Sergeant Driscoll stopped him.

'I suppose it was Constable Power who disconnected the telephone. He's the expert on these yokes, isn't he? I hope he can reconnect it again so as I can phone the hospital.'

'I'll see to it, Sergeant. Immediately. And thanks.'

283

The older man held the younger's gaze for a moment. Then they smiled at each other before Pat turned and left the office.

A little later, after giving the sergeant time to have made his phone call, Pat knocked again on his door and went in.

'Well, Sergeant, how is Mrs Driscoll? Any news?'

'She's well, Pat, thanks be to God. They thought something might have been happening this morning and they were going to get in touch with me, but it was a false alarm. Just as well, says you. They'll let me know if they want me.'

'That's great news, Sergeant. Great altogether. I suppose there's nothing we can both do now but sit and wait.'

'Ay, Pat, sit and wait. Patience. It's a great gift, but a trying one.'

'Especially when you're hungry,' Pat rejoined. 'We've had nothing since breakfast, and the soldiers weren't allowing anyone into the barracks so we won't be seeing Mrs Hogan. I'll get Andy to cook something for us. I'll let you know when it's ready.'

'Ah, sure I couldn't eat any food,' the sergeant told him. 'I'm too nervous altogether.'

'Well, maybe you'll have a cup of tea anyway.'

'Maybe a cup of tea, then. That'd do me.'

Sergeant Driscoll had his cup of tea; the men had scrambled eggs and fresh bread, a meal they devoured eagerly but mostly in silence. They seemed to have exhausted conversation. For the rest of the afternoon the scene in Gortnahinch RIC barracks was much like any other quiet uneventful day, except for the police and soldiers still in the front yard.

Then at nearing six o'clock they heard the telephone ring. What little talk there was at the time was stilled as they waited to see if the sergeant would come into them. If he did, it would likely be news of Lucy or news of the takeover. Which? And would it be good or bad? Pat closed his eyes, crossed himself and said a prayer. Some of the men followed suit. They waited.

After a few moments noises from the front yard made them all crowd to the window. The Crossley tenders were being revved up, the police and soldiers were climbing back in, and then with roaring engines the four vehicles swept out of the gates.

The men didn't know whether to cheer or not. Pat wasn't sure what the departure meant.

As he turned from the window Sergeant Driscoll appeared in the doorway.

'They're gone, Sergeant,' he said.

'Ay, lad, they're gone. And, what's more, they won't be back.' Sergeant Driscoll's face broke into a smile. 'That was Tralee on the telephone just now. Colonel Smyth has countermanded his own order. You bate them, boys, you bate them!'

Wild cheering broke out. The men hugged one another, clapped each other on the back, danced around in triumph. Sergeant Driscoll moved among them, grabbing a hand here, putting his arm around a shoulder there, his eyes bright, his face glowing.

'Listen, lads, listen,' he said, making them pause momentarily, 'I think we deserve a little celebration tonight. Aengus, let you go out to McCarthy's and get a couple of dozen bottles. It's a special occasion. Tell him I'll fix up with him later.'

'I'll go and gladly,' Constable Rafferty said.

'And I'll go with him,' Andy Doyle offered. 'He'll need help to carry it.'

To shouts of 'And don't drink any of it before ye're back', the two policemen left.

Pat Howell leaned forward to the sergeant and touched his hand.

'With luck maybe we'll be having a double celebration, Sergeant.'

Sergeant Driscoll looked into his eyes but said nothing. What he was thinking, however, was clear to Constable Howell. May God grant it, his expression said, may God in His goodness grant it!

285

16

It was a quarter past ten when the first shot rang out.

Constable Fahy was lying on his bed. He had just heard the chimes of the quarter-hour sound from the clock in the lower hall and was wondering if he was going to be lucky enough to have an early night. He certainly needed one; never before in his life had he done as much walking as in the past week. Mercer, he knew, was in his room, and it was surely very unlikely he'd be going anywhere this late. So that was Ambrose out of the way.

That left Elizabeth. As far as he was aware, she was in her room, too. Preparing to pay him a visit? Somehow, he didn't think so. He had noticed a marked change in her in the last day or two; indeed, the atmosphere in the whole Odron family had suddenly become quite gloomy. He could understand Victoria's low spirits – Pat's sudden recall had brought to an abortive end the romance Tom had seen was quickly blossoming between them. It was just as well; in the long run they could have no future together, so separating them sooner rather than later was the best thing that could happen. Victoria wouldn't see it that way of course, and Tom feared for her. Judging by her misery at Pat's departure, she looked like the sort of girl who was capable of brooding on her misfortune for the rest of her life and ending up a spinster.

With Mrs Odron it was different – he just had no idea what

286

could have caused her change of mood. She had appeared to brighten up considerably for a short while, and then suddenly she was back again to the same correct preoccupied manner he and Pat had noticed when they first met her a week earlier – only this time more so.

Elizabeth's turnabout, however, was the real puzzle; she almost wasn't the same girl. There was no more teasing, no more jauntiness, none of her come-hither glances – not for Tom, and certainly not, so far as he could see, for Ambrose Mercer – and a stricken, even tortured expression had overtaken her normally lively features. Her voice was cold and detached whenever she spoke to him – which wasn't often, for he found it difficult to get a word out of her – and Mercer she declined to address at all.

But all these reflections were instantly banished by that first unmistakable sound of shooting. Tom quickly put out the light, took his gun from its holster and rushed to the window. To his annoyance he found that the sky, which had been clear all day and virtually every night since he had come to Odron House, was now quite overcast and it was impossible to make out anything in the grounds apart from the very black outlines of the trees along the front drive. The shot, he thought, had come from somewhere to the left of the drive, but even as he peered in that direction another shot rang out from the other side. He broke a window-pane and poked the muzzle of his gun through it but held his fire. There was no point in using up his limited supply of ammunition too soon; he recalled that there wouldn't be any available in Odron House because months previously all their arms and ammunition had been surrendered to the police.

His door opened suddenly and Mercer appeared, a revolver in his hand. Trust him to have kept a gun hidden away, Tom thought. But just as well he did. For the first time that week Tom was glad to have the man beside him.

'It's the blasted Shinners,' Mercer exclaimed as he knelt at the window beside the policeman. 'How many are there?'

'Too dark to see,' Tom answered, 'but you can be sure there'll be enough of them.'

Just then Elizabeth rushed to join them.

'I heard shots,' she cried. 'Are we being attacked?'

'Yes,' Tom replied. 'And we may be in trouble. We'd better lose no time in getting help. Elizabeth, let you go down and telephone the sergeant. Tell him we're under attack. As quick as you can.'

On her way to the hall, Elizabeth met Victoria, hurrying downstairs, too.

'We're being attacked by the Shinners,' Elizabeth told her. 'I'm going to telephone the police.'

'I heard the shots,' Victoria said excitedly. 'Mother heard them, too. She told me to see to the servants.'

'Is she all right? Is she frightened?'

'I think she is, but she's staying calm. What about you?'

'Don't worry about me,' Elizabeth assured her as she reached the telephone. 'I'll be with Tom and Ambrose. They'll keep the Shinners busy until the police come. You be sure to see after Mother and the rest. And tell her not to be afraid.'

In the darkness of the garden Tim O'Halloran looked up at the imposing mass of Odron House and smiled to himself. The two men he had brought with him to help carry out the first part of his daring plan were doing exactly as he had ordered, moving around as much as possible, stopping only to fire in the general direction of the house and so give the impression that they were far more in number than just three. He had cut the telephone wires before firing the first shot, so no one would be able to get in touch with the barracks. That would give his plan plenty of time – say, fifteen or twenty minutes of gunfire to convince Mercer they meant business and that he'd better get his money together. By then he could have no doubt about what was to follow. And follow it would. The two lads would light their oil-dipped brands, they'd set fire to the back of the house, and hey presto! Mercer would have to escape out the front. It wouldn't matter if he wasn't alone, for he'd certainly be looking to get away from everyone else so as to find a temporary hiding-place for the money. 'And that's when we'll nab you, me boy!' Tim O'Halloran breathed. He had enough men placed in the grounds to keep track of Mercer's movements wherever he'd go. Before the night was out Ambrose Mercer would be no more, and his stolen gains would soon make Tim O'Halloran and his followers the best-armed Sinn Fein unit in the province.

'Are they coming?' Tom Fahy enquired anxiously when Elizabeth came rushing back.

'I can't get a sound from the telephone,' she answered breathlessly. 'It's completely dead.'

'The bastards have cut the wires, I'll bet,' Mercer rasped.

'I thought they might do that,' Tom said resignedly. He turned to Ambrose Mercer.

'Take Elizabeth and round up the women and servants and get out the back while you have a chance. I'll keep the Shinners busy here. I don't think they're minded to kill anyone. They probably want to get us all out so as to set the house on fire.'

'I'm not leaving,' Mercer replied angrily. 'Elizabeth can go, but I'm staying. With the two of us shooting, we can drive them off.'

'Don't be a fool. They're far too many for us, and we have no hope of any help. We can't even see them in the dark.'

'Well, I'm not going. I'll not leave Odron House and I'll not let those bastards burn it down.'

Tom Fahy couldn't understand Mercer's obstinacy. Why should he be so worried whether the place went up in smoke or not? But he didn't have time to think about it. Firing from the front of the house had increased. Flashes were streaking the darkness, and Mercer was already shooting back. And there was still Elizabeth to think of.

'We could all get out together now, couldn't we?' she urged.

Tom shook his head. 'I'll hold on a while more,' he said. He told himself it was his duty. As long as he had enough ammunition left, he should stay and fight – and pray for help, forlorn though such prayer might seem. Besides, they'd surely not set fire to the place when they knew there was still somebody inside.

'If *you're* staying, Tom,' Elizabeth said, putting a hand on his shoulder, 'then I'm staying with you. They'll go away after a while. This is probably just another demonstration, like last week's.'

Tom saw that there was no use arguing. Mercer glared at both of them, furious that Elizabeth's response had been stirred by the policeman's refusal to leave, not by his.

'I hope you're right,' Tom Fahy muttered, letting his free hand linger for a moment on hers. But he had his doubts.

Cook folded her arms across her capacious bosom, complaining irascibly as she plonked herself in a chair beside the range's dying embers. 'Bad cess to them and their nonsense! I was just dropping off when they started. What's the country coming to when a body can't get a decent night's sleep without them shooting off their guns!' Angrily she plucked at her dressing-gown to make sure it was well closed over her nightdress. Her complaints were echoed by Margaret, the elderly housemaid, but young Eileen O'Brien, still suffering from the remains of her summer cold, was snivelling into her handkerchief and shivering with fear.

'Sure they'll go away in no time,' Cook tried to persuade her. 'Didn't Miss Victoria tell us that Miss Elizabeth was telephoning the police? They're the boys will chase them. Can't you be like Mary there? See how calm *she* is, girl?'

Mary Casey put an arm around Eileen and comforted her. 'Cook is right,' she said. 'It's only a bit of sport they're having.' But she guessed there was more than sport involved, that there must be a connection between the attack and the money she had seen under Mr Mercer's floorboards. She'd shed no tears if they took the money – and Mercer along with it – but she wouldn't want any harm to come to the family. She had a nice job with them – even though she hadn't much love for that Miss Elizabeth – and she didn't know where she'd find another if anything happened to put her out on the road again.

'Come on, Eileen,' she urged in an effort to distract her friend, 'you get out the cups and I'll brew a pot of tea. It's best to keep busy. You heard Miss Victoria tell us we'd be all right and to stay here together until it's over. Come on now.'

'That's right,' Cook agreed. 'A cup of tea will settle all our nerves.'

In the grounds Tim O'Halloran was well pleased with the progress of his attack. He and his men had kept on the move, shooting now from here, now from there, and he had no doubt the flashes and firing from one of the upstairs windows were Constable Fahy and Ambrose Mercer trying to frighten them off. Fat chance of that! Now for the next stage.

He paused a moment to gaze up at the outline of Odron House against the night sky. Proud and noble some would call

290

it, but to Tim O'Halloran it was a symbol of arrogance and aggression. For too long Ireland had been forced to acknowledge a foreign master. Well, times were changing, and he was going to help change them, with plenty more like him to make certain that this time the change would be permanent.

In a moment of silence he gave a low whistle. It was the signal his two men had been waiting for. While he kept up his fire, they ran along the back of the house, lighting their brands and hurling them through the windows. For a few seconds nothing seemed to happen, and then suddenly there was a succession of explosions like massive waves tumbling on surf as the flames burst out through the broken glass. Within a minute the back of the house was completely ablaze until from end to end was a blinding inferno, the conflagration climbing hungrily to the upper storey, engulfing everything in its path like a raging vengeful monster. The two men ran back to join the rest of their unit spread throughout the grounds, watching and waiting for Ambrose Mercer's flight. Tim O'Halloran, crouched behind a tree on the still dark front lawn, already could see the glow rising in the night sky, and a long sigh of satisfaction escaped his lips. Odron House was doomed; no one could possibly save it now.

In Gortnahinch RIC barracks the celebrations had started at about the same time as Tim O'Halloran and his men were taking up their positions in the grounds of Odron House. Sergeant Driscoll had delayed their commencement out of a sense of obligation to duty. If there had been a call for him or any of his men while they were busy enjoying themselves with a pint or two, it might have led to a lowering of the high standards he had always tried to maintain. By ten o'clock, however, the likelihood of their services being needed after that hour was remote enough for him to relax and open the first bottle.

In fact the celebration was relatively subdued. The constables, having had a few hours both to shed the day's tensions and to cool down after the elation of their triumph over Colonel Smyth and his soldiers, were mostly overtaken by a pleasant lethargy, and a quiet pint rather than a boisterous bout of self-indulgence suited their mood.

After a while the sergeant left them to their enjoyment and

291

returned to his office, motioning Pat Howell to follow him. Inside, he sat behind his desk and busied himself refilling his pipe.

'You did a great job there this day, Pat,' he said between puffs. 'Not that I was surprised.'

'Ah, sure any one of the lads could have done the same.'

'Perhaps. Perhaps not,' the sergeant allowed. 'If they could itself, 'tis a pity, then, that someone else wasn't chosen as spokesman instead of you.'

'I know what you mean,' Pat commented, sitting opposite the sergeant in response to his nod of the head towards the empty chair.

'You do of course. You wouldn't want much intelligence to guess that you'll not be forgotten – nor forgiven – for this day's performance.'

Pat tossed his head despairingly.

'And it isn't as if they hadn't their eye on me already over the Police Union. I'd say that's well and truly banjaxed now.'

The gloom of his tone was echoed in the sergeant's next sentence.

'The Police Union isn't the only thing banjaxed, my lad. I'm sorry to have to say it, but it's no use pretending.'

Constable Howell looked for some moments at his superior. Eventually he spoke, his voice thick with emotion.

'What'll I do, Sergeant? Is it the end for me?'

Sergeant Driscoll put his pipe down and eyed his young constable. He could guess how the boy's dilemma was already beginning to eat into his thoughts. If *he* had had to face such a decision himself when he was only twenty-two, it would have seemed the end of the world – and at twenty-two his prospects in the RIC weren't a patch on what Pat Howell's had been.

'Well I suppose the best you can hope for is no further action – I mean apart from that transfer to the wilds they had in mind for you anyway before today.'

'And the worst?'

'The worst?' The sergeant raised his shoulders and let them drop with a long sigh. 'They could put you on a charge, a very serious charge. God knows it wouldn't be hard for them; you've given them plenty of cause.'

'And you can be sure they'd find me guilty.'

Sergeant Driscoll's silence was reply enough.

'I haven't much of a choice, have I?' Constable Howell said.

Again the sergeant was silent. He took up his pipe once more, struck a match and applied it to what was left of the tobacco. He seemed to be trying to avoid saying what was in his mind, what was probably passing through Pat Howell's mind, too. To say it would be, for him anyway, like acknowledging its inevitability and having to face losing for ever this young lad who had taken such a hold on his heart. No one else could ever replace him; he didn't mean as a policeman – to the devil with that. There was a lot more to it. Not even the birth of a child of his own could fill the gap the loss of Pat Howell would leave. The thought brought Lucy back to mind – not that she had been far from his mind despite all the day's strange events. He wondered what was happening. God, how long these things take!

Someone in the dayroom started singing. He recognized Denis O'Sullivan's youthful tenor. Denis had a fine voice, and the sergeant could picture the rest of the men, leaning back, coats off, glasses in hand, eyes misting with thoughts of their families. Perhaps Pat was thinking of his own folks up in Leitrim. But he had something far more urgent to occupy him. Colonel Smyth would be quick to pay him back; there'd be damn little time to dither. And the boy was waiting for his reply, his eyes almost plaintive with hope that the sergeant might find some way of keeping him in Gortnahinch.

'No, lad,' he said, 'you haven't much of a choice. Only the one path to take, if you ask my advice. You know what I mean.'

Sergeant Driscoll could have cried with frustration. If only there had been something he could do. There just wasn't.

Pat appeared unable or unwilling to voice the word. The sergeant said it for him.

'At least you'll be safe in America. It's a big place, bags of opportunity; you can make a new life for yourself. There's plenty of our own over there, too, so you won't be short of friends. And when all this trouble is over, sure you can come back then, and your pockets stuffed with dollars as like as not.'

Pat lowered his head into his hands.

'This is my home,' he groaned. 'This is my country.'

'Your home, yes; your country, no. Not yet anyway.' The

sergeant's voice was paternal, but the note was firm. If Pat *had* been his son, he wouldn't have said any different than he was now going to.

'There's no more you can do for Ireland by staying. And, anyway, at the moment it's your own future you have to struggle for rather than Ireland's. It's hard, lad, it's hard. But you're so young. Your life is only beginning. You want to give it a good start, and that's something you'll not be allowed to get here. Not now.'

Pat looked up, the anguish clearly showing in his eyes.

'I know you're right, Sergeant, but. . . .'

The sergeant forced a laugh. 'Ah, well, you're not likely to be in any trouble tonight, so go back to the others and forget about it for the moment. You can sleep on it. In the morning it will all look clearer. Brighter, too, maybe, with God's help.'

Pat nodded. He rose wearily and left the office. Sergeant Driscoll sighed. Taking the pipe from his mouth, he stretched a hand towards the telephone. Then he hesitated and changed his mind. 'We all have our troubles,' he muttered to himself. 'There's no point in bothering the good Sister. They said they'll let me know if they want me, and I'll stand on that.'

Immediately Eileen O'Brien heard the first roar and crackle of the fire she screamed in panic and let her cup of tea fall to the floor with a crash. As Cook tried to calm her, Mary Casey ran out of the kitchen to see how near the flames were. It was clear that there was no time to lose.

'We'd best get out quickly,' she urged, rushing back.

'Oh Jesus, oh Jesus save us,' Eileen gasped between semi-hysterical sobs, 'we'll all be burned alive.'

'What about the mistress and the girls?' old Margaret asked. 'We can't leave them.'

Just then Victoria ran into the kitchen, pulling Amelia by the hand. 'Hurry, hurry, Mother,' she cried.

The noise of the fire was growing apace, and now the acrid smell of smoke was strong enough to heighten their fears.

'We'll have to go out the front, miss,' Mary Casey said. 'The back of the house is all gone up already.'

'Oh, we'll be shot,' Eileen cried. 'I won't go, I won't go. We'll all be shot and killed.'

'Come along now,' Amelia sternly admonished her. 'If we keep together, we'll be perfectly safe.'

'Come on there, girl,' Mary Casey cajoled, pushing the terrified girl towards the door. 'Sure they won't shoot at *us*. It's not us they're after, and if you stay here you'll be burned to a cinder.'

'Where's Elizabeth?' Amelia asked anxiously.

'She's with Constable Fahy and Ambrose,' Victoria replied. 'They won't let anything happen to her. Come on, let's get you and the servants out quickly.'

As flames began to lick at the window-sills, Eileen O'Brien's fear of being shot was suddenly banished and she darted out towards the hall. The others rushed after her, making for the front grounds and safety. At the hall door Amelia paused and turned to gaze back at what she was leaving. Apart from the noise and smoke, everything looked peaceful and secure. She prayed that help might come quickly and save what was left of Odron House. All the unhappiness of her last nineteen years there was forgotten, and she could recall only those blissful times when Alex and she were lord and lady of the manor, growing into their little world, looking forward to what seemed to be a long contented future stretching out before them.

'Oh, Alex, Alex,' she murmured, 'thank God you didn't live to see this day.'

'Mother! Mother!' Victoria's voice reached her from the front steps. 'What's wrong? What are you doing there? Hurry, Mother, hurry!'

Quickly Amelia turned and joined her daughter in the drive.

For Tim O'Halloran things couldn't be going better. The fire had not yet spread to the front of the house, and that suited him perfectly. He had seen some figures emerge through the front door and run down the drive towards the road. They'd be the Odron women and their servants no doubt – though what help they could expect to find out on the road, he didn't know. Even if someone happened to be passing, there was nothing they could do about it. He could see the flashes of the two guns, still now and again firing aimlessly from the upstairs window, but it could only be a matter of minutes before Mercer would have to come out, unless he wanted to be roasted alive. The RIC man would be with him of course, but that made no difference. Mercer wouldn't have any trouble shaking him off, and then there'd be nothing to stop him walking right into the trap.

Inside the bedroom the noise of the fire had now grown awesomely threatening, and the acrid tang of the smoke-filled air was making breathing difficult. Tom Fahy and Mercer still crouched at the window with Elizabeth on her knees behind them, their faces glistening with perspiration. Tom wondered how much longer they could all stay where they were; it was difficult to tell from the front of the house how bad the fire was behind them. If they left, the Shinners could easily pick off Mercer, and Tom feared that that was the real object of the attack. But what if Elizabeth was hit? In the darkness it could easily happen. He had to decide quickly. The longer he could hold out, the more likely that someone might see the fire and get word to the barracks and to the fire brigade. It was only an outside chance, but there was no other. He'd need to know immediately how near the fire really was. It sounded very close, but he couldn't go by the noise.

'Elizabeth, would you take a look at the rest of the house and see how bad the fire is? But be careful,' he shouted as she nodded and rushed out of the room. 'For God's sake, Mercer,' he roared angrily, 'don't be using all your ammunition. We'll have to be getting out soon and I want you to cover me while I get Elizabeth to safety.'

Mercer glared at the policeman, but in the darkness Tom was unable to see the hatred in his eyes. As he turned back to the window Mercer acted quickly. With Elizabeth out of the way and Fahy giving all his attention to the grounds at the front of the house, this was the only chance he'd get of gathering up his money from its hiding-place and making his escape. But first he'd have to take care of that cursed policeman.

He stepped back a few paces so that Tom Fahy's crouching figure was in front of him, raised his gun and aimed. The noise of the fire was deafening.

With a grim sneer on his lips he pulled the trigger. Fahy half-rose, then with a cry slumped on his side, his gun falling from his hand. Mercer stood there, breathing heavily, his eyes burning with triumph. Suddenly something prompted him to turn around. Elizabeth's return had been drowned by the crackling of the fire and she was standing at the door, her face frozen in a look of horror and disbelief.

She rushed over to Tom Fahy where he lay, stretched on the floor, a line of blood trickling from the side of his head.

'You've killed him!' she screamed.

'He won't bother us now. We can say it was the Shinners got him.'

In the darkness her figure was blurred and shadowy. For the first time that evening he noticed that she was attired in her pyjamas and dressing-gown; she had probably been getting ready to pay the policeman a visit when the firing started. Well, there'd be no more of that. She was his for the taking now. She and Odron House, they'd both be his. As he stepped close to her where she was kneeling beside the policeman's body, he could see the pearly shimmer of her bosom rising and falling.

'We can get married now, Elizabeth.' His voice was hoarse with excitement and desire. 'I have money, thousands of pounds. We can get married and live here. I have enough money to rebuild Odron House. Wait, I'll show you. I'll get the money for you.'

He turned to the door.

Elizabeth was suddenly galvanized into action.

'Murderer!' she screamed. Picking up Tom Fahy's gun from beside her on the floor, she fired shot after shot. Mercer staggered forward and then back, his face shocked into a mask of complete incredulity. He clutched at his breast. Slowly he fell, bright red blood spilling over his hand, his still disbelieving eyes holding their glazed stare even in death.

Elizabeth sprang up. With all her might she hurled the gun at Mercer's prostrate body. In a flash she recognized that ever since her mother's confession Fate had chosen her as its instrument of justice. Mercer's death at her hands was the only way the curse that had lain for so long on her mother's life could be removed, the shame buried, the sin redeemed. Her own sin, too. What person might she have been if there were never an Ambrose Mercer to take hold of her life and bend it to his own warped design? But he was no more, dead, gone for ever, and mother and daughter could face a new future, bonded together at last.

She stared at Mercer's body, his once white shirt now a

crimson mass. She turned to where Tom Fahy lay. But for the thread of blood like a vein down the side of his head, he might have been just asleep or resting.

As she stood between them, the picture in the fortune-teller's crystal ball swam before her eyes. This was what she had seen; this was what it meant. The two men struggling had been Mercer and Tom; the cloud of red had been the fire and the blood. That picture had haunted and frightened her. It would do so no longer. Elizabeth suddenly felt as if she had emerged from a long journey through dark choking forests into a clearing where the sun shone, streams ran, the brushwood crackled underfoot. She could feel the heat of the sun, hear the breaking and snapping of the brush. She must tell her mother; she must lose no time in freeing her from her prison and leading her into the clearing.

Turning from the scene before her, she hurried towards her mother's room.

Tim O'Halloran was getting worried. It wasn't merely impatience that was disturbing him, it was a growing concern that five minutes or more must have passed since the little group of people had run down the driveway, the whole of the back and sides of Odron House were firmly ablaze with the flames leaping high into the sky and lighting up the night and the surrounding countryside, and yet Mercer and the policeman had still not appeared. They hadn't fired their guns for some minutes, but he was certain they couldn't have escaped out the back. They would surely have been engulfed in the flames, and even if by some miracle they had got through the fire, they'd have been seen by his men and their escape signalled to him.

He ran towards the house, as near to it as he dared, keeping out of sight behind one of the large stone urns that decorated a corner of the lawn. Through the smoke that was now shrouding the front of Odron House and swirling out of the open door, he thought he saw a form, a human figure. They must be coming at last! His body tensed with excitement and the effort of concentrating his gaze on the doorway, trying to make absolutely sure that he really was seeing something, not just imagining it. Yes! There *was* someone there, staggering out, no doubt almost overcome by the smoke.

The figure reeled forward. Was it a man or a woman? He couldn't make out which. It tottered drunkenly down the steps and collapsed on the grass, turning to look up at the blazing inferno of Odron House. In the dancing light that lit up the whole scene O'Halloran recognized Constable Fahy. But where was Mercer? He couldn't still be in there and live. He had to come out.

O'Halloran waited. By now someone in the neighbourhood would surely have seen the fire and got word to the police station. There couldn't be much time left before help arrived. He felt sick at the thought that his plan might have failed.

'Curse you, Mercer, you bastard, where are you? Come out! Come out!'

But Ambrose Mercer never appeared.

'Fire! A big fire! It looks like Odron House has gone up!'

The policemen were startled out of their celebrations by the shouts of the two villagers who, breathless from running, had burst into the barracks. They rushed out to the back yard, fearful of what they might see. The sight that greeted them struck terror into their hearts. To the west the sky was lit up with a brightness that was magical to look at but awful to contemplate. It could only have been caused by some immense blaze, and they knew that in that direction there was but the one big building.

Sergeant Driscoll immediately ordered his men to make all haste to Odron House. He himself delayed only to shout at Francie O'Leary to harness up his pony and trap while he telephoned the fire brigade in Tralee. Then, leaving Francie in charge, he set out in pursuit of the others who had gone on ahead on their bicycles.

Facing towards Odron House, the policemen had the glow in the sky to urge them on. Pat Howell pedalled as hard as he could, his heart pumping, his nerves on edge. The fire could only have been the work of O'Halloran and his gang. If Victoria were injured or harmed in any way, he swore to himself that he wouldn't rest until O'Halloran had paid for it.

On either side of him the fields flashed by, resting cattle like dark statues unmoved by their passing. A horse stretched its head over a fence and whinnied at the sound of their wheels, while a stray dog chased after them, barking excitedly. He heard the clatter of hoofs made by the sergeant's pony and, just as he turned the final bend and came in sight of Odron House, Sergeant Driscoll's trap was abreast of him.

Tom Fahy pushed himself up from the grass and took a few deep breaths. His head was throbbing, and when he put a hand to it he felt the blood. He was appalled at the sight of Odron House, now completely engulfed in flames. Despite the heat they were throwing out, his flesh froze with horror at his narrow escape. He tried to recall what had happened. Mercer had shot at him, he remembered that. And he remembered feeling a searing pain as the bullet grazed the side of his head. How long had he been unconscious? It could only have been for a minute but, when he came to, Mercer was lying dead, shot through the heart, and Tom's own gun beside him. How had it got there? And where was Elizabeth? The bedroom had been filled with smoke by then, and he could hear the awful noise of the fire somewhere in the corridor. He remembered praying to God that he'd find Elizabeth while there still might be a chance to get out alive. He had rushed out of the room, shouting her name as loud as he could, but the roaring of the flames had been so great that he could hardly hear his own voice above it. The fire hadn't yet reached the staircase, and he had called her name again. And then – did it really happen or was he imagining it? – she had suddenly appeared through a cloud of smoke at the other end of the corridor.

'Elizabeth! This way! Hurry!'

Why did she stop on hearing his voice? Her hand went to her mouth. He'd never forget the look of shocked amazement on her face. Then 'Tom! Tom!' she had called back. But that one moment of delay had been fatal. Before she could take a step towards him the ground gave way beneath her feet and she plunged into the inferno.

The constable passed a hand over his eyes, trying to make sense of the awful recollection, but he immediately found himself surrounded by a gesticulating group, hurling questions at him. Charles Renfrew was there, supporting Mrs Odron, with Victoria and the servants anxiously asking him if he was all right.

'Elizabeth! Where's Elizabeth?' Mrs Odron cried, looking

around wildly, her voice frantic. 'Where is she? She wasn't with us. Have you seen her, Constable? Have you seen her?' But before he could reply they heard the clatter of Sergeant Driscoll and his men rushing up the drive to join them.

The sergeant was out of his trap and Pat off his bicycle before either vehicle had come to a stop. Sergeant Driscoll, taking in the scene at a glance, despatched two men to see if the stables behind the house were safe, and Sean Hogan ordered others to search the grounds for Sinn Fein men.

'It was the Shinners all right, Sergeant,' Tom Fahy confirmed. 'First it was the shooting, then the fire. Two dead, Sergeant – Ambrose Mercer and . . . and. . . .'

He turned to Amelia.

'I'm sorry, Mrs Odron. I'm very sorry, ma'am. Elizabeth was with Mercer and me. We were trying to fight the Shinners off when they started the fire. After a while she went to see how bad it was, but she didn't get back in time.'

Amelia drew in her breath sharply, and her face lost all its colour. In the eerie light cast by the burning house she looked like a ghost.

'No! Oh, no!' she cried.

Constable Fahy shook his head in commiseration.

'The stairs gave way as she was returning. I saw them go; she had no chance.'

Amelia collapsed into Charles Renfrew's arms and, while he and Victoria were comforting her, Pat Howell looked anxiously at Fahy.

'Are you all right, Tom? Your head is bleeding. Were you hurt?'

The constable drew him and the sergeant aside.

'That was Mercer's work,' he told them. 'He nearly did for me. Shot me when I wasn't looking, Sergeant. Damn lucky I was that the bullet only grazed me, but it knocked me out for a while and when I came to wasn't he beside me stretched out, shot through the heart!'

'So the Shinners got him after all,' Sergeant Driscoll said.

Constable Fahy offered no contradiction.

Charles Renfrew and Victoria were still trying to comfort Amelia. Her eyes were wet, but she had regained control of herself.

'You'll come to my place, all of you,'. Renfrew was saying. 'I have room enough. And you can stay there as long as you like. You know that, Amelia.'

'Yes, Charles, yes. I'll stay there.'

Victoria, seeing Pat Howell, disengaged herself and went to him.

'Thank God you're safe,' he said, taking her hands. 'Thank God. All the way here I was afraid something might have happened to you. I was afraid I might have lost you.'

'No, Pat,' she told him. 'You haven't lost me.'

'I don't know. I hope you're right. But I have to go away, away from Ireland. America is the only place for me after what happened at the barracks today. I can't tell you the story now, but it means I must leave the country immediately.'

'It doesn't matter what the story is, Pat. And it doesn't matter where you have to go. If you want me, I'll follow you.'

Without a thought for where they were or who might see them, Pat took her in his arms and kissed her. It had been a great wild day – a day of courage, triumph, joy and sadness. And love. And he had come through it like a man.

There was a sudden commotion as a bicycle came flying up the drive towards them, its bell ringing madly.

'Sergeant!' Francie O'Leary shouted as he almost cannoned into them. 'Sergeant! It's Mrs Driscoll. The hospital telephoned. She's had her baby, Sergeant, she's had her baby all right.'

Sergeant Driscoll stood as if rooted to the ground, unable to believe what he had heard.

'Congratulations, John,' Sean Hogan cried as he clapped him on the back. 'Go on, let you. I'll take care of everything here. You hurry to the missus and your offspring. Is it a boy or a girl, Francie?' he enquired as the other policemen crowded around to congratulate their chief.

'A boy!' Constable O'Leary laughed. 'A fine healthy boy, they said.'

Sergeant Driscoll was laughing and crying himself as he was bundled into his trap and the reins pushed into his hands. A child! A child at last! And a son, God be praised. Patrick John, that's what he'd call him, Patrick John Driscoll.

The trap gathered speed, and the sergeant urged his pony on

302

even faster. He could hear the cheers still ringing out from the people behind him, but he did not look back. He was going to greet his son.

'Doesn't that just about put the tin lid on it,' Pat Howell said as he pressed Victoria to him.

Before their eyes Odron House was a mass of flames, still burning fiercely; in their hearts, burning just as fiercely, was the fire of their love.